I0577075

MEN OF IRON

THE DARK AGE CHRONICLES, BOOK 1

MJ PORTER

First published in Great Britain in 2025 by Boldwood Books Ltd.

Copyright © MJ Porter, 2025

Cover Design by Head Design Ltd.

Cover Images: iStock

Map designed by Flintlock Covers

A CIP catalogue record for this book is available from the British Library.

Paperback ISBN 978-1-83617-496-7

Large Print ISBN 978-1-83617-495-0

Hardback ISBN 978-1-83617-494-3

Ebook ISBN 978-1-83617-497-4

Kindle ISBN 978-1-83617-498-1

Audio CD ISBN 978-1-83617-489-9

MP3 CD ISBN 978-1-83617-490-5

Digital audio download ISBN 978-1-83617-493-6

This book is printed on certified sustainable paper. Boldwood Books is dedicated to putting sustainability at the heart of our business. For more information please visit https://www. boldwoodbooks.com/about-us/sustainability/

Boldwood Books Ltd, 23 Bowerdean Street, London, SW6 3TN

www.boldwoodbooks.com

For T.R. AKA Terricus. Because I can.

MAP OF C6TH BRITANNIA

R. Trent

GYRWE

R. Welland

SWEORDORA

HERSTINGA

ERMINE STREET

R. Granta

TE

SS WAY

on

R. Ouse

R. Stour

WATLING STREET

ENDRICA

HICCA

NGAS

VERULAMIUM

S

WAECLINGAS

UPPINGAS

R. Thames

R. Medway

CHARACTER LIST

The Eorlingas, a native pagan Brythonic tribe from the west of Britannia, close to the River Habren / Severn

Edern, leader of Villa Eorlingas, now dead

Elen, Edern's wife

Maccus, Madog's son

Macsen, Madog's father

Madog, leader of the Eorlingas

Marchell, Meddi's servant and former seeress

Meddi, seeress of the Eorlingas, former wife of Edern

Merin, Madog's father's father

Rhian, Madog's wife

Sian, a woman of the Eorlingas

Terricus, charcoal maker

Twrch, warrior of the Eorlingas
Urien, warrior of the Eorlingas

The Gyrwe, a tribe from the east of Britain, formerly a *comitatus* invited to Britannia after the end of Roman occupation the previous century
Bægmund, warrior of Gyrwe
Bucge, warrior of Gyrwe and seeress
Burnoth, warrior of Wihtlæd
Cenbryht, warrior of Gyrwe
Eastmund, warrior of Gyrwe
Goddæg, warrior of the Gyrwe
Heafoc, warrior of Gyrwe
Hygebeorht, warrior of Gyrwe
Maggenræd, warrior of Gyrwe
Nothelm, warrior of Gyrwe
Osfyth, warrior of Gyrwe and hunter
Wædel, warrior of Gyrwe
Wærmund, warrior of Gyrwe and son of Wihtlæd
Waga, father of Wihtlæd
Watholgeot, father of Waga
Wihtlæd, leader of the Gyrwe, father of Wærmund

The Beansæte, a native Brythonic tribe from the west of Britannia
Hedrek, their leader

Centus, son of a blacksmith

The Herstinga, a tribe that borders the Gyrwe
Luci, their leader

The Hicca, a tribe in the middle of Britannia
Boddw, their leader

The Sweordora, a tribe that borders the Gyrwe
Dægbeorht, their leader

The Wæclingas, a tribe in the middle of Britannia
Isarninus, their leader

The Weogoran, a native Brythonic tribe that borders the Eorlingas
Corun, their leader

Locations
Corinium – Cirencester
River Habren – the River Severn
Glevum – Gloucester

BRITANNIA AD 540

Rome's reach disappeared from Britannia over a hundred years ago. In its wake, the sophisticated warrior and political society that allowed a far-distant emperor to govern the unruly province has slowly crumbled with the attendant loss of its currency, skills, political elite and, of course, brave warriors who once fought against Britannia's enemies: the Picts from the far north, long held at bay by the snaking walls crossing the north of Roman-held Britannia.

Quickly, the skills and ideals of *Romanitas* have become subsumed by the basic need to survive amongst those who still inhabit the island of Britannia. Some have taken advantage of the weakness of others, although with the work of bladesmith and ironworker lost to all but a few, the majority lack the required weapons or the desire to wage bloody wars against their ancient enemies.

Instead, the men and women of Britannia inhabit the cities abandoned by Rome, forging a living from the soil, reliant on barter. And for those who shy away from the haunted ruins and the lost Roman gods, the even more ancient hill forts of an age before Rome came offer the promise of their protective ditches and ramparts, as well as their familiar gods. Others shelter in the remnants of a once rich and prosperous agricultural landscape doing all they can to grow enough food to survive, daily reminded of all they've lost, as they build ditches and embankments to protect themselves from those desperate enough to risk all for enough food to eat.

To the east, new tribal warriors have emerged, who were once strangers to Britannia, and herald from the northern lands of the Continent. They are not strangers to war. They have come to protect those too weak to fight but with the wealth to pay them in the immediate aftermath of Rome's departure. With a century of no coinage the *comitatus* now lay claim to that which they were once paid to protect.

This is Britannia, a century after the withdrawal of Rome and a century before the emergence of the kingdoms of the Angles and Saxons.

This is the true Dark Ages.

1

MEDDI OF THE EORLINGAS, TO THE EAST
OF THE RIVER HABREN, WESTERN
BRITANNIA, AD 540

'It's time,' the rough voice calls to me through the thin wattle and daub walls of my workshop. I despise its coarse appearance, yet it gives me the privacy I need to perform my secretive rites. I feel my forehead wrinkle, tongue poking through thin lips, examining the object before me with its four leg-like appendages, and fifth projection that I'm convinced looks like a head. There's some magik here. What, I'm yet to understand. But I will understand it, eventually. I need only study it carefully, and perhaps in better light. After all, it is much, much smaller than my finger, and I examine it more by touch than sight. 'It's time,' the familiar voice repeats.

I shake my head. Madog, my half-brother, has the

worst timing. My thoughts are elsewhere. Why does he disturb me like this? I need time to consider this treasure brought to me by the farmer and warrior, Urien, unearthed when he was preparing the hard and unyielding ground for the new crops. Urien knew its home was with me, the seeress of the Eorlingas, the woman who will understand such magiks as this.

'Time for what?' I lift my voice to reply, knowing he won't leave me alone if I don't, endeavouring to keep the frustration from being audible. He's always been the same. My half-brother. Twenty winters younger than me, and yet the leader of what remains of our people, the once mighty Eorlingas of Villa Eorlingas. There was a time when I hardly knew him. That's no longer the case.

'Sister.' The words lack all respect. He shouldn't address me as such, even if it is correct. Well, half-sister would be the proper terminology. The same father, a different mother. I turn and hiss at him as he allows bright sunlight to filter into my darkened hut by lifting the leather door covering, blinding and distracting me, I'm convinced, from some important thought I was about to have. Now it'll take me time to return to the same half-awake, half-sleeping state.

How he annoys me. Younger brothers are all the same.

'By all the gods,' I growl, eyes turning to observe him.

In the half-light, half-shadows of early morning, I see his familiar wide forehead, the russet-coloured drooping moustache that marks him as a man of not inconsiderable means. And then my eyes narrow. He knows his place amongst us. He understands how to stand aloof from the warrior men who serve him, from the farmers who render him barley, wheat, milk, cheese and wool. Who come to him in supplication to ask that his most virulent bull or most stunning stallion service their cows and mares. But now he's dressed for war; even the ancient but shimmering disc of the golden torque with its twin twisted horse heads at its ends that usually encircles his long neck is missing.

Unbidden, anticipation stirs within me.

'It's time?' I question, the item I'm considering forgotten about as it slips from my hands to thud gently to the ground. I think of the deer entrails I examined only yesterday. They spoke of something monumental. I told him as much. There are no secrets between us.

'Yes, sister, or seeress, or whatever you desire me

to name you this day. It is time. Now hurry if you wish to join me. News of his death will quickly spread. We're not alone in desiring the villa.' A curve of his thin lips, so similar to mine, and I know he's as excited as I am. We've been waiting too long for this occurrence, almost since the moment of his birth.

I turn. Marchell's huddled in the corner of the room. She's a creature of no words, but she aids me. Now she presents the ceremonial dagger to me, the copper blade dulled with age. It's been handed down in the female line of the family for generation upon generation, just like the golden torque around my brother's neck, which passes from father to son, with the odd uncle, brother and male cousin included.

I smile and take it from her with the reverence she accords it, hurrying to find my cloak and the most important item of all. The ancient, battered copper breastplate that's tarnished with antiquity but still serviceable thanks to the special care it's received over the many winters and summers of its existence. I'll not fight with copper blade and bark shield. But I must look like I will. Unlike my brother, I keep my twin horse headed torque in place around my neck.

'Tend to Rhian,' I order Marchell. 'Her time is close.' It's this that I thought yesterday's auguries referenced. I was wrong. I also direct this to my brother.

He should be here when his first child is birthed. As should I. But we're needed elsewhere. 'Add the comfrey to the flames,' I direct Marchell, her gaze downcast. I think she'll ignore me, but she nods, focusing again on me. She's a ruin of who she was. She once stood in my place. No more. Now she serves me. She's taught me all she knows. All of it. On pain of death. Our respect for one another is tempered with the knowledge that I can always overwhelm her physically. Now she relies on her wisdom to remain relevant to me.

I admire her but would never say as much. I don't know what she thinks of me. Sometimes, I don't care whether she hates me or not. Other times, I certainly do. There have been moments when she could have ended my life with the concoctions I've allowed her to prepare for me when I was at my weakest. Even then, with her magiks, she must have known what I would become to her, and yet she aided me anyway. Her reticence is something I wouldn't share.

Outside, as I secure my cloak with the precious copper horse pins that are as ancient as my breast-plate, I realise now, the warriors of the Eorlingas have been preparing. They try not to watch me as I emerge from the ruin of my sunken hovel with its dirt floor and step into the brightening daylight. I ensure the shimmer of my copper blade and breast-plate is seen, despite their tarnishing. That my long hair and its tangle of clacking talismans that mark me as a seeress are visible. That the pouch I wear at my waist, containing the secrets only I can ken, are seen. The men dread me and the terrible scars that mar my once beautiful face. They should.

Their women, daughters and mothers know not to fear me, although they do revere me.

Men are frail creatures, like to jump at the smallest of noises. Women know the truth of all. They understand that I know all there is to comprehend, even the reason why the birds fly south in the cold months and return in the warmer ones. They know me. They see me. And I see them. The men do not possess such knowledge. They're not creatures of our surroundings as we are. That's how it should be.

Some warriors are mounted on the few fine steeds that still belong to my people. Many are not. They carry spears on the tip of long wooden shafts, and if they're lucky, a form of shield as well. Shields are needed but difficult to make without the required copper or iron and the skills to form them. Instead, the bark from a willow tree must be just right. The tree must be the correct age, with enough of the bark showing to ensure that when it's stripped away, it will continue to flourish. We can't kill the tree in the process, or it's counterproductive. Why kill a tree to protect a man? Warriors can be grown far more quickly than a willow tree can be nurtured from its smallest branches.

The bark must be bent back on itself but not too far to cause it to snap. Too many potential shields have been broken by those inattentive to the task. The bark must be just wet enough, just malleable enough. These are the secrets to making a good shield from the bark of the willow tree. Not everyone possesses them. Some of the warriors have other, heavier shields made of copper or iron. They're old and tarnished, like my breastplate and dagger. Treasured family heirlooms. Special items gifted to the most successful of my brother's warriors. Or the most arrogant. My brother is not above rewarding men who I would rather see dead in battle.

I eye them appraisingly. We're not a huge force. We've always lacked a good quantity of men to fight for our people, but since that bleak day, almost coinciding with my brother's birth, I've tried to bring more fighting men within the tribe. I offered what little we had to tempt them, and sometimes used my skills to bring their women so that the men must follow. Now we'll not be overtopped by the enemy. I pray to all the gods.

The day isn't far advanced. I've been awake all night. I might regret that with all there is to accomplish today.

I turn to my tall brother. He nods, a smirk on his familiar face, as he tells me the news I've been desperate to hear for most of his lifetime.

'It happened late last night. Now, we must hurry.'

My cream-coated mare's brought forth by one of the young boys who won't be joining the attack. She's a gentle creature. She should be cantankerous and difficult as behoves my position as seeress, but she and I have been friends for over ten summers. We know each other too well.

Carefully, my brother holding the reins, having taken them from the boy, with a smile I mount and make myself ready.

'Men of the Eorlingas. Today, we take back what was stolen from us long ago. Today, we will triumph. Our revenge has been too long delayed, but no more.' Ragged cheers greet my words, a distinctly feminine soft grunt of pain following on behind from within one of the run-down buildings. I look to my brother. He shrugs. The work of his wife will be done while he's absent. It's to be hoped that both he and she and the child in her belly will survive this day.

I look at his stronghold. The buildings with their thatched roofs in need of repair. The dilapidated grain store, waiting for fresh produce to fill it later in the summer, to the enclosure where his bull grazes, alone. There should be cows there for the animal to service. To the enclosure where the horses should graze, but every single one is currently being ridden. We've fallen low since my brother's birth. I don't lie when I say that this day we will be victorious and restore ourselves to the former glory we held. Our neighbours will fear us. We'll no longer be afraid. We've suffered. We will triumph now.

With his arm raised high, the sunlight shimmering off his breastplate, and the iron at his waist, Madog leads us as we ride out. His warriors hasten to join him, some running, others riding; I follow, urging my pliant mare onwards. I must witness today's success. It'll be as much mine as Madog's, for all he'll provide is the strength of his warriors to reinforce that of my new life's work.

My lips curl as I consider those who currently hold Villa Eorlingas, and who have changed its name to Villa Edern as though this would make it theirs and wipe out the decades of my family's control. I've been hungering for Edern's death for many summers. Unconsciously, my hand sweeps over my cheeks, feeling the deep cuts there that have forever scarred me. The ones that ensure I never risk looking in the shimmering surface of iron or gold as one of my calling should do. And they're only the visible marks, the others are hidden beneath my dress and between my legs from view. Even I dare not look at them. But I feel them. Every day. All the time. They've made me who I am.

I grip my copper dagger tighter. How I wish I'd wielded the final blow that ended his life. Damn the bastard. Edern should have died many winters ago. His continued existence has forced me to doubt myself and my gods. But no more.

We ride through the desultory defences of our home. The wooden struts atop the ditched embankment need replacing. The ditch clearing. But my brother's concern is with the fields and streams running towards the vast River Habren that provide him with produce. He says he must feed his people. Only then can he consider other matters. It's taken much persuasion on my part to ensure the men were trained to fight and had the equipment they needed for this day. He argued the wars are over. He stated the warriors are all dead, or gone from this shore. On this, we disagreed.

The eyes of women, old, young and meek, watch their men leave. They incline their heads when they see me or meet my gaze fully. The older women know not to fear me. I've seen them through many tribulations. Those who are even older perhaps feel more conflicted. They owe Marchell much more than they do me. All the same, they expect much from me. I'll see it done.

The journey's accomplished quickly. The sweat coating the bodies of those who run is an unwelcome reminder of men and their desires. My lips curl. Not that it's their fault. They've never harmed me. They wouldn't dare lay a hand on the seeress of their tribe. The woman who sees all, even into their hearts' desires.

The sun illuminates the red tiles that still adhere to Villa Eorlingas' roof ahead, the vast river glinting in the near distance behind the villa. This was once my home. It hasn't been for many summers. I note how some of the tiles on the roof have been replaced with grass. I growl. The fool. I told Edern to seek new tiles – well, old tiles that could be freshly applied to the roof, having been robbed from long-abandoned buildings within Glevum. Not that he ever listened to anything I said. The bastard.

Our arrival's met with shouts and shrieks from those tending the growing barley within the haphazard enclosure, the flock of thirty sheep out grazing, and the ten cattle mixed among them. Bright eyes seek out my brother, leading his warriors, shimmering with the protection of his position. With short commands, his men are sent running forward, skipping over the ditch and ramparts as though little more than pebbles.

The warriors of the Eorlingas need not kill these people. But these people must not defend themselves either. Over the last twenty summers, Edern's strength slowly waned. Now we'll reap the rewards of his continued arrogance. If ever a man thought time changed nothing, it was him. He didn't see the ruins of his plans as clearly as I did.

Those on horses ride onward, their speed increasing. I allow them to carry on ahead of me. There's work to do before I can be assured of my arrival, although those who see my brother and recognise him quickly look for me. I note a few bow their heads low. Others appear confused. They're too young to remember. They should have been taught better by those older and wise.

I note the granary store, as devoid of produce as my brother's. I look at the horses. There aren't as many as there once were, perhaps only twelve, and a few ponies mixed amongst them. What has the fool done with the wealth he stole? Lost it, no doubt, as he has everything else. But my eyes are drawn to the still-standing red-tiled building time and time again, and the complex of buildings close to it, neatly arranged in lines. I know what I will find inside Villa Eorlingas. I smile to know it will soon be in my possession once more.

Not, it appears, that Edern's few remaining warriors are to permit it to happen without bloodshed. Again, I curse them for lackwits. They should allow this to unfold peacefully. After all, it's never been doubted.

My brother and his swiftest warriors leap into the mass of twenty or so outraged men, forced from their hall, drunk with grief for the lord. Edern's body will not yet have been sent to the afterlife. I think of all I'll take from him. I think how powerless he is to stop me. I wish I could have done this while he lived, but it was impossible. He must have known, as he lay dying, that he'd lose all. He should have lost it long ago. Even in death, a man may not evade the consequences of his actions.

Ahead, my brother skewers one of Edern's warriors through the chest, hair wild, arms reaching with his knife. I recognise him, and snarl. I'm glad he chokes his last on the dust of the horse's hooves. More and more fall. I watch this pathetic fight with amusement. The shrieks of these men are like ravens circling overhead. They don't concern me. They might tell me a lot, but I don't see it. Not yet.

'Sister.' Blood-splattered, mouth open in a broad grin revealing the black of my enemy's blood on his teeth, my brother invites me to dismount a short while later. The smell of death permeates all. Chickens cluck through the enclosed courtyard, pecking at splatters of pooling madder as though grains. Two dogs argue over the severed hand of one of the dead men, muzzles bright maroon. Edern's hunting hounds. Soon they'll be mine to command. We'll find the best deer. The most vicious boars. The remaining bears.

'The way is clear. Villa Eorlingas is yours to command.'

I squeeze his hand tightly, as I dismount, pleased with him. He's become the man I always hoped he would be, even when he was a small child, wobbling on unsteady legs, and I placed a wooden spear in his hand, much to the disgust of others.

'Where is she?' I hiss. If I couldn't bring about Edern's death, there's another whom I'll sate my bloodlust upon.

'Inside,' Madog offers. 'All the women are. Untouched, as you once ordered.' I turn to eye the warriors who surround my brother. Sweat beads their skin, burgundy shimmering on hair and weapons, hairy chests heaving, eyes alight with bloodlust. I know what they wish to do. They'll not do it. I'll not allow it. They know it, yet their blood runs hot. They would be better at home with their women. I'm sure they'd enjoy seeing their men so filled with vigour.

'Come with me,' I urge Madog, stepping into Villa Eorlingas. I look down, my bare feet walking over the familiar tokens of an age I don't remember. Of an age few recall. This is myth beneath my feet, but it belongs to me now, as it should always have done.

As ever, the small coloured pieces of stone forced into an intricate pattern have been swept clean. They shimmer with brightness once more, the local stone colourings of white, grey and brown, the additional pieces of startling blue and occasional baked red depicting a stallion in its prime, and a mare in hers. Edern's pride and joy, more so than his bull and his stallion. Mine now as well. I will make the correct use of them.

I stop and examine the images picked out in the shiny pieces of stone, some bright, others dulled with age. I would bend and run my hand over it, and welcome it as a long-lost friend in a warm embrace. But I don't. Today is momentous enough, as I always knew it would be. It has taken longer than it should. These stones beneath my bare feet will wait a little longer.

'Seeress,' Madog intones, reminding me there's more to do and, before these people, using my title, not my relationship with him. For all I think him young and foolish, in this he shows much wisdom.

The main room, glistening with bright light from the remnants of white paint, yellowed now with smoke from the hearth at its centre, where it should not be, is filled with sobbing women and children, bowed low, not daring to look at me, while the fountain stands silent. I shake my head to see that. It should trickle with the water of life, and not the blackened remnants of the fire placed at its heart. It appears the fool had even lost the ability to warm these rooms using the correct means.

Edern's there, laid out for all to see, awaiting his burial. Small iron tokens have been placed on his eyes to ensure he's unseeing. With relish, I remove them. I consider pissing on his ugly face, revealing my secret wounds to him in this moment which he inflicted upon me, but stop myself. This room is mine now. I'll not soil it further than he has already done. He's not worth it now he's dead.

Edern's as unsightly in death as he was in life. He was always a tall man, bulky with a bulbous nose and small, hooded brown eyes. Now that they see nothing, they hold more life than when he lived. He was a cold and calculated man.

A woman wails close to him, unheeding of my arrival or that of my brother. I know what some of Madog's men would do with her. I'll not allow it. Edern showed me the worst of all men. I strive to ensure my brother and his adherents don't make the same mistakes.

'Elen.' I snap her name. She looks up, lower lip trembling, pale, thin face revealing red-rimmed green eyes despite the artful arrangement of her dark hair. There's a fine twisted golden torque encircling her neck, and twin penannular brooches on her shoulders, in the form of horses, hold the rich fabric of her bright red dress in position. I grimace. They once belonged to me. I showed them off better. She's too thin to fill the dress as it should be worn.

Hungrily, I eye the collection of iron keys at her waist, the little bag beside them containing all I once claimed.

'Meddi,' she spits, finally realising what's happening.

'Indeed. I see the bastard's dead, at long last,' I retort, chin raised. I would not suffer many people to speak to me like this. She should use my title, but I know her ways. This is meant to anger me.

'You witch. You killed him. You always said you would,' she shrieks, maddened with grief, but more likely fearful he's barely cold and already her worst fears have come to fruition.

'And how did I do that when I'm only just arrived and he's stiff in death?' I kick his body, just to prove the point. A loud fart sounds. There's fury in my voice but I smirk at the familiar noise from a body that should be silent. She bows down, covering her face, wailing again, as though my arrival has allowed the sound to ensue, while I wrinkle my nose at the stink erupting from the corpse. She's always been a bloody fool.

'You,' she begins on looking at me once more. 'You,' she continues, flailing for words. Madog moves through the other women, keen to take his place as the leader of these people. I don't watch him. My focus remains on Elen. She and Edern. Both bastards. 'What are you doing here?' she demands, even though it's self-evident.

'I've come to take what's mine.' Bending, I reach down and yank the girdle of her dress undone, deigning to use my iron blade to cut through it, even though I have to saw at it because the edge is so blunt. I snatch the pouch and the keys from where they tumble to the floor.

'Villa Edern isn't yours,' she howls, no doubt looking for her warriors to defend her. She was always slow to realise what was happening around her. I once suggested to my brother that someone who cared so much about her appearance had no wit to look further than her own nose. His laughter cheered me, even if it was forced. Men have always desired Elen. I don't know why. Her beauty is far from unsullied.

'A little late,' I murmur, running my hands through the pouch, and feeling the familiar weight of the keys which once marked me as mistress of Villa Eorlingas.

'What will you do with us?' she shrieks, scrambling back on her knees, no doubt to merge with the other wailing women, only to come up against the unyielding legs of my brother's warriors. They've separated her from the others, as I commanded. She's to face her future alone. She's not truly one of these people.

'They'll be welcome. You will not.' I don't hide the scathing glower from my face. 'You should join your dead lord.' She shudders, hand going to her belly unbidden.

I laugh.

'Really, you're with child?' I question. Edern was an old bastard. That there's no son to take his place is down to his failure to prove his fertility despite his best efforts. He'll not have managed it now, so close to death.

'I...' She once more fails to take advantage of her position.

'Lock her up in the grain store. We'll reveal the truth of that possibility. She's to have water and one meal a day, nothing more.'

'The grain store?' Madog questions while Elen continues to fumble, desperate to evade the reach of my brother's warriors. Urien bends to obey my instructions to take her away, accompanied by Twrch.

'Once we know you're as hollow as I was, you may be allowed to leave,' I offer, dismissing her with a flick of my fingers. I wish to breathe in the air unfouled by her presence.

'That might take until the harvest,' Madog counters, his voice betraying conflicting emotions.

'It may. Or it may not. If she's with child, he or she must not live.'

A shriek of outrage and a lower murmur of unease from the other women.

'Perhaps it would be better to kill her?' I turn a furious gaze on them. They've not known a seeress for twenty summers. They must be reminded of the magiks I possess. I would much sooner she was dead. It was my intention to have her killed, if she still lived. But, if my brother blanches at keeping her captive, I know I'll have no luck ordering her death. Not yet, anyway.

'No, no,' Elen cries desperately, finally apprehended between Urien and Twrch, two of the strongest men who serve my brother. 'Lock me in the grain store.'

'You heard her?' I flick my fingers again. The men show no unease, although they do perhaps eye her small heaving breasts with too much appreciation. My brother remains conflicted, watching her being led away, emotions rippling over his face.

'You will kill any child?' he questions, no doubt thinking of the babe his wife now labours to bring forth and perhaps mistrusting me to allow it to flourish.

'I'll kill any child of this foul union and disperse it alongside its bastard father. Perhaps alongside its mother as well. It would be better if Elen was dead.'

My brother's forehead furrows, but he bites down on his complaint. I also have power over him, even if he doesn't like to acknowledge it as often as he should.

'Ensure no one touches her,' I instruct my brother, mindful men are fools where their cocks are concerned.

'No one will touch her,' he reiterates, face twisted with disgust at the thought.

'Now, I've other tasks to attend to,' I inform him, sweeping my gaze over the bowed heads of the women who clutch one another in grief and fear. 'Is Angharad here?' I question. A shuddering sob greets my words.

'No mistress,' one of the women is brave enough to tell me. 'Edern bed her and she died in childbirth.'

My fists clench. The bastard lived too long. Admittedly, I doubt the child was actually his, but people tell themselves the stories they need to hear, even Edern. While women will do what must be done to earn a position of respect.

'You'll assist me, then,' I inform the woman, noting the streaks of grey through her once auburn hair. She was perhaps beautiful when she was younger. I don't recognise her, though. She's not lived here for the span of my brother's life. She came afterwards. 'Tell me your name?' I request.

'Sian, mistress.' She pushes to her feet. I note her sagging breasts and half-ripped dress with a snarl.

'Find yourself a new dress,' I order her. 'Take what you will from Elen's clothes, and meet me at the workshop.'

She bows her head, eyes glimmering. She's quick to realise what I've come for.

Edern's death will return something most precious to me and something he should never have deprived me of possessing.

2

WÆRMUND OF THE GYRWE, CLOSE TO THE WASH, EASTERN BRITANNIA

I eye the smoking ruins of the great circular hall and dwellings of the settlement with a wolf smile on my lips, aware as I grin that blood tinges my face, pulling it tight as it dries, perhaps masking the purple stain that's marked me since birth.

Waga thought to disparage me, but I've repaid him for that kindness. The pale and marbling flesh of those who served my brother calls to me. I've triumphed here. I've overwhelmed the snivelling wreck I always knew him to be, despite his posturing and him having my father's support.

'Heafoc,' I call to one of my men. His long hair is blond but stained dawn red, his right arm slashed and flooding with blood, although he seems unaware. He was the first to swear his oath to me last summer. He was the first I recruited to aid me in ending my brother's life and taking my vengeance against my father.

'Wærmund.' His booming voice is flushed with triumph. It's too soon for the fatigue of his endeavours to make itself known.

'Are they all dead?' I stand, blade to hand, shield resting on the ground before me, beside the cooling body of my damn brother. The arsehole. I feel no remorse for killing him. If anything, I'm embarrassed for him. He hardly put up a fight, and yet he thought to send me from this place of water and fens, damning me as cursed by the gods because of my birthmark, in mimicry of my father. I can hardly say it was a difficult fight. He barely knew which way round to hold his seax.

Now there's nothing left of this settlement. No one will wish to dwell in this dead place on a slight rise between two surging streams. I confess I've perhaps done more damage than I expected. I reason it this way. My brother was the leader here. My father would never have allowed me to command in my younger brother's place, even when I proved his weakness. And so I've done the only thing that made sense. I've killed him and his people. I've ensured the settlement they called their own is inhabitable from this day onwards.

'All of them,' Heafoc confirms, raking in the rest of the men who stood with me, as well as a few women. I nod, pleased, and bend to cut the long blond hair from my brother's head and, in the process, release the wealth of silver and gems he wore mingled with it. They clatter together, a gentle sound against the violence of moments ago. He did nothing to earn such riches, but my father rewarded him all the same, just because he wasn't forever marked by the gods, as I was.

I spit on Waga's upturned face. How I hated him. My father named him after his father, as though even his very name should make him a future leader of the *comitatus* of the Gyrwe, as though not giving me the name, even as the older son, marked me as inferior. Now I've had the ultimate revenge against him, and my bastard father. And his father before him. They all treated me as though I were shit on their boots because of my birthmark. I'll have the last word on that. A pity really only my father lives to see it.

Black smoke billows in the cloudless sky, driving away the irritating insects that leave itchy welts on my skin. It won't be long, and all will see this rising from the flat fenlands, not just the insects. No doubt my father, Wihtlæd, leader of the Gyrwe, will summon his warriors to join him in determining why the settlement of Waga burns. But I don't plan on being here then. He'll find my brother's dead body. It won't take him long to understand why his beloved son is dead.

'We must find it,' I urge Heafoc. He nods and, likewise, spits on the cooling body of my brother before him. Waga wasn't above tormenting others my father had cast aside from his *comitatus*. Both of us pant from our exertions. We've killed and done what needed to be done. Despite my confidence and bold words to those who pledged me their oath throughout the last year as I plotted vengeance, there was never a guarantee we'd triumph. I'm grateful we did, but now I must take what I need to continue my life elsewhere. I've accomplished what was needed first; my brother's death.

Striding onwards, I stop before the round wooden hall my brother once called his home. It's not small. Luckily, it doesn't smoke. Yet. I stamp inside, but I know better than to find what I'm looking for within. But I want something else as well. Something denied me because my brother had it.

Forcing aside the animal-skin flap that covers the

door on a summer's day to prevent the flies from getting within, I make my way to the other room, the one at the back, where Waga once slept.

Here, there's another door, a flimsy thing made of willow sticks. I sniff the air when entering, smelling all that's left of my brother's life like a hound on the hunt.

'He smelled like a bastard as well,' I mutter to myself.

Animal skins and some woven blankets cover the bed, but it's not there that I go. I stamp to a wooden chest, opening the lid with a creak of ancient, distressed hinges, to be greeted with a large enough pile of clothing to keep a man adequately covered for three lifetimes, not just one, and a fresh smell of cut wood to drive out the stink of my brother.

I eye the tunics and trews, the bright colours arresting my attention, and realise my warriors would welcome these. I don't want them. I want nothing my brother owned other than his life, his treasure, and one more thing.

The sword I find when removing the clothing isn't a finely wrought weapon. If anything, it's pitted with rust spots and needs a new hilt and guards fitting over the tang to make it possible to use as a weapon. But what it signifies is important. My father should never have given this to my brother. It's the weapon of a warrior. Or it will be, in time. Now it's mine, and I'm the warrior to wield it once it's repaired.

'Hurry,' Heafoc calls to me from where he paces close to the leather covering over the door. He doesn't fear the arrival of my father's warriors. I inhale, smell the burning thatch and realise this building hasn't escaped the ravages of fire despite my earlier thoughts. How could it when the entire settlement burns and the outside is hotter than a furnace, even without the addition of the flames?

'I'm coming.' I glower, pulling the clothing bundle into my arms and carrying the sword as well. Only then do I pause and stride to the bed. It might be the last thing I want on a day such as this, but I pull the blanket free. It's of good quality. It'll have taken the women an entire winter to create using what little daylight there was, the loom weights clacking against one another rhythmically. I can't allow that to be incinerated. It's worth more to me than those lives which ended here this morning.

'Is that it?' Heafoc questions, jerking his chin towards me.

'It is, yes. Have these, share them out.' I thrust the clothing at him. He eyes it with a smirk of delight and I notice the rip in his tunic, from shoulder to waist, as I stride past him and out into the daylight, the sun almost obscured with the thick black smoke. 'Come on.' I lift my voice to bellow to my warriors – well, those who still live, for no doubt we've lost some. Not all the warriors I enticed to my cause were fine fighters. 'We must leave.'

I realise then I questioned Heafoc as to whether or not the enemy was dead and not whether or not my warriors live. I curse myself for that. I need to be more careful. I can't reveal such a lack of thought to those who serve me. Our relationship has, until to-day, been held together by the flimsiest of promises of what would happen when my brother was dead.

As I scowl down at the man who lies below, the ground blood-soaked where he's been sliced through his belly, I know a moment of rage towards him. He assured me he could fight when joining my warrior band. I see that wasn't entirely correct.

I bend and pluck the shield still clasped in his hand. I won't be abandoning that, although I will leave his body behind. He can fester in the sun like the rest of them. Only then do I pause. No, once more, I remember my father wouldn't countenance this, and neither should I. I might hate my father, but he's a leader of men, and a fine warrior.

'Goddæg,' I call to the closest of my allies.

'Wærmund,' he replies quickly, that single word filled with respect, even though his chest heaves with exertion.

'Help me. We can't leave him like this.'

A quiver of sorrow touches Goddæg's lips as he sees the dead man. 'A pity,' he suggests, and it is a suggestion. None of these men knew one another well. They were not raised together. We've not even fought together before today. I collected them in a piecemeal fashion since last summer, as my vengeance formulated. Only last night did each warrior eye the others. Only last night. As such, Goddæg's sorrow is more for a dead man than someone he knows. Perhaps it's also for being reminded as to how fleeting the life of a warrior can be.

'We'll burn him. Help me put him beneath those eaves there.' I jut my chin where I intend and he nods and judders. It's not the way of our people to burn the dead, but instead to lay them beneath what earth can be found between the meandering rivers and sodden fenlands. I've no time to offer the dead man, whose name I can't recall, that respect. 'Think of it as a pig carcass,' I comment.

He nods again and bends to take the corpse's feet. I grip the hands and wish I weren't so close to the forever staring eyes. I don't shiver at the feeling of the cooling flesh, but I'd like to do so.

'Come on,' I heave, and it's a huge effort to get the long corpse anywhere close to where I thought would be a good place for his remains to burn. I wish I'd not done so now. There's another task I must complete before my father's warriors rush here to see what's happening.

Finally, we drag the dead body almost to the position, but by now the flames are licking along the moss-stricken thatch.

'Put him down. We'll roll him from here.' I fear my eyebrows will singe if we get closer. The sound of the body dropping to the ground resounds wetly. I grimace as the head knocks the hard-baked earth and blood pools from the open mouth.

I look up, considering if my ancestor, Woden, watches this. I hope he's happy with what's befallen these people today. He must approve of my need for revenge against my brother. My father has named me as cursed by the gods, Woden amongst them. I'll show him even those believed to be cursed might well be beloved.

Quickly, I kick the body as close as I'm going to, only just avoiding a piece of falling wattle and daub fracturing from the burning building rather than being consumed by the flames.

'At least he'll burn well,' I offer, as it covers him, the hungry flames coming closer.

I'd say a few words, but I didn't know him. He gave me his oath and said he'd fight for me, but other than that I recall almost nothing about him. It's possible his family are dead. I really don't remember the life stories of all these men and women. That, I realise, is something else I'll need to improve upon if I'm ever to be more than just a landless man taking his pickings wherever he can, cast out from his tribe for being a kin-slayer.

Again, I recall my father and my brother. Both of them knew how to make men loyal, but I've never possessed that particular trait. And my brother's ways were very different to the means my father employed. But then, as can be seen in the detritus, the men loyal to my brother were not warriors. If they had been, they'd not lie dead and forever staring now. No, my father saw what he wanted to when looking at my brother. He didn't notice the weaknesses, the posturing, the failure to do more than bask in the glow of our father's successes. All he saw was a boy who lacked the birthmark covering much of my cheek, and which only now can I attempt to cover with the beard I'm growing.

'Hurry.' Heafoc's voice ripples through the burning dwellings, the thickness of the smoke almost making it impossible to see. I run back to where I think I found the body of my dead warrior, but I can't find the blanket or sword I wanted. Turning, I curse my stupidity and then kick something metallic that makes me hop, but at least it's what I'm seeking.

'This way,' I shout, hoping those who still live and are loyal to me will heed my call. But not too quickly. I still have something to find.

Pulling the blanket bundle into my arms, coughing on the dense smoke, I hurry away from the confines of the ditched enclosure, although I don't stand outside it. Instead, I look around me. I know where it'll be, or rather I know the location that will have been chosen. I still need to pinpoint that spot.

The ditch, the dwellings, the grain store, the hall my brother once ruled the few people here from, they all look one way.

I feel the wolf grin on my face once more as I rush towards the side of the ditch, close to where men and women would come within and where a piece of wood acts as a bridge over the sodden ditch.

The ground here is well trodden by footprints and hoof prints.

'There,' I mutter to myself. I'm sure in the winters it's been hidden, the ground will have been filled in, but all the same, there's a slight depression. Pulling my war axe from my weapons belt, I crash it into the hard earth. It's been a dry summer, but the dampness of this place is persistent. It takes more than one impact for anything to happen, and then it's only a shard of dark earth that comes away, releasing the stink of dankness from beneath the crust.

From close by, I hear the pounding of approaching footsteps. I need to do this quickly. Perhaps, I realise, I should have trusted someone to help me, maybe Heafoc. Definitely not Cenbryht. I don't want him to know my promises of reward were dependent on this. I needed him, because of his warrior prowess, but he was reticent. I assured him of payment. He eventually agreed to come with me. He was the last of my warriors to join my group only four nights ago.

I scrabble at the earth, and now bigger and bigger chunks come away, and slowly I create a hole, and then, with a final dull ting, what I'm hoping to find is revealed before me.

Grinning, I spread out the blanket, and hastily

scoop all I've found into it, mindful of the hempen sack disintegrating under the dank soil, before gathering up the sides of the blanket, and holding it tightly, the broken sword in my other hand. At the same time, I kick the mud back into the hole, hoping to obscure it before my surviving warriors arrive. I hope Heafoc's brought my shield.

With a final kick, I realise I'm no longer alone. I'm grateful I thought to turn my back on where I've found my treasures.

'Is everyone here?' I question, aware more than the burning man is missing. The numbers loyal to me were small anyway, fourteen of us. Now they've declined even more.

'Those who live,' Heafoc responds without rancour, his eyes appraising me to ensure I have what I came to take, holding my shield alongside his. He knew of my intentions. Only he understood nothing was assured.

'Good. Now, back to the horses, and then we can get away from here before my father's warriors come to inspect what's happened.'

I think Cenbryht might complain, but he snaps his thick lips shut, running a hand through the blood-encrusted beard covering much of his chin. His cheeks are a web of scars. He's a man who's

fought throughout his life, but has never been rewarded as he thought he should be by my arrogant
father. I promised to change that.

'Come on.' I turn and, with nimble steps, run
from the burning inferno towards where we secured
the horses we rode here earlier and left outside the
ditched enclosure. There'll be enough animals for
everyone to ride away from this place. Perhaps it's
better that a few of the warriors perished. At least
we'll be able to travel more quickly than if hampered
by those on foot. And we need to travel quickly. To
evade the anger of my father, Wihtlæd, the leader of
the *comitatus* of the Gyrwe. I allow a grin to touch my
gods-cursed cheeks.

He shouldn't have dismissed me as he did. He
should have accepted what I was, and stopped
blaming me for being the cause of my mother's
death. My brother was a weak man and not fit to
hold any claim to the men and women oath-sworn to
my father, by ties of family or even those who had no
choice but to serve him.

Now I must continue in my endeavours. I didn't
think I'd be overwhelmingly successful, but desperation and pure rage urged me to attempt this. Now I
know my future can be made, just like my father, and
his father, and his father's father, all the way back to

Woden from whom I claim my descent. But not here. I must leave the only place I've ever known. I can't say I'm sorry to do so as I swat aside yet another of the pestilent buzzing insects that have plagued me each and every summer of my short life.

Perhaps, I reason, there might be a place where I can live from now on that's free of the persistent flies, as well as my arrogant arsehole of a father, who thought I deserved only to be swatted like one of these insects.

3

MEDDI OF THE EORLINGAS

I find the small workshop much as I left it, having forced open the shrieking wooden door and the pile of detritus built up against it. For a moment, my anger sparks. Edern took this from me and then failed to show the respect it was due. The bastard.

Sian assists me with the strength of her firm arms. I turn, hoping no one sees my triumph turned to desperation, thwarted by a bloody stupid door.

As soon as it's finally open, Sian and I share a look of shared victory. I bow my head, touch the ceremonial torque around my neck, and then stand to brush the stone lintel over the doorway with my fingers. I mutter soft words under my breath, audible to no one. Sian stands reverentially aside as the smell of an enclosed space fills my nostrils. A strange combination of the herbs stored within, alongside other, less pleasant aromas.

'Can you find a besom?' I ask softly, as I realise the tiled floor is thick with dust and the leavings of other animals. I can smell rat droppings and the astringent stink of their piss. No doubt, there's mice within as well.

'Mistress.' Quickly, she scurries away. Alone, I stop myself from stepping within. I need to do this correctly. It's been too long in the making to rush it. I will wait until I can walk over the remnants of the tiled floor and touch all that was once mine.

I should not feel so relieved to see it as I left it, but I am, despite my fury that Edern's not respected its importance. Elen has not used this space. It remains as I left it on that dark day. I curl my fingers into the balls of my hands so my nails dig into my flesh, holding myself away from what I long to do. I'll wait for Sian. Not that I'll let her clean the space for me.

In the distance, I hear my brother and his men taking control of the settlement. Madog will welcome knowing he's the leader here. He's too young to have ever made this place his home, but this is where he should have spent his summers and winters until now. We shouldn't have been banished from here to our poor settlement to the south. Edern should never have had command of our home.

Sian returns quickly. I notice how she limps, favouring the left leg.

'Mistress.' She indicates a desire to go ahead, as she holds a besom tightly in her hand.

'No, no. I'll do it. Please, find hot water and a cloth. We'll need to clean the whole space before it's suitable.'

She nods, not offended by the request. I don't know her, but already I believe we think alike. I don't fear her. She doesn't appear to be apprehensive about being with me, either. It's a good start. My relationship with her will be different to the one I share with Marchell despite Marchell teaching me almost all of what I know.

I grip the wooden handle of the besom firmly, my eyes fixed on the harsh bristles, and then I step beneath the roof. The coolness of the room envelops me as I start scraping the detritus through the doorway. I feel past impressions through my feet as they touch the area where no tiles remain and close my eyes, allowing the rhythmic nature of the action to transport me to another time and place – when I was many summers younger and lacked the scars that mark me now.

For a moment, a smile plays on my lips and my hand moves to cup my belly. I'm surprised when there's no gentle curve there. I feel a tear drip onto my lips and lick it clear, straightening my shoulders defiantly. I'll not allow who I was to influence me now. I am different. I am changed. But my ambitions remain.

Opening my eyes, my movements are firmer, harsher, a cloud of dust blowing up around me. I direct it towards the open doorway, the scent of burning reaching my nostrils. The fires have been built up in their correct spaces. There'll be hot water, and food, soon. There's no need to light the fires that will keep the floors warm. After all, it is the summer.

With a satisfying scrape, I fling the rat shit and other items, a myriad of dead flies amongst them, through the doorway.

'Whoa,' my brother exclaims. I fix my eyes on him, startled from my reverie.

'Apologies,' I offer, smiling. He grimaces away as my eyes narrow. My brother isn't used to seeing me as anything other than the fierce and fiery seeress I've become. No doubt, my appearance as besom wielder shocks him.

'Is all well?' he asks, the words revealing his surprise.

'It will be,' I assure him. 'And you?'

'Yes, Edern will be burnt tonight. Elen's under guard. We hold Villa Eorlingas. Now we need to protect it from others who we might have pre-empted.'

'Place two of your shields showing your emblem of the horse at the junction with the road,' I advise him. 'Then they'll know Villa Eorlingas is once more in the hands of its rightful tribe. They'll fear to come closer.'

'Truly?' he questions. I see him with fresh eyes then. He's my fierce brother, but he's also a small boy, asking for my advice. I was always rough with him. He needed to be forged into the man he had to become. It's taken much perseverance, and patience, which even I freely admit I lack.

'They'll dread us. They'll see this for what it is. We're not the cowed people we became. You'll have a son soon, perhaps even by now, although I doubt it. The first child always takes longer to finally arrive. And I'm here, as well. We're restored and will keep what we have.'

He grins then, and the winters are driven back from his young face. Not that he's old, but the responsibility of my expectations has weighted him. 'It

is a fine place,' he announces decisively. 'We'll live
here and make much more of the land available to
grow fine crops and even better horses, sheep and
cows.'

'We will, yes.' I see Sian and two young lads carrying heavy containers of gently steaming water towards us. My brother turns and sees the same.

'I'll leave you, seeress. Inform me if you need the
assistance of other, stronger men. If not, you'll light
the flames that cast Edern to ash?'

'I'll enjoy doing so,' I confirm, and we share a
conspiratorial look.

He turns away. I notice his wide shoulders and
firm build. He walks like our father did, when he
lived. Madog will not make the mistakes our father
did. I'll not allow it.

Sian bows her head low as she approaches.

'Please.' I indicate she can enter now, as I move
outside. 'Direct the boys as you would. Ensure everything is cleaned of dust and debris.'

She inclines her head and quickly orders the
boys to help her. I continue to sweep the mess aside
from the doorway. I don't want it anywhere near this
special place. I stand then, and survey Villa Eorlingas, besom to hand. It is, as my brother said, a fine
place. The ravages of Edern's occupation are clear to

see. He was never far-sighted. His lack of a son proves that. He thought of only one thing, and once he gained it, that was it. He had no intention of doing more. A man such as him will be quickly forgotten. In time, we'll not mention him. He'll be dust in the wind.

My brother, and his son, will rule this place and rule it well. There will be everlasting monuments of what they accomplish, added to those who went before us, aside from our father. He's lost to us. He's certainly dead, but his remains were never interred as they should have been. I hate Edern anew for that.

The fields will quickly flourish, and the animals will grow fat and provide good meat, milk and cheese, as well as youngsters. I'll breed horses from my fine mare as well as bartering for better animals to swell the herd. I'll restore the wealth and connections of my tribe. We're a proud people, whose horses were much in demand from others. We were wealthy because of that. We will be again.

And I'll do it with the most precious thing that I've been deprived off for all these winters.

My child never walked with me, or spoke with me, or did anything with me after I held her briefly in my arms. Edern saw to that. But I was able to inter her where she'd stay close to me. When Sian and her helpers have finished, I'll bend and check she still lies beneath the walls of this small building, once roofed with tile, but now the place of this tribe's seeress.

The warmth of the sun touches my face. I lift my head upwards, allowing the light of the precious sun to dance on my closed eyes. I welcome the searing madder-red playing along my eyelids. I greet it as my rebirth.

Edern took my daughter from me, but now, I'll take all from him. If Elen is with child, that child will perish. I'll not scar her as Edern inflicted on me. But I'll not allow any spawn of Edern's to breathe a single breath. It would go against the will of our gods. Never again will I allow another to take control of my future. Never.

4

WÆRMUND OF THE GYRWE

My brother's treasures weigh heavily on my horse as we travel. The landscape opens up before me, flat but marshy, rushes rising high, almost to my shoulders, even when I ride. Bird call rings loudly in my ears, including the harsh shriek of gulls, and every so often our passage sends some of the birds squawking into the air. It's unfortunate, as it will give away our location, if we're already being hunted. I hope we're not. The sun touches my cheeks, and I feel the aches and pains of my triumph as my body slowly cools from this morning's exertions. I'll not be able to fight again, not until I've allowed my body time to recover.

And so, I must decide what to do next, other than

following this path westwards towards the border with our neighbouring tribe.

I can't rise up against my father, Wihtlæd, the leader of the Gyrwe. He's too strong and has too many warriors who would fight us, especially now. They'd overwhelm us far too easily, just because for every one of my warriors, my father has several.

But I'm also now a warrior, and I have my own collection of loyal men and women. To keep them, I must reward them. And ensuring they live and aren't cut down by my vengeful father is one of the ways I can do that.

I recall all my father ever told me of his father, Waga, and his father's father, Watholgeot. Or rather, all he ever told my brother and which I only heard by chance. Those men were of this land, but their ancestor, Woden, was not. He came from over the sea, to the east, and inveigled himself into a position of authority amongst those who already claimed this place as their home.

I must now do the same. I have the ceremonial sword, passed down from generation to generation since the days of our ancestor, Woden, never entrusted to the ground with the death of a fighting man for it was too precious. With it, I will forge my place here, even if I must find the means to restore it to its former glory. My brother should have done so many summers ago. And so should my father before him. The bloody fools.

But first, there are more basic requirements.

The day draws on as I fight a path through the fenlands of my home. We'll need somewhere to sleep and food to eat, far from where my father's warriors might find us. The complaints of those who are now my warriors but aren't used to riding reach my ears. They too are tired and exhausted. The horses do the work of their legs, but their bellies are rumbling, and they can't keep on forever without needing sustenance. I remind myself of my decision to earn the loyalty of my warriors other than by promising them rich rewards for joining me. I must make them respect me as they once did my father, before he dismissed them from his service for one slight or another.

I turn, relieved to at last realise the black smoke from the burning settlement which has risen high into the sky is no longer visible. We've travelled far enough.

'Here,' I call, eyes alighting on a rare cropping of thick trees that'll provide cover and fuel for our own fire. Deep within those trees, there must also be animals to capture and butcher, as well as water suitable for drinking. We also need food for the horses. I'd not considered that. I've no oats for them. That's an unwelcome oversight. I should have stolen those from my brother's settlement as well rather than letting them burn. I hope I won't regret the mistake.

I dismount quickly, slapping the horse's brown shoulder as I do so. The animal offers a soft whinny as I lead it to a stream I find by listening to the tinkling of running water. I sniff the air, and content it's untainted by the salt of the sea, allow the animal to drink.

I turn and eye my collection of men and women. Heafoc's the only one to incline his head towards me respectfully, but then he's been a warrior all of his life. He knows warriors need to be led and have one person who'll reward them with food, weapons and clothes to keep them warm. My father was a fool when he told Heafoc he was no longer a member of his *comitatus*.

The others bitch and complain. I'll need to keep an eye on Wædel and Cenbryht. I already mistrust their place here. If I'd had more choice, I wouldn't have brought them, but Cenbryht can fight better than any man I've known. It was vital he joined me. I held out on enacting my plans for him. Wædel, I fear, has always been too close to my father. Even now, I know Wædel would happily re-pledge himself to him, if only my father would have him. But I was desperate, in the end, and took Wædel because he convinced Cenbryht to join with me.

The two women, Bucge and Osfyth, speak quietly to one another. Osfyth sports a bloody gash on her chin. Bucge hobbles as she dismounts. They're not women I'm likely to wish to bed. Both have proven themselves unable to breed despite any number of bedfellows. They're a fine addition to my small force. Osfyth and Bucge have skills other than just being able to kill with a blade. The same can't be said for Wædel and Cenbryht. I'll watch those two closely. All they can offer me is their blades. And their loyalty is far from assured. I consider whether I'd have been happier had they been the ones to die during the attack. Wædel, perhaps, but I hope to win Cenbryht to my cause.

'I'll find food,' Osfyth informs me, already striding beneath the trees with their green leaves, having left her horse in the care of Bucge. Bucge murmurs to the two animals she leads to water. I can't hear the words, but a shimmer of unease courses down my body. Bucge knows things no man should know. She understands things my father was once desperate to hear, until he was displeased with her answer, and banished her from his side.

I open my mouth to argue with Osfyth, but she's a good hunter. And why would I tell her no, other than I didn't order her to do so? I bite my lip. This leading might be somewhat problematic. I'll have to ensure she looks at me as more than a man young enough to be her child, had she ever borne one herself.

Eastmund speaks next. 'I'll find wood and kindling.' He runs a grubby hand over his singed black beard. He got too close to the burning buildings, which hardly reassures me he's the best to start a fire.

'What of the horses?' Heafoc questions, his eyes penetrating. 'We've no oats. We burned them.'

'They'll be content with water and grasses, for now,' I suggest as he joins me while my horse continues to drink.

'Where will we get oats from?' he questions, eyebrows high. It's not quite a complaint. But it is almost one.

'We'll barter for them,' I say with more assurance than I feel.

'From whom, and with what?' he chuckles, his hands sweeping across the expanse before us. He's right. We're nearly a full day away from all I've ever experienced in the territory of the Gyrwe. Here, there'll be tribes I don't know, and men and women will be wary if we ride amongst them with our weapons and shields. I imagine my father's reputation, and that of his father, Waga, and his father's father, Watholgeot, will have penetrated even here. They'll not know that we're outcasts from the Gyrwe. They'll think we were sent to steal from them, as Watholgeot once did before some of our people became farmers.

'Then we'll fight them,' I interject, chin held high, chest heaving. I've enjoyed my triumph for less than a day, and already I'm being questioned by those older, and perhaps wiser, than me.

'That's more like it,' Heafoc concedes, striding towards long grasses swaying in the gentle breeze, tinged with the salt of the ocean. I steady myself, licking my lips, my thoughts turning to my father again.

I'll need to banish the spectre of his presence. I'll need to build my own following. Fighting for oats is hardly the stuff of fireside stories, but it's what's required. I'll need to find another tribe, like my father's. I'll not kill them as I did my brother's men. Or perhaps I will.

I consider my followers. There were fourteen of

us in total. Now there are twelve. We have the same number of horses. No more, and no less.

With the smell of smoke from Eastmund's fire filling the air, I retrieve the blanket and all wrapped within it, including the sword I took from my brother which should have been passed to me, not to him. I must reward these men and women, as I said I would. But I can't give them everything I took from my brother's treasure. No, a man who means to do as I now do must have the means to entice others to his side. I lick my lips again, tasting the salt of the day's efforts. Where will I find more men and women to join me? How will I tempt them other than with shimmering silver and gold and the iron axe heads? They're valuable indeed, with the correct person to make handles for them. They should never have been cast aside as these have. I understand why. My brother intended to claim his village and the ditch encircling it by burying his portable wealth within it. I'll not be repeating his mistake. These war axes should be used. They'll be used, I see now, in what must happen next.

'I'll take this, and this.' Wædel bends to collect the items he indicates. I startle. I shouldn't have allowed him to sneak up on me.

'You will not.' I move to snatch the silver pin and

iron lump back from his grubby hands, but his fists close over the two things – well, not the iron lump, but he turns his hand over so I'm faced with his knuckles. It's taken little time for him to turn on me. Once more, I realise I shouldn't have included him in my intentions. If I'd been able to get Cenbryht without needing Wædel, I'd not have allowed him into my grouping to defy my father, and kill my brother.

'And what will you do about it, little bird?' Wædel taunts, his face twisted in defiance. I'm not little or frail like a bird. I am quick, though not as quick as Heafoc, who, despite his bulk, can move more swiftly than a stag in flight. He reaches over Wædel's shoulders, and places his hands over the smaller man, squeezing tightly. I see swift fury on Wædel's dirty face, but it's quickly replaced with a wince of pain. His shoulders strain beneath his filthy tunic, as he tries to prise his arms apart.

'Drop them,' Heafoc breathes into his ear. I don't understand what I've done to make Heafoc so fiercely loyal to me, but perhaps it's nothing I've accomplished. It's just his nature to be loyal. I don't deny I'm grateful.

'I can't while you hold my hands.' The altercation has drawn the attention of the others, even Osfyth, who comes towards us, hands bloody from where she's been butchering the animal found to feed us. In the dimming light, she holds more menace than the tribe's wise man, with his strange shuffling gait and clacking of whatever he wears beneath his long tunic, who's replaced Bucge because he speaks the words my father wishes to hear. His sightless eyes never stopped him from perceiving everything. I consider if he knew of my intentions. If he did, he warned no one. Perhaps then, as Bucge states, he was nothing more than a fraud. My father should have relied on the words of his wise woman, not those of a man who stumbled into our tribe one day four winters ago. Since then, he's beguiled my father, and my brother. I'd have liked to kill him, but he was lucky enough to be with my father, and not my brother, when we attacked my brother's settlement.

'I'll release you, and then you drop them,' Heafoc announces in his surprisingly placid tone. He has the menace of a wolf, but the voice of a man who knows no fear. Of anyone.

'Release them,' Osfyth adds, her words cracked and harsh. I consider if she spoke with a more pleasant tone when she was younger. The scars marking her throat perhaps make her sound rough. Or so I've long suspected.

Wædel does as he's told, lips twisting with disgust. He spits on my fine collection of treasures.

'Is this all you have?' he glowers. 'Is this what you won our support with? I should have asked to see more before I agreed to your task. We'll be hunted by Wihtlæd and killed for such an act, and for what?'

But the others don't share his dismissive attitude towards my brother's treasures. Bucge stands beside Osfyth, unheeding of the blood dripping from her hands, and I see a smirk of triumph on her face, hair pulled back tightly, and threaded with talismans. I hope she'll aid me with the wisdom she enjoys, even if my father dismissed her. I know she possesses a sight I don't.

The others are pleased. Their smirks and smiles reflect the shimmering treasure I have before me, now displayed for all to see. I didn't intend to present it to them in such a way, but Wædel's actions have brought all of my remaining men and women to my side.

'I promised you much,' I retort, unsettled by Wædel but pleased by everyone else's reactions. 'You can take a treasure now and leave to go wherever you wish or stay with me, and we'll find others like this. We'll grow our numbers and then we need not fear my father's retribution.'

'Agreed,' Bucge announces quickly, while Osfyth nods. Osfyth's another my father dismissed. He's always been determined only the youngest and brightest should serve him. Those, like Osfyth and Heafoc, he scorned as too old, although he has the same number of winters to his name. He never rewarded them for what they'd done. He expected them to beg for scraps upon which to eat and live. He was foolish in that regard.

Wædel's face scrunches angrily. I have my hand on the small shimmering iron discs I'll present to him. They were once decorated, how I don't know, but now the edges are thinning and whatever was on them is only glimpsed in the brightest of sunlight, the indentations only perceptible with my nail.

'I'll stay,' Heafoc announces in his slow tones. Others also nod, amongst them tall Goddæg, and short Nothelm, although one other than Wædel shakes his head. Cenbryht. I knew to doubt him. He was slow to commit, and I anticipated he'd be the soonest to leave. Where he'll go, I don't know. But I needed him, and now his task is complete. My brother is dead, and I have the treasures he had. And the sword that should always have been mine from when I was old enough to hold it.

Eastmund, the only one not to join us yet, as

Hygebeorht, limping Bægmund and madder-haired Maggenræd are already close, makes his way from where the familiar crackle of flames over twigs can be heard.

'I'll stay,' he confirms. 'There's nothing for me in any of Wihtlæd's settlements.' There's no anger in his voice, only sorrow.

For a moment, none of us speak. Eastmund's grief is new, and understandable. He thought to become a father but now has no wife and no child, both dying in a shriek of blood and pain all within my father's settlement heard only two weeks ago.

'I will not,' Wædel announces. 'I'll take what's mine,' he reiterates, bending down to snatch what he wants.

This time, I reach across and stop him, holding his hands firmly in mine, threatening to overbalance at the same time. My arms strain with the action, my knees crying out for me to stand, but Wædel's not to belittle me, here, as men and women promise themselves to follow me. Not my father, or my weak brother who my father was adamant would command the tribe after his death.

Wædel's arms thrum with their strength. I can already feel myself growing weaker, but I need to overwhelm him or lose face amongst these few men and women. They could take all from me if they wanted to do so. No doubt Wædel and Cenbryht realise this. Cenbryht's close to Wædel, poised to strike with his blade. I'll fight him if need be.

'I'll give you what I promised in exchange for fighting at my side,' I growl, aware my arms are shaking, but that Wædel can't overwhelm me. He, like Heafoc, was thought too old by my father to continue in his *comitatus*.

'You'll do more than that, or I'll run to your father and tell him of all you did, and what you plan now.' As Wædel speaks, spittle lands on my face, but I still hold him distant from stealing away what I took from my brother.

'You can take what you were promised,' I menace, my low voice surprising even me with the threat contained within it, 'or you can die now, with a blade at your throat.'

'You little runt.' Wædel lurches towards me. I fear he'll knock me over. Only, at the last moment, I sense movement at my feet and with a litheness that surprises me, snatch up the blade sent towards me to hold it away from Wædel's throat by no more than a finger's width. I'll thank Osfyth for this later. She didn't need to help me as she has.

'I'll end your life, and wash my treasures in your

lifeblood,' I threaten, the words even lower, the promise in my voice only slightly offset by the tremor in my seax hand.

Wædel holds my gaze for a long moment. I almost wish he'd force me to do this or come closer so I can do as I warn. But he values his life too greatly to end it in an argument over second-hand silver and iron.

Hands to either side of him, raised close to his head, he steps away from me and the promise from the small, sharp blade.

'I'll take what's mine,' he announces with finality. The tension evaporates as the smell of meat cooking fills the air.

'Then that's settled. You'll leave at first light,' I huff, pleased to have triumphed here. 'Any others?' I ask.

Cenbryht surprises me by shaking his head. I thought he'd leave with Wædel. I think Wædel did as well, because he startles.

'Then I'll give you your share.' I incline my head towards Wædel. 'But if you seek my father, and he comes looking for me, I'll repay you only with a blade through your neck.'

I extend my hand, the shimmering discs held within it. He snatches out his hand to take them, a slow grin of appreciation turning his dour lips upright.

'My thanks, Wærmund,' he mutters, his warm hand gripping what I offer.

After that, I watch him for a long time where he sits close to the fire, holding up his treasures so their wealth glitters with the flames. Even while everyone moves aside and the meat's cooked and ready to eat, I continue to watch him. He must know I survey him, but gives no indication. Only then do I cover the rest of my treasures with a clink and clank, including my brother's sword, and turn to meet Heafoc's gaze.

He nods and shares a wink with me.

I know what he's thinking. I'm sure I'm considering the same.

Wædel's not to be trusted. It would, perhaps, be better to kill him now. But in the morning he'll be gone. I can't decide which option is to be preferred. Killing him might make those who've decided to stay uneasy. But Wædel might just tell my father where I am. Would I sooner lose more of my warriors or risk my father finding me and ending my life? I decide it's better to lose warriors than have my father find me. I must do all I can to evade my father's reach. My life depends on it.

5

MEDDI OF THE EORLINGAS

'Brother.' I approach him later. It's been a long day, but one I've waited for throughout so much of my life that fatigue is banished in my triumph. I've ensured all is well in my workshop. I'm content. My daughter lies there, or rather, her remains. No one has touched her. I consider if Edern feared the small bundle of what is now bones for he knew where I interred her. The thought brings a smile to my face. I hope he did. I hope he spent the last half of his life fearing to visit there. The workshop certainly has the feeling of long abandonment.

'Seeress,' he replies, but with no malice. Instead, his face is glazed. I almost wish I could capture him like this, here and now. This moment of peace and contentment will not last. How can it, when others still hunger to hold Villa Eorlingas despite my telling him to place two shields proclaiming our return close to the roadway.

Edern wasn't the first to attempt to take my father's villa, and I doubt he'll be the last, even if, so far, he's been the most successful. It's long been a source of anger that my tribe held the richest, most fertile villa of those still standing in the local area. It's long been a problem that could gain momentum in a heartbeat, but few could do anything about it, until Edern came along. Before then, my father had been the strongest of all men, the one able to hold back the threat of violence from others. It helped that aside from a few rusty blades, few during my father's life had the ability to mount an attack, while my father possessed the finest stallions and mares from which he could mount an attack or defend his holdings. Now there are even fewer blades, but more desperation. Food's less plentiful. The weather, despite all attempts to win the aid of our gods and goddesses, is not always kind to the crops and animals we cultivate. The most recent summers have been wet and windy, and the subsequent harvests poor. It has made people weaker than they should be.

But Edern didn't steal Villa Eorlingas with a

blade. No, he stole it by killing my father and dishon-ouring the accord between guest and host that en-sures the safety of all who trade between the different villas. Once that was done, Edern kept hold of it by brutally stamping out any who thought to take it from him. And by claiming me, my father's daughter, as his wife, as though this made his actions somehow acceptable. Madog's mother escaped in the resulting confusion, spirited away by Marchell. Even now, I think Marchell knew of what was to happen to my father, but she never offered any warning. Per-haps what befell him was his destiny. It's taken me many summers to forgive her.

And I? I didn't take kindly to being Edern's wife, bound to him at the point of a dagger. Neither did I welcome sharing his bed. I even resented the child growing in my belly until she was taken from me, and deemed worthless by her father. When he took out his anger on me, causing such terrible injuries, I vowed to have my revenge, and somehow, wounded and cast out, I was found by those of my father's people who'd managed to escape on that terrible night. They took me to Marchell. They allowed Marchell to save me. I'm grateful to them, even now, I lived to see my half-brother grown to manhood.

But ours isn't the only tribe to have been harmed

under Edern's commands. Neither, it appears, am I the only woman he took to his bed and defiled. What Elen willingly consented to, Edern stole from others. How she could lie with him, knowing what he did, I do not know. It's another reason why I despise her so much.

'I'm a father,' Madog announces, meeting my eyes, which shimmer in the dying rays of the day's light. 'A boy, as you promised.'

I nod, trying to appear sage, but inside, a part of me is thrilled. This is the next part of our tribe's survival. First, we had to dispose of Edern, and when we were unable to do that, lacking the strength of enough warriors, we had to wait for him to die. Now my brother has a boy child who can lead the tribe after him. I want to laugh joyously but content myself with embracing him. He's my leader, and I'm his seeress, but I wiped his arse when he was a boy, and while I lost my daughter, when I was sensible after my healing was completed, and my grief dispersed, I welcomed Madog as her replacement. I doubt he knows the depths of my feelings for him. Even to myself, I endeavour to keep it hidden.

'And your wife?'

'Both well.' He grins even wider. 'They'll journey here as soon as they're able.' He waves his arms at the expanse behind him. I nod. This is my home now, but it is also his. This is where we belong, and not in some humble and decaying settlement to the south. No. This is from where we came. We were the ones, long ago, who took Villa Eorlingas, not that it was called that then when the original owners left these shores. It was said they'd return one day, but it never happened. Knowledge of who they were has long since been lost, although we happily shelter beneath the tile roof and firm walls they caused to be placed here. And, of course, from the wealth of their horse-breeding stock. But this is our home. Even my father never feared another would assert an old claim to Villa Eorlingas. Alas, he should have been seeking an enemy closer to home.

'Then I'll welcome them and perform the rites when we're assured of his strength,' I intone. Madog's grin widens.

'You always said this day would come.' He speaks with the excitement of a boy with his first pony.

'I did, but we must be wary now. We've much to lose if we're not careful.'

'I know, seeress. I've set guards, firm guards. I trust Urien. And those who remain and were once subjected to Edern will pledge themselves to us or face banishment. We'll only allow those who are loyal to reside here.'

I consider this carefully. There are some elements of our reinstatement I've not fully considered.

'We'll need slaves to tend the crops and animals,' I inform him.

'We might. I'll not be hasty,' he affirms. Then he quietens and doesn't meet my eye. 'Was everything as you hoped?'

His question surprises me. I didn't believe it was any of his concern. I thought his intention was merely to take back what was stolen from our father. From us.

'It was, my thanks. I'm content but know to be cautious.'

'Was, was...' And his voice trails off. I offer him a soft smile.

'All is as I left it, apart from the obvious. The bones are where I left her. I feel complete once more.'

A flicker of sorrow touches his cheeks. I understand that today of all days, as he becomes a father, this must be suddenly poignant for him.

'Now, are we going to burn the bastard?' I recall him from such melancholy thoughts.

'Yes,' he announces decisively. 'Yes, we'll burn the

bastard. All is ready. Seeress, should Elen witness this?'

I growl. I don't wish to be reminded of her. I hope never to hear her voice again.

'She'll smell it,' I affirm, steely in my resolve.

'Seeress,' he confirms, nodding as though my determination is wise. I'm not sure it is, but I don't wish to see her. Not until I can be assured she's a barren husk. Only then will this be complete.

We walk towards the funeral pyre together. We've not gathered the material together. It was already done, waiting for the body of Edern to be laid upon it, perhaps with the dawn, perhaps with the sunrise. Now he'll burn and light the night sky and, in the morning, instead of carefully curating his ashes, to gather them together in an ancient bowl and seal them in the mound of the Eorlingas, he'll be scattered to the wind. His burnt remains will be dispersed. No one need remember him and what he did. In time, the horrors of all he wrought will be forgotten. There's no one to recall his memory. No one will even want to do so.

All those living near to the River Habren will see the flames from the pyre. They'll understand what they mean and then, tomorrow, we'll have to fear repercussions. Not for killing him, although I wish I could take responsibility for his death. No, they'll come for the wealth of Villa Eorlingas and for the secrets hidden beneath the surface, for not all are as obvious as the stallion and mare mosaic which decorates the entranceway with its dulled colours and depictions of horses, manes glistening even though the image is solid and passes beneath my feet whenever I walk within. It must be cleaned, thoroughly.

They'll not have Villa Eorlingas. It is mine. And my brother's.

'Seeress.' My brother indicates it's for me to light the waiting kindling.

I nod, taking the brand from Sian. She bows slightly. I see the flicker of triumph on her face. She's as pleased as I am Edern's dead. I'll remember that. I've found a new ally in the most unexpected of places.

I touch the leaping flames to the kindling and tufts of greasy wool pulled from a sheep by a hedgerow, and with a satisfying whoosh of hot air, it catches. I take a final glance at Edern and the face I've hated for all these winters and summers. I stay close, not heeding the heat as the flames leap forward, consuming the kindling and his flesh, watching him melt away to nothing but ash, and then I laugh, and look upwards, into the darkness of the coming night, and the vast expanse which assures me he is a small man, already forgotten about in the huge space above my head.

'It's about time, you bastard,' I murmur, unbidden tears rolling down my face as I stroll away. The people of the Eorlingas don't stand witness to his burning. None of us need to honour him. There'll be no priceless gifts to send him to the afterlife. There'll be no offering of grain alongside his ashes. No. Come the morning, he'll be dispersed by the wind and forgotten.

There's still much to do to restore Villa Eorlingas and its reputation, and I need consider Edern, and all he did to me, and my defenceless daughter, no more.

It may have taken the length of the life of my younger half-brother, but Edern is gone, and Villa Eorlingas is ours. Now we need merely hold on to it. It might not be as easy as I hope.

6

WÆRMUND OF THE GYRWE

I pretend to sleep when we've eaten the meat Osfyth gathered and Bucge cooked. I'm wary of Wædel and his intentions. Yet he ate with us and seemed reconciled to the treasure he received, and to the fact this will be his last night with us. I still suspect him, though. He'll want more. I'm sure of it.

So, rather than closing my eyes and resting after the day of success, I wait as darkness coats the land, descending between one blink and the next. Here, we're protected beneath the trees. Someone might smell the smouldering fire, but I'm confident they wouldn't wish to attack us. How could they determine how many of us there were? Unless they could see the horses, which now move and rustle as they try to rest in the unusual surroundings. This isn't what they're used to, far from it.

Unless, of course, my father is already hunting for me to seek vengeance for killing Waga, firing Waga's settlement and stealing his treasures. I'm confident my father will already know of what I did. The thought isn't a comfort.

But no, the sound I listen for isn't that of someone coming to seek revenge, but instead, the furtive movements of an alleged ally trying to escape with the contents of my treasure. If that happens, I'll have failed before I've begun. The scraps of iron, the shimmering if dulled circular discs, the axe heads, which lack handles, and my brother's ancient sword. My future is dependent on them. I must keep them near. I have them close to my body, wrapped in the vibrant blanket I took from my brother's bed. If Wædel means to steal them, he'll have to kill me, either with a blade at my throat or a stabbing action into my chest. It'll not be quietly done, even if he intends it to be.

Heafoc and I haven't spoken of our thoughts, but I know we share them. Heafoc isn't near to me. But he also pretends to sleep, I'm sure of it. Hygebeorht keeps guard, with his reassuring bulk, but he won't be looking inward. I don't know him well enough to inform him of my fears and worries. I can't appear weak. I've only just gained his regard with my success against my brother, and the promise of the very treasure I fear Wædel means to steal. Bucge also keeps a watch but from the other side of the encampment. Her task is to secure the horses, not us.

The sounds of night are reassuringly normal: the call of bats, the hoots of owls, and the occasional sharp snap of other winged creatures in the air. The rustle of four-legged night-time denizens can also be heard, even the lapping of water from the nearby stream, but nothing troubles us other than the pesky buzzing insects.

I feel myself lulled by the noise. I fight to stay awake. My breathing slows. My body aches from the day's exertions. I think of the men I killed. I consider my brother gasping his last breath like a fish out of water, disbelief on his face as I ended his life. I feel no remorse for his death. He shouldn't have been such an arsehole. He shouldn't have blindly followed my father in dismissing me, the older brother, but the one with the huge birthmark colouring half of his face which, my father told all, meant I wasn't beloved by the gods.

And then I sense it. My body stiffens. I fight to slow my pounding heartbeat and calm my worried

breathing. Anyone coming close would quickly realise I'm not asleep. I have my blade close to hand,
the edge of the seax sharp enough to kill if I stab
with it. It lacks the keenness to slit throats – a pity. I
dream of owning a blade like that. I know my father
has such a thing, but he's the only man of his people
to have such a deadly weapon. It was his father's before him, and his father's before him. He even said it
was once owned by our ancestor, Woden.

I'll need to have the sword I've reclaimed tempered by the magik of a bladesmith to make it even
half as good, as well as having a new hilt and guards
fitted. I know a bladesmith could restore the sword to
its former keenness and beauty, unlike the weapon in
my hand. The metal it's constructed of is poor-
quality iron. It doesn't shimmer in the sunlight, and
even has pieces of the blade missing where I've used
it to stab before. Those distortions shimmer as
though with silver but that's not a good sign. It
means the blade has been cold-shorted and is likely
to break from a too heavy impact. It signifies the iron
was not of the highest quality. Perhaps I shouldn't be
surprised my father gave me such a poor blade. He
never liked me. No doubt, he hoped I'd pick a fight,
and then be surprised when the weapon failed and I
bled my last.

But for now, I have the seax, as poor as it is. I know where it is. I don't reach for it. Not yet. It's just there. I need only snake out my hand and grip it.

The sound comes closer, a shuffling noise. Does Wædel not realise he needs to be quieter?

A questing hand runs over the hard-packed ground close to me. I keep my eyes tightly shut. He's close, breathing audible, but not near enough. My heart thuds louder.

I consider if Heafoc is as alert as I am, if Hygebeorht hears as I do, or if Bucge is aware of what's about to happen.

Still, I wait.

I can hear Wædel breathing, the sound ragged. I would laugh to listen to it: despite his inability to mask his actions, he still thinks about taking what's mine. He no doubt means to win my father's regard. How he intends to account for his involvement in my brother's death is something he'll have to consider when faced with my father's wrath, for Wihtlæd will be beyond furious when he discovers.

Not that Wædel's going to succeed.

Wædel fought well today. He took several lives. It's a pity he won't live to see the sunrise, just like those he killed.

Finally, I can wait no more. His hand is working at the knot, holding the blanket tied together. It won't be long, and he'll have his hands on what he wants. I'm surprised he doesn't intend to take everything. It would have been easier, but perhaps he fears the items clanking together. The noise would wake every-one. I surge upwards, my seax blade extended to stab.

The cry of shock on seeing my blade doesn't sound like it comes from Wædel. I narrow my eyes, using what little moonlight there is beneath the scudding clouds overhead, to see it's not Wædel be-fore me at all.

'What are you doing?' I demand, furious now I see another intends to betray me. I can sense others waking from their sleeping, even Hygebeorht coming closer. Heafoc's alert, his war axe ready to take a killing blow.

'Taking what's mine,' Cenbryht replies angrily, sitting back on his heels, facing me with defiance etched into the hard angles of his face as lit by the moon overhead. Why, I consider, didn't Cenbryht simply ask for his treasures when Wædel did? Why has he determined to steal away my fortune now?

'There's no more. Not for anyone,' I counter. I hear Osfyth murmur her agreement as the fire flares, someone either kicking it to life, or adding fuel to the smouldering embers.

'Wædel has more.' Cenbryht's reply is defiant. Once more, I regret needing him to attack my brother's settlement, but of us all, Cenbryht is the one with the skill of a true warrior. I knew he'd be able to overwhelm my brother with his fine blade, a gift from my father before he too was cast aside for being too old and slow with his actions. At least my father didn't take back the blade.

'Where is Wædel?' I question quickly. I expected it to be him who attacked, but as I peer into the gloomy shadows, I can't see him, although I can count the others of my loyal warriors.

'Wædel,' Heafoc calls into the darkness, but there's no reply.

'He went for a piss,' Hygebeorht replies. 'I don't know if he returned.' Now Hygebeorht sounds confused. I should be furious.

'Then we must assume he didn't,' I mutter angrily, focusing on Cenbryht. With Wædel missing, Cenbryht's actually in a better position than if Wædel were here. There's no need to kill him, but neither can we have someone such as him with us. I need loyal men and women, not those who would take what's mine the moment my eyes are closed.

'What will you do?' Heafoc questions. That's the problem. What will I do with Cenbryht? If Wædel has already gone, which seems to be the case, I fear what he'll do next. Will Wædel go to my father? Would Cenbryht mean to do the same? Cenbryht's recent banishment from my father's *comitatus* still burns him. It's raw. I took advantage of that, but what if Cenbryht meant to be restored to my father by telling him of all I've done?

'We'll tie him up and decide in the morning,' I announce while Cenbryht growls at the touch of Heafoc's rough hands on his wrists. I have no rope, but I tear a strip from my brother's blanket. I need to bind Cenbryht if I'm not going to kill him immediately.

I sense the unease of the others. Even Bucge has come to cast an eye over what's happening.

'We'll double the guard,' I decide. Now we know to expect something from Wædel, either tonight or in the coming days, I feel we should be more alert. 'I'll take it,' I sigh when no one offers to aid Hygebeorht and Bucge. I bite my lip, wishing my voice didn't falter with unease at the lack of a response from amongst my warriors.

'And what of Wædel?' Heafoc demands, even as Cenbryht twists beneath his hands.

'Stay still,' I glower, struggling to bind Cenbryht's hands tightly enough. He pulls and turns, and I fear he'll escape before I can restrain him.

'Here.' Osfyth's suddenly before me, her eyes flashing in the moonlight. She has Cenbryht trussed up more quickly than I could ever manage. She offers me a grimace. 'Like one of the boars I hunt.' And now Cenbryht's still, although he could risk running from here because his legs aren't bound, only his hands. 'I'll also keep guard with Bucge and Hygebeorht,' she informs me. 'We'll keep Cenbryht close to us so we can be assured he doesn't escape. You can get some sleep.' With that, she hauls Cenbryht to his feet and marches him beneath the trees. I turn to Heafoc. He nods, or at least I think he does.

The others, some of whom haven't even bothered to stand upright, offer no further caution and quickly go back to sleep. I slump to the ground, my hands feeling all around the blanket, looking to tie it again around the treasures. They fumble, and my legs shake. I feel cold and then too hot. I look around the small campsite in the light from the flames, seeing the bundles of the men who rest there because the two women are on guard duty, aiding Hygebeorht.

Should I suspect more of them? Should I even remain here with them, or try and escape? Now that

I've been successful in killing my brother, I need to decide what to do next. Are these people the best to plan my future with, away from my father's tribe? I grimace at the thought. They were easy enough to bring to my side, mostly because my father belittled them as much as he did me, but people who lack all faithfulness won't necessarily remain loyal to me either. Not now I've taken them away from all they've ever known.

'Get some sleep,' Heafoc rumbles.

I startle at the sudden noise. In the near distance, I hear the sound of footsteps and what I suspect is the angry scuffling of the captive Cenbryht.

'Get some sleep,' comes again. 'In the morning, you must decide what we're doing next.'

Slowly, I lie down, pulling my cloak tightly around my shoulders. My breathing slows. I stop shivering, but I can't shake the trickle of fear that shimmers down my spine.

I was in two minds about including Wædel but I needed him to bring Cenbryht and his superior warrior skills and blade to my side to be in with a chance of success. Now I wish I'd had the stones to tell Wædel no and encourage Cenbryht without him, using my position as Wihtlæd's disgruntled son and nothing else. Wherever Wædel's gone, he means me nothing but trouble while Cenbryht has the loyalty of a hound dog when the bitches are in heat.

There were twelve of us after our success at my brother's settlement, but now there are truly only ten loyal to my cause. That'll not be enough to counter my father's warriors when they follow our trail. Not that they need even do that if Wædel leads them directly to us.

In the morning, as Heafoc states, I must decide what to do, with Cenbryht, and with the rest of my warriors. I thought to escape my father by stealing my brother's wealth which was denied to me when I was passed over as my father's chosen successor. Now I must get far away from my father, while endeavouring to make my force formidable. We might be few in number, but we've achieved much already. I need only remember that, despite such setbacks.

7

MEDDI OF THE EORLINGAS

I sleep beneath the roof of the workshop. I find it comforting to be here and not within Villa Eorlingas. The villa was where Edern took all from me. Here, I feel safer, with the bones of my daughter sheltered beneath the wall and the faint aroma of the herbs that should line the walls, and will soon enough. Even though I've watched Edern's body burn and turn to ash, I still sense him here. I hope it won't take long for the feeling to fade. With a good wind today, his remains will be dispersed. There'll be no ceremonial interment for his ashes inside a priceless pot and then beneath the sheltering embrace of the earth's soil. He'll not be causing me any more problems. Ever. I must keep reminding myself of it.

'Seeress.' I'm woken when it's barely daylight. I turn to peer at the sound, and appreciate my brother calls to me. I notice he doesn't step inside the door. I've taught him well to respect the possessions of the seeress. The workshop is now my home. He'll treat it with the same regard he did my feeble hovel at our old settlement.

'What?' My voice is thick with lack of sleep and fatigue. I'm not sure when I last slept all night. It's been a few days.

'They're coming.' His voice is urgent.

'Who?'

'The Beansæte.'

'Already?' Irritation makes my voice acerbic as I struggle to my feet. The floor isn't the most comfortable of places, but there's no bed within. I'll have to get one made or dragged from within the main building of Villa Eorlingas. I don't plan on sleeping beneath its tiled roof if I can help it. 'Ready the warriors. I'm coming,' I call, stretching my back and working to drive some heat into my body. It's not cold. Or it shouldn't be, but I'm tired and hungry. 'Haven't they seen your shields?' I mutter, angry to find my suggestion has come to nothing. But Madog doesn't answer. He's already organising his warriors.

Sian's also stirred to wakefulness. I told her she could sleep within, in her usual place inside the main building, but she refused. I consider why, but perhaps she merely means to be as helpful to me as possible. She doesn't wish to share Elen's fate. And Elen has been far from quiet. When she smelled the smoke last night, she howled, more akin to a wolf than a woman. I almost rued my decision to let her live. Who cares if she's with a child? Her continued existence is an affront.

'Did you hear that?' I question Sian.

'I did, mistress.'

'Then take yourself within the villa. You'll be protected there.'

'I should stay with you,' she starts.

'Don't argue with me. Do as you're ordered.' My words are cold with fury. I should have been firmer last night. I'll not have Sian think she means more to me than she does.

'Mistress.' And she bows her head and quickly moves aside.

I busy myself, collecting my breastplate and the dagger I brought to claim Villa Eorlingas, ensuring my torque is in place, as well as the talismans of my position. From outside, I hear my brother and his men readying themselves. They've no intention of being overwhelmed, as we were able to do to those guarding Edern's villa yesterday. I'm resolved to ensuring it doesn't happen as well. No one else truly has a claim to this place aside from my brother and me. This is where I was born. This is where my father oversaw the tribes who looked to him as their leader. This is where Madog should have first entered the world as well.

All the same, Edern wasn't popular. I imagine every group in the local area would like to do as we have done and assure themselves the bastard is dead and gone.

Striding from the workshop, I take myself to the front of the main villa building, where my brother and his men wait just in front of where the two protruding sides of the villa end. The warriors don't look at me, although Madog eyes me with some unease.

'You'll not fight,' he cautions.

'I'll do what must be done,' I counter, hands already busy within my cloak, gripping talismans and items I can use to drive the claimants from here.

'You'll not fight,' he repeats, his words colder than a shard of ice. I don't deny him again. We'll be united in our stance against the newcomers.

'They've travelled all night?' I question.

'It would appear so,' Madog agrees, peering towards the trackway we progressed down yesterday. I realise almost half of his warriors stand at the ditch and embankment protecting the settlement. We came over it yesterday as though it didn't exist, but we had horses. The Beansæte don't. Certainly, I can hear no sound of hoofbeats. I do hear the bleats and lows of the sheep and cows as they graze.

As the shadows lift with the growing daylight, I see our opponents. They stride confidently along the trackway running in front of the River Habren. The man who leads them is much older than my brother, with a long greying beard that reaches almost to the middle of his stomach. He carries a shield with a dulled boss at its centre and a spear in his right hand.

Behind him follow fifteen men and boys. They're similarly equipped with spears and shields. None of the shields are bark, but all are old, small and made of metal. They'll protect a man's chest, or his cock, but not both at the same time. I eye them, chin raised arrogantly. I'd recognise Hedrek anywhere. He thought Edern was his ally. Edern proved him wrong by stealing away his blacksmith and prized stallion as soon as he was in control of Villa Eorlingas. I believe both the blacksmith and the stallion are now dead, but Hedrek's desire for revenge is entirely un-

derstandable. I'd welcome him, but my claim for revenge is stronger than his, despite the fact Edern also
took many of his people. Hedrek has had to rebuild,
just as the Eorlingas have needed to do.

The sunlight gathers and grows as a gentle breeze
touches my cheeks. I'm tempted to smile as it alights
on my breastplate, causing every eye to turn towards
me, but I keep my face purposefully blank.

'Seeress,' Hedrek starts, head already bowing,
while those behind him quickly follow suit. I don't
believe they see me as an individual, but rather what
I represent and, even then, he's not entirely respectful. A moment later, his hate-filled eyes rest on me
and my brother. 'This isn't your place,' he roars. 'I've
waited for this for too long. I'll not be stopped.'

'Then you'll fight us,' Madog announces without
heat. 'For we were here first, and as you can see, we're
now in control of Villa Eorlingas as we should always
have been.'

Madog's warriors hover close to the gap in the
ditch. They've parted just enough to allow Hedrek to
see me and Madog. They'll merge quickly enough
should Hedrek use his fury and not his sense.

'Give me my stallion, or one of the stallions get,
should the animal be dead. And the blacksmith,'
Hedrek shouts, the words still heated but tinged with

acceptance. He knows we all have a grudge to bear. He appreciates he has been beaten, and now tries to make the best of it.

'There's no stallion. The horses are weak and feeble, and all mares,' my brother replies. 'The blacksmith has long been dead.' I'm pleased Madog knows this.

Hedrek's face clouds with fury, his grey and white beard buoyed by the wind. Like me, he's grown into his fury against Edern. Like me, he was once much more but Edern took it from him. I pity Hedrek, but he's too late. Villa Eorlingas is ours. If he had half a thought in his head, he'd realise that. His intentions throughout Edern's life should only have been to restore my brother and me to Villa Eorlingas. In doing so, Hedrek could have earned our high regard. But not now.

'Then I'll take all Edern once possessed. Give me Elen.' His lips curl upwards. I swallow my unease. She's a bitch, but she still has worth for what she signifies. Hedrek will not have her. Any consolatory feelings I have towards him evaporate like dew beneath the heat of the sun.

'You'll have nothing unless you take it from me,' Madog rejoins, his voice thrumming with conviction.

'Then I'll do so,' Hedrek shouts, face flushed with

fury and spittle landing on the ground. 'You're nothing but a child. I'll best you and your weak warriors, and then this place will be mine.'

I step in front of my brother, dagger held before me. Despite Hedrek's words, Madog and his warriors will have no problem overpowering Hedrek and his men. Hedrek's men are all menace without substance. Yet I think enough have died because of Edern.

'Leave here with your lives,' I order Hedrek, making sure I meet the eyes of every one of his fifteen frightened warriors. It's one thing to face Edern and his fighters. Quite another to find a seeress in his place.

'You bitch,' Hedrek roars, hastening to a run, his weapons extended before him.

'Get out of the way,' Madog urges me, pushing me behind him with no regard for my position.

I hiss under my breath, but I'm no warrior. Well, I am, but they need not know that. Not unless it becomes imperative I kill to protect myself and my restored villa.

'Attack,' Madog shouts, hurrying to join the rest of his men defending the ditch. I turn aside consideringly, and while men crash blades and shields, I look to where we burnt Edern last night. The funeral pyre is little more than warm ashes, but there's something there besides.

Moving towards it, I lean into the lingering heat from the ash, and pluck what remains of Edern's skull from within, using the end of my dagger. I shouldn't be surprised his skull didn't burn. It's thick and heavy.

I grimace at the blackened remains pooling from the empty eye sockets and hollow space where his nose once was. Holding my trophy before me, I stride to the front of Villa Eorlingas and pull one of the spears free from within the doorway. Hooking the skull over the spearhead, I march towards the fighting.

My brother and his men are engaged against Hedrek's. Already, shouts and screams of pain flood the growing daylight. This should be a day of triumph. I'll not allow more men to die, and certainly not my brother's warriors, just because Hedrek wishes to sate his bloodlust for all Edern visited upon him.

'Stand aside,' I shout, aware of those watching me from the doorway of the villa. I walk straight, the spear held out in front of me. I don't wish to be tainted with Edern's filth. 'Stand aside,' I roar once more, and now my brother hears me. He turns, mouth opening in shock, the helm covering his head dented and dull, but adding a yellow glow to his face.

'Stay back,' he shouts, but I ignore him. And now Hedrek and his warriors stop their assault. I sense even more eyes on me, some belatedly bowing heads as my talismans clatter, alerting the gods and goddesses to my presence.

I thrust Edern's white skull towards Hedrek, who stands with spear and shield. His eyes narrow with disgust.

'Villa Eorlingas has been restored to the correct owners,' I inform him coldly. 'You must enact your revenge on all that remains of the man who took so much from you. Here, you may take his skull and piss in it for all I care.'

A gleam of malice flickers on Hedrek's face.

'I want Elen,' he repeats defiantly.

'You can take Edern's head, or we'll ride to your settlement while you're here and take it as well, slaughtering all your animals, women and children. The choice is yours.' My brother's quick to reinforce my intentions with such threats. While Hedrek's face shows no emotion, those behind him look horrified. So far, only one of their number limps while another bleeds from a cut on his cheek. It's not much. They can save themselves and their families if

Hedrek relinquishes his foolish assertion to Villa Eorlingas.

Madog breathes heavily, but from what I can see, he doesn't bleed.

I knew others would want Villa Eorlingas. That's why it was so important to get here first. We'd had people watching the villa for many winters and summers before Edern did us the service of dying.

A muttering of voices has Hedrek turning angrily to glower at those with him. I notice his warriors are more alike in age to my brother. Hedrek's the last of his kind to still live. No doubt, those who would come after him don't wish to bleed for a long-dead stallion and blacksmith. I remember the blacksmith. His death was horrifying to witness. So much magik contained within his mind. Edern had his head bashed in with his own axe, despite my efforts to prevent him from killing the man who knew how to make the fine edges so rarely found on blades. Since then, Edern's not had the ability to reward warriors with good blades. No one has. But that's another of the reasons Edern had fallen so low in the winters before his death.

Now all must contend with weak cutting edges. Not even Marchell knows how to form blades with the sharpest lips. Not even Marchell knows how to make nails to hold everything from boots to roof tiles together. That magik, for I deem it such, was not of her ken. Edern was a bloody fool to kill the only man who knew the secrets of the small grey stones he could forge into blades, nails and even locks to prevent treasures from being stolen.

'We'll take the skull,' Hedrek acknowledges unhappily, reaching for the grey-stained item. 'We'll take and do what must be done to have our revenge on him. But tell me,' and now Hedrek's voice is cajoling, 'the blacksmith. Are his tools here? There's another who could make use of them.' I look from Hedrek to Madog. He's deep in thought. My eyes narrow at Hedrek. He came here to demand the blacksmith and yet says he has another? I'm astounded. Blacksmiths are rarer than a winter without snow.

'Who?' I question. Hedrek bows his head again, seemingly determined to win my favour by showing such respect, even if it is belated.

'His son. A mere boy when his father was taken. He says his father shared the magiks with him.'

This, I realise, could prove useful. Before my brother can reply, I speak. 'Bring him here. If he can prove himself, he may have the tools, and then he can determine who he'll serve.'

Hedrek's eyes narrow before revealing a flash of respect. 'Seeress, I'll return with him in two days' time.'

'I'll have the equipment uncovered if it's still here.'

'He'll owe me his loyalty,' Hedrek reiterates belligerently.

'But I am the seeress,' I caution him.

Hedrek and I have known each other for a long time. I know the man he is beneath his bluster. Whether he can discern my thoughts so easily is highly doubtful.

'Two days,' he shouts, carrying the skull on his own spear, while two of his men aid the wounded man to his feet. Blood has been shed, but not much. No one will die from this small fight.

'Two days,' I confirm. 'Bring the boy. He'll have it if it's in my power to gift.'

Madog glowers at me. 'You weren't to get involved,' he huffs angrily.

'Perhaps,' I reply. 'But no man will die today, and in two days' time, you might have a bladesmith to aid you in keeping Villa Eorlingas secure from all who think to take her. Not everything must be resolved with blade and shield, although, admittedly, the threat of them can also be enough.'

Madog grunts softly, collecting the spear I used to bring Edern's skull to the limits of the ditch and enclosure. 'And sometimes, it must be blade and shield,' he rejects.

I nod, pleased to know my brother is prepared to fight to keep what is mine. Or rather, ours.

8

WÆRMUND OF THE GYRWE

The next morning, I'm groggy and ache all over. Rising as though awoken from the grave, I stretch and grimace before taking myself away to piss into the undergrowth. The sound is loud and long, and despite the alleged loyalty of those who haven't turned on me in the night or fled from our camp, I turn and peer suspiciously back through the trees to where my treasure lies.

I need to find a way of hiding it from everyone, but equally, it and the battle in which I killed my brother are the reasons for the grudging respect my warriors currently hold for me. It's a perplexing problem.

'Where to today?' Heafoc calls as I emerge from

beneath the trees. He's standing beside the horses, peering into the distance. I know he's seeking out Wædel. I'd like to do the same. And if not looking for Wædel, then Heafoc is, no doubt, trying to determine if my father, and his warriors, already follows us.

'Westwards, towards where the sun sets each night,' I offer quickly. I don't truly know. Now, in the cold light of day, I can be honest enough to admit I didn't expect to be so successful in my endeavours. My dreams and ambitions had truly gone no further than ending my brother's life and stopping his constant derogatory remarks about me and my father's steadfast refusal to notice them. I hadn't thought of what would happen today, or tomorrow, or in the future. I've erred in that.

What will happen amongst the tribe of the Gyrwe, now my father's favourite son is dead, and his least favourite is gone, I don't know. I can suspect it easily enough. All the same, I won't face my father's wrath if I can avoid it. He's virile enough to have more sons. All he needs to do is live long enough to make any newborn son a warrior, and then he can die, happy in the knowledge the tribe will continue to be ruled by his descendants. I'll never return there. Not willingly. My future no longer lies with the

Gyrwe. I've made myself an outcast, just as I was always deemed one anyway.

'And what then?' Heafoc's insistent today. I turn
to snap a reply at him, but stop myself. He's appraising me, but not with malice. He's testing me. I
try to recall all I know about Heafoc. He's a fine warrior. Or, at least, he once was. He too has grown old.
My father has never seen this as giving warriors
wisdom and expertise. Instead, he's derided men
who've known him since he was a child. I might have
failed to consider my future, but my father's a damn
fool not to consider what he's made of the few warriors who've lived as long as him.

Rapidly, I consider what the future could hold for
us and then step closer to him, softening my tone.

'My father, Wihtlæd, and his father, Waga, and
his father's father, Watholgeot, made a name for
themselves. I'll do the same.'

'How?' he questions, but again it's merely interest
and not scorn making him query my response.

'As they did. We'll become warriors of renown,
men to be trusted and paid for fighting the battles of
those too weak to protect themselves, but with the
means to finance others.'

He arches an eyebrow, a hint of amusement on
his lips at my stark ambition. 'You'll need to do more

than kill your own brother to claim to be a warrior. Most look unkindly on kin-slayers. I'd not share that knowledge when selling your services.'

I nod. I realise this. He needn't remind me of what's brought me to this moment. I know it well enough. I can still see my brother's death throes. I'd like to say it grieves me, but it doesn't. He was the first man I killed. He'll not be the last. 'Then that's what we'll do.'

We eat what remains of last night's meal as prepared by Osfyth and Bucge, and turn our horses towards where the sun will set later that day. It's turned grey and menacing, but remains warm. I'd welcome some rain to clear the tension. None question where I lead them. I don't miss some uneasy glances between others of my warriors. It behoves us not to be too trusting of one another. Not after the treachery of last night, and Cenbryht, trussed to his horse, remains a very visible reminder of that. Of Wædel there's no sign.

The treasure I carry is a heavy load. I'm unsure what to do with it. It needs hiding, as my brother did on the boundary of his settlement, beneath the ditch, until such time as I can make use of it. But we aren't settled here, and I don't plan to be either. So I must keep it with me until I find a more permanent home. Where that might be, I don't know.

'Heafoc.' I call him to my side. He's hunkered down beneath his cloak, eyes appraising our passage. Perhaps he wears his cloak to protect him from any possible attack from one of the others, or to stop the insects from biting his skin. He's tried to wash away the blood from his wounded right arm, but I see the dull maroon on it. The insects can smell it too. He should bind it, I think, to keep away the insects and to allow it to heal, but I don't advise him to do so. He'll have endured many such wounds before in his life as a warrior. He'll know what's best for him.

We've seen few men and women so far today, busy about their tasks in field and dwelling, but they've watched with mild curiosity, not fear, and we've not ridden close enough for them to know who we are. I consider if we're still in the territory of the Gyrwe. I don't believe we are. If we were, I think we'd have faced spears by now, and perhaps a mounted host as well. Not this uneasy regard, which has no doubt turned to relief as we've ridden around their homes and crops without threatening them.

'Wærmund.' His reply is almost terse. I speak all the same.

'Tell me of all you've been told about our ancestors.'

He quirks an eyebrow but shakes his head, whether in surprise or denial I'm unsure, until he replies. 'Speak with Bucge, not me. She knows much more.'

I nod, but don't immediately call for Bucge to join me. I don't want to say she scares me because she doesn't. However, I'm uneasy in her presence. I'm astounded she united with me to attack my brother and his settlement. She informed me it was impossible to remain within the Gyrwe after my father's denouncement of her skills. All the same, I'm not alone in fearing her and what she knows of the future, and the past.

I look for noticeable signs we've crossed from the region of the Gyrwe to the next closest neighbour, the Sweordora, but there are none. I don't believe I'd have missed whatever warning might have been placed on the mutually agreed border, be it a line of sheep or cattle skulls or something even more intimidating, but perhaps I have. It's not always easy to see everything in the damp landscape. The sound of water rising or falling is never far from my ears.

Eastmund rides to the rear of our small collection of men and women, his gaze slowly sweeping over the flat landscape behind us, where the pestilent flies that love the water and our warm flesh so much continue to buzz and irritate me and my horse. Eastmund shouts no warnings. We're not being hunted. Yet. Bucge, Osfyth and Hygebeorht are somnolent as we ride, the exertions of last night telling.

I suspect my father will come for me. Or perhaps he won't. Maybe it would be his ultimate revenge to entirely dismiss what havoc I've wreaked on his son, my brother. If only Wædel were dead, I could reassure myself of that, but if Wædel lives he'll rile my father to take action. Cenbryht remains bound. He could prove useful. Eventually. And I won't allow him to escape with more tales he might tell my father, adding his voice to Wædel's. No, Wædel knows little of my plans because even I didn't know what they'd be. But Cenbryht understands enough to cause problems, if my father's damaged pride demands retribution.

And then, ahead, my eyes do alight on a border symbol between the Gyrwe and the Sweordora. I ride close to the collection of gleaming white skulls, arranged on wooden posts and flat stones, beneath two huge oak trees, branches stretching far overhead which speak of longevity and permanence. It's a bold statement, no doubt meant to scare people away. But

I'm unsure of the animal these skulls belong to. They're not the familiar sheep or cows I'm expecting. Nor are they horses. And they're certainly not those of people either. I know what the skull of a man or woman looks like.

Heafoc rides closer. 'Boar,' he offers without too much consideration, his eyes narrowing. 'We're passing into the territory of the Sweordora.'

'And what do we know of the Sweordora?' I won't admit I know little more than their name and that their collection of settlements borders those of the Gyrwe.

He offers me a sly look. I know what he'll say next.

'Ask Bucge,' I growl softly, and realise I've not asked her the questions of earlier either. 'Bucge.' I call her to my side as we ride through the border symbols. To travel towards the setting sun, we must go this way.

The horses haven't long been allowed to drink from a wide and deep stream, of clear water flashing brightly in the daylight. It tasted differently to the water I've drunk all my life. Fresher, somehow. I hope it will continue to be so refreshing, assuring me with each hoofbeat that we're leaving the only home I've ever known.

Our pace is far from fast, but it's consistent. The animals can continue at such a speed over vast distances but I don't want to overextend them. We need the horses to transport us. I can't allow them to become winded, or wounded.

Bucge heeds my call, appraising the skulls and muttering something beneath her breath. I don't ask her what she says or what it means. It could be a curse, or a whispered word against any magik with which the Sweordora have infused these skulls.

'Wærmund.' Her tone's reserved at being summoned to my side. Perhaps she also fears me as I do her.

'Heafoc tells me you're the one to ask about our ancestors.'

'What do you wish to know?' She settles a telling glance on Heafoc, but he purposefully avoids her gaze.

'How did my father become leader of the Gyrwe?' I've only ever heard my father's explanation for why he was the leader of the Gyrwe. I'm curious as to whether he spoke the truth, or not.

'His father was leader before him, as you know.'

'And before him?'

'Your great-grandfather.'

'And before him?'

Now she stills. I know this, but I wish to hear the details from her. 'Before your great-grandfather, Watholgeot, the Gyrwe were not from this island. They came from over the sea, far to the east of here, in ships made of good wood, like the ones they still use on the fenlands.'

'So this island was deserted?'

'I didn't say that. No, there were others. The Gyrwe came to aid them against their enemies from the north, they were *comitatus*. But they were weak in the end. The Gyrwe now rule where that tribe once did.'

'And what about elsewhere?'

Bucge doesn't immediately answer. I almost re-peat the question, but then she does begin to speak. 'There were others, alike to your ancestors. The numbers weren't vast, but they didn't need to be. Warriors with iron to hand can overwhelm those who don't fight or have no knowledge of how to fight. The people of Britannia grew weak under their mas-ters from Rome. They thought only of wealth and fine food, and not of how to defend it when those from Rome disappeared, which was destined to hap-pen. No man can rule so far from where he makes his home, and this Rome is far, far from here. Over seas and huge land masses.'

'So, the same happened everywhere?' I know this island is vast, bounded by seas pounding against its encircling shores.

'In some places. But you lead us west, I believe. The tribes there are different. The men and women bicker amongst themselves but would be wary of accepting your assistance for fear of being overwhelmed as happened to their neighbours long ago.'

'So, I shouldn't present us as a *comitatus*?'

'Oh no, you should certainly do that. But, you might not be welcome. Is that what you intend to do? Forge your own *comitatus* in imitation of your ancestors?' She asks the question with mild curiosity. Again, I consider why she joined my attempts to overwhelm my brother. Did she, like me, not think we would succeed and therefore gave no thought to the future? Did she think her death would come then? Did she believe it was better to die in battle than live reviled by those of her people who should have revered her? Or, did she perceive we'd succeed? I never asked her to tell me the future, if she did know it. I wished to have no prior knowledge of whether I'd succeed or not.

I shrug my shoulders. 'I want to know what I'll find to the west, that's all.'

'I don't know the answers to that. The traders

who visited the Gyrwe came mainly from the east, across the sea, from our ancestral lands. I can tell you where they came from and where we came from, but not what lies ahead in any more detail than that. The Gyrwe weren't overly friendly with their neighbours.' That's something of an understatement, but I don't question her further.

'Then we'll discover what there is in the west,' I state, puffing out my chest, allowing the clink of my treasure clutched on my lap to flood the air.

I sense Bucge's gaze on me, her eyes trailing from the treasures to my face. 'It would aid us if you had a beard or moustache,' she mutters. 'Perhaps I could find the means to help you grow more than tufty hair on your chin as though you're a child.' It remains unsaid it would also cover much of my huge birthmark. A beard would make me much less easy to identify as my father's son.

'I...' I begin, and then falter. 'In my family, such facial hair is slow to arrive,' I eventually comment. She chuckles darkly. I'm surprised by her amusement.

'A pity but you're right. Your brother looked like a boy.' She veers aside from me, making it clear she doesn't wish to speak about this further. 'One more thing,' she calls a little time later. 'I've heard terrible stories of the leader of the Sweordora. Be wary with your arrogant attitude. It might cost you all that remains in the pile of treasure to win free from him and his warriors.'

'You could have told me sooner,' I glower darkly. Her chuckle greets my complaint. I sense no unease amongst the rest of my allies – well, apart from Cenbryht. And no doubt he's merely uncomfortable and would sooner be unbound from where he bounces atop his horse. I can't allow that. It'll not be until we're many days away from the territory of the Gyrwe that I'll allow him any sort of freedom, if I decide to do so. We must be far from where my father might think to seek us.

Briefly, I consider whether we should turn back, perhaps go around the Sweordora. Only then there's no possibility of doing so. Ahead, I see a pall of smoke rising high into the air followed by the familiar sound of hurrying hooves over the road we ride upon. It seems the Sweordora have found us easily enough. I doubt they'll be welcoming. This will be our first test outside the lands of our birth. I hope we survive.

9

MEDDI OF THE EORLINGAS

Rhian, Madog's wife, arrives later that day. She clutches her son tightly in her arms, wincing slightly with the movement of the horse beneath her. She's a strong woman to endure the discomfort, but then my brother needed a strong wife to aid him in our ambitions. I note Marchell remains close to her. Marchell knows her worth amongst our people. Afresh, I admire her resolve. She could have tried to escape when I determined to replace her, and in the many winters and summers since then, but she hasn't. If there's one woman who knows her value, but is also loyal to our family, it's her. I almost wish I could treat her more kindly. But no. I can't allow any weakness in my dealings with her.

I greet the small party. Madog had sent half of his men back to our former run-down home to retrieve all that was needed after the altercation with Hedrek. The horses are weighed down with our treasures, and the oxen and sheep have also been corralled along the trackway. They're allowed into the enclosed space encircling Villa Eorlingas. A few of our people will remain behind at our old settlement to tend the planted crops. We can't allow others to take them. The previous summers have been wet, the harvests suffering. We need all that can be grown. They're brave men and women to hold steadfast when news will soon spread of Madog's success, and others will wish to emulate it, perhaps starting with overrunning our former home.

I walk sedately towards where Madog and his wife embrace, before she steps back to allow him to inspect his son. I do the same. It's important I accept Madog's son within the tribe. Marchell has already performed some of the task by ensuring the child lived through the perils of birth. Marchell mutters under her breath as I pull back the animal coverings and gaze at the small pink face, a dark shimmer of hair covering the child's head.

For a moment, I stagger, too easily reminded of when I gazed at my daughter in the moments after her birth. The boy child shares the same full lips, the same pert nose and the identical chunky chin. But then, I now know, all babes look like this. I've seen more than enough of them. There's nothing special about this boy other than he's the future of this tribe. Provided he survives his childhood.

I nod, once, running my hand over his small face, the smell of his soiled loincloth and the yeasty smell of milk almost unpleasant.

I turn aside, and hear the murmurs of relief from all around at this initial easy acceptance of the boy. I don't miss my brother's expelled breath. Did he truly expect me to turn against his son? I gaze at Marchell. She must know I'm there, for all she doesn't acknowledge me.

'All was well?' I question her.

'Mistress,' is Marchell's mumbled reply, which I take to be assent. I stride once more towards my workshop, aware she follows on. It's time for Sian to return to her duties. I have Marchell now.

But Sian's already gone when I dip beneath the low lintel, touching it once more as I enter. I narrow my eyes. I've not set her a task yet, but perhaps she's already performing one for me.

I turn abruptly, almost colliding with Marchell, who enters behind me, her hands reaching, running over all within the small space. I step aside and allow her the time to acquaint herself with this hallowed space. Before Edern, she made this place her home. Like me, I imagine she feels relief at once more being here. We've never spoken of those events.

'Everything is as you remember?' I ask.

'Mistress.' She bows her head again. I pause, and watch her. Here, she could do untold damage to me. Here, there must be secrets she's never shared with me. Perhaps even magiks I've never even considered she knows. I feel myself relenting in my firm stance against her.

'I would thank you,' I find myself saying, the words tasting like ash on my tongue. 'For tending to the boy child. He's a welcome addition to our depleted family line.'

'Mistress,' she mutters, but takes the time to face me. I see the gentle breeze buffeting what remains of her thin white hair, and for once her gaze is sharp as she truly appraises me. I find myself standing taller beneath such an inspection. 'All will be well,' she offers, more than her usual reply of 'mistress', intended to show respect, but also a means of masking her true thoughts. That she speaks so openly now is unusual, to say the least. 'It's the way of our people that one must always replace another. Your father would be proud of you.' And then she turns aside. Her words astound me. 'But I'm not sure you'll live to see it,' she continues before I can say anything else. The unexpected foreshadowing sends a shudder down my spine, and all pleasant thoughts towards her are banished. I imagine she might even smile a little as she delivers her verdict on my future.

'I will return,' I snap, grateful my voice doesn't waver from such a threat, ducking below the low lintel again, and emerging once more into the sunlight. The wind's stronger now. My thoughts wrench from thinking about Marchell and what her words imply, to the treasures of the blacksmith.

'Mistress, this way.' A young girl rushes to me, her hair wild in the wind, and tangled. I pity her mother trying to force a bone comb through that.

'Where?' I complain. Her breathless voice lacks the respect I expect. I narrow my eyes, seeking out someone who claims the child as their own. I might have words with them. Only then she bows low, recalling herself.

'Mistress.' She dips. 'Sian bid me find you.'

'Then take me to her,' I command, half an ear listening to Marchell moving in the interior of my workshop. I bite my lip, abruptly unsure of myself. There's much to do. I can't allow my careful planning to unravel, just because of Marchell's unsettling words. I watch the activity around me for a moment: the cows being led to the fields after milking, the women with their looms sitting in what sunlight there is wrapped in cloaks, although the work will warm them. All is as it should be, even so soon after Madog seized Villa Eorlingas, and Hedrek tried to take it from him. Yet I sense an undercurrent of uncertainty. 'Show me,' I instruct, determined to do something to banish my unwelcome unease.

The girl leads on, almost reaching for my hand to drag me before reconsidering. I note her bright eyes, but sallow cheeks. I'll speak to my brother with regard to apportioning the food we have more equally. Edern has evidently been hoarding it to himself, if the size of his belly when we burned him is anything to go by. Others have suffered while he grew fat and bloated.

We pass the grain store. I hear no sound from where Elen's being kept captive, but notice Urien's giving her water and food. He sees me while closing the door behind him, and offers a slight bow when assured the door is firmly shut and our prisoner can't escape. I incline my head towards him. I hope Elen wore herself out with last night's shrieking while we burned Edern. All the same, I should be keeping a closer eye on who has access to Elen. The sooner we know the truth of whether she carries a child or not, the sooner I can have her banished. She has no place here.

The girl leads me almost to the end of the villa complex, her feet kicking up puffs of dust. I notice she has no shoes on her feet. Admittedly, mine are old and often repaired, and I often cast them aside, preferring to feel the ground beneath my feet, but it's another sign Edern has been an inadequate chief. This place was once so vibrant and rich. He's done nothing but consume the produce and make Villa Eorlingas poor and feeble. I should have realised when I first saw the treasured horse mosaic, laid out on the floor of the main entrance and covered with the passage of the dirt of hundreds of feet. I must ensure it's carefully cleaned and the brightness of the ancient craft brought to life once more.

'In here,' the girl offers. From within, I hear items being moved about. Some of them heavy enough to need dragging.

'Sian,' I call, just to be assured she's the one I've come to see.

'Mistress. Come, I think I've found it.' I'm impressed she's been hunting for the items when I didn't order her to do so.

I duck low then, and emerge into a room with light streaming into it through some gaps in the walls, the animal skins usually there, held back to allow the room some brightness.

'What is this place?' I know what it is, one of the smaller rooms used for storage, with the painted walls dulled and dirty. I need to know to what purpose it's been put since I left here.

'This is where Edern put everything he didn't know the purpose of.' Sian's words are filled with disdain, as she stands upright, hands resting on her hips, her weight on one leg.

I walk amongst the random collection of hempen sacks and wooden boxes, the sides rotted away. I'd like to know what can be found within each one. I'll inform my brother of this. Madog will be keen to see what else Edern was too foolish to keep close to him, and which he dismissed of no importance. If he couldn't eat it, or drink it, or bed it, Edern would have disdained it.

'Is this it?' Sian asks hopefully.

I look at where she points. In the far corner of the room, there's a collection of items. The signs of pulling things aside is easy to see in the trails of disturbed dust and dirt, even last winter's leaves – brown, old and shrivelled – filling much of the space.

The leather covering over the door has been little use. I'm sure there was once a wooden door here. Where that is, I don't know. It wouldn't surprise me to learn Edern burned it one cold winter night.

There's a rusty cauldron, and a collection of other items, blackened and clearly made from metal. Some look like farming equipment, others have a more obvious purpose, the hammer for one. There is also, I realise, a heavy-looking object, resting on the ground. It's too heavy for me or Sian to lift. It's pitted and covered in orange rust spots, the flat top assuring me it must be something the blacksmith uses, the indentations on its surface perhaps made with the hammer I lift, also marvelling at its weight. I hold the hammer over the flat surface, lowering my head, to line up the edges of the hammer with the marks on the flat top. It's evident the two are used together. For what purpose, I'm unsure. My eyes narrow and I stand upright.

'Yes,' I confirm, confidently. It's been many years since I saw a blacksmith at work, but I recognise these items all the same. I thought there would be much more, however. The magiks of the blacksmith are so important I feel they should amount to more than a collection of hammers, tongs and, perhaps, old bars of metal waiting to be turned into other objects, abandoned here after the man was murdered by Edern.

'I recall the man,' Sian admits. 'Edern was unwise to kill him when he couldn't do what was requested. After all, he had many other uses.' Her lips are downcast. I'm finding few here thought much of Edern, aside from Elen. It warms me to know Edern was hated by all. I find myself being more conciliatory towards these people. I no longer believe my brother should make slaves of them. Yet I also consider how weak our tribe must have become to allow Edern to prevail against us. Why was my father unable to better protect us from him? After all, Edern had only a small collection of warriors to aid him. I'll speak to Madog about it. We've already faced one opponent who thinks to take from us what we've just regained. We'll need more warriors, I'm sure of it. We won't allow Villa Eorlingas to be overwhelmed again, even if Edern did use treachery.

'This looks heavy,' I marvel, bending low to examine everything. I run my hand over the old cauldron, feeling the coolness of the metal under my hands, before turning to Sian. 'He'll need heat to perform his magiks.'

'He will, and not just from a cooking hearth.'

'Will he know to bring the black rocks that burn so brightly?'

'Charcoal, mistress,' she informs me, offering the word, one I've forgotten, but which I now recall. 'And I doubt it. He'll be focused only on the items here and not on how the magiks themselves are performed.' She mirrors my thoughts.

'Then that's likely a problem.'

'Perhaps there's some, within this room, the blacksmith brought with him all those summers ago.'

'Will it still burn? Will it not be as damp as everything else in here?' Edern did no favours to these items he dismissed. The smell of rodent piss and shit is sharp on the back of my throat.

I'm beginning to realise the endeavour is likely to be much more complex than I first thought. It's not just about knowing how to do it. It's also about having all the required items to encourage the flames to work their magik on the metal.

'There are items to be melted down, look.' She points to a sack, the ramshackle contents spilling through the split sides. There are twisted pieces of metal, perhaps once put to some other use I now can't determine.

'Then that's what he'll have to start with.' I bite

my lip, surveying the room. I feel as though there's much more here. If Edern killed the blacksmith, what else did he cast aside when it didn't perform as he anticipated? He was never a far-sighted man. His gaze was always only his own comfort. The damn fool. 'I'll have Madog send some of his warriors to help us drag the items free from this room. And then, Sian, I'd ask you to sort through everything. Anything that's too decayed must be thrown away or burned, as you see fit. We'll rid the building of rats and mice before they cause us more problems,' I confirm.

She bows once more. I realise the girl remains in the far corner, watching all with wide eyes.

'Don't we have the material to make shoes?' I'm reminded of my anger about her feet.

'I'll find it,' Sian confirms. 'Edern kept all such finery to himself.'

'Shoes aren't finery,' I almost spit.

I've hated the man for upwards of twenty summers. Now my fury towards him is growing with everything I hear about how he's treated these people within Villa Eorlingas. If we can win the allegiance of the blacksmith, and if he can truly remember all his father taught him, then we can once more dominate our neighbours by having access to items almost impossible for others to possess, unless passed from one generation to the next. It will make us wealthy, and others will be keen to ally with us, rather than fight us. With such resources, and the restoration of the fine breeding horses which will be my labour using the horses brought from our previous home as well as the few still living here, we'll return Villa Eorlingas to its former grandeur.

'My thanks,' I call to Sian and the young girl, determined to seek out Madog now.

'Mistress,' they both intone, but I hardly hear them. My mind whirls with possibilities. Reclaiming Villa Eorlingas was the first of our endeavours. Now we must consider how we'll retain our hold, and how we'll grow wealthy in more than just foodstuffs.

10

WÆRMUND OF THE GYRWE

'Who are you?'

I eye the lead rider who speaks with interest. His horse is young and restless and doesn't like being brought to a stop. Now the man tries to control his beast with his thighs and the reins, but the animal remains restive. My mount is much better behaved but perhaps not as well bred as the other animal.

'I'm Wærmund, and these are the warriors of my *comitatus*,' I announce without preamble. The man is at the front of a force matching mine. If this comes to a fight, we can easily overpower them. I hope. All it will take is for one of my warriors to kill one of his. I already have my eye on his horse. I'd look fine riding a beast such as that.

'And why are you on the land of the Sweordora?' he demands.

'Who are you?' I query, not yet prepared to answer his questions, and aware I've offered him my name but he hasn't given me his.

A swift look of fury touches his face, and another figure, standing beside him and unmounted, moves to stamp forward, a spear held in his hand, although I see the rust on it from here. I doubt it could skewer a dead pig with such a poor blade.

'I'm Dægbeorht, commander of the Sweordora.'

'Well met,' I call, astounding myself with the calmness of my voice. I sense Heafoc close to me. Bucge, as well. I also realise Dægbeorht's watching the bound Cenbryht closely. That doesn't surprise me.

'Why are you here?'

'We seek a tribe to fight for,' I offer with a confidence I don't feel. I should have realised how quickly my resolve would be called upon and that I'd need to be assured. He looks at my face, lips twisting with disgust for the birthmark covering so much of my right cheek.

'Why?' Dægbeorht's voice is filled with unease. 'What have you done to your own tribe? Where are you from?' he quickly adds, voice flecked with suspicion. I should have ensured Cenbryht and his bound hands were out of sight. Dægbeorht has already noticed.

'We've been fighting in the east. We completed our task, and apprehended the enemy. Now we look for a new task.'

'You're lordless men?' Dægbeorht's lips twist even further. The noise of his warriors securing a firm hold on their blades is far from comforting.

'No,' Heafoc interjects smoothly, when I hesitate in my reply. 'We fight for our commander, Wær-mund.' I'm grateful Heafoc doesn't name me as Wærmund, son of Wihtlæd. That would be awkward.

I sense Dægbeorht sizing me up. I must look like a boy child, only weaned from his mother's breast recently, and with a large mark covering much of my face. Perhaps Dægbeorht thinks the same. My appearance is as far from a warrior-lord as it's possible to be. And yet I do have blades, horses, shields and warriors who evidently fight in my name. Perhaps, I reason, I don't look quite as young and untried as my pounding heart implies.

'We've no need of warriors here,' Dægbeorht eventually announces, a sneer accompanying the statement. 'The Sweordora have no enemies who could better them.' His arrogance is misplaced if these are the best of his warriors.

'Then we'll ride on.' I reclaim the conversation from Heafoc, inclining my head respectfully. Dægbeorht's eyes narrow, although it's obvious we're following the path of the roadway.

'To where?'

'West,' I reply evasively.

'There's no one in need of the help of warriors from over the sea in the west.' I don't add I'm not from over the sea or that I was born in the lands to the east. I don't mention my father is the true lord of our warriors. No. I must forge my destiny. This is the first real encounter with someone who'll live to tell the tale of meeting me. Or who probably will.

'There are always tribal leaders in need of assistance, even if it's just to pierce a boil on someone else's arse,' Heafoc chuckles darkly. I settle myself. I must remain confident, even if I don't feel it. Heafoc reminds me it's not all about who has the sharpest blade.

Dægbeorht's face clouds. No doubt, I realise, he fears what we might do if one of his enemies thinks to employ us. 'You'll not come this way,' he announces decisively.

'You deny us access through your lands?'

'I do, yes,' Dægbeorht announces, lifting his chin defiantly high, revealing his neck. I eye it menacingly. He's brave to reveal such weakness. No doubt, he believes his posturing reveals his strength. I'd argue with that. His neck should be covered so none can sever it and release the flood of lifeblood from it. I hear Heafoc growling angrily beside me. I consider what to do. I could turn tail and leave this place. I could order us to attack. We might overwhelm Dægbeorht and his few warriors. But what would I do then? I'm not far enough from my father's lands. No, we must travel further west and make our wealth far from where my father might think to seek revenge for murdering his favoured son.

'Is there another path westwards?' I eventually capitulate. At the moment, I don't feel the urge to fight Dægbeorht unless he thinks to attack me first.

'You should return to the east,' he instructs me implacably. I shake my head.

'That isn't the way our path leads.' I offer a friendly smile. Well, what I hope is a friendly smile.

'Then travel north, and you'll find another route,' he advises me. 'The Herstinga are far more welcoming.' I don't miss the gleam in his eyes. No doubt he sends me to fight someone who might be better able to counter me. It's clear he doesn't wish to risk his warriors in battle against me and my small force. I take that as a compliment, I think.

'Good day,' I call, but remain where I am, watching him. I'll not move aside until he does. He sits and appraises me, while his horse walks forwards and backwards, uneasy. The spear wielder's face at his side is tight with fury. I doubt the warrior has the strength in his arm to throw far or even to jab up close. And behind the pair, the other men are equally motley. I don't fear these alleged warriors. However, I don't wish to fight them yet, if it can be avoided.

Heafoc and Bucge support me, but it's Eastmund who growls, 'We should fight them,' so the enemy hears. Abruptly, we face a wall of rusting spears and poorly maintained metal shields as Dægbeorht calls his warriors to order. Dægbeorht labours to dismount. I notice his belly overhangs his weapons belt. That gives me pause for thought. My father's chest is rigid with muscle. He won't allow himself to become too weak to fight in order to protect all he holds sway over. Indeed, it's one of his most frequently used reasons for dismissing those few warriors lucky enough to live to a grand age. He won't allow men grown fat to fight at his side.

'What do you think?' I murmur to Heafoc. I trust his judgement in this.

'We leave,' he advises. 'This land is poor. The animals aren't worth fighting over, aside from the one horse. There's evidently no bladesmith, and the weapons they have are inferior as well.' He speaks much more quietly than Eastmund.

'We'll leave.' I hold out my hands to show they're devoid of weapons. 'Lower your weapons, as pitiable as they are,' I add derisively. 'We ride north to the Herstinga,' I inform my warriors, turning away from Dægbeorht and his warriors even though my heart pounds loudly in my chest at such arrogance, I'm sure they must hear it. I've seen my father act like this. I thought him weak then, but I realise it takes much more assurance to turn your back on the enemy.

With a clatter of iron and wood, we move aside, Heafoc the last to join me, as he holds the gaze of Dægbeorht. I carry myself firmly on my horse, mindful I can't turn and look behind. That would show weakness. Instead, mirroring Dægbeorht's jutting chin and confident air, I encourage my horse slightly northwards, as he indicated, the sound of hooves ringing loudly in the air for some of this pathway is lined with small stones, although it's not the same as the road I hoped to follow west.

I'm very aware Dægbeorht has directed my next steps. I don't appreciate that. Perhaps, I realise, we should have gone south, after all, to whoever rules there, or ridden through his small guard to continue on the stone road we were following.

'Arsehole,' Bucge mutters when we're finally out of sight of the baleful glares of the leader of the Sweordora. 'We should take all they have under cover of darkness.'

'They have nothing,' Heafoc counters aggressively. 'Their weapons are poor. I suspect Dægbeorht owes his allegiance to another. Perhaps to whoever he's directing us towards.'

'Then they'll fight us?' I question. My warriors are riding in a close formation, even Cenbryht's alert to our conversation. I wonder if he's regretting his actions of stealing. Should I allow him to prove himself to us so soon?

The landscape's familiar; and yet I see it with new eyes, appraising all there is. Before us stretches a sea of grasses, possibly crops, and the occasional murmur of a stream assures me it doesn't lack for access to water. But where are the grazing animals? Where's the dense woodland to provide fuel to burn and, perhaps, even charcoal to allow a bladesmith to produce fine blades? No, there's none of that. Admittedly, we didn't see Dægbeorht's home. Perhaps the wealth is kept there, behind a ditch and embankment. Or perhaps there's none, as Heafoc suggests.

'Potentially. Is that what we want?' Heafoc asks. I consider this. My ancestors came to this island to fight on behalf of others who lacked their skills. Since then, my family has taken command of a settlement and its wealth, but has done little else. My father is feared. So feared my weak brother could hold his village without the worry of being attacked by my father's enemies until I surprised him and overwhelmed him.

But there's no point in fighting for nothing. What I need is a bladesmith to restore the ancestral sword to its former glory, oats to feed my horses and somewhere rich in pigs, sheep and cattle. What I need is somewhere that can grow me grains to feed my warriors and horses. I don't see that here. And it was always something my father had to barter for with other tribes who did have access to rich farmland.

'We want to be feared and then grow wealthy,' I announce decisively. The words are greeted with mutterings of agreement, even from the bound Cenbryht. It seems none of us have enjoyed being assessed on the quality of our weapons.

'Then,' Heafoc affirms, 'we need to learn to fight much better.' I turn and glower at him. He offers me a grin. 'I think we'd all agree we were lucky. Your brother's men were incompetent warriors. Some of our allies died. We need to learn to fight together to prevent losses as great as that.'

'So, we'll not fight Dægbeorht today?' This frustrates me. Now I've decided what I hope to do, I want to do it. I am, after all, the leader of these people, not Heafoc. Yet, instinctively, and because of his experience, I know to follow Heafoc's advice. When I gathered him to my cause, he came willingly, a man not yet past the peak of his warrior's capability. If even he cautions me, I must heed it.

'No. We'll find somewhere to stop, close to this track. And then, we'll learn to work together, using our shields and weapons to ensure no enemy can isolate one of us and kill us one by one.'

'And why should we listen to you, Heafoc?' Osfyth questions angrily. 'Our pledge is to Wærmund.'

'Because, while you've been hunting prey since you could hold a spear, I've been learning to fight and kill my enemy. Your father, Wærmund, might well command his warriors and their families with military might, but he didn't always know how to do so. Neither did his father, or his father. Much of what I know has passed to me from my father, and his father, and so on, but it doesn't change anything. How to stand and fight together hasn't altered in that passage of time, despite what Wihtlæd of the Gyrwe might think.' Heafoc's words are filled with suppressed fury towards my father.

I absorb this, frustration thrumming through my body. But, perhaps, after all, Heafoc, a man I realise has stood at my father's right-hand shoulder since before I could walk, although not in recent summers, is correct.

'We'll do as Heafoc says. We'll learn to fight, together. And then we'll overwhelm our enemy.'

Mutterings of agreement fill the air, and no one, not even Cenbryht, complains. Until, that is, Heafoc forces us all to dismount and stand together, side by side. We've made our way beyond the boundary marker of the boar skulls. We're no longer on land under the control of Dægbeorht. It might mean we're back in the territory of the Gyrwe, but I'm not convinced of that, either. I've never been here before.

The horses are pulling up grasses and chewing contently. I realise I still need to find oats for them.

Something else on my list. But for now, my focus is on Heafoc.

He appraises us all, shaking his head, or nodding at what he sees, depending on whether he's happy or not, his cloak flung aside, so we can all see his severed flesh, and how it knits together on his right arm already.

'Loosen your grip,' he informs Osfyth, the hunter, as she clutches her shield close to her body. 'If you don't, your arm will quickly grow stiff, and your fingers too tight and unresponsive.'

He turns to Eastmund.

'Put your weight on the front of your feet,' Heafoc advises him. I furrow my forehead, confused by his orders. I step free from the line he'd forced us into and really look at my collection of warriors.

We are few, that can't be denied, and yet we've had a great victory. Why then does Heafoc make such observations? He turns to me, grinning once more, as he advises Bucge to hold her spear further down the ash shaft. And on he goes. Adjusting a grip here, a stance there, even going so far as to tell Goddæg his tunic is too loose and will flap when he fights. Goddæg grunts and quickly replaces it with a tighter one from the collection of clothing I took from my brother's sleeping quarters. Slowly, I begin to understand what Heafoc's seeing.

'And me,' I urge him, standing proudly with my shield and seax. 'What am I doing wrong?'

A murmur ripples through the line of watching men and women. Heafoc quirks an eyebrow and then narrows his eyes. The day's advancing. If we mean to eat tonight, we'll have to find something soon or go hungry because it'll be too dark to hunt.

'You hold your arms too rigid, you expose your chest with that grip on your shield, and you need to secure your boots more firmly to your feet.'

My mouth drops in shock, while I hear Cenbry-ht's delighted laughter at such a summary. I've allowed him to stand with us, although his hands are bound so he holds his shield with both of them.

'I...' I stutter.

'You asked,' Heafoc announces firmly. 'I tell you only what I see. You can fight well, but every warrior here can fight well, alone. What we need to do is to become the best at fighting together, as a group. That way, whoever attacks us, or whichever tribe we fight against, will lose. Now, return to your warriors. I wish to see who should fight next to who.'

Muttering darkly under my breath, I join the end of the line of men and women. With Heafoc directing us, there are eleven of us in total. It's not a huge number. But my father has only double and he's a leader of a much wider area with many more warriors and craftspeople.

'No, you stand in the centre,' Heafoc urges me. I want to ask why, but he answers me before I can. 'All should know who leads. I'll stand next to you.'

Briefly, Heafoc inserts himself into the line of men and women, causing those to my left to shuffle away.

'Yes, yes,' Heafoc confirms, nodding happily at his decision. 'And then, Osfyth, you come next to me, and Goddæg next to her. To the other side of Wærmund, I want Eastmund and then Bucge. Cenbryht, if you're part of the battle line, will be at the end of the right-hand side. You have the most experience, and you know how to fight like a dirty bastard.' I expect Cenbryht to complain, but instead he smirks and struts to where Heafoc thinks he should stand. That leaves only Hygebeorht, who let Wædel escape, Bægmund, Maggenræd and Nothelm to position along the line. Heafoc does so quickly, Bægmund and Maggenræd slotting in to my right, and Hygebeorht and Nothelm to the left. Heafoc nods, content with his selection.

'So, this is how we'll stand if we face a shield wall

of warriors. If not, we'll fight in smaller groupings. But, for now, we should learn to move forwards as one and overlap our shields, if we have them.'

'Don't we all have shields?' I startle. I'd not realised that. How I've overlooked it, I don't know. I asked these men and women if they could fight, when approaching them to join me. I didn't, I realise, query if they had shields and blades with which to do so.

'No,' Nothelm answers quickly.

'Then we need to get you one as soon as possible.'

'But you have a good spear,' Heafoc confirms. 'The blade is sharper than most. It'll serve you well, and you can protect Hygebeorht and Goddæg with it. Now, raise shields.'

And we do so. I crash mine into Eastmund's and he grins. Heafoc stands to my left and his joins mine more smoothly.

'We need to make that less like we're shouting for Woden's attention,' Heafoc offers gruffly. 'Drop them, and try again.' And so it continues until the sky shades towards night, and so far all we've done is try and bring our shields together in a smooth action that doesn't have one or other of us dropping the bloody thing.

I'm sweating from holding the heavy item, and Heafoc's general demeanour has grown less and less happy.

'We should stop if we intend to eat tonight,' Osfyth eventually calls. She's not the only one thinking of her belly. My stomach growls angrily.

'We should,' I confirm, eager to throw my shield down and relax my shoulders.

'This isn't going to be as easy as I hoped,' Heafoc complains, as he too steps clear from our small line of warriors. 'In the morning, we try again,' he confirms, already circling his shoulders to alleviate the pain in them. I do the same. The only ones who look happy are Cenbryht and Hygebeorht, and that's no doubt because they only have to place their shields against one other. Even Heafoc's not exactly good at performing the task.

As conversation grows, Osfyth takes her spear to hunt something to eat, while Bucge bends to gather stray pieces of wood. Maggenræd tends to the horses with the aid of the bound Cenbryht. I check my collection of treasures, but don't open the bundle to reveal them, or my brother's sword. I'll show these men and women I trust them, even if some of them need to prove themselves.

Heafoc gathers his spear and seax and glowers at

them. In the gathering gloom, I'm unsure why he's so interested in his weapons.

'See.' He shows me the spearhead. 'The blade's no longer smooth. The iron flakes from it.'

'So, we need better equipment, as well as a shield for Nothelm.'

'Yes.'

I look at my spear and seax. I can tell the edge on the seax is sharper than the one on Heafoc's. But it also has some marks on it. I also realise it flashes with my brother's blood.

'You need to learn to clean them,' he advises me, pulling up some long grasses. 'Did no one teach you to tend to your weapons?'

'I've been a little busy,' I glower, not answering his question.

'No man or woman should ever be too busy to clear away the blood of their enemy. Dulled blades are no use to anyone.' With his words ringing in my ears and the aroma of something cooking over the small fire, I set to the task, even though my arms ache with the repetition of the movement.

I quickly realise the others are doing the same, aside from Osfyth, who watches the roasting pheasant. I can't image there'll be much to go around, but it'll be better than nothing. Even Cenbryht labours to polish his shield despite his hands being bound. He's not had his blades returned to him, aside from the knife on his weapons belt. I've examined it. It's not sharp enough to saw through his bindings. In a fight to the death, the hilt might aid him, if he's lucky. It's not really worthy of being called a knife.

'Here, use this.' Heafoc hands me a stone which he's been using to sharpen the blades now they're free from blood and the remnants of pale flesh. I fumble the first attempt, but then find my rhythm, even though I'm gritting my teeth because my arms are heavy and exhausted. 'Tomorrow, we'll try once more,' Heafoc announces to everyone when we're eating the hot meat, which for some reason tastes better than anything I've ever tried before, even though there are few enough mouthfuls of it. 'And then,' he mutters, 'we might even move on to fighting with our spears together.'

'And what of travelling westwards?' Osfyth asks.

'We can do that as well. But, until we learn to fight together, it'll be a risk. We've been lucky so far. But luck will not always win,' Heafoc warns, with all his summers of experience. It's far from reassuring.

11

MEDDI OF THE EORLINGAS

The blacksmith's equipment is arranged before us. I eye it, as does Madog. I sense nothing special from the hammers, anvil, pliers and other items found with them, and yet I know there's magik within them. If not, they wouldn't be reserved for the employ of a blacksmith. Neither would they have been cast to one side by Edern but put to better use. After all, these items are made from good iron. They would have worth, or could have been employed as farming equipment.

There's also a pile of small kernels of what Sian assures me are long-abandoned pieces of charcoal, no bigger than a berry. They're old and crumbly, but might be of some benefit. It's something I realise we need to set right. We must have the means to make charcoal in order to forge blades and tools from the indeterminate shards of ironstone and some already forged iron that, for now, seem to offer nothing other than something heavy to drop on my foot. Or trip over. Looking from the small pieces of charcoal to the ironstone and few fragments of worked iron, I don't truly understand how the one can have any impact on the other, although I appreciate charcoal must be set aflame to work.

'They'll be here soon,' my brother mutters. It's taken some convincing to ensure he understands how important it is we keep the young blacksmith within Villa Eorlingas, whether he truly knows the skills of his father or not.

'Hedrek will have promised him much. We must promise more, or we'll hold Villa Eorlingas for less time than it takes the blacksmith to forge sharp blades with which Hedrek and his warriors can sever our throats and end our lives. Think of your son.' I know the words are cruel. My brother comprehends it as well. He judders at the menace in my voice. I wish I could reassure him, but I can't. 'Unless, of course, the boy knows absolutely nothing, and then it won't matter.' Madog nods, biting his lip, making him look like an unsure child as he eyes the random collection before us. To those who don't know, it appears to be a jumble of stray items. How would anyone know that from this can be brought forth blades sharp enough to cut a man or woman's throat without having to consider the best means of applying pressure on a blunt blade? No, it's a great talent if the boy truly possesses it, and knows what to do with these things. The labours of a blacksmith have been denied the Eorlingas for many summers.

'They're here,' Urien calls from where he's been tasked with watching for Hedrek. Madog and I peer along the small trackway towards the single ditch and embankment protecting us from any enemy. The people who once owed their allegiance to Edern have been quick to abandon him, the promise of better food and treatment ensuring none mourn him, especially as it's been explained they won't be our slaves but our equals. Now they witness Hedrek's arrival with uneasy eyes. Even my treatment of the bitch, Elen, doesn't offend anyone. They realise how much Elen helped Edern assert control over them. Madog and his wife have a much more gentle approach. Even now, the small children are being given good clothing and shoes to cover their feet. Sian has also been instrumental in encouraging the surviving women to direct their labours towards helping others. The women sit beneath the protection of the roof, and the columns keeping it aloft, taking advantage of the warmth of the outdoors, while the dazzling brightness of the sun is kept from their faces.

Elen's fed and watered, albeit grudgingly, by Madog's warriors, with Urien in overall control of who has access. Soon, we'll know if she's with child, and then a fresh decision can be made about her future.

'Hedrek,' Madog greets, as the small collection of potential enemies is allowed within the protective ditched boundary. I stay beside Madog, seeking out this boy who knows his father's secrets, although, of course, the boy is no longer a boy. As we meet peacefully, none of us wear or carry shields, breastplates or spears. Hedrek's warriors have left them with two men who stand to the other side of the ditched embankment.

'This is Centus,' Hedrek offers with a gleam in his eye, after he and Madog have exchanged what could be termed pleasantries. He peers at the same assemblage Madog and I have been assessing, which we've had brought from the storage room to the forecourt of the villa, now swept clear of all detritus. The women of the tribe sit there to stitch clothing and prepare food.

Whether Centus knows what these items are, I'm yet to ascertain.

'Well met.' Madog greets the man with half a smile, his voice warm although wary. 'Hedrek here says you know how to use this equipment.'

The man's older than Madog, but not by much. He's well built, with shoulders broader than the door on the granary store. He's also tall, overtopping everyone there. For a moment, I feel I should run my hand over my hair, aware there are elements of grey threaded through the dark mane, but I hold my hands in place, remembering I'm shrouded in my cloak and hooded. With the men and women beholden to Hedrek in attendance, I must become the seeress of the Eorlingas. There can be no familiarity with them while they're our guests.

'Madog.' Centus speaks in a booming voice to match his appearance. He moves forward to look at all before him, a look of concentration on his face. 'May I?' he asks. He's wise not to presume.

'Is it all here?' Madog questions too eagerly, but Centus makes no reply. I sense Hedrek eyeing me, but I keep my gaze on Centus, determined to see if he's evasive. I hope he's wise enough not to hold any secrets close to his chest.

'I don't know, Madog. I'll need to try and work the

equipment, and only then will I remember all the intricacies. We've brought charcoal. Fresh charcoal,' he adds quickly, dismissing the powder-like stuff we've found in the foul storage room. I wish he'd not done that. I wish I knew from where he'd managed to get new charcoal. Madog would do well to find some charcoal makers to aid us. Even I know it's not a simple process. As I know the magiks to bring forth a healthy child from a mother's womb, so charcoal makers know the intricacy of wood and fire, and everything else that makes the blackened fuel from seasoned wood. I imagine the smirk of triumph on Hedrek's face. He has something Centus needs and we don't have it. We'll need to remedy that quickly. Well, if Hedrek was responsible for the charcoal, we will.

My eyes narrow consideringly. There's something I know thanks to Sian, who shared the knowledge she had. Producing charcoal is a slow process. It can't be done overnight. The wood must be seasoned. The charcoal must be allowed to form beneath the weight of earth and with the heat of fire. So, I'm even more suspicious of Hedrek. Did Hedrek know more about Edern's death than we did? Did Hedrek have warning and begin to prepare long ago? I wish I knew. I'm grateful we were quicker to reach Villa Eorlingas.

'Is there a place for me to labour?' Centus questions. I sense he's eager to begin the task. My eyes narrow. I consider who I should fear the most, Centus or Hedrek? Who's told the most half-truths to get the other to aid them?

'Outside and to the rear of the villa,' Madog's quick to reassure. 'We brought the equipment here so you could make an initial decision, but if you believe you've enough to start with then, yes, you, Hedrek and I, alongside the seeress, will begin the experiment.'

'What of my warriors?'

'What of them?' Madog questions Hedrek, chin defiantly jutted out.

'They would watch as well.'

'No. They can remain here, under guard, of course, or they can come within the villa, also under guard, or they can wait beyond the boundaries of Villa Eorlingas with their weapons and your other warriors.'

Hedrek's lips twist. He's unhappy about this, but he's brought more than the fifteen men and boys with him than when he first came to ask for the equipment. It's a show of strength now he has what he wanted within his grasp.

'I'll have half of my people remain, and half may wait beyond the boundaries.'

'We'll provide food and ale,' Madog concedes.

For a moment, everyone looks at one another; only then Hedrek mutters under his breath and begins to divide his warriors. At the same time, Centus bends and continues to examine the haphazard collection of items found close to the old, seemingly useless, charcoal. I've added some additional stray items amongst the finds, just to see if this Centus truly knows what he's doing. I can't see he'll need to make use of the iron spoons or even the half-cracked pot nestling amongst the two metal cauldrons. Or the collections of soft pieces of wool that can be used to apply patterns to clay pots with the aid of heat, and so nothing at all to do with the magiks of the blacksmith. I'm curious to see how he manages. It would be a definitive advantage for my brother if Centus could truly do what he's promised.

'We'll help you move everything.' Madog quickly stops Centus from collecting everything in his hands in one go. Sian and the girl who is her shadow hurry forward to do just that. I notice Centus collects the heavy ironstone pieces, as well as the already worked iron bars. He eyes them with interest, turning one piece from side to side as though the glint of the sun on it will make it reveal its secrets to him. The iron-stone's more black than shimmering. It needs heat and other actions to make it produce what we want. The iron bars glint dully.

In a cacophony of dropped and collected items, my brother leads us to the space laid aside for Centus. Already, we've decided if Centus stays he'll have the use of a small outbuilding, similar to the one I use, but to the far side of the rear of the villa buildings. Still within sight of everyone, and certainly within the defences of the place.

We don't go there now, but rather to a space cleared of debris close to the room where Sian found the items, but still outside. Centus hardly seems to notice where he's being directed. Sian, Madog and Hedrek place the items Centus picked from the random collection on the ground, and soon I hear something heavy being dragged towards us. I eye Hedrek. He offers a mocking smile.

'The charcoal,' he informs me. I gasp softly. Compared to the small pieces of ironstone Centus chose, and even the lengths of worked iron bars, there's vastly more charcoal. Indeed, two full hempen sacks of it. 'There's more, as well,' Hedrek continues to mock.

I seethe quietly, but Centus pays no mind to

events happening around us. Centus eyes some of the rocks and stones, and then astounds me by digging into the hard-packed earth using one of the hammers. Or, rather, he attempts to do so.

'Get him a spade,' I direct Sian. The small girl who's her shadow rushes to do just that. When she returns, Centus takes the item gratefully, and moves larger clumps of soil aside.

When he's happy, he carefully places slabs of rock and stone found while digging, almost like the tiled pattern of my horse mosaic within the villa. There's almost no gap between the stones and rocks, so closely packed together are they. I find myself growing impatient as he works to ensure the best fit for them. This isn't what I expected to see. Far from it. I thought he'd light a fire and produce a blade from the ironstone or iron bars. How wrong I was.

I lean towards my brother, already growing weary of standing and watching the younger man work. 'Send Sian to me when something is produced. And I'd get comfortable if I were you. This won't be a quick process.' My brother nods but hardly heeds me. He's watching Centus too keenly. I told him to show less enthusiasm for the task, but no doubt, the thought of what could be accomplished with sharp blades and a blacksmith at his beck and call has driven all such restraint from his mind.

I return to my workshop and Marchell. She lifts her chin as I enter, sniffing as though a hound.

'It's me,' I murmur, in case her eyes fail her this day. She's rummaging through boxes and sacks, looking for something or perhaps just testing what's here and what isn't.

I return to the small item I was examining on that fateful day when my brother informed me of Edern's death. While Rhian might have been keen to be re-united with my brother, and show him their son, she ensured, alongside Marchell, that everything was brought to me from my old hovel. That's what con-cerns Marchell right now. But I need to understand the small object. I curse my brother for disturbing my ruminations a few days ago. It might have been for a good cause, but this small item must have some meaning. I only wish I knew what it was.

The sounds of the settlement fill my senses. The crying of the babies, for there are more than Madog's young son to care for, and the lowing and baaing of the animals. There's the smell of pottage cooking, flavoured with last summer's herbs, and also the noise of men and women working the ground to plant seeds or weed around the short growths already starting to show. If not for the presence of Hedrek, everything would appear calm and orderly, and as though this villa has always been our home. I would even enjoy it, and perhaps allow my suspicions to dissipate.

But there's something out of place. I listen carefully, and realise it's Hedrek. He talks to Madog, his voice rough and persistent. I can't decipher the words, but I imagine he tries to barter for Centus even now. He wants Centus' skills. I want them as well, provided they exist.

Marchell nudges me. I turn to her. Her gaze is on the small object in my hand, and her eyes narrow. I'm sure she must have seen it before, when it was brought to me, found by Urien when weeding, but perhaps she hasn't seen it.

Her eyes narrow, and her thin tongue pokes through her lips. She fondles the item, rolling it in her hand which easily absorbs the impossible weight of such a small thing, and then she hands it back to me.

She offers nothing else, as I sense the latent heat of her fingers in my hand. A soft sound comes from her lips, a gentle song or incantation, I'm unsure. I watch her, considering who she is, and what she's done for me, and why, despite everything we do share, I can never be friendly towards her.

And all the time, I hear Hedrek's loud tones, and they disturb me even more than Madog when he dragged me away from examining this small item, and reclaimed Villa Eorlingas for me.

I place the item down on the wooden boards serving as a sort of counter for all the herbs and pots I have. Surely, if it were significant, I wouldn't be so easily distracted from observing it. Perhaps, after all, it's not important.

12

WÆRMUND OF THE GYRWE

Heafoc works us hard over the next few days. We remain at the temporary encampment despite worrying my father could find us easily so close to the Gyrwe, or that Wædel might lead him to us. I'm too exhausted to demand we move on at the end of each day of training, even though I wake each morning determined to do so. Throughout the long day, my thoughts evaporate as we hold shields in place, and then spears, and learn to move together. We must become a single beast with many eyes and protrusions, or so Heafoc bellows. Osfyth keeps us fed on meat thanks to her hunting skills, but it's hard going. Eventually, I start to realise the movements do come more easily. Heafoc has less to shout at us about.

Which is good, because resentment is building, and not just from me.

The horses grow fractious at having little but grass and the occasional find of wild oats to eat.

'We need to get better food,' I eventually announce one evening as we settle before the fire, limbs exhausted and with more than a few bruises each. It's been a cool day, the promise of rain from the low-hanging and dark clouds making everyone grumpy. We don't have the clothing to spend time outdoors if the weather should change. We'll be drenched should it rain.

'What do you suggest?' Heafoc demands. He too is grumpy and poorly fed. I've also heard complaints about the lack of ale. I'd like to think Bægmund would have thought to bring ale from my brother's settlement, but I doubt it. He just expects it to be there.

I don't like my answer, but it's the right one. 'We'll test our skills and take ourselves raiding, in the morning,' I announce, because I'm their leader and I must be the one to make such decisions.

'Where?'

'Back to the land claimed by the Sweordora. We'll ride to Dægbeorht's village and take what we need.'

Heafoc's lips are downturned and yet he eyes me

respectfully, even nodding his head. 'If we're lucky, everyone will live through it,' he confirms. They're not exactly words filled with confidence, but we either feed the horses or eat them. The horses are valuable. I'll take the chance on feeding them. I notice no one else offers a complaint, not even Cenbryht, whose hands remain bound, although not his feet. He could run from here. He's chosen not to do so. Yet.

I've been waiting to be hunted down by my father, but I've seen no one I suspect in recent days. Wherever Wædel is, he's taking his sweet time to exact his revenge if that's what he means to do.

'We'll ride in and then dismount, using the skills Heafoc's taught us. Two of us will watch the horses while the others get what we can,' I announce.

'Do we kill everyone?' Eastmund queries with a grin on his face, the thought of fighting where blood can be shed without complaint from men and women he lives amongst seemingly pleasing him. He's still an angry man since the loss of his wife and unborn child.

'We kill those who get in our way, the warriors. All we want is the oats for the horses and some better food and ale for us.'

'Is that wise?' Bucge questions. 'It would be better

to kill everyone, man, woman or child. We already know Wædel's out there, somewhere, and no doubt your father as well. We don't want the survivors of our raid to hunt us down as well, do we?' She makes a fair point, but I shake my head, surprised by her vehemence and desire to kill indiscriminately. Especially the women and children.

'If we must, we'll increase our efforts and kill any who attack us, as we did at my brother's settlement. If not, we take what we can, and ride westwards. We've better horses than them. They only have one horse. We should take it.'

'And who'll watch our horses while we're fighting?' Heafoc asks. He's always the one to question my decisions, and yet I sense no malice there. He simply likes to have every possible scenario answered.

I hesitate this time. I want to have Osfyth and Bucge stand guard over the horses, but they'll abuse me if I suggest them. They're valuable though, and as more than just women who are warriors. Bucge's knowledgeable about affairs that only a wise man, or *seith*, should know and Osfyth can track better than any hunter I've ever met. I see the curve of Osfyth's mouth, daring me to name her. I swallow down on that suggestion.

'Who are the weaker fighters?' I direct to Heafoc.

A groan of dismay runs through those waiting to know their fate. He's hardly comforting at the best of times, let alone when asked to make a determination like this.

Heafoc eyes everyone consideringly. Cenbryht isn't the best, but he's hampered by the ties around his hand. And I don't want him alone with the horses, for he'll take them, and then I'll lose the horses, which I'm prepared to kill for to feed better.

'No one is any worse than the other,' Heafoc eventually concedes. 'I suggest Hygebeorht and Nothelm for the simple reason they fight well together at the end of our shield wall. We'll not disrupt the formation we've been practising other than Goddæg will become the end of the line.'

'Then it's agreed. Hygebeorht and Nothelm will watch the horses. The rest of us will fight.'

'We don't even know where their settlement is,' Osfyth reminds everyone. 'We might need to ride for days to find them.'

'No, I suspect it's close.' I speak with more confidence than my limited knowledge should allow. 'We didn't come upon Dægbeorht by chance. He was not far from his settlement.'

'We don't know what it looks like. Does it have a ditch? A palisade? Are the dwellings built of stone or wattle and daub? Is it protected? Is it on a slope? Is it close to a river?'

'I know,' I confirm. 'But we need to get good oats for the horses, or they'll grow too weak to be useful, and grains for us as well. We can't live on whatever meat Osfyth can capture. We'll take the risk. We can't be seen trying to scout the place. Then Dægbeorht will be alert to us. This way is better.'

I can tell not everyone is happy with my suggestion, but I'm the leader here. I'll not allow them to argue with me. The horses are important. We must prove we can fight together in our formation as opposed to when we attacked my brother's settlement, and we were, it must be admitted, bloody lucky to survive, and no one is more surprised than me that we did.

* * *

The following morning, we mount up before it's fully light. The horses are slow to respond and I sense I might have left it too late. We need their speed and stamina to succeed in my intentions to flee my father's lands. I hope I've not let their hardiness drain away while we learned to fight together better.

'They'll recover quickly.' Cenbryht surprises me

with his reassurance. I remain wary of him, especially as he's doing his best to become useful. 'A few days of grass will not kill them. But go carefully. They're tired and lacking their usual resilience.'

When I'm mounted, I turn to my small band of warriors. It's not the most reassuring of sights. Nothelm still lacks a shield, although he won't be fighting, while the spears and shield we do have, no matter how often they've been cleaned since our attack on Waga's settlement, show their age. Bægmund's spear haft is far from straight.

'Go easy with the horses. They're suffering, as we are, from lack of good food. Once they're fed, later today, they'll be quickly restored. Until then, don't push them too hard. Our pace will be slower than I might like, but it'll serve us better than speed.'

I sense the eyes of all the horses and my warriors on me. No one comments, although my mount emits a whinny, perhaps in agreement, perhaps in agitation, I'm unsure.

'Come on.' And I direct us to retrace the steps of only a few days ago. Almost too quickly, I find myself at the skull markers demarcating Dægbeorht's territory. Unlike last time, there's no one to greet us as we cross them and venture along the road running through their territory.

'We get as close as possible before dismounting and attacking. Remember, protect one another.' I don't object to Heafoc speaking as he does. He's proven himself to be wise regarding the warriors I have at my command. While Osfyth might have initially questioned him, even her complaints have subsided.

'We do as Heafoc says,' I agree, meeting the gazes of my men and women. This will be our second attack together. For the first one, I gave little thought to how we'd triumph. Rage drove me onwards. My brother not only didn't deserve what he had, it wasn't by rights even his. My father should have thought more of me rather than my brother. My father shouldn't have announced I was cursed by the gods because of the mark on my right cheek. Now that I'm away from him, I'm determined to show the mark is a sign I'm blessed, not cursed.

This time, I want to win and ride from this place not just with treasures but with the oats we need to feed the horses and good food for us. And some ale. Such will allow us to become better warriors. Perhaps not the ale, mind.

'We'll prevail, but be alert to your shield, brother or sister. Keep together and fight well. Hygebeorht and Nothelm, if you sense the horses are needed for a quick escape, bring them into the attack. If not, stay away and protect them. We can't allow others to steal them from us as we try to steal from them.'

So spoken, I move along the road Dægbeorht must have taken to reach us. I see rich pickings in the greyness of early dawn. Horses have come this way, perhaps cattle as well. I lick my lips, considering eating beef when we slaughter one of the animals.

The smell of smoke is the first indication we're close to Dægbeorht's settlement. No brands are lit. I narrow my eyes to make sense of the buildings before me. It seems similar to my brother's holding. There's an enclosure to the side of the road, and a ditch and embankment, behind which there are sloping roofs of at least five buildings and perhaps more. It's not easy to see.

'Dismount,' I order my warriors. My horse whinnies softly, perhaps with pleasure I won't ride him further. The grasses we've been feeding the animals have been plentiful but far from the highest quality. It's too early in the season for that. I hope there are oats left within Dægbeorht's settlement from last year to restore the animals to their vigour.

I wince at the loud clatter of sound as my warriors dismount, wishing I'd ordered everyone to be quieter as they prepare with shield, spear and seax. I hand the reins to Hygebeorht. He offers me a grimace for he's still displeased with his orders, but takes command of five other reins alongside his own horse without protesting further.

'Do what you think is best,' I murmur to him while the others prepare themselves. 'But remember, no one wants to walk.'

With the caution given, I focus on my blades and shield. There will be nine of us. We'll all have shields. I look to Cenbryht. He's still bound, and it would be better if he weren't. I step to him. He moves aside to let me pass, but instead I place the shield he grips on the ground and saw through the bindings on his wrist. I smell his rankness. It's not been possible to keep clean. None of us has more than a single spare set of clothing to wear despite the clothes I took from my brother. We'll have to see to that as well when we're triumphant.

'Don't let me down,' I growl. 'Or I'll slice through your throat with the bluntest weapon we have. It'll take time, and you'll howl in agony.'

'Wærmund.' Cenbryht half bows. I detect some mocking in it, but swallow my sudden unease.

I slip into place beside Eastmund and Heafoc, noting Heafoc glowering at Cenbryht as I do so. But he offers no caution for my actions. Neither does anyone else.

'Now,' I urge my warriors quietly. We've been lucky not to be seen so far, but it won't last forever.

As one, shields locked together as Heafoc has taught us, and has taken us too long to master, we stride forward. We try to be as silent as possible, but we're forced to separate at the ditched embankment to gain entry inside through the narrow opening. I'm perplexed as to why the entrance isn't guarded.

'Hurry.' I urge my warriors back into position and direct my gaze towards what is surely the grain store. It's lifted above the ground, the roof hanging low but not low enough vermin could climb within it effortlessly and ruin the crop.

Only then movement to my right catches my eyes. Now I realise why the entranceway was vulnerable. Dægbeorht and his men are more alert than I'd like them to be. They come at us from both sides of the settlement, appearing from behind dwellings that have kept them hidden. I growl as the two sides meet together. Dægbeorht's force far outnumbers my nine. He has more warriors than when we first encountered him. Even with Hygebeorht and Nothelm, we'd still be outnumbered by two to one. For the briefest of moments, I reconsider my intentions. The horses aren't suffering that much. We could ride from here and find somewhere else from which to steal oats. But then there's no more time for thought.

'I told you to bugger off,' Dægbeorht roars, his cry taken up by his fellow warriors in a cacophony of rusting iron hitting metal shields. In the growing daylight, they reveal the marks of previous fights. Dægbeorht isn't untried in the art of a bloody good fight. I also notice their clothing. Some have ancient, dented and far from well-polished breastplates protecting them. Others lack that but wear heavy, padded material to cover them. One or two even have helms so dulled with age they appear blackened. The men seem huge, their taunts making my legs tremble as I taste bile in my throat.

I swallow heavily, determined to show no weakness. We stole into my brother's village. We killed men and women of our tribe while they slept and before a shout of warning could be given. This is going to be altogether different, and we can't run from here. If we run, I'll forever be known as a weak man who scampered away at the first sign of true resistance. I'll not live with such a reputation. After all, my brother had that slur levied against him, and it made me resent him every single day of his life. I'm a warrior. I'll prove it. Now. Even if my intention was merely to steal supplies.

I do wish I had a helm to cover my hair, even if only to stop it blowing into my eyes.

'Advance,' I roar, and my warriors keep step with me, their blades hitting the edges of our shields. 'We'll triumph,' I encourage, pleased my voice doesn't tremor. For a moment, I'm a child once more, watching my father's warriors with their weapons and blades, in awe of their skill, worried I'll never fight as well as men with scars on their bodies to show the battles they've survived. But no, I'm a man. I've killed, and I will kill again. Now is the time to prove it.

I hear Heafoc at one side, Eastmund to the other. I hold my shield firmly, pleased with the grip I have on it. It's heavy. Even with the training undertaken under Heafoc, it remains uncomfortable in my hand. One day, I vow, I'll have a lighter shield to hold that's easier to manoeuvre. One day. When I make a name for myself to rival my father's, and his father's and so on, all the way back to the time when this land wasn't our home. I've listened to the stories of those times told over hearth fires in the depths of winter, with storms raging against the wooden and wattle and daub walls. I'll be a warrior like those long-dead men were. I'll have a name to strike fear into the hearts of others.

'Advance.' I hear Dægbeorht's answering cry, and likewise, his warriors crash their shields together.

'This'll be dirty,' Heafoc calls to us, with his summers of battle experience. 'Protect the man to your right. Don't be afraid to draw blood and hit bloody hard.'

And then there's no more time for thought.

I see the feet of my enemy before I clash against my foeman. I don't believe it's Dægbeorht. I think Heafoc has the honour of facing him.

A spear point jabs against my shield with a reverberating bang. It throbs along my left hand, and I grit my teeth, sweat already beading in my hair. At the same time, I sense something passing over my head, threatening to scour a line through my hair. I lower my head, almost below the edge of the shield, and jab with my spear. It's an unwieldy object with only one hand. It's much easier to fight with two hands. It passes through the enemy shields without resistance. I growl low, jabbing it back, while Heafoc jostles me, and I almost lose my grip on it.

I'd sooner fight with my seax, even as blunt as it is. I can make much smaller movements with it and have more control over its path. But no, first I must use my spear, as does everyone in the shield wall. I can only see the tip of my spear, and little else other than shuffling feet. The rest is all in the feel of the shield wall. It holds firm, even while my warriors fight, jabbing with their spears and prodding with their shields.

The air between the two sides is fetid. I swallow the salt of my exertions as I retrieve my spear and jab again. Once more, it passes through nothing, yet there's a rusting edge close to me. I watch it, unable to tear my eyes away as it comes closer, closer. I stagger, and try not to veer aside. If I do, I'll knock Eastmund and he in turn will knock others. No, I stay in position and then watch it being retracted. A little further, and I'd have felt the thrust of it, if not been cut by its frail edges.

Heafoc's firm beside me, his movements calm and precise. From him, I sense no sign of panic or worry, just the intention to better our enemy who, I realise, is indeed Dægbeorht.

'Hold,' Heafoc orders. I bite back my reply that I am. Whether it was the intention or not, Heafoc now commands the fight. I'll obey him even if I should be the one to shout such orders.

Belatedly, as I take deep breaths and try to still my fluttering heart, I realise why the order's been given. The limping Bægmund and Cenbryht are struggling. As I glance along the shield wall, I realise I can't see them. It's curved back. They must draw level, or we'll be overwhelmed and the enemy will get around us. Even now, some of our foes might be running behind us. I hope Hygebeorht and Nothelm shout a warning if that happens. I consider if they're still there, minding the horses, or if they've taken them and ridden away, content with my treasures and the vast number of horses. I banish the thought, pleased when I see Cenbryht and Bægmund fight to draw level again.

'Seaxes,' Heafoc orders now.

'About bloody time,' I huff, pleased to drop my spear and reach for my seax instead. Despite the lack of a keen edge, I can do more with such a weapon in my hand. I killed my brother with it, savagely ending his life with jagged thrusts into his neck and cheek. He died gargling his own blood. I smile with the memory. A poor death, for a terrible warrior.

'Steady,' Heafoc shouts. I sense his scrutiny from

where I'm already preparing to lower my shield and jab at the enemy.

Dægbeorht's also ordering his men, but differently. Once more, I feel a spear coming closer, and with my seax, strike against the wooden shaft. I don't believe the wood holding the spearhead will break, or the blade shatter, and I'm astounded when it does. Now my foeman has only a blunt piece of thin wood, admittedly with shards sticking from it, which could give me a nasty wound, likely to fester without the aid of honey to heal it.

The shaft retracts and now I aim for the man's head. He lacks a helm and wears nothing but a hood to protect him. I thrust forward with my seax. His seax comes up to counter the move, the tangs intertwining. I jab my blade back quickly, aware Heafoc's fighting hard against Dægbeorht. For a moment, I feel a tingle of jealousy and unease. If Heafoc kills him, he'll take the acclaim of my fellow warriors, and that should be fine. But I've not killed my foeman yet. When I've done so, perhaps I can overwhelm Dægbeorht. He's a huge man with a straining belly. He's strong, despite his girth. Even Heafoc's struggling.

A crash on my shield, and I realise my foeman has untangled his seax and now batters against me. I

snatch back my hand, not wanting to risk him jabbing upwards unexpectedly. He clatters his blade
against my shield, each stroke sending shock waves
of pain along my left hand. I reorder the grip on my
seax, bring it up before my neck and then jab from
left to right against my foeman's head. He's not expecting it and makes no effort to protect himself.

A reddened mark quickly reveals itself on his
forehead, but I've not drawn blood. Not yet. I repeat
the action, only this time I jab into his nose. The
movement's uncomfortable, my wrist bent back the
wrong way, but the impact makes his nose explode. I
spit aside the taste of his blood and follow up with
more and more punching actions. My shield slips in
my hand, temporarily leaving me vulnerable, but my
enemy's too busy coughing and choking to take advantage. The man beside him is more alert.

For a moment, I meet the glowering gaze of Dægbeorht, his own seax, with a somewhat sharper
blade, coming perilously close to my cheek. I jerk
backwards, grateful when Heafoc's blade intersects
the attack, and I can concentrate on my foeman.

I jab and stab, shield and seax working together,
my seax getting lower while my shield gets higher.
The man attempts to counter me, his seax blade
hammering against my rising shield. I growl low,

sweat streaming into my eyes, my breath so hot even I find it distracting as I'm forced to re-inhale what I've just breathed out.

I sense the shield wall advancing, but Heafoc offers no other words of command, too focused on overwhelming Dægbeorht. And then, with a final crashing blow against my foeman, using the hilt of my seax more than the blade itself, he's stunned and abruptly falls below my feet.

Quickly, not thinking, I jab into Dægbeorht's side, my blade seeming to effortlessly glide through his tunic, where the shimmering breastplate doesn't protect him.

His eyes open wide. I grin in triumph, but he lurches at me, forgetting about Heafoc and his shield, a seax to either hand, both of them coming towards me as though he intends to slice my head cleanly from my body. I jerk backwards, tangling my feet in the still body of my foeman. I struggle for balance, and just as I'm about to surge upwards once more, I feel the passage of air over the very top of my head, so close I watch strands of my blond hair shimmer to the ground.

'Watch it,' Heafoc huffs. While Dægbeorht's men have decent enough weapons and shields, the bastard has a blade that's sharper than any other. I see my blond hair fall with unease, and only then right myself, grateful Heafoc's claimed Dægbeorht's attention so I can finish off the warrior I knocked to the ground, but hadn't yet killed. The blade slides into his body with difficulty, and the man's eyes flutter with pain before he dies with a wet gargle. I pull on my seax, but the blade's well and truly stuck.

'Bollocks,' I huff, but my eye catches on the dead man's weapon. I snatch it from his slackening grip and meet the next enemy with my shield held before me and his ally's seax blade to hand.

The shield walls are disintegrating. This is becoming a one-on-one fight, and Heafoc has urged us not to allow that to prevail. 'We're better together,' he repeated time and time again.

'Together,' I shout, and then repeat myself when my order's hardly louder than the flap of a butterfly's wings. 'Together,' I roar, finding some command for my voice. I sense Eastmund bring his shield next to mine. It's difficult with the dead man beneath my feet. It takes too long for Heafoc to join me, but to his far side, Osfyth and Goddæg have crashed their shields together. They face at least three warriors, but they're gaining some protection from the ditch at their side. The enemy will be disadvantaged if they step into it because they'll be open to an attack on their heads, instead of their bodies.

'Bastards,' I hear Dægbeorht shout. I can't help thinking if I could kill him, this fight would be over, but now more of his warriors are moving in to aid him that won't be possible.

And then Heafoc slides his shield alongside mine once more. He's breathing heavily. I glimpse the shimmer of blood in the corner of my eye. He's bleeding, or Dægbeorht's bleeding. I'm unsure which.

'We need to end this,' I growl, unhappy my intentions have come undone, and we're in danger of being beaten. If I should meet my end here, my father would laugh with delight, praising Woden for aiding him. I can't allow it to happen.

'Then we must work together,' Heafoc huffs. I want to check him over. I'm suddenly fearful it's his blood and not Dægbeorht's. I can't lose Heafoc. Since the attack on my brother's settlement, he's become important to me. I know my father once esteemed him before deciding he was too old. I'm grateful to have him with us and for everything he's taught us.

I lower my shield and eye the men we fight. They're as ragged as we are. They're fine warriors. Well, some of them are. What they know is how to fight against us, but I don't believe they truly appreciate the power of the shield wall. Even now, some enemies grumble unhappily and refuse to link shields with the warriors to their left. We can take advantage of that. I hope.

'Together,' I command once more. 'We keep the shield wall tight and fight as one. Be wary of one another, but kill the enemy. Advance,' I cry, and we do so. I feel it as a shiver against the shield wall, the crash of iron and wood, the smell of sweat and exertion.

'Advance,' I repeat. The dead man is behind me now. I'd welcome Nothelm or Hygebeorht coming to drag him away, but no, they must keep the horses safe. The enemy could escape and take the animals from us, and we need them.

'Advance,' I cry once more. The thunder of wood and iron meeting wood and iron is louder now.

'Advance.' With one more step, we're butted up against the enemy.

'Advance,' I shriek. Heafoc says nothing. I take it for approval of my tactics.

It's harder now, much, much harder. The enemy belatedly appreciate our intentions. They try and stand firm, their shields held together. Even if the men hate one another, they don't hate one another enough to allow us to overwhelm them.

'Advance.' But it's impossible. I see the feet of my enemy beneath my shield. I note the wrappings covering them with strange detachment. They look comfortable. I detect the hint of sheep wool acting as some sort of cushioning.

'Attack,' I huff, feeling the strain in my left arm, along my shoulder, aware of Heafoc swinging his blade over his right shoulder, of Eastmund doing the same to my left, and I copy them. I crash against my enemy with my blunt blade. I hammer it against his uncovered head, his shield wedged between the two men beside him so he can't lift it to protect himself. His angry cry floods the space between us with his hot breath and foul aroma.

I bash again, using the flat of the blade and its dulled edges. His blade also comes for me. I keep my grip tight enough I won't lose the blade but free enough I can move it from side to side. It's more hacking than stabbing, and still, he holds firm.

This is going to be hard. I breathe deeply, try and ignore the fatigue in my arm, the ache in my back, the sweat running down my face and back, sitting uncomfortably in a wet patch where my tunic meets my trews.

And still I hack and bash. Beside me, Heafoc roars. I sense some give in the shield wall. Eastmund hollers as his enemy falls still, his fighting arm slowly dropping from sight. The shield wall wavers once more, those who've felled their enemy eager to take the next step, but Heafoc and I still have bastards to kill.

Dægbeorht's becoming desperate. His blows are wild. One of them even hits me, making my vision blur and allowing my enemy to land a blow against my left cheek. I feel it as a dull pain and I'm sure I bleed, but it's impossible to tell with the sweat running down my face.

I snarl low in my throat, lashing out to land a whacking blow against Dægbeorht, ignoring my foeman for the time being. He continues to rain strikes on my head, but if we kill Dægbeorht, or mortally wound him, this will all be over.

'Leave him to me,' Heafoc urges as another clout knocks my head dangerously forward, almost banging my chin on the shield I hold.

With strength coming from deep inside me, I finally hack into my foeman's head, my blade wedging in the top of his skull, blood gushing forth while his eyes flicker and lose all focus. He's on the ground and now only Dægbeorht prevents us from meeting the

few remaining warriors who hover uncertainly behind us. I can't see the women or children of this
tribe. They must be hiding.

I focus on Dægbeorht, but suddenly he's not
there. I turn wildly, seeking the leader of these warriors, but he's gone.

'Where?' But the question dies on my lips.

Heafoc sags beside me, blood pouring from a
wound on his cheek, his eyes wavering.

Osfyth moves to keep him upright. I do the same.

'Finish this,' Heafoc growls. My eyes alight on
Dægbeorht. He's had his horse brought for him, and
labours to mount up while his remaining warriors
rush towards him. I see frightened eyes peering from
inside doorways, and my rage pools to fury. He's
abandoning his people, the very women and children I urged my warriors not to kill unless it was absolutely necessary.

'Break the shield wall,' I urge my warriors. 'Stop
Dægbeorht from fleeing.'

This began as a need to get better food for us and
the horses, but it's become much more immediate
now. Dægbeorht needs to die, not just because he
fought us, but because he's feeble and thinks only of
himself. I find, in that moment, while I hate my father for deriding me and mocking me as cursed by

our gods, I admire him. He'd never leave his women and children to face the enemy with little more than a weaving beater, farming hoe or sickle to defend them.

'Hurry,' I call, half a thought for Heafoc, whom Osfyth's lowered to the ground, her expression filled with concern as she examines his wound.

'Get the bastard,' Heafoc shouts, and I urge my legs to a run and surge towards Dægbeorht.

13

MEDDI OF THE EORLINGAS

It's not until almost dusk that Centus announces he's ready to reveal his findings. I thought it would be much quicker, but of course, he was a boy when Edern brought his father here, and then had him killed. He's only slightly older than Madog. What Centus believes can be remembered must have been dredged from long-ago memories.

Behind the villa buildings, where we stand, expectantly, I see many changes have taken place since I returned to my workshop. Centus has equipment arranged around him, a collection of blackened iron hammers, tongs and other things I don't understand. There's also a wooden board stretched over two pieces of tall stone, and upon which I notice a beaker of water and a jug, no doubt containing more. It seems Sian has been ensuring Centus had all he needed.

The pile of charcoal Centus brought with him, and which appeared so vast, is much depleted, and the heat rising from the hole he dug into the ground, and then lined with flat pieces of stone, is intense, and covered with soil so I can't even see the flames. I assume there must be a fire, from the sweat on Centus' face, but I can't see it. I have my cloak around my shoulders to keep warm in the approaching dusk and shiver slightly. Only Centus is warm. Hedrek has been summoned as well and Centus inclines his head respectfully towards Madog, who's been standing here for much of the day, if I know my brother.

'My lords,' Centus begins. 'There's much here I needed. Thank you, Madog, for allowing me to make sense of it all.' Centus speaks well. He's neither snivelling nor lacking respect as he focuses on the two men.

'Have you?' Hedrek questions too eagerly. 'Made sense of it?' He's as keen as my brother for this to succeed.

'I'll only know when I complete the process,' Centus offers, although his words remain respectful.

'Then we'll watch?' Madog asks. I know what we're all expecting, or rather, what Hedrek, Madog and I are anticipating, but I suddenly feel a sliver of unease. I don't believe Centus has the same hopes as us. He came here to see if he could remember all he learned from his father. It wasn't necessarily to bring forth a much superior sharpened blade to any we now have available.

'I thought it best, yes. The furnace is burning well. I've been adding the charcoal and also some small pieces of ironstone which I hope to melt, but I believe the furnace could be warmer. I've laid aside the iron bars. I don't have the heat to melt them. But, these can be used for the small pieces of ironstone.'

He lifts a flat item which also opens up and smells faintly of animal skin. I can hardly tell what it can be for, only then Centus shows us, brushing air over our faces with the actions as he pumps the two sides together. The effort needed is immense as his strong arms quiver. A terrible smell of disuse, and perhaps rat shit, wafts from it. I thought the item was of no use, but I added it to the collection of found objects. It seems I was right to heed Sian's urgings.

'It goes here,' Centus informs, not noticing my grimace, bending low and holding the item close to an opening in the hollowed-out and stone-lined ground, from which flames do lick hungrily. I hope the flames are well contained by the pieces of stone and soil covering. I wouldn't like them to spread to the priceless tiled roof covering much, if not all, of the villa complex. But no doubt, I reason, that's why there's a stone lining. It will contain the flames, just as would be used in the kitchen or even to heat the floors we walk over in the winter months. Or rather, will walk over when we've amassed enough wood to burn, and found people willing and trustworthy enough to tend to the fires. I recall such luxury from my father's days. Edern never made use of it, or indeed of the baths that also benefited from such heating.

'I'll do it,' Madog affirms quickly. This surprises me. I'd have expected him to get one of his many warriors to perform the task, perhaps Urien, but of course, he wishes to show himself amenable to Centus and reveal his regard for the magiks Centus understands.

'Here, then.' Centus shows Madog where to stand, or rather crouch uncomfortably, his knees on the ground, as the part of the strange contraption is thrust through the small hole. I shuffle away from Hedrek and his scowl. Madog holds the unfamiliar object. He gives it a few experimental compresses and then nods, satisfied he can do what's required. Hedrek would never be able to crouch so low, not in such a position. Madog can squat, his balance much better. After all, he has less than half as many winters to his name as Hedrek. I keep my face expressionless. I don't want Hedrek to realise how amusing I find this.

I realise then Marchell is beside me and Sian hovers not far away. I beckon Sian closer. This is the sort of thing we should understand. As secretive as the art of producing iron from ironstone is, the only way the knowledge can be kept alive is to have more and more people aware of it. Until Hedrek arrived with Centus, I'd thought it impossible for Madog to ever have someone with such skill as part of our tribe. I've heard of no one else forging new metal for many summers. Since Edern did away with Centus' father, these magiks have been lost to us. It's been somewhat easier, I know, to melt down old iron and make it conform to some new use. But that's been far from successful, especially in the art of producing sharp blades. And even those who know how to do that are far away from Villa Eorlingas and require huge recompense in barter. My brother would never allow such exchanges. He thought it more important to feed his people. Grudgingly, I admit he was no doubt correct.

I watch the flames dance above the soil roof of the fire as Centus urges my brother to work the bellows, as he calls them. In no time at all the few visible flames through the cracking surface covering the hole go from yellow and dancing merrily to burning with the heat of the coldest blue, the hottest of flames. And then Centus gets to work once more, pouring copious quantities of charcoal into the bowl-shaped hole through a small gap, but only small amounts of ironstone, which perplexes me.

All the time, Madog works the bellows, sweat running as much as on Centus' face. Time seems to drag, the darkness of night closing in around us, although Centus never stops. His expression remains intense. Even I grow warm and step aside from the effects of the flames. Only then do I realise we're no longer alone. Night has drawn in, and every member of our tribe stands and watches in hushed awe, even Rhian with her small son.

'You can stop now,' Centus offers. Outside the bright circle of the flames, all is black, and yet he can see.

Madog stands, still limber, showing no ill effects from his labours other than the sweat on his face.

'Stay clear,' Centus murmurs. I consider what he'll do next. Perplexed, I watch him take hold of a huge metal item. 'Keep the children back,' he also commands, as I sense we all lean closer. Even Hedrek's alert.

More quickly than I think possible, Centus knocks aside the remaining soil covering the hole and plucks a flaming object from its centre, before moving it quickly to the heavy anvil, as I've been informed it's called, also found in the storage room.

'Can you hold this?' he asks quickly, and again Madog steps forward to do as he's requested. Centus moves swiftly then, bending for another object, the huge hammer he initially used to dig the soil out that he swings against the heated heart of the flaming lump of what I take to be the iron. Sparks fly, and Madog's quick to order buckets of water brought to stop anything from setting alight. The night rings with the mighty thuds of the action, a dull counterpart to my enthralled breathing. I see it then. I see the shape starting to form and realise whatever part of the process this is, there'll be no sharpened blade this night. I was correct to fear Centus had other intentions, or rather, the process wasn't as simple as I thought it would be. I should have known better. Nothing is simple in the magiks, as I know.

Finally, Centus heaves in a deep breath and turns to face Hedrek and me while Madog leans perilously close to the still-glowing lump.

Centus offers a wry smile, his face backlit by the open flames from the furnace which are slowly dying down now the bellows aren't being used.

'This is all I need, for now. Tomorrow,' he says, nodding to himself. 'Tomorrow, this will become a blade of good iron.' A smattering of surprise rings through the assembly, while my belly growls. Madog's too involved in the reddened shape to notice the unease of his people.

'We're all hungry,' I call quickly. 'We must eat and be about our beds. A new day will bring us closer to what we desire.' As I turn to face the men and women of the Eorlingas, I see little, blinded by the bright flames so the darkness of night is impenetrable. I hope these people are pleased with what's been achieved so far. For myself, I hardly know what to think.

The image of the shimmering red shape is never far from my mind. Centus says he's made iron, and can then forge a blade from the cooling mass. My doubts remain, however. During the blackness of night, I creep towards the bowl-shaped hole, eyeing it warily, aware the flames lick at its edges although there's little to no charcoal remaining. I see what's left at the bottom of the hole. I don't touch it, the heat driving me back, but I see it, and I worry that what's been left behind is, indeed, the iron needed for blades. Is Centus not aware of this?

I sleep poorly, my mind consumed with images of fire as I fear my dreams of triumph for Madog will amount to nothing.

* * *

The following day, I return to Centus and his outdoor working area as soon as I've eaten, conscious I can't appear too keen. Marchell and Sian dog my steps, but I offer no complaint to either of them. Centus is already busy at work, Madog and Hedrek watching him, although the rest of the tribe are busy with their daily tasks. I realise I should have remembered to caution Madog about seeming too keen again, but it's too late now.

Centus holds the reddened lump he formed yesterday into the flames of another fire with the use of the tongs, this fire separate to the one he used yesterday, which still puffs intermittently. He rotates the substance until it turns dark and menacing and then lifts it onto the anvil, before hitting it heavily with a blackened hammer. A solid *thunk* fills the air, and we all lean forward, to watch him repeatedly hit the lump. It takes some time, but it appears the substance is becoming thinner and thinner, and no longer the awkward shapeless bulge from which I thought nothing could be made because he'd left the iron within the bowl-shaped hole. It seems that wasn't the case. I don't know what that other stuff was, though. Perhaps something left over from the magiks of the process of producing iron.

I watch Centus' expression as he works, not the item he's producing. I see the flash of pride on his face which instantly disappears as the thinning iron fractures in two.

I see the confusion in his eyes, and the biting of his lip, and then he stands tall, his shoulders somewhat deflated.

'I'll need to try again. My apologies.' He inclines his head respectfully.

Hedrek huffs and storms away but Madog and I both scoop forward, intent on collecting the separate pieces of iron in our hands. I'm astounded by the effort that's gone into bringing forth such a small amount of the much-needed substance.

'It'll be hot,' Centus warns quickly.

'It's too thin,' Madog suggests, snatching back his

hands as though already burned, for all he's not yet held the iron.

'It needs something else.' I speak with a confidence I don't feel, considering all the remedies I've learned from Marchell. It rarely takes only one ingredient to cure illness. 'Something added to the ironstone, or perhaps, just better ironstone.' Again, I recall, sometimes, only the freshest of ingredients will produce the best results.

Centus' face clears as he realises we aren't angry with him.

'I'll consider both suggestions,' he replies. 'Perhaps more of the base material, the ironstone, but also something else within it.'

'Here, look at my blade.' Madog pulls it from his weapons belt. 'I know the edges are too thick, the blade not sharp enough, but I've always wondered what caused this here.' And he points a finger at a thicker band running through the grey metal.

'May I?' Centus questions and examines it when Madog hands him the blade. I watch him, and turn to Madog.

'He'll decipher how. I know he will.'

'He will, yes, but perhaps we need not tell Hedrek that,' Madog suggests with a gleam in his eyes as he whispers.

I smile in return, nodding my head slowly and with consideration. 'Indeed. This will work to our advantage. I'm sure of it.'

'We'll leave you.' Centus nods absent-mindedly at Madog's words and we share a conspiratorial look. Centus is consumed by the desire to recall the magik of making good iron.

I walk with Madog towards the main villa building, my eyes appraising it. It could do with some fresh paint, and a thorough clean. I don't know what Edern's been doing for all these summers, but he's not been ensuring the building was maintained.

The cry of Madog's son brings another smile to his lips, but my focus is on Hedrek. He's taken himself along the trackway leading to where half his warriors wait, excluded from entering Villa Eorlingas, and seems to march from one end of it to the other, frustration evident in the way he stamps and swings his arms.

I direct my steps towards him, murmuring softly to Madog of my intentions.

'It was always going to be difficult,' I inform Hedrek, bringing him up short, so his familiar eyes glare into mine.

'He said he knew the magiks.'

'And do you recall what you were taught while no taller than your father's knees?'

'Yes,' he announces firmly, but I sense the waver in his voice.

'You've no idea,' I growl. 'You shouldn't expect so much from Centus. His failure is merely another in a long line of men and women who've thought they knew the magiks but had no true idea.'

'No. No.' Hedrek shakes his head so violently his fat chin wobbles beneath his long white and grey beard. I watch the rippling effect until it settles on his wrinkled neck. 'He knows the magiks. He'll be successful.' And then his eyes narrow. 'I should have known you'd be quick to dismiss his efforts. It'll do your brother harm if Centus can forge good iron and make superior blades. He'll lose what he's only just gained.' There's a triumphant gloating look on his face, his anger banished.

'It will not. Even if Centus determines how to do what he suggests, it's unlikely he'll be able to do more than produce one or two such blades. Have you realised how much charcoal and ironstone he used to produce so little? That's hardly going to bring my brother's leadership into contention. After all,' and I shrug nonchalantly, holding my hands to either side, aware of the jangle of bangles and talismans as I do so, the clacking of the items I wear threaded through my hair, 'where are you, or Centus, to find more ironstone and charcoal and whatever else he needs? Do you even have more charcoal to heat the ironstone? Do you have enough to heat the iron bars we found? No, Hedrek, I'm happy to play host to this attempt by Centus, but whether he succeeds or fails is irrelevant. The materials needed to make enough blades to threaten Madog are sadly lacking. If they weren't, those items wouldn't have lain dormant for almost twenty summers, would they now?' I speak without anger. I'm curious as to how much, if anything, Hedrek has kept from us. Does he have more than just charcoal at his disposal?

He nods, reluctantly, a grimace on his old face. Again, I recall how, if Hedrek had aided me many summers ago, Edern need not have kept my villa for as long as he did. Perhaps Hedrek acknowledges that now.

'You're right. I admit it. We've just enough charcoal. We didn't even have any lumps of ironstone for Centus to examine, let alone iron bars.' He stops, eyeing the smoke spilling above the roof of Villa Eorlingas, and looks at me appraisingly. 'You look well, Meddi, or seeress, as I should term you. It's been a long time coming, your return here.'

'It has, yes,' I acknowledge, my voice even. Hedrek and I have known each other for more than half our lives. He knew me before I was seeress. He knew me when I was my father's daughter and assured of a good marriage and an easy life, before I even considered becoming a seeress.

'He was always a bastard, Edern,' he mutters. 'A bastard that was impossible to stop. If I could have done, I would have done so.'

'Perhaps,' I murmur, not wishing to follow the line of thought. 'It was a long time ago. Now isn't the time to dwell on it, but rather, to make right all he did wrong, and not merely to me.'

'Yes.' Hedrek nods. 'We'll do so. And, your brother is a fine leader of your tribe. Your father at least chose the mother of his youngest child well.'

I nod once more, not trusting my voice. 'Come. We should eat,' I suggest.

'As you will.' Hedrek bow is long, and I find a reluctant smile on my lips at his respect for my position. It's a pity, really, I must deceive him. There was a time I wouldn't have even considered it but I know the ambition hidden by his wobbling cheeks and wrinkled neck. I'll be mindful of him and not only with regard to Centus and the magiks of iron craft.

14

WÆRMUND OF THE GYRWE

The settlement of the Sweordora

Dægbeorht's horse is frightened and fast, but I hasten onwards, calling Eastmund and Bucge to help me, hoping the need to avoid buildings and animal enclosures will slow him down enough to catch him. The others are making short work of ending the lives of the other warriors Dægbeorht fought beside before abandoning them. My eyes sweep to find Cenbryht, relieved to find him fighting beside my other warriors.

I feel sweat dripping down my face and resting in my growing blond tufty beard and moustache alongside the blood of those I've killed. But for now, I banish such worries and urge my legs to pump faster. I must stop Dægbeorht, for if he escapes, he'll send warnings of my intentions to other tribes in the west and, perhaps worse, seek out my father and tell him I live. So close to the lands my father controls, it wouldn't take long for word to reach him of our current whereabouts. I'm astounded we've not yet been found.

No, Dægbeorht must die. If we'd managed to steal what we needed without being detected, he could have lived because he wouldn't have known it was us. But not now. Too much of my hastily decided future depends on us being able to present our force as a *comitatus*. Gaining a reputation for stealing will not aid that.

I rush through the collection of dwellings, some rounded and with a peaked roof, others longer and thinner, the roof more squat to the ground, covered in turf. I'd not realised how large the settlement within the ditched enclosure was. The lowing of cattle and the baas of the sheep also reveal the wealth Dægbeorht has at his fingertips. I allow a smile to curve my lips. This will all be mine once Dægbeorht's dead. I'll take as many of the cattle and sheep as we can control between us.

Ahead, Dægbeorht kicks his mount to greater

speed. I regret leaving my spear behind. And my horse. Without them, I won't be able to stop Dægbeorht. His horse is fleet-footed, and if I throw my seax towards him, it'll not reach him with the blade in a position to pierce or even knock him from the back of the horse.

Only then, I hear the sound of thundering hooves.

'Ware,' Nothelm cries from the back of his grey beast. The horse is quick, eyes wide as it avoids the buildings and dips, almost gaping holes, in the hard-packed earth walkway that runs through the settlement.

I veer aside to avoid being trampled, growling because I want to kill Dægbeorht. Heafoc thought to kill him, and I had to allow it because they faced one another in the shield wall, but with Heafoc wounded I want to end Dægbeorht's life.

Nothelm races onwards, encouraging the horse to greater and greater speed, Dægbeorht turning his head to see he's being chased. Just as I fear Nothelm will thrust his spear towards Dægbeorht, the animal Dægbeorht rides crashes to the ground in a shriek of pain, his rider tumbling forward, and failing to leap clear. I hear the sharp snap of broken bone and arrive, out of breath, to see the horse staggering to its feet, lips pulled back to show its teeth, while Dægbe-orht lies on his back, bleeding where he fell, his right leg at an impossible angle. Already, the light of life is leaving his eyes.

'Bollocks,' I roar, frustration boiling within me because I've failed to kill him myself. I must build a reputation. I must become a warrior who can kill more than the weak and already dying. All the same, I bend over him, and push my seax through his chest, while his mouth opens and closes although no words issue forth. It's no great victory to kill a dying man. If anything, it's a sign of weakness but I do it anyway. I killed my brother, and now I've killed a wounded man. My reputation is hardly growing as my father's did, and his father's and his father's father. It's essential I become a warrior with a warrior's renown, but today isn't to be that day.

Breathing heavily, I turn to eye Nothelm, Bucge and Eastmund, who watch my actions, Nothelm from atop his horse.

'A triumph,' Eastmund mutters darkly, blood covering his clothing, a wry smirk on his lips as he breathes deeply, his chest rising and falling quickly.

'A success,' Bucge equivocates, nodding towards me.

'Better it's done and the bastard dead,' I growl,

my thoughts suddenly returning to the wounded Heafoc. 'Leave him. We take what we need, including the animals.'

'What? You won't hold this place?' Nothelm questions, eyes narrowed in disbelief from atop his grey beast. Dægbeorht's horse watches us warily.

'No. We came for grain for the horses and food we could transport for ourselves. We'll take the animals and the food. I don't want to make my home here. It's too close to the tribe of the Gyrwe.'

Bucge understands immediately, turning aside to follow my orders, but Nothelm looks ready to argue.

'If you wish to have the place, take it,' I state. I'm not going to argue with him about it. 'But I'll only leave you what treasures I already promised and some share of the animals and grain. If you want to command a tribe with nothing to support itself in the wake of our victory, then so be it. We'll part as friends. On this occasion,' I add, the menace clear to hear in my voice, although it's not entirely my intention. Nothelm bites his lip, considering my words. I see him surveying all there is from his vantage point. It's a fine settlement, I don't deny it. But I didn't start today's fight to become commander over something I must in turn safeguard, learning to work with the people who live here and what resources they have available to them.

Indeed, our triumph here and at my brother's settlement has revealed something important to me. It's perhaps too easy to attack and kill. It's protecting what you possess which is more difficult. The ditched enclosure here was no deterrent. Men with blades to hand were no restriction. To be victorious and hold something against those who think to take it, there needs to be more than rusty iron, ditches and embankments.

'No, I'll come with you, Wærmund,' Nothelm quickly corrects himself, the ghost of a smile on his face, revealing he also lacks many of his front teeth. 'You're correct. We must travel further west. There we'll make a name for ourselves.'

I nod and bend low to pull Dægbeorht's seax away from his slack hand. 'Help me,' I ask Eastmund, who's not moved aside, when I'm satisfied the sounds of the fight have subsided. This tribe's warriors are dead. Now we'll take what wealth in blades and iron they had and put it to good use as we forge our path ever westwards.

With much fumbling, we pull the breastplate from Dægbeorht and also his weapons belt, although I leave the rest. I don't want his boots. I do gather an arm ring from his wrist, too narrow to go around his bicep. It's heavy but the metal's too tarnished to determine if it's silver or iron. I suspect iron, but it might come in useful too.

Striding back towards the rest of my warriors, with Eastmund at my side, I remember Heafoc's wounded cheek and hurry to check he's well. Osfyth looks up as I approach and nods once. Although Heafoc's awake and watching everything, he doesn't speak. His arm wound has barely healed and now he has another injury. Perhaps my father was correct to think him too old to fight in his war band. But no, I need Heafoc. He has the experience I lack to make us into a fighting force. But, immediately, my attention is taken elsewhere. The shouts of women and children flood my senses. I turn and witness them emerging with frightened eyes from beneath one of the peaked roofs.

The leading woman shrieks on seeing me, a child cradled in her arms. I don't think it's the blood dripping from my seax, but rather the mark on my face that so terrifies her.

'Where's Dægbeorht?' she demands fearfully.

'Dead,' I reply quickly. 'His body's over there.' I jut my chin to where his corpse is cooling, but instead of rushing to what I assume is her husband, she launches herself at me, nails out to scratch my face. I wish her luck with removing the mark from my face. If only it were that simple, I'd have done so long ago. 'What?' I huff in surprise, hands lifted to ward her off me, mindful my seax remains clasped in my right one. Nothelm's fast to intervene having dismounted, but it's Bucge who pulls the woman away, arms pressed tightly to her sides, so Nothelm has to move quickly to gather the child into his arms before it hits the ground. If the child had died, it would have been another death I was responsible for but which would hardly have cloaked me in the glory my father can ascribe to his name. I'll prove myself worthy of the title of warrior, no matter my father's derision.

'You've killed him. And the other men. What about us?' Her voice is hard edged and angry.

I shake my head. 'It's not my concern,' I remonstrate with her. 'Your men and your warriors were too weak. We'll take what we came for and leave you.'

'You'll steal our animals and food? You'll curse us as you've been cursed by the gods?'

'Yes,' I reply simply, wincing at the mirroring of my father's bitter words towards me. More and more women and children erupt from the building. I see them watching me sullenly, although the tracks of tears can be seen down dirty cheeks. But I don't much care. In fact, I turn my face towards them, ensuring they see the mark placed there at my birth. 'Get the cows and the sheep,' I call to Eastmund. He nods and moves off, beckoning for Maggenræd to join him.

'You can't take our sheep or our cows,' the woman protests, fighting free from Osfyth, although Osfyth hovers close by. The woman's snatched back the child from Nothelm now she's free, and the babe cries, the harsh shrieks adding to the general wailing of the other survivors, making me wish I'd set the building ablaze.

'We take what we won,' I growl, glancing towards Bucge to ensure Heafoc's well enough to ride from this place. I want to be gone from here. The day is still young. We can put a good distance between us and Dægbeorht's settlement. I'd welcome doing so.

'It's ours,' the woman announces with a stamp of her foot.

I look at her then. She's older than me, but not by much. She's clearly the widow of Dægbeorht and I pity her being saddled with such an old man. She's not beautiful. Indeed, her belly sags, and so too do her breasts. I realise then the child hasn't long been born. It's unlikely it'll survive now its father is dead.

It's probably better if it doesn't. Her hair was hidden beneath a cloak, but now it pokes free, and I see the brightness of it in the growing daylight. Still, I don't want her, or the child she almost dropped.

'It's ours, and that's the end of it. You can't fight us for it. You'll all die if you attempt it. We'll leave you with one cow and two sheep. If you don't hush your mouth, we'll also take them.'

I see her take in a deep breath, as though to argue, but an older woman, bent-backed and hobbling, lays a hand on her arm. Something passes between them, and the woman bites back any further complaints. I don't plan on shouting about the grain. We'll just take a good quantity of it. But we don't need all the horses, I realise. Well, apart from Dægbeorht's animal which, despite its fall, is a good breed.

'You can keep most of the horses too,' I announce, about to stride off, only then I stop and look at the woman and the other women and children. Their eyes are fixated on something close to the ground. I smirk. Dægbeorht's not been keeping his secrets very well if all know where his treasures are hidden. 'Bring me a spade,' I call to Goddæg, grinning. He returns my grin, understanding quickly, and scampers off to find such an implement from wherever they keep their farming equipment. Now the collection of ancient men and women have grown sullen. But I don't crow over them or even scrutinise where they're unable to stop looking. With the spade to hand, an old thing, the wooden handle worn reedy with long use, and the metal lip of it almost too thin to be any use, I walk to the building opposite the one the people have all sheltered within. I smile as I do so. This looks like nothing more than an open-sided storage area, yet they all eyed the place close to the front wooden pole. I thrust the spade into the hard-packed earth, surprised by the keenness of the ancient blade. If they could make equipment like this, then why did they fight with blades that were flimsy and likely to shatter if they were ever used with violence?

Almost immediately, I hear the sharp ting of the blade hitting something iron or metal and dig quickly, pulling forth a rotting sack into the open. Once more, all eyes are on me as I root through it. There are no stores of silver or gold, but there's something else, and I think it's probably even more valuable. I'll add the riches to those I took from my brother. They'll come in handy, soon.

'Get me a better sack,' I command Goddæg, handing him back the spade. Perhaps, I think, we should take the spade with us, but no. I dismiss the idea. It'll be unwieldy to travel with. Bad enough to have spears without adding more long and often useless items to the horses' backs. Admittedly, we could dig our own defences with such equipment, but I think it's better to rely on the speed of our horses than digging ourselves into a position which might be hard to defend.

I hear a murmur of conversation from amongst the survivors, whom Nothelm menaces with his blade, but no one speaks. Perhaps they fear I'll take even more from them, maybe their women as slaves. But I don't want a shrieking widow at my side. For what I've planned for my warriors, I don't need a woman. The other male warriors might think differently, and if they want to share their food with a woman, I'm not about to stop them, but for now I want no children and no women. We ride westwards, and we have grain and more stolen pieces of treasure, which I suspect are pieces of iron, to take with us.

All we need do now is find someone who can forge better blades, and also repair the blade I took from my brother. I glance around the settlement, but I don't believe there's a blacksmith here, and if there ever was, he's dead in the fight.

I stride to Heafoc. His face is sheeted with sweat and blood, but Bucge helps him to his feet, which I notice makes him wince. But I'm not going to leave him here either unless he asks me to do so.

'Come on, we have what we came for. Now we leave. We can still ride a good distance today, especially now the horses have been fed oats.' Osfyth has taken responsibility for the task, although she doesn't work alone. Hygebeorht also aids her as the animals are eager to feed well.

Heafoc makes no complaint.

'Hygebeorht, bring the horses,' I call and, shortly, the sound of hooves approaching can be heard, as I scrutinise the rest of my warriors. Some of them are bloodied, others are bruised, but they all stand. Heafoc's the most badly wounded. I even offer Cenbryht a nod of recognition. He's fought well, and the fact he's not stolen one of the horses and run from here speaks of someone who's determined to make amends for his earlier treachery. He bends, grabbing one of the few clucking chickens trying to feed on the blood splatters and all the time holding my eyes, wrings the creature's neck with a sharp snap.

'To flavour the pottage,' he explains. I nod, although his casual violence does unnerve me despite the cooling bodies of the men we've slaughtered.

Bucge and I help Heafoc mount, and then the rest of us gather much of the remaining grain from the grain store in sacks, not plentiful, but enough to help the horses, as well as the warrior equipment we've taken from the dead men. Nothelm's taken Dægbeorht's shield, so I need not worry about him any more. I also add the bag of treasures to the cloak carrying what I took from my brother. It's heavy now. I'm grateful I have the additional horse to carry the load. Cenbryht's made himself useful gathering the sheep we mean to take, with the aid of his shield held before him to stop them from escaping as they're funnelled between the horses. The cows have had ropes tied around their necks by Eastmund and Maggenræd, and can be led as easily as horses.

With the sun high overhead, we leave the settlement behind, and in our wake the harsh shriek of ravens can be heard as can the wailing of the abandoned women, older folk and children. I close my ears to their cries.

We have what we came for. We have even more than that. I hope I don't live to regret not killing all those we've allowed to live. Some might say I have a soft heart, but perhaps my kindness is misplaced. With no one to protect them, and with the loss of many of their animals, they'll probably starve come the dark times of the year, if they survive until then without being attacked by others. Maybe, I realise, I should have been kinder to them, and killed them all, no matter how much it might have pained me and damaged my quest for a warrior's reputation. Maybe.

15

MEDDI OF THE EORLINGAS

Once more, I'm woken by the sound of iron hitting iron.

'By the gods, he's determined,' I mumble to myself.

Shuffling forward on my bed, brought into my workshop only yesterday, welcoming the creaks of the wood and the rustle of straw beneath me, I sense I'm alone within the workshop. Where Marchell is, I don't know. Quickly, I rise and dress, tending to my requirements before meandering towards where Centus labours, no doubt waking everyone within Villa Eorlingas. I can't imagine my brother's wife welcomes the clamour, not with a newborn babe who'll hardly sleep at the best of times.

Hedrek, I see, is already standing, eyes bright with excitement. Sian's also there, continuing to assist Centus. Madog's absent. Centus, I quickly realise, hasn't slept all night, his actions are slower than yesterday, exhaustion tempering him, just as he attempts to temper the ironstone. I see there's another curved depression in the ground. He's evidently been trying to free the iron from the other pieces of ironstone.

'Success?' I ask, even though I doubt it. Even if Centus stayed up all night to make fresh iron from what little remains of the ironstone and charcoal, I can't see he'll be ready to try and make a blade.

'We'll know shortly.' Hedrek's all gruff and ambitious his tongue poking through his thick lips, between the grey white of his beard and moustache.

'Summon Madog,' I instruct one of the youngsters who's come to try and glimpse the magiks. His face clouds, but he knows better than to disobey me.

'Yes, mistress.' He bows and rushes off. I notice his feet are also encased in shoes now. That pleases me. I'll have to thank Sian for her labours.

Once more, I watch Centus as he toils. With a clamour making my head ache, he works on what must be the labours of his second attempt at extracting the iron from the ironstone. This does at least look better. He must have knocked aside all the elements of the process he doesn't need, and is slowly flattening what he does have with the force of his hammer strikes so sparks fly. Every so often, he returns the lump to the cracked open furnace which still burns to heat it, and then brings it away, to hit it with the hammer once more. Sweat beads his face, and the manly smell of him is brought to me on the gentle breeze, scented with smoke. I wrinkle my nose. It's an unpleasant reminder of my time with Edern and the stink of him as he grunted above me.

I wince at the noise, but I don't look away, entirely focused on Centus' actions. Only belatedly do I realise Madog hasn't come. I turn to find the youth, but he's also absent. And that's when I hear it, in a lull, as Centus takes a moment to recover his breath and swill water into his mouth before resuming his banging.

'What's that?' I glower, but I recognise the sound of fighting easily enough. I turn to rush away, catching Sian's eye as I do so, the command to remain behind unspoken but understood by the quick nod of her head.

I hurry towards the main villa building, all the time my heart hammering wildly and without the rhythm Centus employs. The closer I get, the louder the cries, and I realise I'm correct. Hedrek came here with his warriors, but evidently he wanted a peaceful resolution to enable Centus to see if he could work with iron and the tools of his father's trade when he realised he couldn't claim Villa Eorlingas, his stallion or the dead bladesmith. Not so much the man who stands before my brother now with his prancing warriors close to him.

I growl low, and hastily return to my workshop for my breastplate and dagger. I never expected my brother's position to remain unchallenged, but twice in about as many days wasn't my expectation. I doubt this warrior will be as pliable as Hedrek. As ever, there are always arseholes keen to emulate men such as Edern, and the leader of the Weogoran is just one of them.

Madog will need to overwhelm him and his warriors. He must win another victory. And then he'll be forced to impose his will over yet more people. I know he'll prevail. But I'll aid him, with all the knowledge I possess, and feel no compunction for the men for whom today will be their last in this world.

Marchell's within my workshop. I consider where she's been. Silently, she hands me my breastplate. I pause, as I strap it to my body, considering her.

Marchell has always had the gift of foresight. Did she know of this? Did she not tell me? Or was it so obvious Marchell thought I didn't need informing? I'd question her about it, but would be wasting my words. Marchell doesn't speak to me of anything important, not any more.

I take my blade and stalk away, listening to the voices raised in anger from the ditch and embankment protecting Villa Eorlingas. To remain here, Madog will have to fight all who think to challenge him. Hedrek's more peaceful arrival made me forget how precarious our position is.

Striding through the villa building, my feet welcoming the familiar feel of the cool tiles and double horse image below them, I hear the worried voices of the women my brother protects, including his wife and son from the main villa room into which they've been sent for protection. While they're concerned, they're not fearful. I smile. Our tribe has always been able to rely on the strength of its women. My father knew that. For some time, after my father's death and when Edern abused me, I worried we'd lost our way. I no longer feel like that.

Outside once more, the doors of the villa pulled shut behind me, so I stand beneath the shade of the veranda where the women would usually be working, I look towards the ditched embankment. Within the confines of it our animals can graze and be kept safe. But now the animals are all corralled close to the villa and I see the enemy to the other side of the ditch. They posture while summoning the courage to attack the blades of my brother and his warriors. They wait within the enclosure, with even Hedrek hurrying to gather his men and battle gear. I realise all of his warriors have been allowed within the boundary of the villa. It's better to have Hedrek's warriors fighting for us, as opposed to against us. Admittedly, he'll be doing so to protect Centus. If we should die, he won't shed a tear, provided he and his warriors survive.

'How many are there?' I question Madog, as I stride to his side. He eyes me without unease, not even bothering to tell me to stand aside. I'm pleased he's learned the lesson already.

The enclosure has been sealed with a small wooden gate. To our side of it, it's been reinforced with anything that can be found, from heavy pieces of metal Centus said was nothing to do with his work, to two stone barrels for collecting water for the animals, placed there with some considerable effort, if the marks in the soil are anything to go by. Still, we glimpse our enemy over the top of the gate. The banked walls aren't that high as to prevent us seeing them.

'Fewer than us now Hedrek and his warriors have joined us.'

'Then you'll prevail?'

'Always, seeress, always.' He half bows. I smirk to see the confidence in his stance and on his familiar face. He's dressed for war, carrying his shield and spear. 'They have poor blades. They think to overwhelm us with a few rusted spears and even fewer shields and seaxes, look.' He indicates what he means. I nod, considering the enemy. Madog's correct to be dismissive of the might of this force.

'That's truly all they have?'

'Yes, Twrch saw them early this morning coming from the south. No one has separated from the group. They ride together or walk; not all have horses.'

I nod, but still I can't shake my unease. 'Be wary. There are more tricks than that,' I caution.

Madog inclines his head, but his focus is on the enemy. 'Corun of the Weogoran, why are you here?' he shouts to the leader of the collection of men and three horses, standing to the far side of the gate.

'We've come to take command of Villa Edern. He's dead. This now belongs to me.' Corun indicates the villa and lands with a wide sweep of his arms, chest puffed out in arrogance. He's dressed for war, a shield in one hand, his spear shaft planted in the earth, upright, in the other. Beneath his cloak is a thick, padded tunic. He's a wide, barrelled man, his muscles bulging where they're visible.

'Villa Eorlingas,' my brother corrects, 'never belonged to you. It was my father's, and now it's mine.' Madog's words thrums with menace.

'And you have the warriors to protect it, do you? I don't think so. Your family is weak and poor and has been ever since Edern took your bitch of a sister as his wife. You've done nothing but live off the leavings of those who had more than you,' he disdains while his warriors cheer him.

At those words, my heart stills, but I stride confidently to the fore, chin raised, determined to show no fear or trepidation at having the agonies I suffered shouted by a man I despise.

'Meddi, I should have known you'd be behind this,' Corun calls, his lips souring at the sight of me. I stand proudly, weapon to hand, my breastplate heating the front of my body where the sun beats down on it. But my hand reaches for something else, the collection of talismans worn at my waist. Corun tries not to watch, but unbidden, his eyes stray there. I hold my smirk of triumph in place. He comes here with his blades and shields, all hot air and wind, but he's as terrified of my powers as all men should be.

Madog, sensing his distraction, speaks once more.

'Leave now, Corun, or you'll be little more than smoking ruins by the time the sun sets.'

Corun tears his eyes away from me. I don't dance and prattle, as I've known other seeresses to do, although never Marchell. There's no need. Our power lies not in our outward appearance but in what we have within us. Corun knows that. All men know that, although whether they like to accept it is another thing.

He swallows visibly, a nasty scowl on his face, while those behind him jeer and encourage him. Admittedly, their eyes glance my way. I pull the thread holding the talismans at my waist into my hands, running the triangular spangles from one hand to another noisily so the warriors keep glancing towards me, uncertainty on their faces. My brother knows what I'm doing but doesn't so much as look at me.

Here are the marks of my position and powers. Here, I make myself useful to my brother and his men, even if I don't intend to fight beside them with blade and shield. There are other skills I possess.

'She has no power over us,' Corun roars, but it's forced and his voice cracks. I keep my face expressionless. I'll show him no rage or fury. I won't even reveal my disdain for him. Instead, I crash my blade against my breastplate using my right hand, the sound rich and reverberating. Again, all eyes look my way. I sense my brother and his warriors preparing themselves. Rising onto the balls of their feet, they're ready to launch a quick strike against Corun and his men; even Hedrek and his few warriors are alert to what I'm doing in distracting the enemy.

'Now,' my brother calls. I watch, continuing to bang my blade against my breastplate, as Madog, Hedrek and their men advance on Corun and his small force surging over the banked enclosure rather than trying to straddle the blocked gateway. Despite the blades and shields they have to hand, Corun and his warriors are caught unprepared by the actions of the fighting men of the Eorlingas and Beansæte.

I raise my voice, ululating, the sound eerie and seeming to come from all around and not from my throat at all, punctuated by the crash of blades meeting and the shrieks of wounded men. Madog jumps the ditch outside the banked enclosure, his men with him. I'm aware of others joining their voices to mine. The women of this tribe support their warriors in the ways they can. Some, I know, would sooner take blades to hand and fight beside their brothers, fathers, husbands and sons, but for the time being I've forbidden it. The talents of the women of this tribe are as secret as the skills I possess to ward against the anger of our gods, and the vagaries of the weather.

We can use them if there's no other option. Women have skills that must be used elsewhere unless they're proven to be barren or past the years when they can bear children, like me. But we still have our uses.

It's almost over before it's begun. My brother, sweat-stained and dripping with the blood of our enemy, turns to grin at me, eyes bright with battle joy from outside the ditch and banked enclosure. I notice even Hedrek has killed, as blood drips from his seax. I consider what he'll expect in repayment, but banish the thought for the time being. What was important was the survival of my brother and his warriors and that Corun's attempts to steal Villa Eorlingas were quickly stopped.

'All dead?' I question, as though I speak of the pigs to be slaughtered and not men.

Madog shakes his head. 'No, Corun lives. We'll send him on his way back to what remains of his tribe now his warriors have been dispatched and hope he lives to tell the story of what happened here. We'll take the horses and blades from the dead. Some of the blades are ancient and free from rust. They have fine, sharp edges.'

Even now, Corun's being shoved onto the back of his wide-eyed mount by Urien and Twrch. The horse's almost white coat is smeared in the pink of Corun's blood, seeping from a wound on his right side. His padded tunic has merely delayed the inevitable. His eyes are clouded, although they watch me coming towards him warily, as the gateway is unblocked, and I walk freely towards the enemy.

I keep my expression bland, my one hand again tinkering with the talismans at my waist, muttering beneath my breath, while I hold my dagger with the other. Corun's face twists in pain and fury. I reach towards him, having first bent to run my dagger hand through the bloody wound of one of his allies.

I lean towards him, smearing his face with the stuff, my words too quiet for any to hear, even him, but filled with the mysteries I know. He tries to jerk away, but it's impossible with the two warriors supporting him. Then I raise my voice.

'Tell your people the tribe of the Eorlingas will welcome them into Villa Eorlingas if they come in peace and with deference. They'll become subject to Madog, as their commander, and to me, as their seeress. They have two days, or we'll come to your village and take your animals and what meagre wealth you have. They'll be left with enough to survive until the end of the growing season. Nothing else.'

I think Corun will spit towards me, his mouth working, his cheeks concave, but instead he emits a shudder of pain.

'Go quickly. Or they'll never receive this message and then pay the ultimate price for your failure. The tribe of the Eorlingas is restored. We'll triumph against all who think to steal from us.'

I nod towards my brother, slapping the backside of Corun's mount to encourage it on its way.

'His people will never accept me as their leader,' Madog comments as the sound of hooves fades away with the distance covered. The air's buzzing with flies come to feast, the sun dazzling my eyes and making me thirsty.

'No, they won't. And yet they must be given the option,' I confirm, eyeing the women of the Eorlingas with pride where they stand within the enclosure. They're quieter now. A few lead forward children old enough to see what happens when blades encounter flesh, while some shudder and hide behind their mothers' skirts. I note them keenly. Those too young to understand and old enough to hunger for a blade in their own hands are the most keen to walk amongst the sightless gazes of the dead. Those in between are too scared. Tonight, they'll wake from nightmares, but in time, just as I was forced to, they'll become accustomed to it.

'We'll burn the bodies,' Madog announces, 'just as we did with Edern, and we'll make the flames leap high enough Corun will see them and know his warriors are all dead and have been sent to the afterlife without the means to celebrate their deaths.'

I nod, showing I agree with Madog's announcement. It's not always the way of our people to burn the dead, but these warriors don't deserve to be interred with their blades and shields, with the respect due to those who died defending their tribe. No, these men will have nothing with them when we set their bodies ablaze. Just as Edern was shorn of all he held during his long life.

Hedrek, puffing heavily, bleeding from a shallow cut on his lower arm, walks to my brother. I eye him, unsure why he gesticulates so wildly and why my brother shakes his head. I walk closer, eyes narrowing.

'He wishes to know how long Elen will be held captive. He says he'll take her and allow us to keep Centus.' It's a beguiling suggestion. Hedrek is no fool. He's seen we want Centus to succeed. He's seen Madog has fierce warriors to protect him. He means to take what he can while he can. But he's a damn fool if he thinks I'll allow him to have Elen.

'No,' I announce without preamble. 'Elen remains here. And Centus will make his own decision about who the better man to serve is.' I stalk from Madog and the slaughter field, the women of the tribe reaching towards me as though they can absorb some of my power. But I'm keen to see if Centus has had any success with his experiments. The matter of Elen hasn't concerned me for the last few days, but clearly, there are others who think to gain from having her join them. I allow the fury to pool within me.

Hedrek will not have her. No one will have her. But before I consider her future, I must be assured she has no child within her belly. There's to be no debate about who'll lead this tribe after my brother has gone. It'll be his child and no one else's. In that way, I'll ensure the correct line is restored, lacking the taint of Edern, for everything he touched turned rotten. I need only look at this once fine villa to know that. When not fighting, men and women labour to restore the roof, clean the tiles of the horse mosaic, and ensure the animals are fed well. When not fighting, they, just like me, labour to re-establish the fortunes of our tribe. Never again will another take what's been ours for generations, all the way back to when Villa Eorlingas was newly built by our ancestors grown wealthy on the profits of trading in horses, gleaming beneath the sun, nestled in the valley that shelters it from the fierce winds, close to the wide River Habren that stretches out before us. Never again.

16

WÆRMUND OF THE GYRWE

We camp that night in a sheltered treeline away from the road we've been following since leaving Dægbeorht's settlement. We saw few people after the battle. If there are more Sweordora, they knew to stay away from mounted warriors.

After the fight, my body has slowly seized up, and aches and pains are making themselves known. I'm grateful to dismount as I find the trees, and Bucge quickly builds a fire from loose-lying pieces of deadfall and begins to make a pottage in a copper bowl she took from the destroyed village. Maggenræd offered to cook, but Bucge informed him she'd rather eat her own shit.

The smell of good food cooking causes my stomach to growl. The familiar sound of strong horses' teeth over their oats rings throughout the temporary campsite. I smile to hear it, pleased they'll soon recover from their recent privation. Today has reiterated how important the horses are for us. We've ridden far since our fighting this morning, along the roadway depicted in stones and with wide ditches to either sides of it, as opposed to using sheep tracks. I'm convinced in just one day's travel, we've moved through and out of the territory of the Sweordora. We leave two sets of enemy behind us, but I doubt the Sweordora will ever have the capacity to seek vengeance against us. Not unless they join with a tribe who do have warriors.

I wince as I lift my arms over my head to ease the ache in my shoulders from holding my shield and seax so tightly during the battle, and then riding so far. I move to where Heafoc lies on the ground, eyes fluttering in pain, his cheek wound pink and red, fresh blood weeping from it.

'How are you?' I question him.

'I'll be well,' he growls through gritted teeth.

'We have more ironstone and treasures,' I announce, squatting beside him to share the confidence in the growing glow of the fire, my seax on my weapons belt, but cleaned and ready to kill again, should it prove necessary.

'But no one who knows how to make the iron-stone into blades,' Heafoc huffs. His forehead is beaded with sweat. It's evident he's in a great deal of pain, and talking angers his wound.

'Did we take any ale?' I call to Eastmund. He and Osfyth gleefully sort through the goods we took from Dægbeorht's village because there's not been time before now.

'Only a little,' Eastmund announces, hefting a pottery container to show me what we have.

'Ale?' I question Heafoc. I think he'll refuse, but he bites his lip and nods, only to regret the action.

Quickly, I stand and take it from Eastmund.

'Is this all?'

Bucge replies, 'Don't give him too much because we won't have enough to get him through all his healing. Tonight, dulling his pain will aid him, but it won't always be this way. I need to find some comfrey to aid him when the ale is gone.'

'I'll pour the rest into a water skin,' I announce decisively. 'It won't taste as good, but it'll make it easier to carry than in the container.'

Alongside the copper pot, bubbling with pottage,

my warriors have taken other items to aid us in living outside of any one settlement. I grab a wooden beaker and take it and the small container of ale to Heafoc. He lifts himself on his elbows, the sour smell of his sweat washing from him. Quickly, I fill the cup and offer it to him. He drinks greedily. I sense others looking my way, licking their lips. We've not had ale since leaving the remains of my brother's settlement.

'If you want ale, you can have one beaker, but no more. Water will keep us alert to our enemy,' I call, the scent of the ale twitching my nostrils. I could happily drink it all, but that was my brother's downfall. He liked his ale, mead and rare carafes of wine from distant lands far too much. Already weak and ineffectual, drinking to excess only exacerbated the problem. My father never allowed himself to indulge. He ejected warriors who took a liking to too much ale with regularity, amongst them Cenbryht and Maggenræd. As such, I remain astounded by his inability to see my brother for what he was. Perhaps Waga's face, devoid of the blighted mark, was enough for my father. The bloody arsehole. I hope he curses me now. I wouldn't want it any other way.

Cenbryht comes forward for his share, much restored in the estimations of all after his part in the battle, as does Maggenræd. It's only then I realise

Maggenræd's also wounded, a hastily tied piece of cloth around the top of his left arm.

'Has Bucge looked at that?' I ask as he winces on taking the beaker from me.

'Not yet. She was busy with Heafoc.'

'Bucge,' I call, and she lifts her head to meet my gaze. 'Another one with a wound. Can you take a look? We can't have him losing his arm to wound rot.'

She nods, eyes narrowed. 'When we're fed.'

Maggenræd grunts and turns aside, ale dribbling into his red beard so his tongue darts out to grab the dregs.

'You have a way with words,' Heafoc groans, closing his eyes against the agony showing in his tight lips and shoulders.

'I speak the truth.'

'So, if I get the wound rot, you'll leave me here to die?'

'I'll have no choice but to do so,' I grumble. A silent moment passes between us before Heafoc's eyes open and he nods.

'You're more alike to your father than either of you care to think. You'll make a fine leader if a harsh one. And provided you hone your battle skills. There's still much more for you to learn, even though you've taken two victories.'

'I know,' I muse, not angered by his announcement. I'm a keen spear wielder, and good with my shield, but fighting Dægbeorht and his men, even with the instructions from Heafoc, was a closely won battle. We triumphed because Dægbeorht died, and it wasn't truly at my hand. We have his horse to thank for that.

'You'll continue to train us, even while you mend. You'll be able to better direct us from watching instead of taking part.'

'I will, yes,' Heafoc announces, closing his eyes again.

'You need to eat before you sleep,' I order him, rising to survey the cook pot and its contents. Now we have pottage flavoured with the Sweordora's chicken Cenbryht killed before leaving, I realise we have a problem.

'Do we have bowls?' I call to Eastmund. He gapes at me, and then understanding flashes, even as Bucge grumbles with the realisation we have nothing to eat the food from. In the distance, the sheep and cattle have been corralled between the hanging branches of three huge trees, with the horses to the remaining open side, including the animal that once belonged to Dægbeorht. The cattle graze happily enough on the grasses growing there.

'We have three more beakers,' Eastmund informs me, striding forward. They're similar to what Heafoc drank from, so hardly large enough to hold pottage. I hand them to Bucge who eyes them warily.

'They'll have to do,' she admits. 'Perhaps next time, we should get some bowls, unless you have any amongst your other prizes.' She juts her chin to where I've placed my wrapped treasures on the ground.

I shake my head. 'Alas, no. Just hunks of metal.'

It takes a long time for everyone to eat, but the food is good and hot. I eat quickly, handing back the beaker for Bucge to refill for someone else, as I take myself to the nearby stream and plunge my fingers into the cold water to clean them afterwards. My hands, I realised as I ate, still showed the blood of my enemies. It added a metallic taste to the pottage.

'What next?' Cenbryht demands, his eyes starting to lose focus now he has hot food and some ale in his belly. I won't bind his hands again. I think he's proven his loyalty, for now, although I remain wary of his ultimate intentions, and remember why he was so beloved by my father. There always has to be one warrior more lethal than the others, if only to encourage them to fight more keenly. A pity he took to the drink.

'Next?'

'We have horses, oats, cows and sheep. What next?'

'Bowls,' Bucge mutters and I chuckle.

'We continue to ride west. But tomorrow, we'll allow Heafoc a day of rest. We'll train more. Hygebe-orht and Nothelm didn't fight in our shield wall to-day. We'll make sure they know how to do so.' Nothelm chuckles at my words, licking pottage that's halfway up his arm at the same time. 'And, we might teach him to eat better as well,' I suggest, and laughter floods the encampment.

Two victories. Neither of them expected or, if I'm honest with myself, exactly earned. I must ensure we don't become too confident even while enjoying the sensation of being triumphant and having warriors look to me as their leader. How much better it would have been for my father if only he'd been prepared to look beyond my marked cheek.

* * *

It rains in the night. I rouse and move myself under the trees sheltering the animals but I'm already drenched by then. When we wake, much later, the fire is a ruin, and cold white faces greet mine. No one's cheerful, and Heafoc, I realise, is sweating even more, his cheek wound red and swollen, while the rest of us shiver from the cool breeze and damp drenching our clothes. Heafoc's been restless throughout the night. If not for him, the rain might not have woken me.

'Bucge,' I call. She stands with a shriek of protesting sodden cloth and comes to where Heafoc lies, tossing and turning beneath his cloak.

'I feared this,' she confirms, bending to sniff the wound and then grimacing. 'We need heat to seal the wound. If not, it'll only get worse for him.'

I eye the smouldering remains of our campfire and appreciate today is going to be spent finding enough wood to burn to the required heat rather than in training my warriors further. Although we're beneath trees, there's little wood on the ground, waiting to be consumed by flames. Much of the deadfall was consumed by last night's fire. 'We'll have to chop branches from the trees.' I wince, thinking of the laborious task, when my arms are already tired from yesterday's fight.

'We will. Or he might die, not today, but perhaps in seven days, or even ten. It'll be slow and painful. I also need to find comfrey, as I said.'

'We can't have that,' I announce, head turned upwards to look for something suitable to cut free from the trees. The animals are restless in the rain, and I avoid them, not wanting to have them startle and run into the low-hanging cloud promising rain all day long. I don't want to chance frightening one of the sheep and causing all of the foolish creatures to dart away from us. It'll be impossible to find them, and we'll merely hand a free meal to the wild denizens of this place in a day or two.

I bend and gather an axe into my hands from the collection of items taken from the Sweordora. It's hardly sharp, but it's what we have. With it swung over my shoulder, I march beneath the trees, grateful here, at least, the heavy raindrops don't land on my head and trickle down my shoulder blades, chilling me as they slide down my back.

Quickly, I can hear little but my breathing and the shuffle of my feet through the leaf litter. I eye the trees. There are many low-hanging branches, but they're huge. My poor excuse for an axe won't cleave through the wood easily. The smaller branches are higher up the trees.

I mutter darkly beneath my breath, shivering as I realise the requirement to climb higher to find what I need. I could, perhaps, order one of the other men to perform the task, but I don't foresee them doing a good job of it. Maybe they don't wish Heafoc to survive his wound, but I do. He has the knowledge I require to forge these men and women into a fierce warrior band, a *comitatus* to rival that from when my great-grandfather first came to these shores, across the iron-grey expanse of the vast, sweeping sea separating us now from that homeland. Or rather, my ancestor's homeland, for this is my home.

Wiping my hands on my wet trews, I slip the axe through my weapons belt, and grip the highest branch I can reach. Water falls onto my face. I shake my head like a wet dog. I test the branch and, convinced it might hold my weight, I pull myself upwards. It sags, but not enough to break and so I push off the ground, weaving a path through the damp leaves, which leave my back sodden. I grit my teeth, cursing myself for a damn fool. I must learn to command, as my father does. Doing this myself does not show others I'm worthy of being their leader. But I've started, and I'll complete this task.

Feeling the strain in my arms, fatigued after yesterday's fight, I slip my feet onto the wet lower branches and climb higher. I don't look down, not as I slide upwards, my breath getting hot and clouding my vision. Finally, I reach a level where I might be able to cut through a narrower branch. I know I've sent no end of water and broken-off leaves down to the ground, but that won't sustain a fire. They'll do little more than smoke if we attempt to burn them. Holding tightly to the branch I've selected, I remove the axe from my belt and begin hacking at the wood. It's not easy. I should have realised it wouldn't be. I'm stretched out, my arm reaching above my head, standing on tiptoe so every time I make a wild strike, I risk severing my hand holding the branch as steady as possible.

'By the gods,' I mutter and pull myself higher again, ensuring I can get some force into my swing. Only now, my body weight rests on the branch and if I cut it too quickly, I'll be slithering to the ground alongside the wood.

Taking a more careful aim, I force myself to strike calculated blows, slivers of wood flying free. At the last possible moment, I move aside, hanging on to the lower branch as the one I've cut free falls downwards. It does so slowly, and I have to kick it free because it gets tangled in the other branches.

'So much for worrying I'll fall,' I glower. I'm soaked. If the fire I want to build doesn't catch, I'll be cold and shivering while Heafoc's hot and shaking.

I find another branch and begin again. This time, my arm's more used to the work, and the branch breaks free when I've only half cut it, adding my weight to it so it gives with a sharp crack. I grin and then grimace. It's still not enough.

Up so high, I can almost see my surroundings. Or I'd be able to if the clouds weren't so low and the greyness quite so complete. I hear muted conversation and, for a moment, worry we might be under attack. But then I recognise Cenbryht's voice.

I peer downwards, trying to see whom he speaks to, but it's impossible. I can't even see his head through the thick leaves and branches.

From below, Eastmund calls to me, 'This is good.' The noise of the branches being dragged away drowns out all other sound. I focus on two more likely-looking branches and quickly have them cut free and heading for the ground. Only then do I realise how high I am and that many of the branches I've cut are those I used to work myself higher.

'By Woden,' I growl, eyes wide, seeking a careful path back to the ground. It's slow going. By now, my arms are cold and shivering, and my legs are as well. My stomach's hollow and every time I see the woodland floor far beneath my feet, I taste bile. 'This better be bloody worth it,' I mutter, closing my eyes and forcing myself to let go of the branch. I land roughly, hands grasping for purchase on the slick leaves, feeling hurts along my hands and feet.

'That's more than enough,' Eastmund hollers.

'I'm coming down,' I reply. I hear his noisy footsteps cease. No doubt he waits for me.

When I finally land on the ground, Eastmund startles, proving me wrong. 'I thought you were up that tree,' he exclaims, voice too high with fright, as he points to one on the far side of us.

'No, this one,' I huff, pleased to feel the steady ground beneath my feet, hands on my knees as I fight for breath.

'There's a fire going. You look like you need it.' He steps forward and pulls twigs from my damp hair. 'Heafoc's awake, but he's mumbling about shit. Bucge says the fever's bad.'

'Have you seen Cenbryht?'

'Cenbryht's been largely absent for the morning. I thought you'd set him some task.'

I shake my head. 'No, I didn't. Can you find him? I heard him talking to someone, but I don't know who it was.'

Immediately, Eastmund understands my concerns, although he hardly looks pleased with the request. I fear I'm imagining things because of my exhaustion, poor night's sleep and worry for

Heafoc. I'll feel better when Eastmund's found Cen-bryht and assured me he's not in the act of be-traying us.

'Here,' I offer. 'Take this with you. It scarcely has a keen edge but you might need it.'

With a wry smirk, Eastmund grabs the axe, and I drag the remaining two branches through the trees to where I can smell the heat of a fire, and see the pitiful smoke trying to lift clear of the ground. It doesn't get far before the dampness hanging in the air forces it down again.

Heafoc watches me, but his eyes lack focus. I see streams of sweat on his body from here and Bucge looks worried.

'I'm nearly ready,' she confirms. 'I also found comfrey for when the wound is sealed. It'll help Heafoc and Maggenræd.' Gratefully, I hold out my hands towards the heat of the fire, wishing they didn't sting from the sap and tiny splinters em-bedded in them.

'I need to clean my hands,' I mutter, wincing at the pain.

'I have water ready. I've been gathering it. This rain is torrential.'

With her help, I clean my hands and look for something to dry them on but everything is wet. In the end, I hold them towards the fire and wait for them to warm through.

'Will you hold him?' Bucge asks me.

'Yes, give me a moment.' I prepare for Heafoc's strength. My shoulders are pulsing with my exertions. I could get someone else to restrain him, but everyone is absent, no doubt trying to keep dry or tending to the animals.

'Grip his head,' she commands. 'I'll sit on his body. You keep his head straight. Be careful, or you'll be branded as well.'

I hardly need the caution. We lie Heafoc down. His eyes are closed as he mumbles to himself. Bucge straddles him and I grip his head between my two hands as she reaches for the knife in the fire, bundling the bone handle in layers of damp clothing spluttering unpleasantly. The smell's already terrible, and it's nothing compared to the sizzle that erupts as the blade touches Heafoc's red and infected cheek. Heafoc startles. It takes all my strength to hold him immobile and avoid the length of the heated blade.

'Hold still,' I urge him, the smell nauseating. His eyes greet mine, acceptance in them that only disappears as they close, his legs bucking beneath Bucge, his body stilling as he loses all sense.

And still Bucge holds the blade. I see her lips

tighten with pain. The blade is undoubtedly too hot for her to grip for much longer.

She flings it aside, unheeding of where it lands, as she clenches her hand, waving it in the damp air. I jump aside, and grab some water, but she shakes her head.

'It's not that bad. See.' She shows me her reddened palm while studying the mark on Heafoc's cheek. The blade's touched his moustache and beard, and the smell of scorched hair is noxious.

'He'll never grow that back,' I mutter.

'That's the least of his concerns. He needs the skin to heal. If we have to cut it away, everyone will see his cheekbones. He'll look half dead even while living.'

The image she presents is unpleasant, and unbidden my hand touches my marked cheek. She watches me, and then pulls my hand away, to peer closely at it. With a surprisingly delicate touch, she manipulates my right cheek, lips pursed.

'Your father was a fool to fear such a mark. It's a part of who you are. It could no sooner be removed than the rest of your skin.'

She releases her hold on my cheek and then tilts her head.

'Anyway, in the right light, it could be mistaken

for being wolf-shaped. I'm surprised he never announced you were one of Woden's chosen.'

I gasp at her words, even as I feel some of my
pent-up tension leave my body. I slap my hand over
the mark, as though I'm the one burned. She shakes
her head.

'Show it proudly. If people fear you, they're the
fools. From now on, we tell everyone you're Woden-
touched.' And she arches an eyebrow and smiles.
'You can tell them your seeress has decreed as much.
Now, we need honey for Heafoc, to work with the
comfrey paste I've made.'

'Did we get any?' I'm not entirely sure of everything we took from Dægbeorht's village.

'Ask Osfyth.' As tired as I am, I realise my task is
far from complete. I stand and walk towards where I
hear the voices of my warriors beneath the trees.

I step into the temporary animal enclosure and
notice the sheep and cattle there. They look as damp
as I feel. I don't see anyone else though, other than
Maggenræd, and he's lying on the ground, rain hitting his boot, but otherwise leaving him dry. His loud
snores are a counterpart to the drumming of the
rain. I cast an appraising eye over his injured arm,
but the wound is merely reddened, and not pink or
inflamed like Heafoc's.

I shudder again. I could do with my cloak, but Heafoc's lying beneath it. I rub my cold hands across my damp arms, seeking the others. I hear voices, but not Eastmund's or Cenbryht's. I know a moment of fear, especially when I make out scampering foot-steps, but it's Osfyth, a triumphant grin on her face as she reveals the bleeding body of an upside-down deer in her hand.

'We'll eat well tonight,' she crows. And then sobers. 'How's Heafoc?'

'Do we have honey?' I question instead, peering into the dark woods.

'Yes, but not much. Has Bucge sealed the wound?' She moves quickly, seemingly unaware blood smears her face, or that, aside from me, her and Maggenræd, there's no else nearby.

'Yes. Have you seen Eastmund?'

'Yes. He's heading that way, through the wood-lands. He told me to tell you he's found footprints.' Her forehead furrows. 'What's he looking for?'

'I thought I heard a voice I didn't recognise.'

She nods now as though something makes sense. 'I thought I heard someone else too. But, whoever it is, is alone. I've been through the treeline. There's no one else.'

'What about the rest of the men?'

As we speak, she's moving towards where our stolen goods have been piled. Someone's moved them beneath the trees, and now she fumbles through the many sacks.

'They've found a shelter, further within the trees. It's drier than staying here. Bægmund came to tell you, but you were halfway up a tree.'

'And is Cenbryht with them?'

'I don't know. I assumed he was, but now you question me, perhaps not.'

She shows me a small ceramic pot containing what I assume must be honey, sealed with a waxed strip of linen. It's very small. Perhaps only enough to sweeten a single pot of pottage. I have to hope it's enough to prevent Heafoc from suffering with the wound rot.

'I'll take it,' she offers, also hefting the dead deer. It's perhaps one of last year's juveniles. It's not very big. 'You find the others. Assure yourself all is well.'

A ghost of a smile touches my lips, and then I'm powering through the woodland, not allowing the darkness of overhanging trees to concern me as I seek out the source of the muted laughter I can hear. I don't have my axe because I gave it to Eastmund. Provided it's only the rest of my men beneath the trees, that shouldn't be a problem.

But if someone is here, I'll have little to defend myself with but my seax, my elbows and knees.

I grimace but press on, trying to banish my worries. And that's when Wædel erupts from the undergrowth beside me, a seax in one hand, wearing a grimace of hatred.

'I'll kill you, you cursed little bird,' he huffs and launches himself at me, his face twisted with fury.

17

MEDDI OF THE EORLINGAS

'Sian,' I whisper to her as I arrive once more where Centus is still trying to determine how to accomplish all his father could once do. I've removed my breastplate and can feel the sweat of my exertions on my body. I've left Madog to organise burning the dead.

'Mistress.' She inclines her head respectfully.

'Tell me. Elen. What do you think?' Sian's eyes darken, and she thins her lips. It seems I've unconsciously found another who hates Elen as much as me.

'It's too soon to tell. She's still ranting and raving about her captivity. I'm doing my best to keep her fed and clean with the aid of Urien. She's not very accepting of her imprisonment.' Without appearing to notice, she lifts her hand to the side of her face, and I detect the faint blossoming of a bruise there I've not noticed before.

'She hit you?' I demand angrily. But Sian's already shaking her head.

'No, she threw her pot at me, filled with piss, calling me a limping bitch. I should have been quicker to move aside. It's not her first attempt. It won't be her last either.'

'I'm sorry for that. Marchell will give you a poultice to draw the bruise away.'

'There's no need,' Sian offers softly. 'I'll wear my wounds as proudly as a warrior, and just as I do my limp.' I allow a smile to touch my lips at her staunch words. Sian's a proud woman. I find I like her. There are few for whom I feel genuine warmth. It certainly doesn't extend to Elen.

'She's still kept guarded? I fear some think to take her.'

'She's very well guarded. The warriors Madog has set over her understand she's not to be allowed to escape. She's too important, while hopefully, being worth nothing.'

'I'm pleased you perceive this.'

'Mistress,' she defers, her eyes returning to Centus, where he hammers loudly, the clanging noise making my eyes close in sympathy for the iron he attempts to urge to obey him. His face is masked in concentration, his strong arms have sweat running down them. I almost feel an unfamiliar stirring for him, but dismiss it quickly. I've no time for such thoughts or urges.

Instead, I stride away once more and quickly encounter Marchell, a collection of items in her hand as she hurries to tend to the wounded. I follow her, wincing to hear the shrieks coming from Elen's prison. Every day is the same. I hope her voice will fail her soon. If not, I'll find something to add to her food. I'm not alone in staying far from the grain store. The men there must be tired of listening to Elen screech to be allowed out. She knows my resolve is implacable. She appreciates Madog will acquiesce to my orders. And yet, still, she howls and shrieks, like a fox in heat.

While Marchell directs her step to Hedrek, I seek out my brother's new son.

The boy's held tightly in Rhian's arms. She offers me a small smile, as I peel back the layers of furs to look at him. His cheeks are rounding, his lips making sucking motions even in his sleep.

'He grows well,' I compliment her.

She preens at the praise from her seeress, and I

make my way to Madog. He's cleaning his spear and blades.

'It'll be the first of many attempts,' I speak without preamble.

'My men grow more confident with each victory,' he acknowledges quickly. He's outside. The smell of death and decay is vibrant in the air and yet no one even looks to where the bodies lie, waiting to be placed on their funeral pyre and set alight this evening. Already, those children too young to fight hurry to collect dry wood and sticks, and anything else to fan the flames, under the direction of one of Madog's older warriors.

He walks now with a bent back and stick to aid him, perhaps older even than Marchell. He can be fiery when he trains the warriors, but first he wins the affection of the younger boys and girls. He's a contrary individual. I still remember the first time I felt the impact of his boot on my arse when I failed in my attempts at defending myself. I'm still wary of him, as are most of the warriors. It amuses me to re-alise all these young boys and girls will one day be scared of his rage.

'Tomorrow, me and my warriors will begin to deepen the surrounding ditch, and we'll fill it with some surprises for any who think to sneak up on us. Corun came too close today.'

I nod, pleased he's realised this without me having to direct him. 'Centus is still unsuccessful. How's Hedrek?' I assume Marchell is tending to his wound within the villa.

'He should live. It bled more than it warranted.' He smirks.

'We must watch him. He has ambitions that surprise me.'

'Can't he have Elen in exchange for Centus?'

'No, he cannot.' I'm fierce in my denial. 'He can have nothing. He must pledge his loyalty to you, and accept you're his commander, even if he's the leader of the Beansæte.'

'Very well, seeress.' My brother bows his head respectfully. I'm grateful he accepts my advice, or rather command. If he didn't, I'd be faced with a difficult decision, but one I would make, if I had to do so. We must labour for the future of our tribe, and not allow such concerns as family ties to interfere. Madog understands this.

* * *

As the funeral pyre lights the night sky later, I take myself to the grain store and temporarily dismiss the guards there. They go, heads bowed deferentially, leaving me alone with Elen, although a wooden door blocks her from my sight. I don't wish to see her. I do wish to speak with her.

'You bitch.' The words hiss through the door. I can hear her heavy breathing, even over the roar of the flames. As we wanted, they leap high into the night sky. They'll be visible to Corun, and those of the Weogoran who still live. They'll know their warriors aren't coming home to them.

'You'd do well to remember my position here.' I speak without urgency, resting my back on the door so I can witness the enemy of the tribe being burned, their ashes mingling with the air, rising high into the darkness. We'll not collect their ashes. They'll not be gathered in a pot and buried under the earth with supplies for the afterlife. No. They'll disperse on the wind, always to be homeless in death, just as we did for Edern. Some might call it a petty revenge, but I know the magiks of ashes and bone.

'And you would do well to remember mine,' Elen hisses.

'You have nothing, Elen. Not any more.'

'Then why keep me here?' Her voice is a whine. I

shake my head to hear it. She knows why her captivity is necessary.

'You were his wife. We must be assured you're not tainted.'

'As you were, once.' If she means to wound, it has no impact. It's been summers since that event. 'I'm not tainted. Not that I'd tell you if I was,' she quickly corrects.

'We'll know soon enough.'

'You can't keep me here until winter.'

'Why, do you have somewhere else to be?'

'I—' she begins, and then stops just as quickly. 'You truly mean to keep me here until the winter, don't you?' she howls, the realisation making her sound feral.

'I'll do what must be done. But your weeping and wailing, and throwing pots at Sian, will earn you nothing. We're all deaf to your cries, so I suggest you halt them.'

'Or what?' she barks, malice dripping from her. If I could see her now, I know she'd be all twisted face and raked nails down her cheeks as she can't reach mine.

'Or we'll have to hush you ourselves.'

'You mean Marchell will,' she gloats.

'No, not Marchell. Marchell's knowledge is in

healing.'

'You said you wouldn't kill me,' she complains.

'I did, then. Now, perhaps things have changed.'

Silence floods back from within the grain store. A smoky cloud temporarily covers me.

'Are you burning me?' Panic infects Elen's voice.

'No. We burn the dead. More fools who think to take what belongs to Madog and our tribe.'

'You dishonour them as you did Edern.'

'Indeed.' I grin, not that anyone can see.

'This will go badly for you, Meddi. I assure you. Edern was well connected. Many were loyal to him. You and Madog don't have the warriors.'

I don't respond immediately, considering her words. Perhaps, I realise, she might be correct. Maybe I've been blinded by my hatred until now and never considered the future with enough thought.

'It will not, Elen. We don't need the numbers when we'll have something much, much better soon. Madog will remain as the tribal chief, and in time, his son will become chief after him. It's how these things should be done.'

I hear her bark of laughter from within, and above the roar of the flames, the scent of burning fat and hair now strong enough to gag, I sense her moving away. For all her screaming, it seems she no longer wishes to speak with me. That's no problem for me. I'd sooner not talk to her either.

I know I'm correct, though. Soon, the men of the tribe will have sharp blades to kill our enemy, thanks to Centus. And the women will have them as well.

With edges keen enough to sever flesh, we'll not need the vast numbers that, I'm led to believe, allowed the enemy Romans to subjugate the men and women of this island so long ago.

I direct my gaze towards where Centus works. The glow from his fire is bright, although I can't see him from where I sit. He slept throughout the afternoon, exhaustion forcing his eyes shut close to his workings. But he's awake now and labouring once more.

No, whatever Elen thinks, the magiks Centus possesses will ensure Madog's survival. With iron and sharp blades at his command, he might not need me.

I'll ensure that doesn't happen. There are other skills I possess of use to him, and if necessary, I'll remind him I'm his sister, not just his seeress.

18

WÆRMUND OF THE GYRWE

I raise my arm to counter the thrust, my seax already curling in my hand.

Wædel stinks. I've no idea what he's been doing, but living wild off the land for a few days shouldn't make a man smell as he does.

'I'll kill you, you cursed little bird,' he repeats, spittle landing on my face as we close on one another. I can feel the strength behind his attack despite his noxious smell.

'It would be my pleasure,' I retort, kicking out to connect with his lower leg, so his balance falters, although he doesn't immediately go down.

'I'll drag your lifeless body back to your father, and he'll reward me with all the treasures you stole.

You'll be left to rot, exposed for the carrion crows to gnaw upon. There'll be no burial for a son such as you.'

'We both know that's not going to happen,' I huff. I kick out again but Wædel's moving aside. I'm the one who almost overbalances, not him.

He smirks now, seeing my failed attack on him.

'Lackwit,' he taunts. 'You've been lucky so far, but I know how to fight and defend myself. I'll end your life, and then do the same to the rest of the men and women who've decided to pledge themselves to you. I'll allow the women in Dægbeorht's village to piss on your dead body and then your father can do what he wants with you: abandon you in a deep ditch where the wolves, ravens and other small animals can feast on your corrupt remains, if he so decides. You'll have nothing in the afterlife.'

'My thanks for sharing your wishes for the after-life with me. I'll know what to do with you when you're dead beneath my blade,' I huff through tight lips. The images he presents don't worry me. I'm younger than him and stronger as well. If I don't yet know all of Heafoc's tricks, it's only a matter of time until I do. Until then, I'll counter Wædel with my strength. It will win.

Wædel chuckles darkly before propelling himself

at me once more. It's all I can do to avoid his well-aimed strikes, moving backwards, blade raised. He's a dirty fighter – he always has been – but that doesn't make him ineffective. I should have been paying more attention to what he was doing, as opposed to considering my next moves.

I feel a thud on my left shoulder, and realise while I'm watching his knife, he's punched me. I growl low in my throat.

'I'll best you,' he roars. Now his knife flashes darkly. His left fist is also bunched. He means to attack me with his iron and strength. And damn it, he's bloody strong. Already, the sensation in my left arm's fading. His hot, fetid breath makes it difficult to take a deep inhalation without gagging.

I curl my fist to strike him, but then reconsider. He comes closer and closer, dribble flooding down his untidy bearded chin. I flinch and turn aside, at the same time lowering myself. My left hand on the ground behind keeps me upright. He thinks I've crumpled because of his attack, but now I kick out. My foot tangles with his leg. He lurches forward, almost landing on me, both arms splayed wide to stop from hitting the ground. I push myself upwards, just avoiding him, only to be distracted by the shimmer of blood on my arm.

I've not even realised I'm cut. It was a bloody lucky blow, I'm sure of it.

I jump on his back, legs to either side of him. He bucks beneath me. His arm is outstretched. I realise he's lost his blade with the force of that landing. I wish I'd known that before I jumped on him. I punch into his back with my left hand, and at the same time attempt to land a slicing blow with my blade, but he moves too much to risk the stabbing motion. I might cut myself. Already, my blood drips onto his back.

My punches don't stop him. It's almost as though he doesn't feel them. And then he's gone from beneath me, scrabbling forward to grip his knife and turn on his back, legs bent before him, kicking out.

I jump upright and hurl myself at him again. This time, I smack his knife hand hard on the ground. The knife once more springs free. But so does my seax. Neither is within easy reach. I can try for my blade, or I can punch him. As his fists come up to hit my chest, I strike him with my right hand, all of my strength behind it.

He coughs, once more releasing stinking, hot air into my face. I punch again, straddling him and holding him down. Wædel's face is dark with fury.

'You little cursed bastard,' he roars, feet drumming the ground like that will help him.

'You are,' I counter, clutching his throat with one hand, trying to tighten my grip and keep him still beneath me. But he continues to strike, his blows powerful, even while his face purples as my grasp tightens on his throat.

I punch as well, wishing I could risk reaching for my seax to stab him, but I can't. I've barely got him under control. About now, I could do with Heafoc coming to my aid, or really, any of my warriors. I have to hope Wædel's alone. If someone appears to help him, I'll be gutted.

Abandoning punching my chest, he thumps straight up with one of his hands. My grip falters on his neck. Before I can redouble it, he sucks in a deep breath and continues to pummel me.

'Eastmund,' I manage to roar. 'Eastmund, get your arse here,' I shout. I can hear him striking wood close by. As much as I don't want to admit it, I need his help. Or someone's.

'Little cursed bird can't kill me alone?' Wædel taunts. My fury pools within me, but just as I'm about to punch him, he slips free from my grasp, rolling onto his front. I still straddle him, but now he pushes upwards using his hands and feet. I reach for his hair, pulling it back tightly to lift his head to expose his throat, but I need my blade to kill him.

Distantly, I'm aware of running footsteps. I hope it's Eastmund, or perhaps Bucge. It'd better not be someone coming to Wædel's aid. The cock needs to die, and now.

Wædel pushes and pushes upwards, despite my grip on his hair and the pressure of my body over his. I feel myself lifting and realise I look like a child riding their parents' back. Still, the sound of footsteps comes nearer, but not close enough.

I'm almost standing, even while I slide along Wædel's back. I'm losing control over him, and any moment now he'll be able to reach for one of the blades. And mine is the closest. I refuse to die at the hands of my weapon.

'Bollocks,' I exclaim, abruptly jumping free, hand reaching for my seax, and scooping it up before he can claim it. Panting heavily, we stand and face one another. I have my blade. Wædel doesn't. Indeed, his knife has skittered far along the woodland floor. He can't reach it without getting through me. I'm not going to allow that.

His face is smeared in dust and leaves from the ground. His lips twist in a derogatory grin. 'First blood goes to me,' he hoots. I wish he'd not managed to blood me.

'And the last will go to me,' I rebuff. He's shaking

his head. There's still no one to help me, but any moment now I expect someone to emerge from the trees. I want to kill this bastard before then.

Trying to recall everything Heafoc's taught me in recent days, and before that, everything I learned from watching my father and his men train together, I spin into Wædel, seax extended. Only, in the time it takes me to move, he darts aside, eyes gleaming as they fix on his blade. I have little time to stop him before we'll be back to where we started. Despite my youth, I can sense myself weakening. I need to end this. Now.

I lick my salt-crusted lips and dive towards him, taking down his legs and once more tumbling him to the ground. He goes down with half a shriek of fury, akin to a pig being led to slaughter. I work myself up his body, stabbing every piece of flesh I can see and those protected by his tunic and trews. My arm trembles with the effort, my left arm pulling me upwards time and time again, my right skewering him. The hot aroma of blood fills the air, and still he fights me. He's dragging both of us forward. Soon he'll have his hand on his blade, and I'll be weakened from the struggle, and will still need to overwhelm him.

Only then, I see a pair of dirty boots before me, and look upwards, expecting to see Eastmund, but it's not him. No, it's Osfyth, a mirthless grin on her lips as she bends and runs her blade over Wædel's exposed neck. He stills almost instantly, a wet gurgling sound coming from his mouth. I roll off him, glancing at the wounds I've caused him, feeling the sticky slickness of his blood on my fingers, and gasp in a much-needed deep breath.

Osfyth doesn't move aside from Wædel, waiting for his drumming legs to be entirely still. Only then does she speak. Only then does she say what I've been thinking.

'You were bloody lucky there, again,' she offers, holding out her hand to aid me to my feet. 'He's always been clever with his blade.' She makes no other comment. I'm grateful for that as Eastmund finally surges through the trees, his eyes taking everything in, switching from me to Osfyth to Wædel.

'Where did that bastard come from?' he questions, words tipped with fury.

'I don't know. He jumped me,' I huff.

'And you killed him, with only a little help,' Osfyth comments, already bending to cut Wædel's trinkets from around his neck and also grabbing his blade, eyeing it with detachment. 'Where did he get this?' she questions. 'He didn't have it when we parted.'

I look at the blade then, noticing the unmistakeable design on the hilt.

'He's been back to my father,' I mutter darkly, suddenly fearful we're being watched, and Wædel's only the first of many to attack us.

'Perhaps,' Osfyth comments, her lips pursed in thought. 'But whatever he promised your father, he's failed to deliver it.' By now, more and more of my warriors are appearing, eyeing Wædel's lifeless body with surprise.

'Where's Cenbryht?' I question. He's the only one missing. I recall Osfyth's assurance she'd seen and heard no one else, but my hand tightens on my seax all the same. My warriors mirror my actions, and then Cenbryht steps into the clearing, head down, eyes looking at whatever he's hauling behind him.

He twists, sees us all and shudders in surprise. But my eyes are on what he's dragging.

'I found this,' he offers, perplexed, and we all turn, looking down.

I feel my mouth open in shock, but it's Eastmund who speaks. 'Bloody hell. He's a big bastard.' The boar Cenbryht's found is very definitely the largest beast I've ever seen.

'You killed it?' Osfyth asks, her voice dripping with disbelief while Cenbryht grins.

'He was enjoying a nap in the sun. I made sure it was the last one he ever took.' Only now does he realise we have our own corpse. His mouth curls with displeasure. 'I think mine will be tastier,' he offers, and without a backward glance hauls his kill through the woodland to where we've left Heafoc. 'We'll eat well tonight,' Cenbryht calls. I allow my stance to relax, and abruptly, I feel a thousand hurts, and the cut on my arm stings as though I've got salt water in my eyes.

'Come on, before you fall down,' Osfyth orders me. 'You can come back and deal with the body when you're not in danger of toppling over.'

No one compliments me on my kill, or rather, Osfyth's, but equally, no one looks unduly concerned. And yet unease gnaws at me. Has Wædel spoken to my father? Has he told him where I am? Will my father come after me if Wædel has told him my intentions? Why have I still killed no one aside from my weak brother?

Perhaps, I realise, it's time to move on even more quickly using the good stone road we followed to reach here. I would welcome many days' travel between my birth land and where I mean to make a name for myself as a warrior. Grudgingly, I admit I need to increase my fighting skills. They're not yet as good as I think they are. When Heafoc recovers, we'll have much work to do.

'What by all the gods is that?' We hear rumble through the trees, and I smirk, despite my exhaustion and worry this was altogether too close for comfort.

'Is he feeling better?' I question. Osfyth cracks a smile, and together we make our way back to Heafoc and Cenbryht. If Cenbryht thought he was going to be regarded highly because of his kill, he's very mistaken. Heafoc's voice is loud and filled with complaints. I'm just grateful to hear him sounding like his old self.

19

MEDDI OF THE EORLINGAS

In the morning, there's little but ashes to show Madog and his warriors were ever attacked by the men of the Weogoran, under Corun's leadership.

Once more, I take myself to where Centus still labours, his face sweat-streaked and red with the heat of the fire. For all I'm convinced he can recall much of his father's talents, I'm concerned it's taking so long.

Hedrek joins me there, his face bleached after his wound, but other than that, well enough.

'How's your arm?' I ask, just to be pleasant.

'It'll heal,' he grumbles, wincing, as though I've reminded him it hurts. He says nothing further. I assume he doesn't intend to converse with me, but when he next speaks, I realise it's been a debate about how to phrase the words. 'I fear Centus knows none of his father's skills.'

I chuckle, although there's little humour in it. 'You brought him here to extract iron from ironstone and then to forge blades with sharper edges than anyone can currently produce. You should have realised it wouldn't be an immediate thing. How could it be? While there's some charcoal and ironstone remaining, we should allow him to do what he can.'

'You believe a child no older than four winters at his father's death can recall the processes? If you do, you're a bigger fool than me. I've realised the error of my ways.'

I flash him a quick look, surprised by the dejection in his voice. He winces once more and goes to run his hand over his wounded arm but stops himself from doing so.

'I shouldn't have brought him here,' he exhales, Centus unable to hear above the hammering of his equipment and the roar from the fire. I notice he also has another firepit now. He's busy.

'I disagree. We should leave him to experiment. In the meantime, we can do other things. We need to produce more charcoal and find more ironstone.'

'And a bladesmith who knows what he's doing,'

Hedrek mutters darkly. I grimace, but then turn it into a smile. If Hedrek's so determined to give up on the idea, perhaps I should agree with him as opposed to trying to prove him wrong. When Centus recalls the requirements or determines what he's not doing but needs to do, he'll become a member of my brother's tribe with no affiliation to Hedrek. That's worth considering.

'Will you bring your people here?' I skewer the conversation. Hedrek's led the men and women within his settlement of the Beansæte. They could unite with us.

'Not yet,' Hedrek decides. 'If you'll forgive my caution, your brother has only been in position for a few days. So far, he's fought those under Corun, and killed them, although not Corun himself. And, he's been bartering with me about ironstone and the bladesmith. He needs to do more than that, especially when he has a mewling babe for a son and, as far as I know, no one else who could replace him if he met an early death.'

I acknowledge his words with a soft grunt, continuing to watch Centus carefully. He's working the bellows to encourage the flame within the hollowed-out and then re-covered bowl shape in the earth. Soon, there'll be no more room for him to do so. I can't see he's doing anything differently from when my brother aided him during the first attempt, but I believe in him. After all, it's not as though there's anyone else who has even an idea of how to perform the task. If Centus can decipher the magiks, Madog will benefit, as will I.

From the edges of the settlement, I hear men calling one to another as they begin the task of making the ditches deeper to protect those within. I believe my brother also intends to have an outer ditch as well, and then, perhaps, we can graze the animals between the two ditches and keep them safe from attack in that way. It would be good to have them further away so their stink doesn't taint the air as much as it does. Today, they build the ditch. To-morrow, they'll have to seek out Corun's settlement, if the men and women don't arrive before then. There's no point in making threats if they're not followed through.

'Elen,' Hedrek begins confidently, but I'm shaking my head.

'Is none of your concern, Hedrek. I spoke with her last night. She's far from content, but she's my affair, not yours. Don't ask again.' I add menace to my voice. 'I don't wish to sour this new relationship between you and my brother, but if it must be done, then it will be.'

I sense Hedrek clenching his fists with fury, but I pretend I've not realised. I'm more than happy to exert control over him, if necessary. But, until such time, I won't do so.

Sian catches my attention, wearing an expression of concern. 'Mistress, you're needed.'

I incline my head to Hedrek, and follow Sian. I'm unsure who requires me. I thought all were well within the settlement. It seems not. I hope it's not my brother's son. That would crush him when so far, he's had such a successful few days.

'What is it?' I demand, hurrying after her quick steps. She makes no answer but leads me to where Madog and his men are standing in the growing ditch. I narrow my eyes. Why have they stopped working? A sense of dread fills me.

'My lord?' I call, fear making me show him the respect he receives from everyone else. Madog looks at me, expression bleak, before beckoning me over.

I swallow my terror and stride towards him, the talismans at my waist clattering together, so I reach for them to still the unwelcome noise. I wouldn't usually quiet the outward signs of my skills, but there is silence here. It unnerves me to break it. I don't know what they've found. I worry I don't want to know.

Here, close to where my brother and his men fought Corun and his warriors only yesterday, the ground has been hacked open to deepen the ditch. Those with Madog are muddy and sweaty. Their faces show the same apprehension as my brother's. I force myself to look into the ditch and immediately realise why.

'Is it him?' I question, aware my voice wavers. I'm the one clenching my fists and wishing I could fight my way out of this one.

'It wears the torque of the Eorlingas, as you've described it to me,' my brother states. I nod, tasting bile. I shouldn't be asking my brother this. I should be down there, investigating.

I struggle into the ditch, the scent of damp earth flooding my nostrils. At least, I consider, the corpse has been there for long enough the flesh has all been eaten away by time and the creatures living beneath the soil. I reach out tentatively. I don't fear the sightless skull, with the signs of injury evident in the way the top of it has been broken into two pieces.

'Did this happen when you broke through the soil?' I question just to be sure.

My brother shakes his head regretfully. 'No, we found the leg bones and then were more careful.'

I reach out and touch the dirty greenish item around where the neck should once have been. After all this time, and knowing only too well the fate that befell my father, I fear I shouldn't be so angered and saddened to finally see his earthly remains. But I am. Edern was a bastard. He killed my father. He took me to his bed against my wishes. He destroyed our tribe, and all the while, he knew where my father was buried. I wasn't more than a hundred steps from where he savagely took my body every night of our union, even when my child was so huge in my belly it hurt me.

'If he wasn't dead already,' I growl, 'I'd kill him.'

'Then it's our father, Macsen?' Madog queries, just to be sure.

'It is, yes. We'll bury him with honour, amongst his relatives. He'll not be abandoned in a ditch like this,' I announce, replacing the discoloured torque softly against the dirty white bones of his ribs. Tears cloud my vision. In this moment, I feel weak and shorn of the façade I've maintained for near enough twenty summers.

My father was a fine fighter, a lethal warrior, a hard father, but one I adored all the same, despite his many wives and other children, the rest mostly dead now. He didn't deserve this death or this disrespectful burial.

'It will be done,' my brother intones reverentially, coming to stand beside me, his hand on my shoulder, a sign of solidarity, but also support. I tremble where I stand, my eyes flashing from the ditch to the villa buildings my father adored during his lifetime and did all he could to maintain and protect. His name is still spoken with some reverence despite him being gone for so many summers, and his failure to drive Edern away. He was a fierce leader, but a much respected one for those who knew him.

Edern spent all his time trying to denounce my father. Initially, no one would allow it, and yet it seems he took his revenge in other ways.

'I wish we'd not burned the bastard,' I mutter, speaking of Edern. 'We could have done much worse to him than let his spirit escape his body.'

'We could, yes, but he needed to be gone from our lives, and he is, dispersed on the wind. Now we'll right the wrongs done to us and our father.'

I nod, straighten my shoulders, and casually shrug off my brother's support. He steps aside without complaint. I realise the men are all bowing their heads respectfully. It astounds me. The vast majority never knew Macsen. They've been raised listening to their parents lament what befell my father. Throughout all of those years, we were powerless to strike against Edern, where he hoarded the blades and shields my father had once commanded, and broke that which my father had protected.

With the thought, I gasp and bend forwards once more. For not only did Edern bury my father here, in the ditch, a sign of disrespect, in a place normally reserved for cattle bones or those executed for terrible crimes against their own people, he also interred my father's sword.

I wipe the tears from my eyes and crouch low, eyeing the weapon. It's been broken, I can tell, cracked in two somehow. A blade such as this should not shatter. I reach out and pull both pieces into my hands. I turn to my brother, my eyes flashing with resolve, chin high.

'Centus will fix this blade, and with it you will rule our tribe and those nearby. You'll be lord of all our father once ruled. Finding this blade, now, even broken as it is, is a sign from the gods we're blessed in our endeavours. Lord Madog, chief of the Eorlingas, will bring much-needed protection and stability to these lands.' As I speak, I hold both halves of the sword above my head, unheeding the smell of damp and decay infecting the tarnished, green-tinged metal. This sword was made many, many winters ago, and my father would have us believe it was before the Romans who once ruled our island left. It was made with skill by bladesmiths who knew more than just the magik needed to extract iron from ironstone and forge sharp edges. It was made by the best of the best, and since then, this villa and those within it lived under its protection. Until Edern.

Soon, that will be restored.

My brother will command the respect and regard my father was held in before the treachery of Edern led to our downfall and my father's despicable and disrespectful burial.

20

WÆRMUND OF THE GYRWE

We move on the next day. I'm not happy about it because Heafoc remains unwell, but he's determined about it. As displeased as I am, I also feel some relief as we move away from where we've left Wædel's body to be consumed by the denizens of the woodland. His corpse might act as a deterrent to anyone who follows on behind, including my father's warriors. If they do know where we are, they'll have encountered my brother's ruined village, the fight in the settlement that once owed allegiance to Dægbeorht, and Wædel's cold corpse.

Progress is slow with the animals we now have to shepherd on their way, none of it helped by the corpse of the dead boar we've yet to fully consume.

The smell of blood and meat is a heady experience, but not for the cows and sheep, especially as the temperature increases and the grey clouds of yesterday lift. I almost wish Cenbryht hadn't killed the boar. It's difficult to transport the corpse. We ate Osfyth's deer last night roasted over the flames of the wood I hacked from the trees.

'It would be quicker without them,' Bucge comments, half an eye on Heafoc, sweating and swaying atop his horse, his cheek bright pink, although perhaps not as pink as it was. I don't want to convince myself he's healing despite all evidence to the contrary, but I'm sure he is.

'It would be, but this way we're guaranteed to have food to eat.'

She doesn't argue with me. I've deployed my warriors in a tight formation, some behind us, others in front, and even more enclosing the animals moving slowly and without complaint. At least, I reason, the horses are happier with a more varied diet to keep them healthy and strong.

'Has anyone followed this road before?' I question, but no one replies. I feel a prickle of unease along my spine, eyes focused on where we're going. I don't wish to come upon any enemy unexpectedly. Not again. And not when we've not yet spent more time learning to fight well. I thought it better to move on than spend time training.

'Perhaps next time, we should sell our services as opposed to take animals?' I consider arguing with Eastmund's suggestion, but admit it's a good one.

'Are we ready for that?' I question Heafoc. If he's following the conversation, I see no evidence of it. Sweat beads his forehead as he sways in the saddle.

In the end, Eastmund replies. 'We know how to fight and kill,' he asserts confidently. 'That's all we need to be able to do, isn't it?'

The others grunt their agreement, but I'm still not convinced.

'We remain close to the lands of the Gyrwe.'

'And that will work in our favour. Your father's *comitatus* have a fearsome reputation. It'll have travelled far to the west as well as the south.'

I consider all this throughout the long day, and into the next. We eat some of the boar meat and Osfyth instructs Cenbryht on how to butcher what remains and wraps it in leaves after it's been cooked in the same juices as our meal in the copper pot.

In the night, a wolf takes one of the sheep, quietly. We only know about it in the morning when we find the claw marks in the mud and realise the animal's missing, nothing left behind but a wisp of dirty-white wool and the terrified eyes of the animals who remain, sheltering in one corner, close to the horses.

'Were you sleeping?' I question Bægmund, who had watch duty.

'I didn't think so,' he argues but there's no heat to his denial. 'But I must have been.'

'Then tonight, we'll have two on guard duty,' I announce, earning Bægmund some complaints from the rest of our war band. But, as darkness coats the land once more, we find somewhere better to shelter, and carefully the animals are all encouraged inside a raised earth ditch curling around and within which there are tall and lush grasses for them to eat. It's un-likely any of them will be able to crest the steep rise of the exterior, which means they can only escape through a small gap, easy enough for one of us to guard. 'What is this place?' I question Heafoc. His face injury has finally cooled and the rawness of his wound has begun to fade. Not that his ill humour has entirely disappeared. Bucge's tended to my cut inflicted by Wædel, but it's little more than a scratch.

'Exactly what it looks like,' he huffs. 'A place to keep animals safe from predators.' I nod, although I'm still astounded by it. There seems no reason I can determine for it to be here. 'It means a settlement will be nearby, somewhere with a leader. Maybe someone in need of protection from an enemy,' he says, first smiling and then wincing as his wound tugs at his cheek.

'Somewhere we could try out our skills again?'

'Or we could just sell on the animals, or exchange them for something more easily transported. We'd move more quickly then.'

I nod, sensing that, like me, Heafoc believes we're travelling too slowly. If Wædel did reach my father before coming back to kill me, my father will be expecting him to return soon. When he doesn't, and with the few fast horses he has at his command, his warriors would be able to catch us quickly. 'Do you know where we are?'

'No, like the others, I've not travelled this far west before, but as Eastmund says, that doesn't mean your father's reputation hasn't preceded you. Perhaps, this is where that fool Dægbeorht wished you to come.'

We have our answer soon enough. As we're waking the following morning, Hygebeorht shouts a warning.

'Riders,' he calls. I scramble upright from where I've been sleeping, keen to have my hand on my seax.

'Be prepared,' I call to my loyal men and women. I blink sleep from my eyes and focus on those who approach. I can't help thinking Hygebeorht could have given more warning as a small force of fifteen squat horses rides into view. At their head is a rider wearing a much-tarnished breastplate.

The man gabbles something, and I startle because I don't understand a word he says. I glimpse Heafoc mouthing the unfamiliar language.

'He asks why we're here,' Heafoc quickly mutters in an aside. I'm grateful he understands the man's speech. I'm aware the man watches me, his expression inscrutable as he sees the mark on my face. I turn my hands into fists to stop myself obscuring it.

'Tell him why we're here, then,' I urge him.

'And why is that?'

'To find work,' I hiss.

Heafoc speaks slowly. I can tell he must consider what he's saying. I'm uncertain. I didn't expect to have ridden far enough the people who lived here spoke a different tongue to mine. It seems my ignorance is, once more, much greater than I thought. I doubt my father would have made such a mistake. My brother would have done. That gives some consolation.

'You are *comitatus*?' the man says, as slowly as Heafoc, but speaking in our tongue.

'We are, yes,' I respond respectfully and suitably

slowly. 'I'm Wærmund of the Gyrwe.' His eyes narrow, and the stance of those with him becomes more guarded. They must know of the Gyrwe. Perhaps this will be the first time we're recognised for where we come from. Maybe they know of the marked son of Wihtlæd. I can't decide whether it would be a good thing or not. 'Do you have need of our services?' I ask hopefully. But he's already shaking his head. At that moment, an inopportune lowing comes from one of the cows, and it's followed by another gabble of words. Heafoc struggles to understand the rapid beats of them. I don't even ask him what the man says.

'We have no need of your services,' the leader says more slowly. 'But we would like to trade.' Although he speaks with consideration, as though testing the words, his gaze is fierce as, behind us, some of the animals can be heard moving about within the enclosure. I'm sure he purposefully stops himself from looking at my marked face.

Heafoc answers, using the other man's usual tongue, and they speak haltingly.

'His name is Luci of the Herstinga. He'd like to survey what animals we have,' he informs me.

'Then let him.' I turn to my warriors. 'Move aside and allow them to see our riches,' I offer quickly, not wanting to have the men and their horses out of my vision for long.

No one complains. Heafoc and the man continue to speak. I sense Luci's uneasy at our decision. I ponder on his name. It's different to those of my warriors, and the people of my father's settlements. It's something I've never heard before. I doubt he came from across the grey sea to the east, but where he originates from, I'm unsure.

'Tell him we can't let the animals out, or they might escape,' I urge Heafoc. I assume he does so, for the next thing I know, three of the Herstinga are dismounting, alongside Luci. Heafoc moves to greet Luci, and I quickly get into step beside him, alongside Eastmund. Bucge hovers on the periphery, her eyes everywhere, while Cenbryht's to the other side. The horses the men ride are good, sturdy animals, if shorter than ours. They probably can't go as fast as other horses, but maybe here, in this new land where there isn't the constant trickle of water, endurance is more important than speed.

Together, we walk into the enclosure. The animals watch us with varying degrees of interest. The smell is unpleasant but not too noxious. With an appraising eye, I consider what these men see. The animals are in good condition. We've been kind to them as we move along the trackways. None of them shows signs of distress, not even the smaller sheep who are almost impossible to corral as we ride.

The man speaks quickly to his companions. Heafoc tries to listen, but I can tell he doesn't understand everything they're saying.

'We will take all the animals from you,' the man says slowly. 'It will make it easier for you to travel. In exchange, we have oats for your horses, and also cheese and smoked meats. It will speed you on your way,' he offers, with a knowing glint in his eye.

I don't immediately respond, and neither does Heafoc. Abruptly, I realise I'm not sure if this is a good bargain or not. The grain is much needed, and if we had cheese and cured meats, we wouldn't need to hunt before cooking each night to get meat. We could dispose of the remains of dead boar as well. That might get rid of the flies plaguing us. With the weather warming, it'll make it easier for us to move stealthily.

'Can you ask him why he needs the animals?'

'Why? Does it make any difference?' Heafoc questions, not looking at me, but lowering his voice. Without waiting for my answer, he speaks once more in the slow, gabbled tongue. He receives a halting reply. 'They were set upon by a tribe to the west in the autumn, before they could slaughter the animals. They also took the breeding pairs.'

I consider this. They don't want our aid, and yet, evidently, they're wealthy even while facing attack. Perhaps we don't look the part of *comitatus* after all. I find that to be a crushing defeat, although even I'm honest enough to admit our successes so far have been largely down to luck, or perhaps, the aid of the gods.

But before I can reply, another string of words is spoken while Luci's men move amongst the animals, checking hooves and teeth. I consider whether we should have done that before taking them.

'They've sought their vengeance, but alas, the breeding animals were slaughtered by the other tribe who thought only of eating during the dark winter months, and not of the better, warmer ones.'

'Is it a good bargain?' I murmur to Heafoc.

He winces and shakes his head from side to side, lips pursed in a line. 'It could be better. Perhaps some gold or silver, as well?'

Before Heafoc can resume his bartering, Luci speaks with consideration once more.

'We have other riches. Iron.'

This I prefer to talk of grain and cheese, although the thought of good cheese is an enticing one.

'Then we agree,' I respond hesitantly, not wanting to appear too eager. 'We will bring the animals to their settlement and make the exchange,' I announce quickly.

Heafoc repeats my words, and now the man looks perturbed.

'Does he expect us just to let them take them?' I ask crossly as Luci gesticulates while talking to Heafoc.

'No, but he doesn't want us in their settlement either. He suggests we meet, at midday, under an oak tree not far from here.'

'That'll allow them to surround us,' I retort, uneasy at the suggestion.

'He says half of his men will stay with us to show us the way, and the others will gather together the supplies and the iron. He says only four of them will bring what we've agreed to the meeting place.'

'If there are more than four of them, we'll leave, quickly,' I decide.

'I don't think we can leave swiftly with sheep and cows,' Heafoc reminds me. I grumble beneath my breath. I'd forgotten about them.

'So, they might get everything without the bargain being sealed,' I muse.

I glance outside the enclosure, but none of my warriors, or this man's warriors, are doing anything other than eyeing one another with mild interest. There are no angry words. Indeed, there's silence from all. I realise we're all similarly equipped. Some have good spears, others decent enough shields. None of us has a sword, like the one I took from my brother. We're equals.

'We'll do it,' I decide. Whether we run from the place or gain the grain, cheese and iron, we'll be free from the sheep and cows. That'll make our advance easier. 'And, if the bastards play us for fools, we'll find their enemy, offer them our services, and get our vengeance in such a way.' This I say so quietly only Heafoc hears, although Luci watches me. No doubt he can determine where my thoughts have taken me.

With the agreement made, four of Luci's men are left behind, their unease evident to see although Heafoc tries to reassure them with his halting use of their tongue. But, if they understand him, they make no show of it. It seems, the men and women of this land speak a different tongue to mine, and only Heafoc and Luci can converse easily with one another. My attempts at conversation with Luci have been more difficult, and I've been unable to convey all of my thoughts.

As we progress ever westwards, this might become a problem I'd not considered.

21

MEDDI OF THE EORLINGAS

We inter our father with his ancestors, burying into the small grassy hillock beneath which so many of our family have been laid to their eternal slumber. We don't burn him. There's no need when the flesh has all been eaten away by the passage of many winters and summers beneath the ditch.

At my brother's urging, I allow Elen, under heavy guard, to witness what we've found. She must see what Edern did to Macsen. I hope she doesn't already know. That way I'd think even less of her than I already do.

As the daylight fades, torches are lit, their smoke rising into the air, shrouding the work Marchell and I undertake to honour my father. Marchell's cheeks drip with tears. I'm little better. I'm grateful Madog has firm command over the men and women of this villa, and they stand far enough back so as not to see all we do.

Already, I've dipped the bones into scalding hot water, scouring them clean and as white as possible, refusing to allow any other to touch him. My father's torque has also been scrubbed clean of all stains by Marchell. It's a conceit because it will be reburied with him and will soon look like that again, but for now it must shine and be seen in the glittering light of the fires and torches beneath the vast expanse of the darkening sky overhead.

Briefly, I glower at Elen, allowed to bathe and have her long hair plaited before emerging from her imprisonment. I look for the swell of her belly, but see nothing. She must be barren. As much as I despise her, I'm grateful she is. If there is a child, I'll ensure it dies. I'd not welcome bringing about its death, however.

I don my breastplate and paint my face white with chalk before highlighting my lips and eyebrows black with charcoal. My greying hair is also coated in charcoal, as is Marchell's. We look like goddesses of the night, as we should. We've also partaken of our special herbs to allow us to breach the veil between the living and the dead. Or rather, I have. I know Marchell uses little of the substance, but I've rubbed it over my gums and chewed the root of our favoured plant, and now my head is light and I can feel little of my gums and teeth. I feel untethered. Free. Able to honour my father as I should by moving between the land of the living and the afterlife.

My father's bones, cleansed and free from the taint Edern inflicted on them, are carried forward on an old shield, awaiting repair that might never happen, but now put to better use. I've ordered no animals are slaughtered to mark the occasion, as might normally happen for our honoured dead. Being reunited with his ancestors will restore my father more than having one of the horses or dogs executed to lie beside him. Had his remains been more solid, I would have commanded it, but I have half an eye to the future of my father's tribe. We need all the horses and dogs. Indeed, I must see to ensuring the stallion services the mares. It's my particular skill to match the animals well to produce good offspring. Or it was, when my father lived. To fight our enemy, once we have sharpened blades with which to kill them, our warriors must move quickly across this landscape using the legs of horses, not their own.

Marchell and I take either side of the shield and

carry it towards the barrow to the rear of Villa Eorlingas, outside the ditched embankment, where our
ancestors lie, a reminder to all of our longevity here,
aside from the winters of Edern's tyranny. I know the
people of the Eorlingas watch us silently, but neither
of us missteps despite our careful burden, and my
light-headedness. At the preprepared hole, we pause.
Marchell mutters words I can't hear beneath her
breath to summon our ancestors to this special occasion; I add my invocations, shaking my talismans and
urging my goddesses once more to cast Edern into
whatever afterworld will torment him the most. I
hated the bastard, but now I despise him. He was
arrogant to think he'd never need to pay for his actions in murdering my father and burying him like a
criminal.

Within the hollow formed in the barrow, I've already laid a good cloak with a fine white fur collar,
and left offerings of jugs of wine and ale, hard baked
bread and even a small container with grains and
seeds which my father will need in the afterlife. Now,
Marchell and I lift the shield within, careful not to
disturb the cargo. As a final act, I slip the cleaned
torque around the staring and sightless eyes of my
father's skull. I know some of his bones are absent,
but I've gathered what was found in the large exca-

vated area my brother and his warriors revealed. If pieces are missing, I must assume they've been removed before now or stolen away by those creatures that feasted on my father's body when he had flesh as well as bones.

Standing back, Marchell and I both prostrate ourselves on the ground. I feel my heart beating in my chest, but it's the only part of me to feel grounded and tied to this place. I sense Marchell's hand close to me, as though she'll hold me and drag me back to the land of the living, if needed. I risk looking ahead, curious to see if I witness the feet of my ancestors, but I don't. I never have. I believe Marchell, however, can. Behind us, I hear the death song of our tribe, my brother's voice deep but carrying, as he sings our father, a man he doesn't even remember, to the afterlife. Again, tears prick my eyes, and I'm grateful for Sian's foresight in handing me a bag of chalk so I can reapply it when my tears have dried. The people of our tribe don't need to see my sorrow for my father. They should witness me as only the seeress, performing the required tasks to honour the dead. They need not know the deep well of sorrow that's guided more of my actions than I care to admit.

I realise some might wonder why my child isn't buried here, but that's not the way for small babes, dead before they breathed for more than six moons. They stay close to us, where we can mourn and feel them close to us, beneath our feet that pass over them every day, amongst us, but not with us.

As the ululations die away, I force myself to a crouched position and then stand upright more steadily than I anticipate, offering my hand to Marchell for she's old and sometimes slow in her movements. She takes it without fear or worry. At this moment, unlike so many before, we're united in one purpose. She offers me the ghost of a smile for a task well performed. I hold out the bag of chalk, and we both reapply our coverings. She's wept as well. After all, I wasn't the only person who lost much when my father disappeared and Edern took control of our villa.

Two of my brother's warriors move towards the gap in the barrow, and silently close it up, returning the removed soil to its rightful place using their hands and a shovel. I witness the act, and offer them a nod of thanks. Only now do we all walk back inside the ditched enclosure, past where my father had lain, unknown, for so long.

My brother stands before everyone in front of the villa building, the white painted walls behind him shimmering with flames. I notice Elen beside him, held firmly between Urien and Twrch with her hands bound, her ankles as well. Hedrek's to the other side of my brother, and my brother's wife is beside him, holding her son safely in her arms. All of them watch as we walk towards them.

'It is done,' I intone. Now there's an outpouring of grief, as wails and shrieks once more fill the air. We mourn for my father, for the tribal chief who met his end at the hands of Edern, a man who ruled here with an implacable will and little else for years after. I'm again grateful he's dead. I catch Elen watching me, a wretched expression on her face that's too easy to interpret.

'Take her away,' my brother orders his men, and with head slumped, shoulders sagging, Elen returns to her imprisonment. I don't miss Hedrek watching her being led away with a hungry look.

'I won't warn you again,' I whisper to him, too distracted to hear the clatter of my talismans as I approach him. I'm gratified by the way he jumps and startles, eyes wide as he sees me so close to him, my face and hair still black and white from observing my father's funeral. 'I really won't,' I repeat and take myself inside Villa Eorlingas itself, resting to allow my feet to absorb the small stones that together make up the image of the horses beneath me. A feast has been prepared in honour of my father, with the rich aroma of mutton in the air, as well as fresh baked bread and many other delicacies.

As I take my place beside my brother, with Marchell hovering behind me, I catch sight of Centus. He watches all with an unreadable expression, no doubt his thoughts far from here, perhaps with my father, for when my father lived his father was a blacksmith and knew all the magiks of the art he's so desperate to recall. Perhaps he considers where his father's bones lie, but I don't know the answer to that.

* * *

The following day, the work on the ditch is begun once more. My brother's even more determined. 'Let us hope there are no more bones,' I caution him. He nods at the warning. My father wasn't the only man of the tribe to disappear when Edern took Villa Eorlingas. Centus might not share my hope, believing his father's there as well.

'We'll go to Corun's village tomorrow,' my brother assures me. I sense he's right to delay. The construction of the ditch is more important than fulfilling the threat.

I take myself to my workshop and busy myself

preparing concoctions and other remedies, all done in silence, with the aid of Marchell. It's not yet the season for harvesting the goodness of the roots beneath the soil, but it's a good time to gather leaves, flowers and the fruits of the herbs and plants surrounding us, and which give us sustenance. Sian's busy watching Centus, who's returned to his work, although the supplies of charcoal to fuel the fire are almost all gone. I must think about how to replenish them.

I sense Marchell's appraising me. I've always wanted her to fear me, but now we've performed this important rite together, I realise our tribe is stronger with two seeresses rather than one.

My fingers are more nimble than hers as I cut and slice, shred and preserve in precious honey or sharp vinegar, but still, she carries knowledge not shared with me. And all the time, the hammering of Centus rings through the settlement, alongside the shouts of those digging the ditches, and the noises the animals make as they graze in the fields. Villa Eorlingas is alive with activity. I sense the serenity of familiarity settling upon me. These are the noises of my childhood, although other men's voices echo through the villa complex, and other women's hands are busy with spindles.

I think of my daughter, sleeping forever beneath my feet, and almost allow a ghost of a smile to touch my lips. It's been summers since I felt the urge to take joy in my surroundings. I wish we'd killed Edern many winters ago, but he had the strength to withstand us while the harvests were good. Thankfully, the run of recent poor weather, decimated his warriors and reduced his own strength. All are dead now. I wasn't foolish enough to waste the remaining strength of my father's few surviving warriors fighting him, when we had poorer food than him. I've had to wait for Madog to reach maturity and command the respect of new men, and those few older ones who yet live. And for the weather to aid us.

It's taken too long, but now we need never do it again. And when Centus forges weapons with sharpened blades, we'll always be protected.

'Mistress.' A soft voice at the doorway, and I turn to glance at Rhian, my brother's wife, standing hesitantly. She clutches her child tightly to her chest.

'Rhian, what is it?' Immediately, I fear for my brother's child.

'I think it's time,' she exhales softly. I nod, recalled to my position within the tribe. The child has been born and has thrived for many days now, but

I've yet to absorb him into the lineage of my family. I harden my face, for all she's been brave to come to me.

'We'll conduct the rite, starting this evening. Have the women assembled, and the men informed they must not witness this.'

'Seeress.' She bobs her head and moves aside. She fears me in a way Madog doesn't, but then she's not of this tribe. She was wed to my brother only recently as part of an agreement with those who live close to our border. It wasn't a union that saw the exchange of great wealth between two peoples impoverished by Edern's demands but of fresh blood much needed to ensure our future generations are strong. She's proving a good match for my brother.

I consider what's needed for the rite. Some might think it is too soon, but no matter what happens to Madog's firstborn son and whether he survives his first year, he must be acknowledged as my brother's son and my father's grandson. It's most poignant now the burial of my father is freshly in the minds of everyone.

Marchell hums softly to herself as she labours with her tasks. My mind's elsewhere. When Madog was born, I vividly recall her performing the same undertaking. Then, we all believed my father still lived and would come to exact his revenge against Edern. Madog was named and honoured with the weapons of war as well as the grains of a life of abundant food and health. Despite my misgivings in the intervening summers, I never allowed Madog to doubt his place amongst our people.

With what, then, shall I gift his son? Grains, of course, and perhaps other small items as well. Yet my thoughts turn to Centus, and I nod with satisfaction.

Madog's son, when he's named and accepted into our tribe, will be given grains, charcoal, a small lump of ironstone and also the two shattered halves of our father's sword. I'll proclaim him as a mighty and just commander who, after his father and I are little more than white bones turned to dust by the heat of the fire, our essences removed to the afterlife, will rule our tribe and conquer all who surround us with the aid of blades, strong stallions and well-fed bodies.

22

WÆRMUND OF THE GYRWE

'Are you sure about this?' Osfyth questions me when we've been waiting at the oak tree for some time.

I eye the uneasy men of the Herstinga who escort us. Their eyes flicker from our unhappy sheep and cows into the far distance. It seems they expect Luci and the other warriors to have already appeared as well. I've been scouring the horizon for signs of smoke, considering whether he's overextended himself, and now the other tribe have sought revenge against them while half of his warriors are missing.

My belly growls. I thought to be long gone from here before we needed to eat. I confess I was looking forward to devouring pungent cheese and, perhaps, freshly baked bread.

'Where are they?' I question once more, but of course, the men left to guard us don't understand me, and when they gabble words in reply I don't understand them either.

'It'll be going dark soon.' Cenbryht states the obvious in a bored tone. 'We don't want to be here, with them,' and he juts his chin towards the warriors of the Herstinga, 'when that happens.' We're still mounted, but the horses are growing restless.

'I know that,' I growl. I've fought beside these men and women and, I hope, earned their respect, but in trying to barter, I fear I look weak. If only the cows and sheep could move more quickly, I'd already have decided to leave this place. I regret the decision to take them every time I look at them.

The oak tree rests on a small rise in an otherwise largely flat landscape, the gurgle of a stream can be heard behind and below us. The horses have already drunk well, as have we, from the fresh-tasting water. The sheep and cows have also been allowed to drink. It's not a barrier we'll struggle to crest should we be attacked or come under threat. Indeed, the surrounding countryside is remarkably open. I can appreciate it's a good location to meet those not welcome within the heartland of a settlement. But that doesn't explain where those coming to meet us are.

I turn my horse and, in doing so, meet a range of expressions on my warriors' faces, from blank to furious, from puzzled to faintly alarmed. Eastmund's hand is never far from his weapons belt, while Nothelm's half-dozing. He feels no worry. My belly growls once more, and that's when those who've brought us here raise their voices and point. For a moment, I fear attack, but of course, they wouldn't shout to warn us of that. Instead, there'd be a blade at my throat.

I squint into the dying sunlight, and see the familiar face of the man who spoke with Heafoc: Luci. He rides with his remaining warriors, and their horses are encumbered with sacks which I hope contain our supplies. I've ensured the iron I already have at my command is well hidden. I don't want him to know I'm amassing huge quantities of the stuff. It would be much easier for them to take from me than the cows and sheep.

Heafoc brings his horse level with mine and shouts a greeting, which is returned. Another fluid explosion of sound comes from Luci's mouth, while Heafoc nods.

'It took them longer than they thought to gather

the produce. Some problem with the cheese, or something like that,' he offers loud enough we can all hear.

Luci then speaks to whoever leads the four men who stayed with us, and they join the others quickly. For a moment, I'm uneasy, despite the smile on Luci's face. I consider who should go first. I turn to dismount to lead the animals forward, but then stop. I've not seen their side of the bargain yet.

'Ask them to show us,' I direct Heafoc. He does so, and abruptly, sacks hit the ground, heavy ones. They're pulled open to reveal oats, cheeses, the welcome smell of fresh bread and also another, very heavy sack, filled with iron objects. I dismount and inspect the offered goods, remembering once when my father struck a deal with a trader only to discover the sacks were half-filled with pebbles and not a grain at all. He was furious that day. Unconsciously, I run my hand over my cheek where he struck me in anger on my birthmark, even though it wasn't my fault. He blamed the curse he thought I carried. Bastard.

Assuring myself all is as it should be, I turn to my warriors.

'Let the animals through.' With unhappy sounds, and only very slowly, the cows and sheep are forced to walk towards Luci and his warriors. He jumps down quickly from his horse, and he and his men move towards the animals, slipping halters over the necks of the sheep, while the cows already have them. He speaks with Heafoc, and Heafoc replies, and then quickly all is done, and they turn their backs on us to move off. Only Luci pauses, and speaks to Heafoc once more.

Heafoc replies, but doesn't immediately tell me what was said. As the herd of animals lumbers from sight, he speaks.

'He advises us we're not welcome within his territory. He tells us to cross the stream and continue in the land of the Gifla or we'll be set upon by him and his men. He says there are others close by, watching all we do. He says that men marked by the Gods should be wary of his people.'

'Bloody charming,' I mutter, determined not to be angry at the statement, and with the scent of fresh bread filling the air, I eagerly turn my horse. 'Over we go,' I state to my warriors. 'And then we'll have a bloody big feast, but there'll be three of us on guard duty tonight. It seems we can't trust the bastards.' With hooves splashing through the water, my horse stands on muddy soil, the height of the stream evidently usually much higher. 'Come on, we'll find somewhere to stop for the night.'

Despite my unease, I'm not actually angry with Luci. If anything, I'm considering why we weren't welcome to their settlement. Perhaps, after all, I'd like to see it. Maybe they're much wealthier than they portray, just not in animals and livestock. But then, as we've discovered to our detriment, oats and iron are much easier to transport. I'll remember that.

They come in the night. I'm on guard duty, but I doubt any of us are sleeping, despite our full bellies. The bread was a delight, the cheese pungent and fulfilling, and yet, one by one, all of my warriors fell silent with restlessness.

Overhead, the moon's bright, a few clouds scudding past it, but producing enough light with which to see. It's no surprise when we hear the sound of men whispering close by, even if we don't understand the words.

A clank of blades and shields, and I know my warriors are ready for this. I consider if it is Luci and his men who attack us, or whether he's informed someone else of our location, or whether it's my father, led here by Wædel's remains we left in the woodlands. Or because Luci knew who we were, and has sent word to my father.

I don't order my warriors to be prepared. We are anyway. It'll be a test to see whether we fight only for our own lives, or to protect every one of our fellow warriors.

The first spear thuds down not far from where I'm standing. I jump aside, startled by it. I expected them to at least face me.

'Bloody cowards,' I growl low, gripping my shield before me, covering much of my body from below my eyes and down to my middle. My blade is in my hand. My spear is at my feet. I don't throw it because I don't yet know where the enemy is.

The thud of another spear hitting the ground rings through the air, this one coming from the side of me, where Eastmund keeps watch. A soft cry of surprise erupts from his mouth. I hear the unmistakeable sound of shields being lifted, and weapons unsheathed. But nothing else happens, and gradually my heartbeat slows and I catch my breath. I peer into the gloom, wishing the shadows were less dense. Overhead, I squint upwards at the night sky and quickly realise our enemy's intentions. There's a bank of cloud coming close to the moon. They mean to attack us when the light available is noticeably dimmed. I redouble my grip on my seax.

I'd blame myself for this, but until I know who the enemy is, I won't do so. The trade was a good one. If Luci couldn't afford it, he shouldn't have been so greedy with our animals.

I'm not the one to call my warriors to arms. Instead, Bægmund shouts from his position to the right of me. 'Ware,' he calls, and I hear the crash of something hitting his shield. The figures emerge from the gloom.

I see only the moon-silvered edges of the spear tip that stabs at me. I avoid it and follow the wooden shaft towards the warrior who holds it. He has his shield with him and thrusts it against me. I try and land a strike against him with my seax. He's a broad man. I sense his strength as he pulls his spear back towards him. Around me, the sound of a bloody fight erupts from the throats of my warriors. I crash my shield, not into the man fighting me, but against the shaft of his spear, forcing it wide, so I can meet his shield side on. It's like fighting with my eyes shut. I can see so little. I hear my enemy but little else. I can't even see the glint of his eyes or the shimmer of pale flash in the dullness.

'Bastard,' I huff, striking wildly once more, but

my foe is alert to my intentions and, dropping his spear, immediately crashes his shield against mine. I'm sure he must be finding another weapon, but it's impossible to know until the tip of it appears above the rim of my shield, the sound of iron meeting iron the only reason I notice it. If he'd been quieter, I'd be bleeding by now.

I duck low, taking refuge behind my shield to evade his blow.

'Arseholes,' I hear Heafoc shout and spare a thought for him, wounded and having to fight. The horses shift and whinny with fright. I realise while we've been on our guard, I've forgotten to protect the horses, more concerned with keeping our food, and my treasures, from the enemy. That was an oversight. I hope it won't prove to be a deadly one.

The press on my shield grows in intensity, almost dragging me to the ground. I feel the strain in my shoulders, and appreciate the man is much, much stronger than me. I don't want to be forced so low my knees buckle beneath me, but that's what's happening. If my father were here, he'd be laughing at my ineffectual defence, berating me for being a foolish cursed bastard to even attempt to beat someone who's clearly a better fighter.

Forcing myself to cast aside the taunting voices of

my father and brother ringing in my ears, but still unhappy about it, I release the grip on my shield. I rush around it, finally striking my foe in the side, in a huff of hot air. He doesn't react in time, and already I'm hammering another blow against him, a sliver of moonlight allowing me to place him in my mind before it's once more covered.

I jab again, swinging my bunched fist against his face, even as I stab with my seax. Only now does he retract his shield and turn to counter my attack, his shield before him. I take advantage of his reluctance to fight without his shield, and duck low, hand reaching, to grip my discarded spear. I pull it upright, but my grip's all wrong, far from finally balancing the weapon, with the spear tip dipping low to the ground. It gives me an idea, though. I swing it wildly towards where I know he was standing moments ago and feel the wood strike home, vibrating along my arms. A thud, and I dive forward, spear forgotten about, as I hold him down with my body weight. But he still holds his shield, and my legs can't encircle it. Hot pain thrums along my thighs where the sharp edges of his shield have caught them.

'Bollocks,' I exclaim, jabbing down with all my strength, but finding nothing but the wood of his shield. I'm hardly holding him firm, and already he's trying to scurry away from me, taking his shield with him. I grip it with my free hand, yanking it from his grip although I'm still on top of it. It separates us, more effectively than a bronze breastplate. While he labours to wriggle away I slide from him, seemingly attached to the wooden and iron item.

Angrily, I rear upwards, one leg free from the shield, although my left foot snags on it. Again, I launch myself at my enemy, and this time I land atop him; both of us are winded, but I allow a grin to touch my lips as the sharp metallic stink of blood assures me I've wounded him.

He grunts, an agonised sound, and his attack intensifies.

'Will you not just die,' I huff, each word accompanied by a fierce blow until he finally falls still. I drag myself along him, assuring myself no air passes his lips, for it's too dark once more to see the blood. Yet I feel it all the same, hands sheeted in the stuff, as I roll off him, and hang my head between my shoulders, knees bunched up before me.

I hurt all over, but I don't feel the sharp pain of blood. My legs throb enough I could have been skewered, without even realising. I calm my breathing, and allow myself to enjoy my moment of triumph. I hope that would have stopped the taunts from the lips of my father and brother.

I listen for the noises of the battle when I can hear over my heavy breathing, but they're much quieter than I'm anticipating.

'Heafoc,' I call.

'Aye.' His familiar voice reveals no fear, neither does he caution me to silence. 'I think we got them all.' His words reach me across the eerie space, the clouds once more covering the moon so it's too dark to see anyone. Not even the reassuring flash of iron can be glimpsed.

I force myself upwards. 'Bucge.'

'Here,' she calls.

'Osfyth.'

'And me,' she replies breathlessly. And now my warriors shout their names. They come from close by. I pause, deciding who's missing from the shouts.

'Nothelm,' I shout, but there's no reply. I stand and immediately stumble, tripping over a flailed leg of the man I killed. 'Has anyone seen Nothelm?' I call, hoping he's not bleeding his last somewhere.

Again, a chorus of 'no's, rings through the air. I straighten, stab the dead body just to reassure myself, and then feel my way forward. I hear the horses nearby, so I know they're safe, but not Nothelm.

'Nothelm,' I shout once more. 'Where are you? If you're wounded, groan or something and we'll find you.' It's hard to hear anything over my ragged breathing, but I try to catch my breath and hold it in. There's some sound coming from my right side.

I walk that way, using my spear to ensure I don't fall over any more corpses. It knocks against one or two, and eventually I walk into a squatting figure.

'Who's that?' I demand.

'It's Bucge,' she announces quickly, as both of us lower our blades. 'He's not here,' she informs me, her words coming from below.

'Where is he?' I huff, wincing as I walk into the shaft of my own spear which I can't see in the deepening gloom of the night. There are so many clouds above, I think it must rain soon, and still I can't find Nothelm. Has he used this attack as an excuse to leave? Has he rushed to my father, as Wædel did? I confess, I was beginning to like him. Now, when I next see him, I'll have to kill him if he's proven to be less than loyal. I confess, I'm disappointed in the toothless, short man. I really bloody am.

23

MEDDI OF THE EORLINGAS

It's done as the sun rises. A new day to welcome our newest member.

The women of our tribe have stayed with me throughout the night as, with the aid of Marchell, I undertook all the required parts of the ceremony. All apart from one. We've made use of a special tincture to ensure we stayed wakeful all night. Now, the effects are beginning to dissipate and fatigue claws at me.

With the mellow yellow of a new day in the dew-dripped grasses, we process towards the burial place of our forebears, the barrow beneath which those of Villa Eorlingas have been buried since long before the Romans came to this island. Indeed, it's only in the lifetime of my father's father that the barrow has been reused once more.

It's here the remains of my father were placed only two evenings ago. Today, the passing from one generation to another will commence with all the required ritual.

The child has slept throughout much of the night. His mother hasn't, even now, frantic something will stop the rite from being performed. I feel some pity for her fears but believe them ill-founded. The child is well formed, chubby and bright-eyed. He'll survive the night, and indeed, he has.

And now the men of our tribe, led by Madog, as our leader, wait to be formally introduced to his son. It doesn't matter they've all met him before. That they've all held him close and smelt his milky aroma. This is entirely different. Grown men will not bow low to a small babe, but they will acknowledge his connection to every member of our community, and to those who've led us since before most can remember. Apart from me and Marchell.

Fires have lit the starless sky, driving back any who might think to steal the boy from the embrace of his relatives in the perilous night before he became one of us. Now the fires collapse on themselves, little more than ash, the smoke wreathing us so I watch even Madog startle as we women emerge from the gloom as though we've not just walked along the pathway leading from Villa Eorlingas. I shake my head a little, pleased, all the same, that I possess the capacity to cow even my brave brother and his warriors.

I hold the child in my arms. He's heavier than I anticipate. Certainly, he's much heavier than my daughter was ever allowed to grow. The thought doesn't sadden me as it might once have done. What life would she have been allowed to lead with Edern as a father? It's better she was spared that, no matter how much I continue to despise him.

But now isn't the time for such thoughts.

Instead, I pause, and Marchell joins me. We're both adorned with white chalk and the remnants of charcoal, her lips pale, as I know mine are. When we parted from my father, we were white-faced with black lips and eyebrows. Now, to welcome a new member of our community, we're reversed, faces rubbed with charcoal, our lips white. I must try to remember not to lick them for the chalk tastes vile and will make me cough. However, I've once more rubbed my gums and chewed our sacred herb so I can walk the path between the living and the dead. This time, I'm connected to the ground beneath my feet by the weight of Maccus in my arms.

Behind me, I'm aware of the rhythmic chants of the women of the Eorlingas, joined with Rhian's voice as we make this transition. The men don't join in. They shouldn't be here, but I've made an exception to this long-held rite that's always been the responsibility of the seeress and the women of our tribe. They'll never have seen it before. When it happened to them, they would have been older than my brother's son, but still too young to remember.

Today, the men will witness this, including Hedrek from the Beansæte, his warriors and Centus. They too will know Maccus will one day stand where his father does, and where his father stood before him.

Reverentially, even as young Maccus chuckles to himself, wrapping his fat little hand in my hair, he's laid at the entrance to our barrow, not without some difficulty. The barrow's not been opened for many, many summers. It'll not be unsealed today. I hope the next time it sees the light of day, it'll be for my death, or my brother's. We didn't open it for my father. Too many winters had passed since his death. But he's restored to where he should always have been, which gives me strength despite the terrible nature of his death and initial disrespectful burial by Edern.

The chanting from behind grows louder, re-calling me to my task. This division between the men and women sees the men observing their women in a whole new light. It'll take them some time to re-cover from beholding the secrets all women possess over life and birth.

Maccus continues to chuckle, the noise encour-aging him somehow, even though he's there, alone, aside from me. I stand between him and the entrance to the barrow. I'm here to protect him, for now. Soon, he'll be the one protecting me, should I live to see him reach manhood. As the talismans I wear clatter with my swaying movement, I pull my father's blade free from where it's been hidden in the bag I hold slung across my shoulders. All gasp, even though they're expecting this, as growing sunlight glints on the dulled blade. My peripheral vision catches sight of Rhian. She remains terrified but stands proudly.

I move towards Maccus, still not speaking, and with the aid of Marchell to ensure this is done cor-rectly, we place the two pieces of the blade not in the babe's hands, but rather, in the soil, upright, at his head and his feet. My half of the blade slips easily into the soil, and Marchell's even more easily, for all she's old and frail, and her hands shudder in performing the precise movement of presenting the hilt-ended half of the sword.

Eyes alight, I stand, and look from Madog to Rhian, and then back to the men. They're fearful of me, as is right, with the light of dawn casting me into shadow. With my charcoal-rimed face and white lips, I look like something from the afterlife, as is the intention.

'Maccus,' I whisper, only to realise all should hear this, unlike other occasions when I've performed this rite. 'Maccus,' I shout, startling the babe so his fat little arms and legs shoot free from his wrappings. I fear he'll cry, and I don't wish him to do so, but he doesn't. Indeed, his chuckles quickly fill the air again, as he discovers his feet with one hand and pulls them closer to his body. It would be amusing if this wasn't so important.

I arch an eyebrow, allowing all to focus on him before I speak once more. This shows his bravery. All should witness what a strong child Rhian has birthed.

'Maccus, son of Madog, son of Macsen, son of Merin, you're now one of the Eorlingas, and with this blade, you'll defend and protect all, from the lowest slave to your father, and master. Be welcome.' And so spoken, Maccus gurgles even louder, and I exhale softly with relief.

'He's a strong boy, scared of nothing,' Rhian shouts with exhilaration, as the women of our community share their own thoughts on the boy, a hubbub of conversation where all night there has only been chanting or singing. No words have been spoken between us. I catch the eye of Madog, and notice how he grins widely, proud of his son, while his warriors and the other men slap him on the shoulders, congratulating him. I hold the gaze of Hedrek, until he dips his head in supplication. There's a warning there. One he'd do well to heed. He remains a welcome guest amongst our people, and at Madog's and my instigation. But he's not a member of our community. Far from it.

Centus, as I expect, licks his lips and focuses only on the two pieces of the blade that need joining to make Maccus' task possible. I admire his firm resolve. He's a man with one thing on his mind. I still hold out hope he'll be successful in his endeavours, even though the experiments have been long and tedious. And failures to date.

'Seeress.' My brother approaches me, respectful, bowing low.

'Take your son, Madog, son of Macsen, son of

Merin, and leader of the Eorlingas. Raise him to be a brave warrior, and wise leader, to protect the women of his community as well as the children and old people. Make him as you are,' I offer as a final, softer thought. Madog's face, stoic until now, flickers with pride. 'I only say as I see,' I whisper. My position as his sister could make me conceited about the man he's become, but he's so alike to my father I'm astounded my father died while he was such a small child. It's as though my father raised his son, as Madog will hope to do with Maccus.

He scoops Maccus into his arms, no fear at embracing the chubby child, he's familiar with the motion, and he holds him aloft. Maccus continues to gurgle and chuckle, somehow delighted with all this, and it's then I notice the pride on Marchell's face.

She's done well. I should, I admit, perhaps tell her as such. But she's a hard woman, her features always stern. I sense her scrutiny, and meet her gaze. A tight smile touches those familiar lips, but they broker no further closeness. All the same, I incline my head towards her, and she does the same to me.

We are the same.

Although it pains me to acknowledge what my future holds.

24

WÆRMUND OF THE GYRWE

We remain awake all night, waiting.

There's no further attack. The thick cloud cover obscuring the moon and starlight confounds us. We can't see enough to hunt for Nothelm. Instead, we stand alert, silent, no need to fight back exhaustion, for our blood runs hot. I curse myself for a fool, and for allowing us to be so exposed to Luci and his warriors. I should have known much better than to trust anyone. I can hear my father laughing in my mind. He's never been quick to trust any of the surrounding tribes, and they live close together, bounded by rivers, streams and hedgerows. I thought myself a warrior and leader of warriors, but I've failed at this.

As the daylight builds, I begin to survey those we killed, and those of my warriors with injuries.

'Heafoc.' I call him to my side. I notice immediately he's wounded once more, limping heavily, and with his arm cut in the attack on my brother, which had been healing, bloody again. I want him at my side, but he's no use to me with his evident facial scar and fresh blood. 'Sit here,' I order him, astounded when he does as I ask. I swallow back a sudden spurt of fear. I've come to rely on Heafoc. Perhaps too much. I can't afford to lose him now. 'Osfyth,' I shout instead. She stumbles towards me. Her eyes are wild, a livid bruise on her left cheek, as she sways from side to side. Abruptly she stops, and vomits noisily into the tall grasses not trampled by our passage. She rights herself, winces again, but strides with more confidence.

I shake my head, all the same.

'Eastmund, Goddæg.' I call the men to me too. All three watch me, while others turn dull eyes my way, most fighting exhaustion. It seems only I don't require rest. 'Check the perimeter, and discover who our enemy were.' I suspect Luci and his warriors.

'No need,' Heafoc announces in a sullen voice that immediately makes me fearful. 'I know this man.' I realise he's turned over one of the men I killed and hasn't followed my orders. 'It's Burnoth.'

'Bollocks,' I explode, even as the others react in shock, turning to their own dead to see if they've also killed warriors who owe their allegiance to my father, Wihtlæd of the Gyrwe. 'I suspected Luci,' I complain.

'We all did, Wærmund,' Heafoc agrees.

'Nothelm?' I question, fear turning to anger in an instant.

'Wædel no doubt set them on us,' Heafoc states.

'The supplies haven't been taken,' Bucge shouts from where she's checking the goods exchanged with Luci only yesterday. I peer behind us, wishing I could see further, but the almost flat landscape of this place makes it difficult to determine how far I'm able to see. Apart from this slight rise with the trees on it, much is identical. There are few other trees to give a sense of perspective. I'm unsurprised it's been used as a meeting place.

'We need to move,' I inform the men and women of my *comitatus*.

No one argues with me, not even those who are injured badly. There's more than just Heafoc with a bloody wound and Osfyth with her clearly knocked head, making her sway alarmingly.

'Take what we need from the bodies,' I also order

them, counting those who died here and realising my father wasted good men on trying to kill me. I knew he hated me for being cursed by the gods. I knew to fear his reprisals when I killed my useless brother. I didn't realise how much effort, and valuable resources, he'd waste on trying to kill me. Equally, I'm proud of my warriors and myself. We beat them. Now we need to evade any more who are sent after us.

A sense of urgency drives me. I find my fingers refusing to perform the simple tasks of pulling blades from unresisting hands, and the small wealth of dulled shimmering discs and the odd bead from small pouches. I urge myself to calm down, but it's difficult with the thunder in my ears making me believe galloping horses are close.

'Do you think Luci told him where we were, or Nothelm?' Heafoc questions when we're finally mounted, adding the six horses my father's warriors rode to our collection. Six men, against us. It was perhaps not a fair fight, and it speaks to my father's arrogance. He's never believed me a warrior of true worth, laughing with disdain when I attempted to win his regard. I hope he'll reconsider now.

'Probably both,' I growl angrily, considering Luci's instruction to avoid the lands he claims on be-

half of his tribe. The road we were following seems
to run directly through them. As it offers the quickest
means of leaving this place, I'll take it, even though
he told us to keep to this side of the stream. If he
comes to fight us, I'll meet that attack with our
strength. Well, what remains of it.

The horses are reinvigorated with their night of
rest, although we aren't.

'Eastmund,' I call to rouse him from slumber
later. If he falls from his horse at such a speed, his
head will be broken on the remnants of the stone
road we follow. Yawning wildly, he offers me a firm
nod of thanks.

Heafoc's managed to have his arm bound, but the
cloth covering it is already stained with dark blood,
almost black, and the flies buzz around him, desperate to take their fill. Osfyth remains green. She
rides at the back because every so often she has to
bend over her horse and vomit noisily onto the road.
Alongside the trail of horse shit, there's also her
vomit, and the occasional splatter of blood, to mark
our passage. We can't remain in such a vulnerable
location, but right now speed is to be welcomed, not
stealth.

We eat as we ride, sampling the rest of the bread
we've paid so dearly for, pausing every so often to

offer the horses water from fresh-water streams trickling nearby. The sun blazes hotly on my head, and
my group of men and women fall progressively
silent. This is a ride of necessity. It's not enjoyable
and it can't be enjoyed. Every so often, I find myself
unable not to look behind me, but all I can see is the
roadway, and the flat land stretching to either side of
it. Luckily, I see no sign of Luci and his warriors,
which pleases me. Neither do I see any indications
Nothelm, or more of my father's warriors follow us.

Soon we pass another collection of trees and
marker stones festooned with the skulls of sheep or
goats, and I allow myself to rest more easily. Luci's
tribe didn't hold the largest of territories, although it
means we're now in another unknown region. It concerns me, but not as much as evading my father's
warriors, if any of them have survived the attack. His
fury will have redoubled. I killed his favourite son. In
doing so, we devastated one of his settlements and
took all my brother's wealth. We've since killed another six of his men, well, seven if we include
Wædel. If he's not careful, and persists in trying to
track me down, he'll have less warriors remaining to
him than I do. Then, perhaps, instead of travelling
westwards, I could take my own tribe. I could become the leader of the Gyrwe in place of my father,

something he made no secret of refusing to countenance.

But no. That's not what I wish to do. Those people despise me as much as my father does. To lead them, I need to earn their respect and no matter what martial victories I bring, they'd never respect me, but instead see the weak boy, cursed with the mark of the gods, and a child uncared for even by his own father.

Nightfall brings us to an isolated location, close to another stream. With the daylight fading, and my men and women all suffering from a lack of sleep, I call a halt.

'I'll keep first watch,' I inform them as they dismount, groaning and complaining. Osfyth's finally stopped vomiting. Heafoc looks pale once more. 'Then, I'll wake Eastmund, and then Eastmund, you can decide who'll keep next watch. Everyone needs to eat and sleep.'

'You can't stay awake for another night,' Heafoc cautions me, but his words are weighted with exhaustion.

'I don't intend to do so,' I reject. 'But aside from a few of us, we're all wounded and tired. I know I can stay awake longer yet because I'm determined my father's warriors, or Nothelm, will not find us.'

Heafoc subsides too easily, his horse already tended to and now grazing happily, while Heafoc slumps to the ground and is quickly asleep, without even eating.

Osfyth, Hygebeorht and Bægmund are also already asleep. I catch the eye of Bucge as she chews slowly, blinking rapidly to stay awake. 'Too tired to eat,' I call to her and she grunts in agreement, and also settles in her cloak. Soon there's only me awake. The horses have slumped in sleep, some standing and leaning against one another, others lying down. They make more noise than my slumbering warriors.

I blink grit from my eyes, and stride around the implied perimeter of our encampment. Without a hearth fire, and with little thought from tired men and women, we've still managed to cover only a small area. I won't be able to watch everything, but I can keep a firm gaze on the roadway we're following. I eat as I go, one hand on my spear, the other holding bread in it. Chewing keeps me alert, as does the sound of my footsteps over the stone road, through the long grasses surrounding it, and then once more over the stone road. The world fills with the calls of night-time animals, the flap of unseen wings and the cries and yips of animals about their nocturnal pastimes.

The silence – well, the almost silence thanks to the snores and farts of animal and man and woman – allows me time to think. I should never have trusted Nothelm. He's proven himself to be an enemy to my ambitions. Wædel, I should never have approached to join my endeavours. I knew to doubt him but he was a fine warrior – well, he was when I was a child – and without him, I'd never had gained Cenbryht who's proven himself to be a welcome addition, although I do still suspect his intentions.

And my father? Well, I knew he'd resent my actions and attempt to stop me once I proved myself successful and perhaps not cursed after all by our ancestor, Woden. Eventually, fatigue wears me down, and I'm left with no choice but to wake Eastmund. He springs upright. I'm astounded so little rest has reinvigorated him.

'Sleep, Wærmund,' he offers, teeth flashing brightly. 'All will be well, and I'll be sure to bloody wake you if not.' I realise he's prepared himself as I hear him eating. I allow my tense shoulders to deflate. I curl in my cloak and I'm asleep before I even slow my breathing. I'm astounded to be woken by bright sunlight on my face, and Bucge's leering face looking down on me.

'Wakey, wakey, sleepyhead. The day's wasting,'

she assures me. Quickly, I'm on my feet, assessing my force. Not even Eastmund still sleeps and he's had the worst rest of all, being forced to keep guard in the middle of the night.

'Anything?' I call to him.

'Nothing. And Bucge replaced me, and she saw nothing either.'

I catch sight of Heafoc, allowing Bucge to bind his arm. His cheek, I notice, is also really starting to heal, although he'll carry a decent-looking scar from now on. I stretch and take myself to piss away from the water and the horses, squinting towards the west. The land here seems to be less flat, some small hills visible in the distance, as well as increasing collections of thick bands of trees.

'We've travelled a long way,' I murmur to myself, surprised. This place seems nothing like where I grew up. There, the flat landscape is dominated by wide rivers and murky fenlands, the hint of the expanse of sea never really far away. This is altogether different.

I feel a stirring of excitement as I banish the spectre of my father's warriors and Nothelm. If they're to find me, they'll have to venture through three or four different tribal lands. My father and his warriors will need to negotiate safe passage or risk a violent altercation as he'll ride with all his warriors, visibly armed with spears and shields. Admittedly, I'll have to do the same, but at last I feel as though I'm far enough away my father will think twice about doing so. Will he truly wish to deploy more of his warriors to ride through the lands of the Sweordora and the Herstinga and their neighbours?

'Come on,' I call to my warriors, casting an appraising eye over them all. 'We've further to ride today.' Unlike yesterday, my warriors seem almost cheerful. They too can feel the air on their faces, untainted by the salt of the sea, or the buzzing of pesky flies attracted by the water and damp, and by the blood that thrums through our bodies.

They sense we're far from home, and getting further and further away from warriors seeking revenge against us. Now it's time to begin growing our reputation as a *comitatus*.

25

MEDDI OF THE EORLINGAS

'Mistress.' The voice rings from outside my workshop, and I turn, startled from my task of preparing a concoction to guard against the coming winter coughs. With the women of Corun's tribe now members of ours, including the children and old folk, for Corun is dead like his fellow warriors, I know to put more preparation into how we'll survive the winter months. Even with the benefit of hearth fires and the resources to warm the floors within the main villa complex we will require remedies to keep us well.

'What is it now?' I complain, striding to the door. The ringing of Centus' hammer is loud today, and my head resonates with it. I could blame too much wine last night, but I will not.

'We found this,' an excited voice announces, arm extended within my workshop, although no other body part. I look at it with narrowed eyes, feeling my forehead furrow.

'It looks like the stuff Centus works with,' I mumble, and now I see who the proffered arm belongs to: Urien. He's one of my brother's most skilled warriors, responsible for ensuring Elen is well-guarded in her captivity, but most of the time he's a farmer. He understands the soils surrounding Villa Eorlingas. Already, fat beans and peas have ripened beneath the sun and are in the process of being placed in storage for the winter months, once harvested.

'It was found at the bottom of the beans, closest to the stream leading to the River Habren.'

'And is there more?' I question quickly, stepping outside to run my hands over the block of reddish stone. It's heavy, much heavier than it looks.

'Yes, mistress, yes,' Urien's quick to reassure. I offer him a single nod of thanks, and turn towards where Centus works. Urien follows closely behind, bristling with excitement. Already, I'm trying to restrain my flash of hope. Could this be it? I'd not expected to find any new ironstone so close to Villa Eorlingas. If I'd thought it might be here, I'd have had the young boys digging for it throughout the hot summer months since Madog became the leader here.

Centus is standing idly when I reach him, the sound of his hammer having fallen silent. His eyes are unseeing as his hand hovers over what he's working with today. It's not an attempt to repair my father's sword, nor is it any work to create new blades. Instead, he's busy making use of the old iron found in the storeroom, melting it down to put it to fresh purpose, or to repair other items. I know the disappointment of his failure runs deep. He's not alone in being dissatisfied with the lack of good charcoal to superheat the flames to allow him to work on the iron bars.

As of yet, we've found no one with the required knowledge to produce good charcoal. Our attempts have failed. Hedrek, so confident when he brought the charcoal alongside Centus, has been forced to admit he bartered for what he had, exchanging good grain to purchase it. Those who supplied it haven't been seen since. It's a problem that should have been foreseen, but all of us underestimated what was truly needed. It wasn't just about having tongs and hammers. It was about charcoal, good quality ironstone and understanding the magiks at work between flame and metal.

'Centus.' I extend the reddish lump towards him. He jumps, eyes sweeping my face before inclining his head respectfully. Only then does he look at what I hold. He must quickly realise what it is. He leaps forward, eyes sweeping from me to Urien.

'Is there more?' he asks, excited for the first time in many days and weeks. His failure, and the lack of resources, has made him doubt himself. I pity him for that. We've tried to keep our dismay from showing, but Centus feels it keenly himself.

'Much more, yes, come and see.' And with that, Centus and Urien dash from my presence, both stumbling when not far and turning to seek permission. I shake my head sternly, but wave them away, my talismans clacking as I do so. When they're out of sight, I allow myself a soft chuckle. They're like small boys given long wooden sticks with which they're to practise the art of spear-craft.

In Centus' absence, I survey his working area. It's impeccably tidy. Today, there's a small fire blazing. His single attempt to melt the ironstone without good charcoal assured him it was a waste of what supplies of wood we had. Now, I notice, he has a small wooden box in which he keeps his tools. There's also what seems to be a blanket of leather, to wear over his clothes, so he doesn't burn himself. It has hoops on either side, and by that means he can tie it around his waist. I've treated many burns that he's won for himself from the spiteful fire.

I sigh heavily. My father's blade is here, still stubbornly in two pieces, one the hilt end, the other just part of the fractured blade. It refuses to be bound together. I'm almost wishing I'd not made such a fuss about it. Not only does Centus need to learn how to make sharpened blades, he must also repair the old sword as well. But we need to find charcoal, or at least someone who knows the magiks of producing it before we can do any of those things.

From nearby, I hear a soft conversation, and my ears prick. It sounds decidedly covert, as though there's some secret I should know about. Carefully, I sniff the air, eager to decide where the two who confer are. I scowl when I realise the noise comes from the grain store. Elen remains a captive. It's an annoyance. Soon, we'll need it for the grain, and then what will we do with Elen? My brother pushes me to allow her some freedom, but I know Elen too well. She might be as barren as I've been for over twenty summers, but she'll still cause problems for Madog, when she's released.

But the other voice perplexes me. Trying to walk quietly, and not kick up dust or stones from the work yard of the villa, I make my way towards the grain store. I have my suspicions about who talks to Elen. I scowl when I discover I'm correct. But I don't draw attention to Hedrek, squatting close to the barred door, almost lying on the ground to ensure he's not seen. Neither do I stop to listen to what's being said.

I've known to be wary of Hedrek for some time. Why he remains at Villa Eorlingas is difficult to determine. Centus has not made good on his claims. Hedrek should be back at his settlement, but he lingers, even while complaining Centus misled him. Hedrek must trust those who hold sway in his absence. Either that or he's lost his position, but refuses to acknowledge as much to Madog.

Madog's who I need to warn of this. I know we've grown slack in keeping a steady guard on Elen. We've no reason to doubt anyone within the settlement, and now Villa Eorlingas benefits from not one but two ditched embankments to protect it, there should be nothing to fear. Of course, we've forgotten about Hedrek.

I find my brother with his son, both lying on the

ground in the gradually lessening heat of the day as we move towards harvest time, the pair of them giggling as Maccus is held aloft by his father. I don't envy my brother the mouthful of drool that lands on his face, but he doesn't appear to mind.

'Sister,' Madog announces on seeing me. 'See how he grows.' He holds out Maccus to me, but I shake my head. The boy's too heavy for me to hold comfortably. Once he can walk, I'll be able to assist him staying upright, but until then, I prefer not to burden myself.

'Brother,' I offer, running my hand through Maccus' mane of dark black hair, luxuriating in how soft it feels when my hair has grown sparse and coarse in recent times.

'What brings you here?'

The smile slips from my lips as I remember why I've come to the front of Villa Eorlingas, where the women sit beneath the overhang of the building's roof making use of the bright daylight to help their weaving and cloth work. 'Urien's found what he believes is ironstone in the far field.' I indicate where I mean with my chin. Madog looks intrigued. 'He and Centus are examining it. While I was informing Centus, I heard conversation coming from the grain store.' At this a look of swift apology touches my brother's lips. The guards are helping with the harvest or other summertime activities. There are still not enough of us to stand guard and provide for us during the winter months. I know my brother has sent four of his men to coppice the local woodlands, and bring back what wood there is for the winter fires. Now we have the means to heat the floors in the villa, we hope to make use of it when the ground's frozen solid and the water troughs icy.

'Sister,' he begins, but I shake my head.

'I understand, but we must watch Hedrek. He's always been too interested in Elen.'

'Is it not time to allow her to leave?' my brother suggests hopefully.

'No. She'll cause us problems still, and it's still too near to when Edern died. Those who are foolish might believe her even now if she managed to make a child and bring it forth and claim it was Edern's son.'

'None would be so ridiculous.'

I shake my head. 'Ambitious men and women who want Villa Eorlingas won't think of such things. They'll not mind provided it gives them the excuse they need. Perhaps it would be better to ensure

Hedrek returns to his people for the foreseeable future. Surely he must be needed for their harvest? If we don't have enough men, then they certainly can't.'

'Perhaps, sister, yes. I'll speak with him this evening. He's always promised to find the charcoal makers for us. I might suggest he does that now. If not, we'll need to wait until after winter to resume Centus' experiments.'

'Ensure Centus remains here,' I comment quickly. 'When Hedrek leaves, we still must have Centus amongst us. For all the failures, he's too valuable to leave.'

'Of course, sister,' Madog confirms. And then he hesitates. 'Marchell is old, sister. She should sleep within the villa itself this winter, with the advantage of warm floors and solid walls, and not in the workshop, which will be cold.'

'She's mine to command, and will sleep this winter where I tell her to do so. And that's in my workshop.' I hold his gaze, hoping he'll not question me further, relieved when he turns his attention back to his son, although I sense disappointment in how he won't meet my eyes.

'It'll be time to trade soon, at Glevum and Corinium.' He quickly changes the subject. 'What will you have to add to the surplus grains and animals from the villa?'

I grimace at the question. The knowledge I have is always tricky to place a value upon. 'There'll be decorated bone items and other talismans we've imbued with healing powers.'

For a moment, I sense some unhappiness at my response, but then he nods carefully. 'The people nearby lack for a seeress. They'll be pleased to trade some of their flavoursome cheese for the protections of a seeress.'

I wince at having my skills compared to those of a cheesemaker, and I realise Madog grimaces as well. 'If there's something else you require?' I leave the question hanging, tempering my fury. For now.

'No, no,' my brother is quick to deny. 'That'll be adequate, and perhaps for something other than cheese, although it is particularly pungent.'

I huff softly, far from placated, and turn aside. I raise my hand above my eyes to seek out Urien and Centus. Fresh ironstone will be welcome. But Hedrek needs to leave, soon. And, when he's gone, he must be compelled to find the charcoal makers, and if not, we'll need to try ourselves with what wood can be found from the woodlands. To have some share in what Centus will produce, Hedrek must do more than complain about how long this is taking, and cause problems with Elen.

I sigh softly. Much feels as though it's at our fingertips, and yet none of the solutions have yet presented themselves, which frustrates me more than the answers being entirely out of reach.

26

WÆRMUND OF THE GYRWE

For all we're alert to those who watch us from the safety of their hilltop locations in this land so very different from our own, I don't change direction to continue heading west, as was my original plan, but rather follow it south. The road we're following is good enough for the horses to move quickly. It's still marked by stones and drainage ditches. We eat well from the food we bartered for with Luci, and the animals welcome the oats. We all have half a mind to the knowledge we're far from home, so we never drop our guard, but we remain unapproached. Nothelm doesn't make an appearance. And with the growing distance as we encourage the horses to ride all day long, I sense the threat from be-hind us growing much reduced. When my father learns of the failure of his warriors, he'll need to reconsider all he thought he knew about me and the curse with which he believed Woden infected me.

Heafoc's once more unwell from his many wounds. For a warrior of his ability and skill, he's slow to heal, grumbling about his age. Bucge keeps a careful watch on him, which he takes with bad temper. Osfyth is quickly restored to full health, and I'm sure when we're next approached by our enemy, or by those looking for the assistance of a *comitatus* warrior group, we'll be up to strength and able to fight. Each morning and night, I order us to train together before riding for the day, or stopping for the evening.

It takes three days for someone to draw near to us in this new place. We have to be careful because water no longer surrounds us. As well as hunting for food, Osfyth also seeks streams and rivers. I decide I trust those warriors who remain with us, even Cenbryht. Of them all, I find it most enjoyable to spend time with Eastmund. He thinks much like me. And with the distance from our homeland, he becomes less grief-stricken for all he lost and was forced to bury before leaving.

'Ahead,' Eastmund calls to me as we ride through

a collection of small hills, our eyes constantly looking upwards for there are certainly settlements up high. Initially, we thought the smoke was merely clouds, but then we caught sight of people and animals moving about up there. I think it's a good place to make a home.

'I see it,' I reply quickly. I'm keen to determine what they want. Will they be welcoming or violent? I soon have an answer. 'Heafoc, keep yourself to the rear.' It's not a command I like to give, but he doesn't argue, assuring me he approves of keeping himself hidden. 'Everyone else, make sure you have weapons to hand.' I hear shuffling and clanging as my warriors rearrange themselves. There's a difference to riding alert and being prepared to engage with an enemy.

Across the roadway ahead are a collection of warriors. They have no horses. I peer upwards, sensing we're being watched, and see what I think is a banked enclosure, depicted in grey rock against a green background. Whatever is within the enclosure is impossible to see.

'Hail,' I call when I'm within shouting distance, but there's no response from the collection of about fifteen warriors who have spears and shields to hand, although even I can see they're not the finest equipment.

I bring my horse to a gentle halt, my warriors doing the same. I sense their alertness. They have their weapons ready, should they be needed.

A chatter of sound erupts from one of the men, his eyes on my face. I hold myself with confidence, refusing to hide the mark on my face from him. It's evident he's the leader of these warriors, and that while he notes my facial feature even beneath my beard, it doesn't appear to concern him. I shrug a shoulder. I don't understand what he says. Neither do I turn to Heafoc. If he comprehends the words, he'll inform me soon enough.

'Well met,' I call to them. The tongue he speaks is very different to mine. I can't decide if the leader sounds angry or if it's just the harder sounds of his words. 'I'm Wærmund, commander of this *comitatus*,' I offer, mindful Heafoc's not spoken. 'Do you wish to fight, or employ us?' This I ask because I don't know what else to say. I curse my foolishness for not appreciating the speech of the tribes we encountered would differ from that spoken in the east. I should have realised, what with Luci using different words as well.

Silence follows my greeting. The stranger looks

uneasily at his fellow warriors. They're all solidly built, wearing tunics of well-dyed cloth, although only some of them have boots on their feet. Boots, I've come to realise, are almost as complicated as iron and swords to produce. Who would have thought it? Not that their feet are uncovered, but some are clearly merely wrapped in either leather or furs, and sometimes both.

This then is a problem, and one Heafoc seems unable to solve.

I eye the men. They watch us in return. Some look uneasily towards their commander, others glower at us as though it's our fault we can't communicate effectively. I risk a look towards the hilltop, now able to see people watching from their vantage point. I wouldn't like to take the horses up there. It's steep-sided. I consider from where they get their water. There's a river nearby, the sound a gentle murmuration. It'll be hard work to keep taking water all the way up there. And they have animals as well. I see them grazing on the sharp slope. They'll need water too. I decide that perhaps they collect rainwater, or have some other means of keeping everyone sated.

Heafoc's steady rumble emerges from behind. He doesn't speak our tongue. He's trying something dif-

ferent, but incomprehension remains on the face of
the warriors. I recognise it as the tongue Luci spoke.
Still, there's no response. Only then Heafoc tries
something else, and quick understanding shows on
the warrior's face.

'They're the people of the Hicca,' Heafoc announces. 'They don't speak the words of Luci, or our
tongue. But we have a common tongue, although it's
not one they all know.'

'What do they want?'

'They'd welcome you to their home, this hill fort
above. Their leader has a request to make of us. It
seems they seek warriors to strengthen their force.
Their foes, the Wæclingas, have been stealing their
cattle. They wish to reclaim them.' I suppress a grimace at the task. I'd like to fight an enemy over
something other than cattle, but this is our first offer
of work.

'Tell them we'd be open to negotiations,' I confirm, musing on this development. Of course, I realise, we don't know who the Wæclingas are. We
need more information. I don't want to put my warriors unnecessarily in harm's way.

A string of words, and now the man we face
speaks quickly to those with him. They lower their
spears but don't move aside.

'These negotiations will be protracted,' I announce. 'Language is a problem.'

'Perhaps we should seek someone who can speak more tongues,' Heafoc suggests. 'As payment.'

'A slave?' Osfyth is quick to complain. 'We've no need for such.'

I can sense an argument brewing between the two, and I don't want them to bicker in front of these people, the Hicca.

'We'll see what they suggest.' I'm aware a youngster has emerged from some hidden location, and been given a string of instructions by the man who leads here. He hurries up the hillside on nimble feet. Perhaps it's to tell them of our impending arrival. I'd like to be welcomed warmly, with ale and good food. But perhaps that's not the way of these people.

No one speaks for some time, but the tension has left the air. I don't dismount, and neither do my warriors. Heafoc stays behind me.

At some unseen signal, the man speaks once more.

'We can go inside now,' Heafoc explains. 'We'll be received, and then we can begin discussions. We're asked to be careful with our horses. The slopes are steep. They'll take us a circuitous route, around the back of the hillside.'

I consider this carefully, even while the Hicca begin to move towards this path, which I can detect picked out in the beaten-back summer vegetation lining the hillside.

'We'll do as they suggest,' I decide quickly. 'Be vigilant. If this is a trap, we need to realise before we're inside.'

Now I dismount, and lead my horse, and the animal with my treasures on its back as well. I go first, aware Heafoc doesn't like the arrangement, but he's in no position to complain. Almost immediately I feel the strain in the back of my legs from the unusual movement. Our path has been mostly flat until now. I've lived a lifetime on largely level land. This feels very different, and in little time I'm gasping for breath, with sweat running freely down my face. I can hear the heavy breathing of my fellow warriors as well. I thought we could do almost anything, but even this hill has defeated us. By the time we reach the enclosure, far ahead, we'll be unable to fight, which concerns me. I consider if these warriors can have sensed that. Maybe they've encountered people from my former home before? Although, if they had, they'd have realised we spoke a different tongue.

Slowly, we round the hill, and with sweat dripping down my face I absorb all I can see. Here, there's a line of hills running in front and behind me. Below my feet, the grasses are well cropped. The animals usually graze here. It appears, then, they've known of our arrival for longer than we've known we were coming this way. The animals have been moved and penned within the encircling defences. I look forward to peering from the top of the hill to see how far the roadway can be sighted towards the east.

Finally, we near the entrance through the embankment surrounding the settlement. I see there's a gateway. While there might not be any more warriors, people stand there, with whatever they can find to hand, anything from a stone to a heavy-looking piece of wood.

The commander gabbles to them and they draw back. He turns towards me, a wry smile on his face for my obvious discomfort at the walk uphill, and beckons me inside, or at least I think he does. When I hesitate, he speaks to Heafoc.

'He welcomes us,' Heafoc huffs, as out of breath as we are.

'Then let's do this,' I announce, leading the horses through a deep ditch, soggy at the bottom with water, either from the rain or some unseen water sources, and then I'm through the first of the ditches surrounding the stockade on the hill's peak.

The grass here is mostly worn away and liberally splattered with sheep and cow shit. Once more I appreciate their wealth is in animals. To have had them stolen away by an enemy tribe must wound them. Perhaps we could be paid to retrieve them.

Here we pause. There's water for the horses, in huge, hollowed-out stones, assuring me there's access to water, although I'm still not sure from where.

'They say we can release the horses to graze and drink,' Heafoc mumbles. 'He reassures there's nothing to fear from them, but that we go no further.'

I grunt. Here, so close to the buildings of the settlement, wide, round buildings, with grasses on their roofs, I feel we're treated discourteously. Perhaps I might make complaint about that. But I don't. Instead, I release my horses, being careful with my heavy treasures to not make any noise as I lower them to the ground. Both animals walk eagerly towards the troughs, noses moving as they smell the water.

I sense some movement from within the top enclosure, and see women and children bring us food and drink.

'Please, rest easily,' Heafoc translates for us. The babble of a tongue I don't understand floods the space. It sounds harsh although I detect no malice on the faces of these people. I'm handed a wooden bowl filled with a warm and pungent pottage and taste it eagerly.

'It's good,' I call to my warriors.

Heafoc rumbles to the other man. Now he grins, and speaks to those of his people who are close. Pensive faces break into smiles, and soon everyone is eating. While we can't all converse, Heafoc and the man he can speak with come close, chattering together. Heafoc's healing face flushes with pleasure. For the first time, I see an easing of the pain he's been in for much of our journey west.

'Tell me, Heafoc, who is this tribe stealing their cattle, and where can they be found?'

'The Wæclingas.' He stumbles over the unfamiliar name.

'And who is this Wæcling?' I question. I'm aware how such names come about.

'Some bastard, dead for many years. Another, Isarninus, claims to rule them now. Before then, the two peoples lived together, in almost harmony,' Heafoc offers with a wry smirk while the other man speaks.

'And what's our host's name?' I realise I should have asked that before.

'He's Boddw of the Hicca. His family have lived here for generations. Isarninus is an interloper from the south, or so he says.'

'And he's a warrior?'

'He leads a *comitatus*, not unlike our own,' Heafoc admits. I nod. This is all beginning to make much more sense. If Isarninus has the skills my fellow warriors have, as opposed to those of Boddw and his people, I see why they've lost so much. And why the ditches have so recently been made much deeper, some of the churned earth dark beneath the sun and lacking the grassy covering of the rest of the enclosures.

'What have you told him about us?'

'That we're a *comitatus* under the leadership of Wærmund, son of Wihtlæd.'

I startle at that, uneasy at having my father mentioned. It's clear, however, Boddw hasn't heard of him.

'What do you think?' I question Heafoc.

He inclines his head from side to side, deep in thought, and then grins broadly. 'We've been waiting to truly test our skills against an enemy of our choosing. This might be exactly what we need.'

I nod slowly, checking my fellow warriors to see if

they agree or not. 'What will they give us in exchange for risking our blood instead of theirs?'

Boddw listens closely to our conversation, but it's evident he understands nothing of it. Heafoc speaks with him, and now he's nodding, a slow grin spreading over his face, as he beckons for two young men to come forward. They have the build of warriors but are slight, like me, not yet grown into their adult forms. They'll move quickly but are unskilled in fighting their enemy as they lack all scars.

Between them they carry an upturned shield, and on it I see the glint of precious metals, and the familiar sight of axe heads, orphaned from their handles. I nod. It's a rich treasure. More than my brother had amassed even though his father was the leader of the Gyrwe.

'And food for the animals and for us,' I suggest, because if we're to fight, we need to make sure we're all well fed.

Heafoc relays the information. The enthusiastic response from Boddw brings a smile to my lips.

'He also offers you the chance to spend the dark times of the year here, provided you defeat the enemy.'

I nod. I've not given much thought to what we'd

do when the weather turns against us. It seems I no longer need to do so.

'Do we agree to these terms?' I call to my warriors.

While no one cheers their acceptance, there's no complaint either, but muttered 'yes's.

'Tell our friend here he has the pleasure of employing Wærmund's *comitatus*.'

27

MEDDI OF THE EORLINGAS

Hedrek leaves with ill grace two days later, his gaze assuring me he knows I played a part in this. Centus remains behind because we have the equipment he needs, and my brother makes it clear it'll be staying here. Centus, torn between Hedrek and Madog, wisely decides to stay with us. It does perhaps help he's struck up a friendship with one of our women. I might have encouraged her to beguile him. I feel no remorse for that. One day, when Centus has managed to determine how to make good iron, he'll have a prominent position amongst our people, and the girl understands that.

I watch Hedrek and his few warriors as they emerge from the protection of the ditch and embankments surrounding Villa Eorlingas, striking out towards the River Habren. Only then can I breathe deeply, pleased the only person who thought well of Elen is far from where she's being kept captive.

There's so much to be done. Even now Urien scours every field where crops are being harvested for the coming dark time of the year. A small quantity of ironstone has been found, but it's the problem of charcoal that has me seeking out Madog once more.

I find him with Urien, looking at the collection of strange-shaped reddish lumps that have been found. He grins with the delight of a child first sitting upon a horse's back.

'Look at all this,' he states, eyes on the ironstone and not on me.

'It's not enough to have the ironstone if we can't heat it.'

Madog's shoulders slump and he turns to me, defeat written into the lines of his familiar face. 'I don't know the art of charcoal.'

'And neither do I,' I confirm quickly. 'So we must find someone who does?'

'Don't you think if there was someone who knew how to do it, I'd have discovered them by now?'

'Well, Hedrek found someone,' I complain, aware

I sound as reasonable as some of the small children, just learning their independence.

'He did, yes. But he's said he bartered heavily for the supply and those people haven't been seen since. And anyway, you had him sent from here.'

'Because of his interest in Elen,' I explain, but Madog's shaking his head.

'We can learn ourselves,' Urien offers. 'Once the harvest's collected in, and stored, there'll be time to teach ourselves the process.'

I consider this. 'Can it be so easy?'

'I doubt it,' Urien offers, his face cracking in a smile. 'Nothing ever is. But I've some understanding of the process, I suspect. But I won't be able to do it alone. We'll need good wood, and people prepared to help watch the burn. It's not a quick process, and must be monitored or we'll simply waste a valuable resource.'

At this Centus joins us, and seemingly having heard our conversation adds his thoughts. 'I too have some ideas. We should speak at length and decide if what we think we know is correct. Or not.' I sense Centus and Urien have struck up a friendship. It might keep Centus at Villa Eorlingas no matter what Hedrek tries to promise him or if his burgeoning relationship with the girl should falter.

'Then we should do it,' I confirm, eyeing the madder-tainted clumps Madog has. If someone else didn't assure me they were ironstone, I might think them merely large lumps of soil. 'We'll do that, and then we might be able to extract whatever ironstone there is from that.' Madog nods eagerly, his enthusiasm for the task returning.

I walk away quickly. I've set these three men to attempt to produce something not known in our tribe since my grandfather's time, if not before. I pray it comes to fruition, even as a strangled cry comes from Elen's place of imprisonment. I also need to decide where to put her when the harvest is complete. We can't allow our food to be spoiled by rodents. Neither can I allow Elen to leave this place.

Uneasily, I return to my workshop and find Marchell there, her aged fingers fumbling to draw peas from their pods.

'There are children who can perform this task for you,' I complain to her, snatching the bowl of pea pods from her hands. She releases them easily enough, and I set to the task, allowing the pungent aroma to fill the workshop. I'm uneasy with how much of my desire to take back Villa Eorlingas remains undone, and how much of it seems to be impossible.

I'm aware some of the other tribes look this way eagerly. It's not that Villa Eorlingas is unique in the surrounding landscape, other than it remains almost complete, aside from the depravations Edern inflicted upon it. There are lower-level storage areas, but they're too often overrun with vermin to be put to much use. The well in the far corner of the villa complex produces clear, sweet water, and of course, there are many other buildings, all but abandoned under Edern but being put to use once more. It is, I confess, a large complex of buildings. I can understand why others desire it. I'm not the only one who hungers for the colourful horse mosaic marking the entranceway, which reminds any who pass its surface how this villa's wealth was amassed in the first place.

I reconcile myself with the knowledge ditches and embankments will protect the villa until such time as Centus can be successful. I shouldn't have allowed myself to become so swept along with all Hedrek promised. It's clouded my vision of what success looks like to be once more within Villa Eorlingas. There was a time when being able to stand here would have been enough. I could curse myself for refusing to be content with having achieved it.

Unseen, a hand sneaks towards the large and heavy clay bowl, now filled with peas released from their pods, and surprises me. Marchell doesn't look at me as she recalls me to the task I took from her with an admonishing tap of her fingers. I consider how long I've been sitting here, idle.

I shake my head, square my shoulders and return to my tasks.

There's a new child to welcome into the tribe, one older than Maccus, my nephew, and throughout tonight, until dawn breaks, I must perform his welcome rite, no matter the thoughts swirling in my head. And of course, I must still contend with the problem of Elen. Once more, I appreciate it's a pity she didn't put up a fight when Madog and his warriors stormed the villa on Edern's death. Had she died then, she wouldn't remain a difficulty to surmount. Madog would have me release her, but Madog doesn't know Elen's true nature.

I do, as does Marchell. Between us, we'll ensure Madog never gives into his softer sensibilities to release her. She'd do more damage to Villa Eorlingas than a deadly plague, or a run of bad harvests. She'd not hesitate to kill Madog. I can't allow that to happen.

No, Elen will remain here. Until she breathes her last.

28

WÆRMUND OF THE GYRWE

We sleep that night between the two enclosures. I don't complain we're not allowed within the inner area where the people of the Hicca live. In Boddw's position, I'd have banished a force like mine entirely outside both embankments, but Boddw's keen to keep us friendly. Not that I allow us to sleep without guards. That would be beyond foolish. After all, we're somewhere unknown to us, with people who've offered us much to fight on their behalf. Still, it can't be denied we have a wealth of resources they might want if only we were dead. There are many horses and fine weapons.

I anticipate being asked to battle the Wæclingas the following day, but instead we're fed once more, and even brought linen to shelter beneath when it rains as the day turns to dusk. Under Heafoc's watchful gaze, we trained and fought in the morning, but then slept when it was clear we wouldn't be called upon to leave.

'Tomorrow,' Heafoc eventually informs us. He's spoken once more with Boddw, who comes to ensure we have everything for another night's sleep, while it rains heavily, the sound thudding against our temporary enclosure. Here, on the hillside, the rain brings with it a sharp, cold wind.

'Tomorrow?'

'Boddw says Isarninus of the Wæclingas will come tomorrow for more of the cattle. He's a pestilent boil but sticks to a routine of raiding every ten days.'

I nod, and narrow my eyes, considering the view I saw before the clouds closed above our heads.

'Boddw watched us coming this way.'

'He did, yes.'

'What would he have done if we'd not been upon the road, or refused the offer of payment?' I wait for Heafoc to ask the questions, unsurprised when Boddw flashes angry eyes towards me. That speaks of his desperation to better Isarninus.

'They'd have protected the animals within the

inner enclosure, no doubt,' Heafoc suggests when Boddw doesn't speak. As I don't know how large Isarninus' force is, I'm unsure if that would have proven effective. I don't believe Boddw has warriors who number more than the few we saw on first being intercepted.

'Will Boddw fight with us?' I question. My warriors have learned how to stand in a shield wall together. I don't know how Boddw's men will fight, or even if I want them amongst my number.

Heafoc and Boddw speak quickly. Boddw seems uncertain, but shakes his head. I anticipated his answer.

'Not when they're prepared to offer so much in exchange for our services, no,' Heafoc replies.

'And what direction will the enemy come from? The road? The hills?'

'They'll come from the south. Sometimes from the road, sometimes sneaking around the hillside here.' Heafoc doesn't point because Boddw is doing so.

'Early or late?'

'With the sunrise.'

'Then we'll watch for them.' I turn to my warriors. 'It's looking like an early start.' Some groan while others look keen to begin our first official venture as a *comitatus,* Cenbryht lifting his ale upwards as though saluting Woden. This will reveal our true strength as a fighting force. I'm not fearful, but I am curious. I don't wish to die on some distant hill fighting an intertribal battle that's none of our concern. I do want to be paid for our services, and to know once it turns towards the dark time of the year, we'll be fed and offered shelter somewhere safe with food and the promise of shelter against the harsh weather. A warrior can have all the weapons he wants, but he can't eat them. I appreciate that only too well.

* * *

The first hint of a lessening in the dark expanse of night has us standing ready and prepared. Heafoc insists he'll fight. I don't argue with him. There are ten of us now Nothelm's gone. It's not a huge number to counter the enemy of the Hicca, but it must be enough or Boddw wouldn't have put forward such a rich reward.

Those within the inner embankment are evidently also awake. The cattle have been taken within, as have our horses, a concession I demanded from Boddw. He didn't argue too much. Should we all die here, fighting against Isarninus, he'll be able to keep the horses. I hope that doesn't happen.

We hear the enemy long before we see them. Sound moves strangely on the hillside. I think it comes from behind, but then, as the daylight builds, I discover they're far below us.

There are fifteen of them. The man I take to be Isarninus rides, wearing a shimmering breastplate and even a helm decorated with dull-coloured horsehair sticking up from its crest. I suppress a smirk. Already, I don't like this arrogant arse. What sort of protection can such a contraption offer him? He looks foolish, and I only see him from a distance.

Isarninus' fellow warriors have well-made spears and wooden shields edged with iron, but no one has a sword, aside from Isarninus, who carries it on his back, the bone guard peeking over his left shoulder. For a moment I consider retrieving the sword I took from my brother, but it still requires a new guard. It would cause me more problems to try and fight with just the tang to grip. I'd lack a firm way to hold it without folding my fingers so as to make it impossible to jab and hack as I'd like.

'Be on your guard,' I caution my warriors, as we emerge through the gap in the outer enclosure and form our shield wall across the gateway. The wooden gate has been pulled closed behind us. It's protected by Boddw and his warriors, who've reinforced it with blocks of stone lying nearby. They've evidently been put to such a purpose many times. I did wonder why they had the need for so many stone troughs for the animals.

If Boddw and his men fought with us, our combined numbers would easily overwhelm the enemy but I understand why they don't want to do so. They've offered much for us to fight on their behalf. They'd sooner risk our blood than their own.

Catching sight of us, I see Isarninus' visible judder of shock that there are more than just the Hicca to counter. The raised voices of his warriors, joking and laughing with one another, falter to a stop behind Isarninus. A grimace of distaste quickly glides onto Isarninus' face. Then he dismounts, and leaving the horse to crop the grasses at the side of the road, he surges up the hill, far more quickly than my warriors and I managed to do two days ago. His legs are used to climbing such steep hills, I assume.

'Be ready,' I order my warriors, standing at the heart of our number, shield in my hand, spear ready in the other.

'We are,' Heafoc assures me. I see Isarninus hears

our words, and looks from us to the enclosure behind.

'Ah,' he says on drawing even nearer. 'You're a *comitatus*, as my warriors and I once were. You've come to take their cattle as well?' His gaze settles on my face. I wear my birthmark proudly. He grimaces a little. Does he, as Bucge said to me, see the image of Woden's wolf depicted there? Does he believe me cursed, as my father does?

'No, we protect it,' I shout in reply. I'm perplexed he speaks my tongue, but Boddw didn't. But then, if he was once a *comitatus*, perhaps Isarninus' ancestors also came from over the grey sea to the east.

'Whatever they've promised you, I'll give you double if you step aside and come and fight for me,' he promises with an assessing glance, arrogance pouring from him. I can only see a slice of his face beneath the helm he wears. His eyes are appraising. His lips are thin and covered by a neatly trimmed blond moustache. I sense unease ripple through my fellow warriors at being addressed by someone so alike to us. 'I assure you, these bastards have little wealth.'

'We fight on behalf of the Hicca,' I reply quickly, dampening down any urge to accept his enticing offer. I owe the people of Boddw's tribe no loyalty and yet we agreed on a price. We should adhere to the agreement. It's the honourable thing to do. If we're to be esteemed as a *comitatus*, we must prove faithful to those who pay us.

'Hah, let me guess, they showed you a shield filled with treasures, which I assure you are worthless, and promised you food and board for the coming winter. They'd sooner kill you once you've slaughtered us and steal all you have. They're no match for a *comitatus* trained and taught to fight by our ancestors, but they're devious little bastards.'

I really don't like this man, I decide, and not because he quickly fixes on my concerns about fighting for Boddw and what might befall us afterwards. I don't appreciate the way my warriors shift uneasily. From behind, Boddw and his warriors shout curses at Isarninus and his warriors, but their words do nothing to counter the threat Isarninus presents by speaking as plainly as he does.

Isarninus doesn't even hold his shield before him while determining the strength of my warriors. If one of us could be relied upon to do it quickly, we could launch our spear at him, and end his life now. But we don't have those skills. What we know is how to fight together in a shield wall.

'We should join with Isarninus,' Goddæg's the first to state quietly, which I appreciate.

'Shut up,' I hiss to him, but Cenbryht also adds his voice to Goddæg's.

'Ask them what they have,' he demands, standing back from our shield wall. I grimace as I hear Boddw urging us onwards, while Goddæg and Cenbryht weaken our shield wall by dropping their spears and shield.

'I have everything you might desire,' Isarninus continues, eyes rising on his long, horse-like face. 'I've better buildings than these to keep you warm. I've three times as many cattle to slaughter for food throughout the dark times, and I've many women who'll warm your beds at night, as well. You can have as many, or as few, as you like.' He speaks casually. It means nothing to him to offer us this. He is confident.

'Get back in line,' Heafoc orders unhappily. I sense others are also being enticed by all Isarninus has suggested. Maggenræd's the next to stand down. From behind, the cries of Boddw's people become shrill. Why didn't the fool warn me of this? I'd have strengthened my warriors resolve had I known it was a possibility we'd receive a counter offer. 'Don't even think about it,' Heafoc mutters to me. I consider if he'd leave me if I did go over to Isarninus. I can't deny his proposal is welcome.

'I'm one of you,' Isarninus calls. 'I'm from across the sea, not like these people here. They've lived their lives close by, subjected to the Romans and then forced to defend themselves on this bleak hilltop. They truly have nothing with which to reward you. And, if you aid me now, we'll have their women as slaves for your beds, and their cattle for the winter months as well.' Isarninus speaks in a low, beguiling tone, his warriors showing their wealth in weapons and shimmering trinkets adorning their necks. I'm losing my warriors' resolve. Why fight for half of what's been agreed, when we can take three times as much, and we know that Boddw and his warriors don't have the skills to stop us?

'What do you think?' I ask Osfyth and Eastmund. I trust them just after Heafoc, who's adamant we shouldn't change allegiance. There's a long pause, and into it I hear Boddw growing more and more frantic.

'You should do it,' Osfyth concedes, Eastmund snorting his agreement.

'No,' Heafoc roars, in that moment rushing headlong towards Isarninus' warriors. We don't follow him, and just before he reaches Isarninus, the damn fool trips and falls, landing heavily, just within reach of Isarninus, who with gleeful delight steps forward and holds a knife towards Heafoc.

His grin broadens.

'Join with me, *comitatus*, and I'll reward you handsomely, while you fight for me. Or, I'll kill your man.' Again, his words are light. His confidence is astonishing.

And of course, I've no choice but to acquiesce, even though it's unwillingly done. I know I lack all honour, and Heafoc would sooner die than be unfaithful. But right now, I hold his life in my hands, and quite simply, I don't feel like shedding blood to protect the Hicca's cattle, losing my most skilled warrior in the process on the blade of a warrior like Isarninus. Not today.

29

MEDDI OF THE EORLINGAS

Some months later

I wake and yawn, shivering in my layers of furs and cloaks. I should relinquish my determination to sleep within my workshop. The welcome heat from a hearth fire would stop my bones from aching, as would the heat of a warmed floor. But now it's nearly the warm time of the year again. If Marchell can tolerate the cold, alleviated only by a small fire in our workshop, over which we make poultices and potions, then so can I.

I hear a shuffling and realise Marchell's already busy with her day's tasks. I'd welcome going back to sleep, the greyness of dawn still some way off, but I won't allow her to beat me. It's been this way since I took her position as seeress.

Today, I realise, we'll discover if the most recent attempt to make charcoal has been successful. It's been a tedious process but a necessity throughout the long winter months. At least it's driven back the cold as we labour or tend the charcoal where it's been cooked between the two enclosures. If this attempt is successful, Centus can try to repair my father's sword. Madog's looking forward to striding through Villa Eorlingas wearing it before terrifying our enemies with it. And only then handing it to his growing son.

Marchell bends low, and both us of hear the creak of her knees and back. I really should allow her to sleep within the villa, as Madog requested. Her face is pale in the small light from the flames. It would behove me to treat her more kindly.

I take the offered hot water, infused with last summer's berries, and drink it eagerly, the heat spreading through my chest and, I think, even seeping into my distant toes. I notice she doesn't partake.

'I command you to drink the infused water,' I instruct her. If my concern for her startles there's no outward sign of it. I do see her cupping a beaker around her cold, almost lifeless hands. Yes, I realise it's time I relinquished my hold over her. She's old, many, many winters more to her name than I possess. I still need her, despite my firm denials. She must live for many more winters yet. I'll speak to Madog about the transition.

Sian arrives shortly, bringing wood for the hearth, alongside her ally, the young girl who sticks to her side, although the two aren't related. The pair are huddled deep within their cloaks, the air fogging before them, as they deliver the bundle of wood and kindling. The advent of more temperate weather is much delayed. I hope it won't damage the crops already growing in the sullen fields. Certainly, it's not affected the animals. The bleating of newborn lambs can be heard, echoing amongst the confines of Villa Eorlingas. Unfortunately, we must keep them inside, taking up precious space in the storage barns, but it'll ensure they live. It's a pity the smell is so potent. They are at least some company for the horses, and the mares who will bring forth foals soon. It's been nearly a full year since Edern died. The people of the Eorlingas have been busy in that time.

'Today is the day,' Sian states, excitement in her voice, while the young girl looks on with surprise that Sian doesn't name me 'mistress'.

'It is, yes.' I speak more severely, but she knows me too well by now to be dismayed at my sharp tone.

'Everyone is hopeful. The charcoal will fuel Centus' work, and then Madog will once more hold your father's sword. It'll be a fine tale to share in the dark times of the year.'

I welcome the warmth on to my fingers from the leaping flames immediately springing up from the fresh wood. I consider the last year. My brother's son is almost walking unaided. He's a testament to the passage of time. He's strong and healthy. I hope my brother will soon be a father again, if the gentle swell of Rhian's belly is anything to go by. Another son, and then perhaps, a daughter as well. The more sons, the stronger the tribe will become, provided they don't argue. But I'd caution my brother against too many daughters. They can be more spiteful to one another without blades than brothers.

'Centus is already preparing,' Sian encourages, her task complete. Abruptly, I realise I might miss his triumph, and hurry to leave the workshop, mindful Marchell follows me, as does Sian and her young shadow. The four of us are so often together, even Sian's accorded a great deal of respect from the members of our tribe.

'Good day,' I greet Madog, where he stands bundled in furs, and with wool inside his boots to keep his feet warm. He offers me a bright smile. Despite the many occasions we've been disappointed in the past, he's still eager and confident Centus will be successful. Soon.

'Good day.' He bows respectfully, as do others crowding close to where the charcoal is being created, close to the inner ditch. It's taken a great deal of digging and watching, smaller experiments leading to this much larger one. There are containers filled with water to dampen the flames within the covered circle, and only then will we know if the huge pile of wood, so laboriously coppiced and then stacked, has actually been changed into charcoal.

Not that we discovered all this alone. Not long before the first winter storm, a youth came to us from a distant tribe in the west, his face bright red with cold. Terricus assured us he knew the art of creating charcoal and would happily share it with us, in exchange for a winter beneath our roofs. After much discussion, and concern about his intentions, he was welcomed within our enclosures because Hedrek had had no luck in finding his charcoal burners. Although the process has still been slow, today we'll discover if it's been worth it on a scale large enough for Centus to fuel his experiments.

Already, Madog's warriors wait to extinguish the flames that will leap free from the soil covering, and then we'll be able to peer within the structure and see if there is indeed charcoal. A sense of excitement thrums through those assembled. If this works, we'll have accomplished a great deal, and not just for Centus. The same process could be used, I'm sure, to keep Villa Eorlingas heated from below.

'Now,' Madog calls, after Terricus gives a signal the time is right. Urien's one of those trusted by Terricus. Together, they work to shovel aside the hot soil covering the wood, flames leaping high into the sky at being released. Others move quickly to dampen the flames. Marchell and I have spent much of the winter treating livid burns with animal fat mixed with herbs to take away the pungent smells.

Slowly, the flames recede as the pile of discarded material grows to the side. Flames even leap amongst the burned soil and remains of bracken, and Rhian has to grip her son and hold him tight to her side, as do others with children too small to truly understand the threat of the flames.

'Has it worked?' I call, frustration thrumming through my body. No one answers, but I do see Madog, Terricus and Urien peering within. The grin on Terricus' face tells me all I need to know. Now we have charcoal. But still, we must wait for it to cool before it can be put to use.

***

Four days later, I'm summoned to where Centus usually works. It remains bitterly cold, but I doubt he feels the cool air. Centus bends over his bowl-shaped furnace, adjusting the way the precious charcoal has been stacked. I hear him explaining to Terricus as he works. I approve of this arrangement. It's taken Centus some time to entrust his knowledge to others. He and Terricus now share the magiks of iron and heat. Should anything happen to Centus, we won't need to hunt for another to aid us. There are too few who know how to extract iron-stone and force the resultant iron into the desired shapes. It's much easier to use old iron objects and melt them down, but the results are always unsatisfactory.

'Will this work?' Madog questions me. We've been playing this game throughout the winter.

'I'll say yes, and you no.'

'And what if it almost works?'

'Then we'll both be right,' I offer, infected with his good humour.

'I've reports the Husmeræ in the north mean to strike against us soon.'

'From who?'

'The trader who visited us yesterday had come from amongst them. He was vocal in speaking of all our neighbours. There are grumblings to the east, amongst the Færpingas, but I believe them too far away to trouble us and too lacking in fighting men. To reach us, they would need to visit Corinium first, and then we would receive word of warriors on the move.'

'No doubt the whisperings of your growing power have reached them.' I incline my head respectfully. 'It is as it should be. When Centus and Terricus are successful, they'll need to fear you more than they already do.'

Unexpectedly, my brother allows a glow of triumph to suffuse his face. He's not arrogant. In this he's very different to Edern. And because of that, the people who fall beneath his command welcome it – these days.

I chuckle at him, and then stand tall and proud, mindful of eyes watching me. Madog's my brother, but I'm the seeress. I must stand aloof from these people. Well, from some of them. There's no need to show my gentler side to many within the tribe. They must fear me as well as respect me. Especially the men.

I focus on Centus and Terricus. They work together, the one to pump the bellows and encourage the flaming small lumps of charcoal, the other to watch and make sure the colour is correct by adding more charcoal if needed. Finally, the blue-white glow of superheated flames roars within the small space. Eagerly, I watch Centus as he begins the process of melting some of the iron bars found on that fateful day during the harvest. Once that's done, he assures me, he'll use it to bind the two halves of my father's blade together. This is far from the first attempt to add iron to the blades. Those earlier experiments failed because the charcoal ran out, or the iron wasn't correctly melted. Today, I'm more convinced there'll be success. I've been sure of it for some days, a sense of excitement making my stomach bubble.

I watch, murmuring softly below my breath, words that mean little or nothing but which those close to me think aid the work of the bladesmith. Sweat beads my face, trickling uncomfortably down my back, so I want to wipe it away, but I don't. This, then, could also be part of the magik.

Finally, the two ends of the blade glow red and

molten, akin to the blood thrumming through my body, a strange sizzling sound in the air. Then there's a loud clanging, as hammer strikes the heated metal, Terricus adding the melted iron to the workings, sweat dripping from his face, Centus red and puffing himself. It's hotter than the peak of summer, although it's really cold, ice forming in the water containers.

I lick my lips, tasting the salt of my body. I wish I could be closer, more able to see exactly what the pair are doing, as they speak quietly to one another, hammering here, heating there, adding other pieces of molten iron there. Of course, I've seen this all before, but today, well, today it feels 'right'.

Finally, Centus stands back, moves away from the heat of the flames, the sword appearing whole before me, a shimmering heart of fire where it's been welded back together in its centre. Centus' own face shows awe and reverence. I mutter even more, little more than a hum of noise beneath my breath.

Centus moves to the waiting copper cauldron of water, plunges the blade within it, using the tongs to hold it. I see the water sizzling over the surface, a dizzying dance, so alike the sweat coating me I feel somehow connected. Centus lifts the blade free, his face creased in concentration as he next places it on the waiting bed of coarse sand brought from the distant banks of the Habren, where it meets the wider sea. I find myself moving forward, feet shuffling beneath me, desperate to hold the complete sword by the tang. A hand on my shoulder arrests my forward momentum. I incline my head to Madog.

This isn't for me to do. Not yet.

Should the sword prove to be repaired, then it'll need a new bone guard and then I'll bless it. Only then will I imbue it with the strength of our tribe, Marchell assisting me, although I think it'll be done willingly, and not begrudgingly. She's as keen for success as I am.

A heavy sense of anticipation infects those watching. Terricus eyes the sword as though it might move of its own accord. Centus observes it with a surprised expression on his face, and Madog moves towards it, his back to me.

He bends to touch the naked tang and pull it into his hand again. And as he does so, I'm convinced Centus has been successful.

I wait for my brother to turn, to lift the sword and show it to me, and everyone else nearby. I smell the heat of the iron, the strange, enticing smell of the charcoal, the acrid stink of the new iron welded to the two pieces of precious sword.

And I wait to see if, at last, Centus has achieved what he has always believed is possible.

30

WÆRMUND OF THE GYRWE

I eye the man sitting before me, raised high on a small dais, drinking deeply from a horn embellished with little more than trinkets of copper. I believed him wealthy, his tribe as well, but we've been here for many months now, and done little but drink and eat throughout the dark winter months. I'm grateful for that, but also frustrated with the tediousness of this existence. When I agreed to join this tribe, I anticipated some fighting. So far, we've done little but polish our cocks as well as our blades.

'Another feast,' Osfyth whispers to me, leaning over so I smell her washed hair's freshness. With warmer weather approaching, we're all keen to leave off the stink of the indoors. We spent last summer travelling outdoors, despite the rain. I've not enjoyed being trapped, which is what it feels like we've been.

'Another bloody feast,' I agree, aware neither of us drink. I never thought I'd tire of being plied with ale and mead whenever I wanted. But I have.

I acknowledge our time here has allowed Heafoc to heal fully from the many wounds he took in our early days as a *comitatus*. It's also allowed him to grow fat, his face often suffused with the pink of drinking too deeply in his cups. I've tried to speak to him about it. He told me to leave him alone. Well, words to such effect, anyway.

The hall we're feasting within is long and well built of stone. From outside, I hear the cries of the sheep as they birth this summer's lambs. I'm keen to be on my way. I don't believe Isarninus will allow it, however.

Bucge's laughing at something, drinking cup to hand, toasting one of the warriors who owes allegiance to Isarninus. She's made friends here. I haven't. I'm wondering if she'll stay when we leave.

'She won't,' Osfyth announces, somehow determining my thoughts.

'I thought she liked it here.'

'Not that much. She's always been a "make do"

sort of person. She's made do and, when we can, she'll leave with us.'

'Good. There are others I'd sooner leave behind than her.'

'And we all know who that might be.' Osfyth's eyes slide towards Goddæg. He's proven himself an arse. If we don't leave here soon, there'll be an uproar about the child he's about to father. How the girl has kept the secret, I don't know. It won't be coming with us. We have no place for children.

'I don't know how my father endured the tedium,' I mutter. Osfyth allows a slow smile to light her face.

'Why else do you think he made your life so difficult? He did it because he could, and it gave him something to do.' I consider her words, and I'm surprised to discover she might make a good argument, at least for the teasing. Perhaps not for the malicious attacks against me. Changing tack, she speaks again. 'How will you get us out of this agreement?'

'We're due to be paid soon. When he fails to do so, we'll be well within our rights to leave.'

'And you still mean to take all he has stored below his dais?' Her voice drops even lower, little more than the passage of air from her tight lips. I know what she says, all the same.

'I do, yes. He doesn't even know what it is, but I do.'

'But we have no bladesmith.'

'We'll find one, never fear that.'

Osfyth falls silent. Within the hall, a hush has fallen. I narrow my eyes. I know what this portends. I sigh softly, and Osfyth offers me an appraising glance, no doubt cautioning me to mask my ill-humour and unease with what's about to happen.

The man's led before Isarninus, the chains around his hands and arms clinking loudly. I'm astounded the chains don't fall from his skeletal body. His smell reaches me, even here. How I pity the poor soul. His hair is long and lank, falling to the ground. His skin is so dirty I think he's shaded the colour of a chestnut. I can see little but the point of his nose through the white hair covering his face. His beard and moustache are a tripping hazard.

'Why does he do this?' Osfyth grumbles more softly than I make my complaint known.

'Because he can.' I realise he's little different to my father, if Osfyth tells me the truth of my father's reasoning behind tormenting me.

The men and women of the tribe know what's expected of them. They hiss and shout at the pitiful figure. The children run forward and grab his hair, pulling his head backwards. He lands with a sharp snap, hands just preventing him from cracking his nose on the hard tiled ground. Every time. I'm astounded he still thinks about protecting himself.

'Now we'll hear the words of our great educator,' Isarninus shouts.

'How does he know what he's even saying?' I murmur, not for the first time.

Without pausing for thought, a litany of words erupt from the man's mouth. He knows what's expected, again, how, I don't know. They mean nothing to me. They're incomprehensible to all of us, and yet Isarninus takes pride in having them spoken and in having this poor wretch of a man under his command.

I sense Isarninus' scrutiny, his jeering glance, and wish I'd never met him, or agreed to his terms when we should have aided the Hicca instead. I certainly wish I'd never had to kill the warriors from the Hicca. They were far better men than I've found here.

'You still want him?' Osfyth barely whispers.

'Yes, I do. We'll take him with us.' I know she wants to understand why. In all honesty, I want to know why I'm so certain he can help us, but I'm unsure. I feel it deep within. When we leave here, Isarninus will lose his pet. No matter what, I can't abandon the man to be continually tormented by Isarninus.

I listen again, as he speaks, watching Isarninus nod along as though comprehending every word. I've questioned Heafoc about it. He denies all knowledge. Says it's something he's never heard before. None of the others understand either, and I suspect the majority of Isarninus' people don't. This is some sort of conceit. I wish I could grasp its importance.

I pick my moment carefully. The weather's been improving for a few weeks now. I no longer shiver before the hearth fire. It's time to go.

'My lord,' I call to Isarninus as he parades around his ramparts from the high peak, looking down on all below him in the mostly ruined remnants of the settlement. No doubt, he also gazes into the middle distance where his rivals make their home, not that there's much left of the Hicca after such a bleak winter. Even the smoke from their pitiful fires hasn't been seen for weeks now. To begin with, I admired their fortitude. Now I know I'm to blame for the end of their tribe.

'Ah, Wærmund. A delightful day,' Isarninus offers. He speaks my tongue well, although others of
his tribe don't. What else does he know of which I'm
ignorant? Certainly, the majority of his people are
unable to comprehend more than the very basic
'please' and 'thank you's with which we conduct our
day-to-day affairs.

'Perhaps,' I murmur, aware Bucge and Heafoc
hover close by, essentially out of listening distance,
but there to help me if I need them. After all, Isarninus is hardly alone. Six of his warriors glare at me as
I stand beside him. 'It's time for you to settle the
terms of our agreement,' I advise him, watching carefully. I doubt he has the treasures to pay us what he
promised. I've doubted it for a long time, but much
better to be safe, warm and fed, if tediously bored,
than outside during the dark time of the year, especially after what we did to the Hicca. And of course,
my actions also ensured Heafoc lived, although
Heafoc has never thanked me for that.

'Ah, Wærmund, how to sour my mood. I've assured you, I'll settle that when we next raid our
enemy to the south, the Uppingas.' His eyes alight at
the thought of that.

'We'll not fight your battles until we have what's
owed to us.'

Now he scowls, flickering a disdainful look over me. I stand taller, aware I'm a better warrior than him. He's used guile and the blood of others to get to where he is. And his imposing weapon and ridiculous-looking helm. 'You'll not threaten me in such a way.' He flicks a hand towards his six warriors. I hear them clanking and creaking inside their leather byrnies, reaching for blades more likely to shatter on impact than cause a wound. I sense Heafoc and Bucge mirroring their actions.

'You'll not beat us,' I caution him.

'You'll remain here until I deem the task completed. I've paid you in kind. Food, warmth, women and men to keep your toes warm at night. There'll be more than one babe with your foul blond hair and long noses before the dark time of the year returns.'

I chuckle, the sound dark and foreboding. 'We'll not be here to see that, I regret to inform you. Food and warmth aren't worth the cost we've paid.'

'Now look here.' Isarninus stamps towards me, fury and, I sense, fear flickering in his bright eyes. 'The Uppingas will soon launch an attack against us. You'll be here to hold the defences against them and ensure we triumph again.'

'No, we'll not.' I eye the finger he juts in my direction. I realise how easily I could topple him and take

control of these men and women. Yet I don't want
that. A winter here, on this exposed location, with
the wind howling almost constantly, snow, frost and
ice making it hard to crack the lid on the water bar-
rel, has been more than enough for me. If I ever decide to take a settlement as my own, it'll be one that's
far more hospitable and habitable.

'Guards,' Isarninus calls, sensing my determination. I chuckle again. I realise I've grown confident in
my abilities. When we first met this tribe, I believed
them strong and well provisioned. I've since realised
their strength is fleeting, and only Isarninus truly
possesses it. He might once have been part of a *comitatus* but he doesn't have a *comitatus* to command,
aside from us.

'We'll overwhelm you, as we did the Hicca,' I announce staunchly, 'but you're welcome to try anyway.' Only now, I sense something else: a look of
triumph on his face.

'I knew your intentions before you did. You'll do
well to leave here now. Your horses have been taken
away, and the other men and women imprisoned.
And so will you be.' At that, I hear a strangled cry
from Bucge and turn, dismayed to find nearly twenty
men and women armed with whatever they have to
hand menacing Bucge and Heafoc. This is when the

rest of my warriors are supposed to come to our aid, but their absence is telling.

Isarninus steps towards me now, snatching my seax from my weapons belt, and nodding to allow one of his warriors to bind me. I'd sooner this had come to a fight, and I'd died here or killed him, affecting my escape, but my confidence has undone me.

'Now, we'll feed you every so often. I'm not a monster. I won't kill you and your warriors. Instead, you'll sink into a pit of despair, unable to escape, and like so many of my prisoners, you'll learn the only way to triumph is to do what I order you to do. Either that, or the men seeking you will be told you're here. I believe your father would be most keen to see you.' So speaking, Isarninus steps aside, his laughter thrumming through the air. I meet Bucge's wide eyes, seeing the fury on Heafoc's face as well, and shake my head at this unexpected and rapid change of circumstances, determined not to feel even more threatened by the mention of my father. I'd almost forgotten about him. I didn't know Isarninus even knew who he was. No doubt Goddæg has been speaking of my father when deep in his cups, or to the woman he's been bedding.

As we're led away, the men and women of the settlement jeer at us. The children throw mud and stones, and I allow my fury to pool within me.

I'll not be held here. I really bloody won't.

But, for now, I'll allow Isarninus to believe he's triumphed. And then I'll have my vengeance against him. It will be bloody and lethal.

31

MEDDI OF THE EORLINGAS

The blade breaks in two. I sense everyone sag with disappointment, all apart from Terricus, who instead, eyes narrowed, turns towards the heat of the forge, lips pursed. Centus looks defeated. I know a moment of pity for him. We've tried this experiment so many times. All of them, so far, have failed. We've made charcoal. We've found better ironstone and still success is beyond reach.

'It's the heat and the ore,' Terricus mumbles. 'The heat of the charcoal and the quality of the ironstone. Look.' And he points, animated against Centus' defeat. 'Look. It's nearly worked. We must simply decipher what needs to change. It won't be much. We need a higher quality ironstone to bind the two together, and a different means of doing so.' Now Centus looks where Terricus points. I see him nodding slowly, wiping the sweat from his face. Then he turns to Madog, standing straighter, shoulders tight with respectful defiance.

'Terricus is correct. We'll not give up. It's nearly done. The ironstone has adhered to the one half of the sword. All we need to do is make the fixing more permanent.'

My brother's quick to reassure Centus. 'It's called a lost magik for a reason.' I've heard him speak these words many times before. My brother, just like me, is sure we'll soon have the answer. In the meantime, Madog grows in strength, as does our tribe. The amalgamations of our people with others have been peaceful or violent, but those who come to him owe their allegiance to the tribe of the Eorlingas. In time, Madog will have new enemies, perhaps the Færpingas that the trader spoke about, or the Husmeræ. Then it'll become more violent. Then we'll need blades of new forged iron. And my father's sword as a symbol of Madog's prowess.

'It'll come,' I console as well, banishing the spectre of my disappointment. 'It will come.'

Not for the first time, I look to Marchell. She's very interested in the process. I consider whether she knows something and is withholding the knowledge. I can't imagine why, but stranger things have happened. Now I watch her gazing at the small supply of ironstone found by Urien. She examines it with more intensity than I do.

Her actions make me speak. 'Can't we barter for different ironstone?'

I sense Marchell's intense scrutiny.

'What?' Madog replies.

'This ironstone, it might need to be higher quality. We've tried melting down old iron items. That didn't work. This time we ensured there was much more charcoal available, made throughout the winter months. We've tried the ironstone discovered while tending to the crops. What if we need different ironstone? There must be a source elsewhere?'

Terricus nods quickly, considering my words. Centus is slower to react, but I narrow my eyes at Marchell, seeing a quick quirk of her lips. This, then, is the answer. I'm sure of it.

'We'll travel to Corinium and seek out a new supply,' my brother announces decisively. 'It's time we visited anyway. We need to barter for other items as well.'

I consider whether I should go with my brother or not, but I'm unsure. I sense I need to remain here, where I can be assured no one will release Elen from her elongated captivity. There's growing sympathy for her. I said she'd be kept until we knew whether she was with child or not. It's been much longer than that. We even had to find new places to keep the grain and food throughout the long winter months to ensure she remained our prisoner.

'I'll send some of my best warriors, and of course, someone who can barter well.' As he speaks, my brother assesses Marchell. I realise he's noticed her actions too. 'She might be mostly silent, but Marchell knows what she's seeking. She'll accompany my warriors.' I resent that my brother doesn't consult me first, but quickly dismiss my ire. My brother's correct. Centus has learned the art of heating ore. Terricus has brought his knowledge of charcoal. Now we need someone who understands the magiks contained within the hard rocks that can be melted to produce the precious iron. And that someone is Marchell. Mind, I'll speak with her first. She might rarely reply, but she'll heed my instructions.

* * *

They leave the following day, venturing westwards. My brother has chosen six of his best warriors to escort Marchell, including Urien. Madog, and the remaining men, will protect Villa Eorlingas. I watch them ride out, noting how Marchell straightens in her saddle as she almost drops out of sight. I've allowed her to take one of the good horses.

'Do you trust her?' I question Madog.

'I do. Despite everything,' he offers. I find I agree with him. Her loyalty to the Eorlingas is without question.

It'll be a journey of some days, and then they must find what they seek, without arousing the suspicions of others, and organise the exchange, before returning. In the interim, Centus and Terricus are once more busy with their experiments.

I turn and make my way back to my cold workshop.

I've been delaying some of my duties. It'll not help me if I fail in these tasks. As the seeress, I must maintain the secrecy surrounding my skills and actions. I close the wooden door behind me, the silence of my workshop overwhelming me because it's been a long time since I was alone in here. Then I reach for my supplies and begin the task of producing what I need from the collection of early flowering herbs, and those which have been left to dry over the winter, suspended above the fire.

This is no undertaking for Sian. It might have been something Marchell could help me with, but now it's my responsibility. I set to it willingly, aware of the voices from outside, which fall reverentially silent when they see my door closed, knowing I work for the good of my brother and our people.

My thoughts turn to Elen, as they so often do. I know without doubt she carries no child from her union with Edern. Still, I'm reluctant to allow her release. I consider whether I should order her death. She is, after all, a traitor. If I allow her to live, it'll either be in captivity as a slave or far from our villa. But I know Elen and her ways. I fear if I allow her departure, she'll cause problems. What then should I do with her? So far I've delayed making the decision. The weather has been harsh throughout the dark times. There would have been vocal complaints if I'd cast her out then, despite the strain on our resources her continuing to be held in captivity has caused. But now? Well, the weather will soon warm. She can leave now. I could cast her out. Or enslave her.

I can't help wishing I'd ordered her death when Madog reclaimed Villa Eorlingas. It would have prevented the unease of Elen's continued existence from souring some of the relationships within our tribe.

I should have had her killed. My brother's more gentle approach ensured she lived.

I concentrate on my actions, chopping the herbs, grinding them into small pieces, storing them in small pottery jars, the sharp stink of them making my eyes tear. I fear it's not the only reason I cry. I straighten my back.

I will wait for longer yet. Soon, my father's sword will be made anew. The intentional severing of it into two pieces by that bastard, Edern, will be undone.

Only then, when my brother and his warriors have the sharpened blades needed to defeat our enemies, will I need to decide what I intend for Elen.

Only then.

32

WÆRMUND OF THE GYRWE

'Did you know of this place?' I question everyone.

Osfyth replies. 'No.' The sound is simple, sharp, and thrums with more power than a hammer blow.

I anticipate her anger and fury directed at me, not at Isarninus, but it doesn't come.

We've been taken below ground. It stinks within, the smell rank and obnoxious, damp pervading all, and I know we're where the strange man's kept captive, who Isarninus sometimes has perform before his people. I've never given much thought to where he lived. It seems I should have done so.

I feel rage only towards myself. I've allowed another to direct my steps, and those of my warrior men and women. I didn't realise how predictable my nature was. If I'd known, I'd have acted long before now to take my leave of Isarninus. I'm now far too late, which angers me as much as Isarninus' actions towards me. The threat of him knowing who I am and of my father's existence is a worry. I consider who told him and once more suspect Goddæg, but perhaps he's always known.

I believed myself better than this. I've been proved to be woefully misguided.

The rest of my warriors are sullen. If they were angry, their efforts to escape have driven it from them. If they were fearful, their weeping and wailing has long since fallen silent as the nature of our predicament has made itself very clear.

We've been here for, I think, no more than a day. It feels like weeks, perhaps even months. My own feelings have fluctuated from rage to fury to fear. I must escape from here. I'm a warrior, not a prisoner. If I'd wanted to be a prisoner, I could have stayed at my brother's destroyed settlement and waited for my father to come and exact his vengeance against me, which potentially wouldn't have been my death.

The place we've been thrust into is dark and dank. The roof above my head is so low I can't stand upright. The space to either side of me is so narrow I can reach it with my hands extended. There's only an entrance, or rather exit, and it's firmly sealed. All around me is the weight of rock.

'What is this place?'

'A tomb,' Osfyth mutters darkly. I shudder, soft words beneath my breath, an imprecation to my gods that this isn't where I breathe my last.

We've all forced our weight against the door. We've all tried to find something that's not rock through which we can scrabble free. But we're well and truly trapped. The air's too hot, even though the warmer weather has barely begun to seep into my bones. Here, I fear I'll never see the sun again, and yet soon the air will be hotter than a furnace, burning my insides as though I were in a fire.

I shudder once more.

'We'll find a way,' Heafoc calls from wherever he rests his weary body. It sounds as though he's far away, but nowhere is very far away in this cell.

'What is this place?' I repeat, not liking the initial answer.

'A cave, or cavern. They couldn't have built the walls like this. Perhaps the Romans did.' It's East-mund who replies. I notice his voice doesn't ring with desolation. He, then, hasn't given up hope.

'So, what, you think it might be one of their old buildings, somehow sunk into the earth?'

'Perhaps.'

But my mind's busy. I don't know a great deal about the Romans. I know they once ruled much of this island but never all of it. I've seen some of their buildings which still stand, not far from the land my father commands. Now I find myself growing silent, somewhat regrettably, because with none of us speaking, ranting or screaming to be allowed outside, I hear the growl of our bellies. We're all hungry. We're far from starving, but we've been here long enough to need to eat.

I'd also welcome a drink. My mouth is dry. I lick my lips, regret it, and then swallow, only to regret that as well.

But my thoughts have gone to Eastmund's assertion this place was built by this Roman tribe. And if it was, I have my suspicions that, perhaps, it's not quite as impenetrable as it might seem.

Only then my thoughts are disturbed once more. A voice calls from without.

'Have you bastards stopped shrieking and wasting your time trying to escape?' The words are filled with disdain. I clench my fists, dreaming of punching that smirk from the face of the man who shouts to us. 'Move away from the door, and we'll bring you my piss to drink and my shit to eat.' The voice is mocking. I bite my lip, aware my warriors surge towards the doorway. This will set off another elongated attempt to escape, yet I already know we'll fail.

I grip the closest arm to me, a startled shriek from Eastmund assuring me it's him who's nearest. It's too dark to see.

'Tell the others to let them open the door and bring us food and water,' I whisper into his ear.

'Wærmund—' But he bites off his angry reply. He's seeing the truth of my words. He moves aside, grabbing others, and surprising them. More than one startled oath fills the air. I blindly feel my way forward, closer to where the door is, seeking out others to send them away from me.

'Not dead already? Surely?' the voice mocks once more, disappointment thrumming through it. I growl and bite my lip, reminding myself we can't escape this way. The gap is too narrow. We'll need to find another means of breaking out, and I have an idea. Whether it proves possible or not, I won't know. Not yet. What I do understand is our requirement to eat and drink. I need my strength to bring about what I believe might be possible.

There's a loud scrape of protesting wood, and a shaft of blinding grey light floods the small space.

Using it, I look not to the door, but at my warriors. I see them all, noting those with bloody wounds and bruises. I don't believe any of us are uninjured. But I startle at seeing another amongst us, the small old man, the one forced to speak before Isarninus. I suspected he'd be here. Now I know he is. If only I could understand a word he says, it might help me.

He's the only one to come forward to take the food. He's skeletal and thin. I almost wince to hear the shuffle of his feet, fearing he'll fall and snap a bone. But my eyes travel above his head, and then along the confines of this space. Whoever lights the doorway has no idea how much they're helping me, even as my belly growls again at the far-from-enticing smell of cooling food. No doubt, this is what they wouldn't feed to the pigs, but hungry bodies won't care what the food is. And what we must do is ensure we don't become too weak to make an escape.

There's a slosh of something metallic containing water hitting the ground, and then another heavy sound as another cauldron is placed amongst us.

'Forgive the lack of bowls and cups,' the laughing voice jests, flecked with relief at our failure to try to attack him, or so I suspect.

I wait for the door to scrape shut once more, only thinking to move forward to the food and water at the last moment. Better to protect them than inadvertently kick them over.

'What was all that about?' Maggenræd demands once the laughter of our captors has drifted away, as though they've moved away from us.

'We need the food and water,' I advise. 'And I needed the light to see by. Now, come, eat and drink a fair share, although it's impossible to see much, and then we'll begin plotting our escape. The old man is in here with us. Treat him kindly,' I request. I've pitied him before, but now I feel some affinity with him. After all, we're as trapped as he is, only I refuse to accept it as fact. I will escape. I'll even take him with us, whether he aids us or not, and as I told Bucge I would.

Men and women such as us should not be kept captive in a place such as this.

No. We'll win free, even if it takes time, and then I'll have my vengeance against Isarninus and whoever told him of my identity.

33

MEDDI OF THE EORLINGAS

I eye the ruins of Centus, bleeding and bloodied, his head caved in with his own hammer. Briefly, I feel sorrow for the man, his father felled by Edern, and his life ruined by Elen. I allow my rage to pool, my fury to build, and then I turn to my brother and to Hedrek.

Hedrek's little better, but he does still breathe. For now.

'Why?' I thrum with the fire of my wrath. Bloody Hedrek has ruined everything. I didn't welcome his return yesterday, chest puffed out with right-eousness, but he promised much, and brought with him yet more charcoal, his eyes gleaming at the thought of aiding Centus.

His face is black and blue, and that's from the beating he's received at the hands of Madog. Madog breathes heavily, chest heaving, his face white and bloodied as well.

This is a mess, but I'll find order from it. I must.

'She's taken the blade pieces,' Sian informs me, not fearing to let me know that not only is Elen gone, and Centus dead, but the tangible connection with our father has also been stolen.

I focus on Hedrek, clutching the iron hammer in one hand, the tongs in the other. I've a mind to thrash him with both of them, but I lower my quivering arms. Violence here will not undo what's happened.

'Have you sent men to chase her?' I question my brother.

'Yes, half of our warrior strength.'

'Where was she intending to go?' This I direct to Hedrek. He winces at my fury but replies all the same.

'She was to come with me to my settlement.'

'Was she now?' For a moment, my rage is replaced with amusement. 'Did you truly believe a woman such as her would be content with a man such as you? Look at you. You're old enough to be her father.' The words wound more than the hammer and tongs. I drop them to the stone floor, enjoying his judder at the sharp metallic sound. I lick my lips, eyeing the ruin of the place. I've already looked at the grain store. Elen was released with little fanfare. The two guards are both nursing aching heads from being hit with something heavy, thanks to Hedrek. But they'll live. Not so much Centus. 'Why is my bladesmith dead?'

'She wanted the sword.'

'What for?'

'She didn't say.'

'Why didn't she just take it?' I leave aside the question of how Elen knew about the sword. If anything, it confirms she knew of my father's burial place.

'She woke Centus. He fought back.' But this still makes little sense to me.

'How could Elen kill a man like Centus?' Even now, bleeding onto the ground, he's huge. In the time, Centus has been a member of our tribe; he's doubled in size, muscles bulging from the heavy work he'd been doing. Bladesmithing might have been beyond him, but we all benefit from the nails used to secure our homes, shoes and other myriad items.

'We should kill him,' Madog rumbles with fury,

but I shake my head. Here, I'm the seeress. Here, my brother, even though he's the chief of our people, will do as I order him. Just as I was forced to do when he asked me to let Elen live.

'When did you know she meant to take the sword?'

'When she escaped and came this way instead of towards the waiting horses.'

'Where are those horses?' I direct to one of Madog's men, Twrch, a fierce warrior who fights as though possessed.

'We have them, and all of our horses are accounted for as well, aside from those who've journeyed to Corinium.'

'So, she's on foot, then?'

'Unless she's taken a horse from someone else.'

'Is there any sign of the involvement of others, aside from Hedrek?'

'No, mistress. There are no other horse tracks.'

I settle to silence, pondering this. I'm furious. Elen should never have been allowed to leave here. Admittedly, I was considering releasing her to become a slave, or killing her, but now she's gone, I know I needed to keep her close. She should certainly not have been allowed to murder our bladesmith or take my father's sword. With one ill-thought endeavour, Hedrek threatens to undo all we've accomplished since Edern's death. My lips curl angrily at that.

'Tell me, where did Edern come from, originally? I don't recall him telling me that.' I still hate to admit to our union, but Hedrek knew him better than I did.

'To the east.'

'Do we know the name of the tribe?'

'I, I don't believe so. But, he mentioned somewhere, a location, often enough.' Hedrek's eager to please me now. A pity he wasn't when he aided Elen, but men are creatures led by a need to satisfy their urges. Hedrek's proven himself a stupid old fool. And he knows it. 'I'll think about it.' What goes unsaid is the fact he can only think about it if he still lives.

'All isn't lost,' I speak calmly, no matter what it costs me. 'Centus isn't the only one to know the skills of the bladesmith now. He's taught Terricus well. And he understands more than simply how to forge nails, but Elen is a problem. She'll need to be found.'

'My men are looking for her.'

'I know they are, but they'll not find her. She'll evade our reach, for now, I'm sure of it.' I muse over what I've said, realising I believe those words. 'In her absence, we'll concentrate on making our tribe strong enough to withstand any assault she manages to arrange.'

'She is but a woman,' Hedrek moans, angering me because men shouldn't dismiss a woman's skills in such a way. After all, I'm a seeress, with just as much power over life and death as he thinks a blade allows him.

'And yet she's induced you to act like an arse and potentially endanger every man, woman and child who looks to Madog as their leader. Never argue that being "only a woman" will make her ineffective.' Spittle falls from my mouth as I speak, my rage temporarily grabbing hold of me. Infuriated by my anger, I stand straight and push back my shoulders, aware I must present myself in the correct way. These men and women look to me as their seeress, and also to Marchell, I grudgingly admit. I imagine her face will twist with loathing when she returns and discovers Elen is gone.

'Arrange to have Centus cremated,' I intone, 'with all honour, and with some of the accoutrements of his craft but not all of them. We'll need them until more can be forged.'

'So we do nothing else?' Madog asks hotly, voice menacing with his need for vengeance.

'You and your men will seek out Elen. Perhaps a

lucky happenstance will return her to us. But, if not, she'll find men to fight in her name, no doubt weaving a delusional tale about how she came to be cast out. Instead of expending our energy and resources on finding her, we'll seek to defeat that attack, when it comes. Madog,' I incline my head towards my brother, 'you've rebuilt Villa Eorlingas and the standing of our tribe, and people honour and regard you well. We'll use that to build a substantial force. The ditches have been deepened, and the two palisades encircle this place, but we can do more. Terricus will forge what he can with the material available to him. When Marchell returns, we'll have all that's needed.'

'And what of Hedrek?' my brother sneers angrily. 'He's the only one to still live. His men are dead.'

'He'll not be killed,' I reaffirm. 'Instead, he'll be punished. From now on, Hedrek, you'll be Terricus' slave. You'll aid him in everything he does.' A furious scowl touches Hedrek's lips. 'Or if you prefer, we can kill you,' I offer instead. 'Or perhaps, you'd rather be maimed.' His mouth opens and then closes, and then opens, only to snap shut once more.

'Mistress.' He bows low, accepting his fate.

'Tell Terricus his first task will be to craft iron rings to hold Hedrek captive. He was so keen to remove that impediment from Elen he must now wear it himself.'

With my decisions made and Madog offering no further argument, I stride from the ruins of the grain store. I hold my head high, before ducking under the shelter of my workshop. Only once inside do I allow my shoulders to sag and my fists to bunch. Hot, angry tears stream down my face.

Hedrek thought me cruel towards Elen. Even Madog thought me merciless, but really I was too kind. I should have had her killed when Edern died. I blame only myself for this, and still I'm furious. I kept her here to ensure she carried no child within her. It's been more than long enough for any babe to be born, and so I know she's as barren as all the other women Edern thought to bed. Yet she still represents a direct threat to my brother and to the future of our tribe. She might even think to take someone else's child and pretend it's hers. I know it's been done before.

Elen needed to be contained. Her escape is a terrible blow, and I'll need to find a way to reconcile myself to it, to make it advantageous to our people. I only wish I knew how.

34

WÆRMUND OF THE GYRWE

Whether it's day or night, I don't know. Time passes strangely here, with the roof over our heads and the stone sides enclosing us. Sleep takes me on occasion; sometimes, I'm wide awake when others snore. The passage of time seems immediate and yet also slow and elongated. I don't know how the old man can stand it.

We're fed somewhat irregularly. The smell of too many people with nowhere to piss or shit fills the small space. It's noxious. And yet, in the fetid heat, we've discovered a means of getting cool air to us.

Now we labour to widen the small hole. It's bloody hard work. We've nothing other than our fingers to claw away at the gap. We have no light to see, yet we all can feel the cool air percolating through the space.

The old man gabbles. It's nonsense. I don't know what he's trying to tell us. Heafoc's endeavoured to speak to him in the few different tongues he understands, but none elicit a response. I confess, I've tried speaking to him slowly, as though he's a child. I'm frustrated he can live for so long amongst these people and not learn to speak as Isarninus does. We'd be able to communicate with him then. At least none of my warriors resent his presence. And sometimes, when we're all exhausted, and our fingers bleed with the effort, I find him also helping us, widening the space through which fresh air comes.

We've removed some small stones now. The gap's growing wider. When we're fed and brought water, one of us must remove their tunic to plug the growing space for fear our custodians will sense the increased flow of air within our cramped quarters.

Of Isarninus, we've seen and heard nothing since our imprisonment. Neither has my father or his warriors appeared, as threatened.

The guards continue to taunt us, but even they're growing bored with the tedium of our placid acceptance of our fate.

When we manage to escape, which will happen, hopefully soon, we'll astound them. They think us broken. We're not.

'Wærmund.' Heafoc sits beside me. The aroma of his sweat-soaked skin is vile. I wrinkle my nose, aware I smell just as bad and grateful he can't see my disgust. We can't waste what water we're given cleaning ourselves. There's always just too little of it for us to feel sated. Thirst is a constant problem, only relieved when it rains outside and water trickles along our growing exit route to be caught in the bucket we're given, or if the bucket's been taken away and not returned, in our cupped hands which catch the rain.

'Heafoc,' I reply softly. Some of us are sleeping.

'What will we do when we're free?'

'We'll kill them all,' I state, without even thinking about it.

'Is it not better to escape and then seek our vengeance?' I consider this. Heafoc's always wiser than me. 'We're weak and lack blades. Escape should be our focus, not taking our revenge.'

'We'll kill them, especially that bastard, Isarninus,' I growl.

'Oh yes. We'll kill them. Just not yet.'

'You speak as though our escape is imminent.'

'I do, yes.' I realise then Heafoc stinks because he's been busy labouring on our growing exit.

'Are we through?' I ask excitedly, trying to lower my voice so as not to be heard by anyone outside the door or even up above if we have, indeed, finally broken through.

'Can't you smell it? Or hear it?' And I realise I can. Outside, the sound of rain can be easily heard, pinging off the ground and trickling into our prison. I sniff, and also realise I can scent it, despite the stink of Heafoc.

'Is it wide enough?'

'Not yet. But it will be soon. We'll be gone from here shortly.'

'Provided they don't discover it.'

'Indeed. I've left Eastmund there. He's working at widening the space and also making sure we're not discovered.'

I go to stand to reassure myself he speaks the truth, forgetting in my excitement the roof is low, and banging my head, so Heafoc can easily hold me back.

'We don't want to start a rush for the exit,' he cautions. 'Not yet.' Again, I'm reminded of how wise Heafoc is, and has been since we left the lands of the Gyrwe. I settle once more.

'Tomorrow?'

'Perhaps, or the day after. Not that time truly matters. We'll leave when it's dark. We'll take back our horses, and perhaps set fire to the settlement. But, we'll ensure we escape above all other endeavours. You must make that plain to your warriors. We'll not fight if we're overwhelmed by the enemy.'

'We can slit their throats while they sleep.'

'With what?' Heafoc asks, no heat in his voice. He's correct. We have no blades. We'll need to use fists. And stones. There's little else to hand.

'We'll take his treasure,' I state instead.

'Of that, there's no doubt,' Heafoc assures me, and I can tell he's grinning with delight.

'Now, we must keep everyone calm until we can all leave.'

'And what of him?' And I know Heafoc speaks of our fellow prisoner.

'Oh, we'll take him with us. He'll be useful to us. One day.'

* * *

It takes three more days. I grow impatient at the delay. How do I know it's three more days? We can see the sun rising and setting as the void grows bigger. I'm surprised, in the daylight, to discover our prison doesn't lie beneath one of the buildings within Isarninus' settlement. This means, when we emerge, like the dead from their graves, we'll not immediately have to counter our enemy.

I consider whether they even suspect another exit from the prison is possible, or that it might be somewhere else within their settlement.

We eat and drink what we're given, rebuilding our lost strength, or what little of it can be rebuilt. From the warmth outside and the sun's brightness, I suspect we've been imprisoned for a month. It's too long, far too long.

'We go one at a time, and ensure the next warrior to emerge does so without detection.' I speak in a harsh whisper, the gentle breeze of the early evening lifting my dank hair from my back. My beard is thick and riddled with crawling insects. I'll enjoy shaving it away, just as much as I'll welcome being able to cut my hair. I don't even want to consider how long my toenails have grown within my boots. They hurt when I walk, that tells me all I need to know.

'Who goes first?' Osfyth questions. This has been a source of contention. I want the honour. Heafoc says I can't take the risk, but if I send someone else, they might not do what needs doing. Inadvertently, they might alert the enemy to our escape and then trap us again. Neither can Heafoc do it, or even Goddæg. No matter what we do, we can't make the exit big enough for them to slither through. They're simply too broad, and perhaps, and despite everything, too fat. We'll return to the entrance we were pushed through to release them.

'I'll go first,' I announce quickly. Until this moment, I wasn't entirely sure, but now I am. I will be the one. If this goes wrong, it'll be my fault.

It won't go wrong.

Silence greets my declaration. I consider if they disagree. I contemplate if they'll tell me if they do.

'Then bloody get on with it,' Heafoc complains grumpily from where he waits, close to the door. He's desperate to be gone from here. He's not alone.

'I'll go first. Eastmund, you'll come next. Then Bucge. Then Osfyth and Bægmund. Then Maggenræd, Cenbryht and Hygebeorht. Remember, we want the treasure and the horses. We'll come back and kill the bastards when we have the correct equipment.'

I sense the nods of agreement, although I can't see them.

'We have stones,' Eastmund reminds me.

'I know. And we'll use them. A great big clout to

the head for the bastards that put us here,' I growl with remembered impotence. I've felt foolish, and now I feel furious. But I'll temper that fury, just like a bladesmith might, and wait for the sharpness of my revenge to truly triumph over them all.

With no further words, I make my way to where the cool air flows into our prison. The smell of the world above our heads is almost intoxicating. I swear I can see the flavours, but I know I can't. Even though we've widened the gap, it's still difficult to fit within it. That's why Heafoc and Goddæg can't go that way. Even now, I have to roll myself forward while others push my feet. There's a heavy piece of stone, too large to move, and beneath which we must all risk passing. I don't believe it'll fall. If it does, it'll trap those I've left behind until I can get to the doorway.

With my hands stretched out before me, I feel the coolness of the damp night air and the sandy texture of the soil on my hands. My nails are filled with the stuff. I know when I'm in position because I can see through the gap. Above, the stars and moon reveal themselves, not that the moon is bright. We don't want it to be. We need enough light with which to see, nothing more. My hands grip one of the stones we've gathered through our tunnelling. It's flat and heavy.

I suck in the smell of the night and then try to calm my breathing to enable me to listen for anyone close by. I hear nothing, but I still don't move. I strain every part of my body as though it'll make it easier to hear. It doesn't.

I suck in one more breath, and use my hands to pull myself upright. It's not easy. We've experimented. It's not possible to stand upright when I'm on my front. I have to pull myself upwards with my back to the ground. Gritting my teeth, grateful I've tied my hair back in a loose knot, I slowly begin to emerge.

Grass and mud cover my face. I press my lips tighter, determined not to swallow it, and then, between one movement and the next, my hands and shoulders straining with the effort, I manage to find my feet and slither onto the grass, more like an eel than a man.

Quickly, I grip the stone weapon I placed above me first as I listen again for any sign we've been detected.

There's nothing.

I squint, trying to determine where I am. It's not easy to tell. The howl of a dog, and the soft grunts of people in their beds, assures me we're close to a dwelling, but there's not enough light to see more. I feel as though I've emerged from my prison into another dank and dark place. Only here, the wind moves my damp hair. I can smell smoke from a hearth fire, and shit from a latrine ditch. This, then, is freedom.

I hurry back to the opening, feeling for it with my hands, not wanting to fall back into it.

'Come on,' I hiss softly. I hear the scraping sound of someone coming towards the opening. I wish I could see enough to know whether the hole can be enlarged, but it's impossible. Instead, I hover, stone in one hand, listening to Eastmund drawing closer.

He emerges more quickly than I do, but then I'm here to advise him there's no enemy.

Together, we stand and guard as the others make their way out of the tunnel. When there are more of us above ground than below, I take Eastmund with me to find the entrance. I walk the way I think the tunnel follows, but it leads nowhere. Eastmund walks into me.

'It's not here,' I complain.

'This way,' he whispers instead. I wince to hear the noises coming from beneath the ground, but no doubt, the enemy would think it little more than animals moving in their sleep. After all, the strange man has been a prisoner there for many summers and winters. Why would they expect us to be able to escape?

Eastmund disappears from my sight. I turn, unsure what to do, only for a hand to grasp my foot. I startle and then bend lower.

'In here,' he whispers. Now I sense it. Here, there's the familiar stink of damp, cold earth. The smell rising from it is obnoxious. It's not easier to see, but the path down is well constructed with huge stones. Eastmund leads on, his hands outstretched. There are no guards.

'It's here,' he assures me, and now is the difficult element. We must open the door. It'll shriek over the stone ground as it does every time we're fed. I'm sure it'll wake someone.

'Get on with it then.' Urgency floods my voice. I want Heafoc and Goddæg with me as soon as possible. And our incomprehensible fellow prisoner. He's coming as well.

The door opens surprisingly easily as soon as the wooden bar is removed. As it slides open – well, it doesn't so much slide as need kicking by Heafoc within – I realise only a flimsy door prevented us from escaping. They didn't even leave guards to stop us. I feel my rage burble to fury. I'll enjoy taking Isarninus' life when I return to this place.

'Come on, hurry,' I hiss. 'Don't forget him,' I remember. I won't leave a fellow prisoner behind. He's endured too much already.

A figure is bundled into my arms. Frightened eyes blink at me. I hold my finger to my lips and the old man nods. The smell of him is disgusting, his clothing heavily soiled, his beard and hair both so long they've become matted and tangled together. I can't understand him, and he can't comprehend me, but we've endured the same. I'll not leave him to be punished when we escape.

Hastily, we return to the surface. My warriors are there, breathing deeply, enjoying the freedom.

'To the stables,' I hiss, reminding them of our plans.

It's not easy, in the almost perpetual darkness, but we've lived here for nearly half a year. We know the way to where the animals are kept. I hope my horse will be there. I've missed the animal.

More carrying the silent old man than aiding him to walk, we dash through the complex of buildings to the one nearest the enclosing walls. From inside, I hear the soft nicker and whinnies of the animals. Now I taste my victory. But we need the horses, and of course, Isarninus' treasure.

The door opens with barely a screech of ancient

hinges, and we move amongst the horses. It's not difficult to determine which are ours. Isarninus had no more than four horses. There's no time to gather reins and harnesses, but we all grab what we can. I move to force the old man to mount up. But he stops me, his hands surprisingly firm on mine.

'What?' I demand, but he holds his finger to his lips, and beckons me onwards, back outside. I pause for a heartbeat and then follow him. He moves with surprising speed. I always thought him bent-backed and hobbling, but that was an act. Or the promise of escaping has made him young once more.

He leads me with confidence to a small building. I don't know what it is, but it emerges from the darkness, and he skips inside; whatever door there was has long since rotted away. I can't see what he's doing, but I hear him scrabbling around. I have half an idea I know what he's doing.

I don't enter, wary of being enclosed with only him to fight at my side should we be discovered. I can't imagine he'll be much use if the enemy come at us. But the noise from within pauses, and I hear him huffing. Now I enter because I hear the soft sound of horses being led over the grass and know my allies are escaping. The urge to be gone from here is overwhelming.

Hands extended before me, I feel for the old man, and he directs my hands downwards to wrap around a thick sack. I grin and heave. The bloody thing is so heavy, it almost pulls me into its hiding place. And I thought he'd it hidden below his dais. Isarninus tricked me about that as well.

Redoubling my efforts, it comes free, the weight of it making my grin wider.

The damn bastard.

I have his treasures. All I need do now is break free.

Wincing at the metallic clanks, I hurry back in the direction of my horse. And that's when I realise we've been discovered.

So close, and yet I'm still within, and I've nothing but a stone with which to protect myself.

This will become a bloody fight, but one I'm prepared for.

Quickly, I pull the old man behind me, and together we creep towards the entrance. I bring the heavy sack with me because I'm unsure if I'll be able to return. My only desire now is to escape with my life, my warriors, Isarninus' treasures and, of course, the old man.

He stays close to me, perhaps sensing my intentions because I can't speak with him about it.

From outside, I hear the thunder of horses' hooves, and also the angry shouts of those who've realised what's happened. I emerge into the gloom, seeking out my allies, but it's still too dark. No one has thought to light brands yet. That won't last.

'This way,' I order the old man although I'm sure he doesn't understand me. I direct him to where I mean, and he stumbles onwards. I grip the stone I brought with me from our prison, as I try to seek out the enemy, and my allies.

'Wærmund.' It's Heafoc who whispers for me.

'Over here,' I reply quickly, squinting although it's no help at all.

Abruptly, a brand does flare in the far distance, and I blink away from the bright light.

'Get them,' Isarninus roars, the cry coming from even further away. I can't imagine he means to fight me personally. He'll send his six warriors to do that. When we first met I thought him arrogant and confident. He's both of those things, but whether he's a warrior remains to be seen.

I hear the thunder of hooves coming towards me. I hope it's Heafoc with my horse, and also one for the old man. I realise I don't know if he can ride. I have to hope he can.

'Here,' I hiss once more, hoping Heafoc can hear

me over the sound of my warriors hurrying away with their horses.

'Where did you go?' Heafoc asks angrily, rearing up before me, with a spare mount to either side of him.

'I got the treasure.'

'And the old man?'

'He aided me.'

'Good, now we need to go.'

'What of our riches? My brother's sword.'

'You have what you have,' Heafoc answers angrily. 'We'll get those when we return to kill Isarninus.'

'We should kill him now.'

'Get on your horse, and we'll live through the night,' Heafoc menaces, and now I hear other horses coming this way and hurry to push the old man onto his horse, and mount mine. The treasures I carry are awkward but I manage it.

'Do you have Wærmund?' Osfyth calls to Heafoc while the sound of running feet can be heard. I appreciate not all of my warriors have realised my absence. They're coming closer.

'Yes, lead the way,' Heafoc orders. I should be the one doing so, but Osfyth has a brand in her hand,

and is using it to hunt for me. She'll be able to lead us from here.

'Come on,' I urge the old man, kicking my mount to get him to move. The animal lurches forward and does as I order it. Heafoc ensures the old man follows, as I stay close to Osfyth.

Isarninus can be heard bellowing to his warriors, and the people who look to him as a leader have been roused from their beds and clog the trackways leading to the exit. We need to reach it before Isarninus' warriors think to guard the single entrance and exit better.

It feels strange to be mounted after our captivity. It feels even more strange to have no weapon to hand but a lump of stone. The horses lack their harnesses and I bump around on my horse's back, but it's better than walking.

I bend low, gripping tightly to my horse's mane, and urge it to move faster. Osfyth lights the path. I see Bucge at the entrance, alongside Eastmund. There are, I think, the bodies of our enemy on the ground, and then we're through the gap in the encircling embankment and ditch, and racing away. Isarninus won't be able to chase us. He doesn't have enough horses now we have ours. As we ride onwards, I shout to my warriors, checking they're all there, and allow a sense of triumph to flood through me.

We've lost much, but there's now the opportunity to regain it. And then I'll seek my vengeance against Isarninus. I'm not alone in wanting the bastard dead. That, more than anything else, will ensure my warriors stay loyal to me.

35

MEDDI OF THE EORLINGAS

I bend to where my child's bones are contained beneath the floor of my workshop. I've not needed to touch her since my return here. I thought that was enough. But now, with the absence of Marchell, I need to feel the comfort of her presence to counter the rage thrumming through my body. I knew to be wary of Hedrek. He shouldn't have been allowed to return here, but my brother spoke of it positively. With the threat from the nearby Færpingas, he thought it time to grow an alliance with Hedrek and the Beansæte, as opposed to causing more ructions. That Hedrek came with more charcoal, which Terricus stated was of superior quality to what we'd managed to make, made me consent, even if unwillingly, to allowing him within the double-ditched embankment protecting the Eorlingas from our enemies.

I see now we were blinded by the wrong desire. We might want sharp blades to overpower our foes, but that was only important while Elen remained our captive, and we had control over what would happen next. With Elen gone, we've lost that domination. If she manages to encourage others to fight on her behalf, the future of our hold over Villa Eorlingas will be in doubt. And Elen, even I admit, has always been able to entice others to do her bidding. How else did she manage to make Edern take her to wife, when I'd already disappointed him?

Tears drip down my cheeks, running more slowly down the side that's been long-scarred by Edern's anger, and land onto the bundle I reveal. All is as it once was, the small, fragile bones, carefully cocooned in the slowly disintegrating folds of wool, which I replaced with something more substantial.

I close my eyes, and see all I've been denied for over two decades: the soft touch of my daughter's hand in mine, the gentle chuckle of her laughter when delighted with something. It was Edern's fault, but he's dead. It's Elen towards whom all of my rage is directed. How I hate her. But I must admit to my failings as well. I delighted in having her as my captive. It was a heady experience to have her entirely under my control. Hedrek, and his meddling, has ruined that. He's taken away the basis of my new-found confidence. I'll punish him, but being a slave will, for the time being, be penance enough.

Unexpectedly, an old, withered hand settles over mine, and I open my eyes, feeling calmness flood through me, even though Marchell hasn't touched me for years, aside from when returning my attention to the peas last summer.

I didn't hear her return to the villa. I didn't hear her enter my workshop. It must have been while I was contending with Elen's escape. Our search for her was frantic, determined to ensure she wasn't still hiding within Villa Eorlingas, including beneath the raised stone floors underneath which, heat from the fires can keep them warm during the dark months.

'We'll find the bitch,' the hoarse voice informs, startling me for Marchell rarely speaks. Certainly, she's not spoken directly for near enough two decades, our interactions marked by her guiding my steps, as opposed to through conversation. There have been times I would have wept to have her speak with me. Of everyone here, it's only Marchell who's been as poorly treated as I have. 'We'll find her, and then, we'll kill her. Slowly, painfully, allowing her blood to seep between the cracks of this villa's floors.' The malice in Marchell's voice is impossible to ignore, as is her resolve, as she runs her gnarled fingers down the scars marking my cheek, and which she healed, despite the terrible wound rot that infected them.

If there's one amongst us all who should despise Elen more than I, it's Marchell. For Marchell was and is her mother, and Elen forgets that.

I turn and meet her glowering eyes, nodding to seal the bargain. I embrace her, feeling her frailty and allowing fresh tears to stream down my cheeks, as she too sobs. Neither of us have allowed such closeness since the death of my father.

This should all have been accomplished already.

Elen must die. Only with her death can the future of our hold on Villa Eorlingas be reassured. I know that now. I should have killed her when I had the chance. I was weak. I thought of what Marchell would think of me for murdering her daughter. I thought of what Madog would think of me. I thought of what my father would say. I should have ignored those silent voices in my head. I should have been cold, callous, stone-hearted against Elen, and the bitch she became.

But, before she dies, I'll have my father's broken sword returned to me. With Elen dead, and my father's sword in the hands of my half-brother, and after him, his son, I need never fear losing what I've fought so long, and so hard, for.

Marchell and I will see it done.

36

WÆRMUND OF THE GYRWE

The woman stands before me, shivering and sobbing and yet with her chin tilted haughtily. Eastmund watches her uneasily. I'm unsurprised Bucge and Osfyth have leapt to her defence. If Goddæg or Bægmund had found her first, we'd have heard nothing but the screams as they assaulted her. They're both missing the comforts being a guest of Isarninus provided them, aside from keeping us captive against our will.

I lick my lips, uncomfortably reminded of how I came into this world. My father might be a leader. My mother was anything but.

'Who is she?' I question them.

Osfyth stands defiantly beside me, her shimmering blade held out before her because Goddæg and Bægmund prowl like wolves after their prey.

'Stand down,' I order them quickly, aware Heafoc expects me to speak as I do. But, if this woman brings problems with her, I'll order her killed. I won't allow Goddæg or Bægmund to have their way with her. It would sit uneasily with me. Much better to kill her with the blades we exchanged for some of Isarninus' treasures. I acknowledge the decision might seem strange.

'I don't know. We found her while scouting the perimeter. We brought her here because it's better she's here than where the men can get her.' I grunt at that. Osfyth speaks the truth. There's a rift between some of my warriors.

'Have you asked her?' Heafoc questions.

'Of course we have,' Bucge grumbles. 'She doesn't speak our language. Like him, over there.' I don't turn to eye the aged man we've added to our number. He's useless as well. Well, he's useless in that we can't understand one another. But he's not useless in other ways. I have a feeling about him.

'We don't need another addition to this *comitatus*,' Maggenræd grumbles. 'Not one who doesn't speak, and is frail and weak. Look at her. She's not eaten for days.' I notice that, and jut my head towards our friend. We've named him Hljoðr because he's silent. He scurries forward, understanding my intentions easily enough, and offers a bowl of warm pottage to the woman.

The woman, all straggling fair hair and huge green eyes, watches him and shudders back from his approach, even though he offers food. Bucge snatches it from him, and holds it towards the woman. She doesn't take her eyes from me, even as she shuffles behind Osfyth.

'We've no time for this,' I mutter angrily.

'We're not going anywhere tonight,' Bucge argues instead. I realise then she's shrouded the woman in the thick cloak she purchased from the traders we encountered and who provided us with knives, if not shields. I'm already shaking my head. Bucge has made it clear she intends to keep this woman safe.

Hesitantly, the woman takes the offered bowl and eats hungrily, but warily, her eyes darting around her, the flames of the campfire, now the also-bartered-for cauldron's been moved aside, leaping merrily into the darkening sky. It's not exactly warming the space we're sheltered in, however.

'Then she's your responsibility. Make sure she

has no blades or the means to poison our food. And the rest of you can stay away from her, or Osfyth will butcher you like she does the animals she kills to feed us.' Unwelcome groans meet the pronouncement, but I know the men will heed them. They'll do so because Osfyth is a brutal warrior. She kills with the precision of her hunter's skills.

I settle myself before the fire, pulling my cloak tight and wincing against the brightness of the flames. Only I hear a sound and turn, hand already on my knife. The woman, having eaten her fill, has pulled forth a weapon, or rather, a shattered remnant of a sword, its point now broken but perhaps more deadly with its sheen of jagged iron.

'By the gods,' I growl, leaping once more to my feet, Bucge and Osfyth unsheathing their knives as well, but the woman merely holds it outwards and drops it to the ground, another piece quickly joining it. She has a sword, but it's in two pieces and lacks a guard, only the tang visible, just like with the sword I took from my brother, and which Isarninus now has. She begins to speak. The words are incomprehensible to me. I look from Bucge to Osfyth, seeing the same lack of understanding on their faces.

I hazard a look at Heafoc but he shakes his head. Of us all, he knows the most tongues, although I don't know how he learned them. This one is beyond him.

Somehow, I'm unsurprised when Hljoðr begins to speak. I confess, my mouth drops open as I listen to the pair of them, this unlooked-for union of the old man and woman who's older than me, but still arresting, the words falling over themselves as they finally find someone who understands. My eyes narrow.

'Wonderful,' I announce, but there's a flash of comprehension on the woman's face. I hear the name of one of my warriors on the man's lips, and hold my mouth shut against its tendency to drop open as Heafoc listens to some different, halting words of our newest addition. It's a different tongue to the one she first spoke.

'Her name is Elen,' he announces eventually. 'And our friend there isn't called Hljoðr but rather Gildas, some sort of holy man, but not a seeress or a *seith*, as we'd term them.'

'What tongue are you speaking with Elen?'

'British, but he speaks Latin.'

'So what tongue do they both speak?'

'Brythonic.'

I shake my head at this, and open my mouth to question more, but the woman continues, almost tripping over her words in the haste to have them spoken, and this Gildas is also nodding vigorously. A slow smile spreads across Heafoc's face as she then speaks to him once more.

'Well, well, well, Wærmund,' Heafoc offers with a slow smile. 'Elen is from a Brythonic tribe to the west. They're seeking the magiks to make sharp edges and blades, as you are. She hopes to remake the sword and claim the leadership of those people for herself. It's been stolen from her by someone who killed her husband and threatens her. But more importantly, Gildas, for all his mumblings, says he knows the art of doing what she requests. Or rather, he knows where the craft is still practised. He'll aid her, and if we help her in turn, we'll have the means to overpower all those who've belittled us, and we can mount an attack against your father, and Isarninus.'

'Where?' I demand, almost salivating at the idea.

'Not far from here. Our friend here, Gildas' – the name sounds strange on Heafoc's lips because we've been naming him as Hljoðr – 'was captured by the warriors of Isarninus many years ago while visiting a hole shrine in the ruins of the settlement beneath Isarninus' hillfort. If we take him there, and he knows the way, he'll ensure we have access to a bladesmith.'

A slow smile spreads across my face with the news. 'It seems, Bucge and Osfyth, we must be grateful you found this creature.'

The smile transforms into a wolf grin, to go with my wolf-marked cheek, my fury bleeding away. If not for events within Isarninus' settlement, we wouldn't be here now. Then, we wouldn't be about to discover the one thing, aside from our warrior skills, that will see us dominate all who've thought to demean us, holding us captive against our will, and in the case of my father, casting us aside as no longer valuable to him.

'Tell her we'll do as Gildas suggests,' I inform Heafoc.

He shares a grin with me, as I beckon them both towards the leaping flames of the fire, more minded to share now.

'Tomorrow, we'll journey there. And then, if the recompense is adequate, we'll help Elen retake her position within her tribe. And then, we'll also seek our vengeance against Isarninus, and my bastard father.'

* * *

MORE FROM MJ PORTER

The first in another action-packed historical adventure series from MJ Porter, *Son of Mercia*, is available to order now here:

www.mybook.to/sonofmercia

HISTORICAL NOTES

This is not really a story of historical fiction, but rather archaeological fiction. Pick up any book on Britain at this time, and you'll find very little written about what was happening, because we do not know what was going on, other than perhaps in the south and south-west. If it's a book about Mercia, there'll be even less until the seventh century. It's impossible to write about the history of a kingdom when there are no written records. And so we must rely on archaeology.

The decision to write about these formative years in what would become Mercia has been a long time coming. However, it's difficult to determine any cohesive narrative from what is truly the Dark Ages.

Others might look to the stories of the legendary Arthur (no, I don't believe he existed), and Hengist and Horsa and think that's enough, but having read K. R. Dark's fascinating look at Britain at this period, *Civitas to Kingdom*, many years ago, I realised that what happened elsewhere might not have happened in Mercia, and equally, that generalisations shouldn't be used about what would become the Saxon kingdoms in any single part of it. It was an island of petty tribal chieftains. It was not a country or a kingdom. This is an attempt to make some sense of what archaeological findings have been made and devise something that 'could' have happened. These people did not exist as I have named them, although I have adopted tribal names that are recorded in a later document (see below).

All that can be said with any certainty about Mercia is that a narrative had formed by the eighth century which was an attempt by the rulers of that time to explain how they came to be in control of the heartland of Mercia, and then the wider Mercian kingdom. This included many other tribal affiliations: from the people known as the North, South and Middle Mercians, to the outlying areas – the kingdom of the Hwicce, and Magonsæte, being two of the best known. Bede, writing his *Ecclesiastical His-*

tory of the English People, finished by 731, knew some of these details, although he really did not like Penda the pagan – one of the most powerful Mercians in the seventh century – but did grudgingly admit that the contemporary ruler of Mercia, Æthelbald, was a powerful individual, eclipsing the kings in his homeland of Northumbria.

Barbara Yorke has written:

The surviving sources allow us to say with confidence little more than that the kingdom of Mercia was in existence by the end of the sixth century.

— P. 102, KINGS AND KINGDOMS OF EARLY ANGLO-SAXON ENGLAND

How that kingdom came about, we do not know. I've chosen the date of this series carefully. It falls between the Battle of Camlann, said to have taken place in 537 according to the *Welsh Annals*, a later written source, and a later battle between 'kings' which occurred in the 570s and is mentioned in the *Anglo-Saxon Chronicle*, written 300 years after these events. And before the onset of the plague, but after some poor harvests.

Wærmund is a name taken from a Mercian genealogy found in the *Welsh Annals*. There are a
number of different variants of a Mercian genealogy.
This is the one I've used, below.

Woden begot Watholgeot, begot Waga, begot
Wihtlæd, begot Wærmund, begot Offa, begot
Angen[geot], begot Eomer, [begot Icel, begot
Cnebba, begot Cynewald, begot Creoda],
begot Pybba. Pybba had twelve sons, two of
whom are better known to me than the others, namely Penda and Eobba. Aethelred was
the son of Penda; Penda was the son of Pybba.
Aethebald was son of Alweo, son of Eobba,
[brother] of Penda, son of Pybba. Egferht son
of Offa, son of Thingrith, son of Eanwulf, son
of Osmond, son of Eobba, son of Pybba.

Other versions of a Mercian genealogy are found
in the *Anglo-Saxon Chronicle* entry for the year 626
(A2 Version, also known as the G version) when dis-
cussing the later reign of Penda which lists many of
the same names, but has Wihtlæd as the son of
Woden.

I've chosen Wærmund's name somewhat ran-
domly, but with the idea that he wasn't the first of his

family – and that, indeed, he is originally from one of the Wash tribes for which we also have details from the Tribal Hidage. Every time I write a new series, something clicks for me, and in this case it's that whatever the genealogies represent, it needn't be those who ruled Mercia as a kingdom as we recognise it, but those who ruled the 'tribe' beforehand. Yes, they did claim descent from the god, Woden, but most of the Saxon kingdoms did.

The names of the tribes come from the problematic and difficult-to-date Tribal Hidage, which survives in an eleventh-century document, but is believed to be a copy of an eighth-century document. It lists thirty-five kingdoms, which comprise ninety-five different tribal names believed to have amalgamated to form these thirty-five kingdoms, which were then further merged to form the six main Saxon kingdoms of the Heptarchy (the seventh, Northumbria, is not included in the Tribal Hidage).

There are a wealth of Roman villas surviving in Gloucestershire, perhaps most famously Chedworth Roman Villa, and also many Roman mosaics, some of which are not available for public viewing as they have been purposely recovered to them. The tribe of the Eorlingas is associated with Arlingham, just below Gloucester, to the east of the River Severn. As far as I can tell, Frocester is the closest Roman villa ruin to have been discovered from nearby, but with so many of them, it almost feels as though they might have been falling over them – there are fifty-two known Roman villas in Gloucestershire alone.

The idea of an economy dependent on iron had not really resonated with me before, but Robin Fleming's comment that mining, metallurgy and smithing stood at the heart of the Roman economy made me reconsider this. She points out that from the late fourth century (which is traditionally deemed to be the end of Roman Britain – well, 410 is) there is a scarcity of traditional, crucial and once common everyday items – nails, evident in the lack of hobnail boots and also coffins. She does, however, stress the Romans had a successful 'recycling' scheme and that forging iron objects from these re-cycled elements may well have continued. However, pattern-wielded blades (which had largely come to dominate what we believe early Saxon/Anglian kings wielded in their battles) could not be made from re-cycled iron or from a single type of iron alloy, with at least four different iron alloys needed. Therefore, an age 'without' iron almost ensued. It is possible that these skills were lost and then needed to be rediscov-ered. Equally, it is possible the evidence for such occupations as smelting have disappeared from the archaeological record in many places because of the transient nature of the process. I find the lack of nails in the archaeological record, however, very intriguing. It certainly points to something.

Languages at this era are, of course, impossible to reconstruct. It's believed English, Latin, British, Pictish and Irish would have been spoken. It must also be assumed those coming to this island from Scandinavia and Germany would also have brought their languages with them. I've decided to use the terms Latin, Saxon, British, Brythonic and Pictish in the text. There would potentially have been a vast number of local dialects as well, just as there are today.

Sources used while writing this story include: Robin Fleming's *The Material Fall of Roman Britain, 300–525 CE*; Max Adams' *The First Kingdom*; the archaeological site report detailing *Wasperton: A Roman, British and Anglo-Saxon Community in Central England*; a book on the survival of towns, or possible survival of towns, from the third to sixth centuries by Gavin Speed; and many, many Zoom lectures in the last four years, including memorable ones on the Enderby Shield and also on Iron Age hoards and a Derbyshire hill fort. There is definitely a need to write a story based on just what was found at that hill fort. For a fascinating 'living archaeology' discussion of bark shields, have a look at the Enderby Shield. I'm grateful for a Zoom talk I attended for explaining the process of making the shield given by Sophia Adams of the British Museum – I had to include such fascinating objects. It can be seen online at www.britishmuseum.org/blog/how-make-iron-age-shield-out-bark

And there is a shield reconstruction here, which is also fabulous: www.thethegns.blogspot.com/2014/07/the-shield-from-bidford-on-avon-grave.html

I am also grateful to a number of talks given to the Rugby Archaeology Society about the Chiltern Hillforts, the Boughton Malherbe Hoard, the Rutland Villa mosaic, the bath house at Tripontium and potentially many others that I've failed to mention here. They have all added something to this attempt to recreate this very murky period in time. You can find details for the society here, and if you're a local, you can join them for their monthly talks – www.rugbyarchaeology.org.uk I do recommend joining your local society if you're lucky enough to have one – admittedly this isn't my local society, but they did share their talks via Zoom during lockdown.

I'm indebted to two small books I found on Anglo-Saxon smelting and blacksmiths' weapons written by Dennis Riley of Daegrad Tools, *Anglo-Saxon Metalworking Tools* and *Anglo-Saxon Iron Smelting*. There are, intentionally, some errors in how my bladesmith attempts to make blades. After all, he was relearning a lost skill. I must also say a thank you to those who feature in *Aussie Gold Hunters* and *Gold Rush* with Parker set in the Yukon, as it's also taught me a lot about smelting, producing gold bars and about how to find seams of precious metals running through the landscape. Iron is perhaps not quite as shiny, mind.

Any mistakes in detailing these processes are my own, aside from where they've been made intentionally.

I've taken two holidays in 2024 which have helped me 'place' my characters, one to Norfolk, which also included a brief visit to Suffolk to visit Sutton Hoo, and also one that allowed me to visit some Roman ruins in Gloucestershire, and Shropshire.

I have struggled to find references to the religions at this time. Ronald Hutton's *Pagan Britain* contains some useful passages, and I plan to expand on this in the second book in the trilogy. This somewhat leads into burial rites, which are often much of what we know of our ancestors. It does appear confusing – the magnificent ship burials at Sutton Hoo were preceded by burials beneath what is now the visitor centre. Cremation and interment were somewhat haphazardly applied throughout Britain. My own distinctions between peoples are merely an attempt to highlight the differences between them. The depiction of the burial of Meddi's daughter beneath inhabited buildings is a known phenomenon from this period, and written about by Robin Fleming.

I will continue to expand on this fascinating period in later books. I fear my historical notes are already far too long.

ACKNOWLEDGEMENTS

I would once more like to extend my heartfelt thanks to my editor, Caroline Ridding, and Amanda Ridout, at Boldwood Books for allowing me to share this tale with my readers. It's very much a passion project for me, and these don't always correlate to a story that others wish to read. Thanks also to the whole Boldwood family, especially Claire Fenby, and her enthusiasm for everything historical. It feels special to have a fellow historical nerd promoting my stories.

I would also like to thank my copy editor, Ross, and proofreader, Shirley, as well as Shaun at Flintlock Covers who has, once more, made my terrible draft map into something beautiful. I would also like to thank the narrators of this story, Antonia and Simon, and huge thanks to Christine Rauer for sharing her expertise on how to pronounce Saxon-era names. It's a joy to hear them as they should be spoken.

Huge thanks to my brother, AC, for coming to

Sutton Hoo with me, and to EP, for driving me from one end of England to the other to research locations for the book, and for tolerating my sudden shift from Saxon sites to Roman ones. There are only so many Roman walls you can look at, and abandoned Roman forts before they all start to look the same.

Thanks also to my advance readers who all made careful suggestions and reminded me of some elements I may have missed in the initial drafts. Thank you to JF, KM, CS and TR. And to my fellow authors of historical fiction, EA, CE, EQ, AL, DC, JD, RC and PG (I hope I've not missed anyone out), who keep me sane and love to discuss the most minor of details.

And a heartfelt thanks to my readers for continuing to journey with me backwards through time. Would it have been easier to start at the 'beginning' of the Saxon period? I'm actually not sure it would have been.

ABOUT THE AUTHOR

MJ Porter is the author of many historical novels set predominantly in Seventh to Eleventh-Century England, and in Viking Age Denmark. Raised in the shadow of a building that was believed to house the bones of long-dead Kings of Mercia, meant that the author's writing destiny was set.

Sign up to MJ Porter's mailing list here for news, competitions and updates on future books.

Visit MJ's website: www.mjporterauthor.com

Follow MJ on social media:

𝕏 x.com/coloursofunison

⬡ instagram.com/m_j_porter

BB bookbub.com/authors/mj-porter

ALSO BY MJ PORTER

The Eagle of Mercia Chronicles

Son of Mercia

Wolf of Mercia

Warrior of Mercia

Eagle of Mercia

Protector of Mercia

Enemies of Mercia

Betrayal of Mercia

The Brunanburh Series

King of Kings

Kings of War

Clash of Kings

Kings of Conflict

The Dark Age Chronicles

Men of Iron

WARRIOR CHRONICLES

WELCOME TO THE CLAN ✕

THE HOME OF
BESTSELLING HISTORICAL
ADVENTURE FICTION!

WARNING:
MAY CONTAIN VIKINGS!

SIGN UP TO OUR
NEWSLETTER

BIT.LY/WARRIORCHRONICLES

Boldwood

Boldwood Books is an award-winning fiction publishing company seeking out the best stories from around the world.

Find out more at www.boldwoodbooks.com

Join our reader community for brilliant books, competitions and offers!

Follow us
@BoldwoodBooks
@TheBoldBookClub

Sign up to our weekly deals newsletter

https://bit.ly/BoldwoodBNewsletter

www.ingramcontent.com/pod-product-compliance
Lightning Source LLC
Chambersburg PA
CBHW010656100726
47900CB00010B/2688